"You drive me crazy."

She didn't even hide her smile. "Why?"

"Because all I want to do is kiss you."

"More things we agree on." She placed her hand on the back of his neck, went up on tiptoe, and brushed her lips over his. Like a match swiped across the rough edge of the box, a fire lit inside of them. Colt's arms banded around her. One big hand held her lower back. He planted the other right on her ass, his long fingers lay over the curve, inches from the tingling heat building between her legs. He pulled her closer and took the kiss deeper. His tongue glided along hers. She moaned. He growled, titled his head for a better angle, and kissed her socks off.

Luna lost herself in Colt's arms. The first kiss they shared rocked her world off center and left her wondering if what she felt that night in the parking lot was real or just her imagination. Not only was the passion and need real, something opened inside her and everything within her settled.

God, the man could kiss.

By Jennifer Ryan

Montana Men Series
HER RENEGADE RANCHER
STONE COLD COWBOY
HER LUCKY COWBOY
WHEN IT'S RIGHT
AT WOLF RANCH

The McBride Series
DYLAN'S REDEMPTION
FALLING FOR OWEN
THE RETURN OF BRODY MCBRIDE

The Hunted Series
EVERYTHING SHE WANTED
CHASING MORGAN
THE RIGHT BRIDE
LUCKY LIKE US
SAVED BY THE RANCHER

Short Stories
CAN'T WAIT
(appears in ALL I WANT FOR CHRISTMAS IS A COWBOY)
WAITING FOR YOU
(appears in CONFESSIONS OF A SECRET ADMIRER)

HER RENEGADE RANCHER

A MONTANA MEN NOVEL

JENNIFER RYAN

AVONBOOKS

An Imprint of HarperCollinsPublishers

Excerpt from *His Cowboy Heart* copyright © 2017 by Jennifer Ryan.

HER RENEGADE RANCHER. Copyright © 2016 by Jennifer Ryan. All rights reserved. Printed in the United States of America. No part of this book may be used or reproduced in any manner whatsoever without written permission except in the case of brief quotations embodied in critical articles and reviews. For information, address HarperCollins Publishers, 195 Broadway, New York, NY 10007.

First Avon Books mass market printing: October 2016

ISBN 978-0-06243535-4

Avon Trademark Reg. U.S. Pat. Off. and in Other Countries, Marca Registrada, Hecho en U.S.A.
Avon, Avon Books, and the Avon logo are trademarks of HarperCollins Publishers.
HarperCollins® is a registered trademark of HarperCollins Publishers.

16 17 18 19 20 QGM 10 9 8 7 6 5 4 3 2 1

In the end, the best we can hope for is that we've left our mark on the people who matter most to us, that we've loved them so well, a piece of us will forever remain a part of them.

HER RENEGADE RANCHER

CHAPTER 1

Wayne pressed the heel of his hand to his failing heart. A burst of adrenaline and fear raced through his veins. Not long now.

On the surface, he was ready. Deep inside, he wished for more time. A chance to make things better. Time to see his sons married with families of their own. He'd have loved to be a grandfather to a sweet little girl or a rough-and-tumble boy.

The front door slammed as it always did when his boys arrived or left. Reminded him of them running in for food and out to have fun in their youth. Some things changed over time, memories dimmed, and in the end, it was the simple things he remembered. The little things he loved.

He relished the accomplishments, joys, the love he shared with the people who mattered most.

He had regrets, if only's, wishes unfulfilled that left a yearning in his gut.

"Dad."

He'd had children late in life. Maybe if he'd started earlier, he wouldn't have been so indulgent, but more disciplined. Maybe then Simon and his brother, Josh, wouldn't be the spoiled, self-centered men they'd turned into. He'd wanted to give them everything, but he'd only ended up teaching them to expect everything without having to work for it.

"In here." Wayne grabbed his Stetson off his home office desk. He had a date with his favorite girl and didn't want to be late. At seventy-two with a bad ticker, he'd learned not to waste time. He set his favorite hat on his head and turned to greet his beloved—and yes, sometimes annoying and disappointing—sons.

"It's late. Where are you off to?" Simon stood in the doorway, his shoulder propped against the frame.

Josh stood just in front of him, his mouth set in a grim line. Wayne sometimes thought that boy had been born with it. "Let me guess, your date with that waitress. The whole town laughs about it behind your back, you know?"

Wayne didn't appreciate his son's disdainful eye-roll. "I don't really care what anyone thinks. Including either of you. What I do, and why, is none of your business."

"This ranch is our business. We need to talk." Josh moved closer, his hands in his pockets. His relaxed posture didn't fool Wayne. The boy who liked to get his way turned into a man with a mind for manipulation.

"This ranch belongs to me. You've taken little if any interest in this place since the day you were born."

Simon narrowed his gaze. "Yeah, well, things change. If you don't think we've seen the changes in you . . ."

Wayne nodded his head, understanding dawning. "You want to talk about your impending inheritance."

Simon's sharp gaze softened. "What did the doctor say, Dad?"

"Nothing I didn't know already. Don't worry. My affairs are in order. The funeral arrangements have been made. The ranch will continue to run without me here to oversee everything."

"We'll take over when you're gone," Josh stated, like it was a given fact.

Wayne tilted his head. "Not necessary. You've got your own lives. I've found someone to take my place. Someone who understands how to preserve the land, treat the animals right, and who will appreciate all I've built here."

Simon pushed off the door frame and stood at his full height, taking a step closer, his eyes narrowed with concern. "Are you saying you didn't leave the ranch to me and Josh?"

Wayne shrugged one shoulder. "What do you want with a working ranch? You've both made it clear you have no interest in the cattle, horses, or farming I do here."

"You aren't leaving this place to us at all?" Josh swore under his breath and shot an angry glance at Simon.

"I've taken care of you. You'll have what you need to get by and do something with your lives."

"Get by?" Simon scoffed. "What does that mean?"

Wayne held up his hands and let them fall and slap his thighs. "You're thirty-five, not thirteen." He shook his head. "You don't need me to provide every little thing for you. What I've built, I want to see continue, not stripped apart and destroyed. I've made sure it will stand long after I'm gone. Everything else, you'll find out after I'm gone."

"I want to know now," Josh demanded.

"What difference does it make? The life you want

isn't the life I'm leaving behind. Find your own path. Find something you love to do and make it your life. Find a woman who lights up your world and hold on to her."

Josh folded his arms over his chest. "Like the waitress you're screwing lights up yours?"

The anger came swift, heating his face and ears, making his weak heart thrash against his ribs. He clenched his left hand, trying to ignore the pain in his arm. "Watch it. You have no idea what you're talking about, or what she means to me."

"I know you're a fool if you think that pretty young thing spends time with you for any other reason than your wallet." The disgust in Josh's eyes made Wayne even angrier.

"Like your friends and the women in your life, all of them out for what they can get. That's not the kind of man I am. Those aren't the kind of friends I value. I've tried to show you both the significance of the life I lead. I've tried to instill my values in you and still give you everything you wanted. What I should have done . . . Well, it's too late for second-guessing now. You're your own men. After I'm gone, maybe my absence will make you step up and take ownership of your life, instead of always relying on me to give you everything you need."

"So it's not enough that we went to college and have jobs?" Simon asked. "We still don't live up to your lofty standards."

"I'm proud of you for graduating. An education is a good foundation, but you both move from one job to the next when there's too much work or you get bored. You work to get by, and when you can't, you still come to me for money. The houses you live in, I bought. The cars you drive, I provided. All I'm asking is that you don't waste your lives getting by; find what it is that matters to you."

"You say that after you tell us you're letting someone else take over the ranch." Simon shook his head and let his hands fall back to his sides.

Wayne stared at his youngest son and cocked his head. "Are you saying the ranch is important to you? You want to run it?"

"Better that than you just giving it away."

Wayne shook his head. "Trust me, son, I'm saving you a headache. You don't really want it. It's work. Hard work. If you don't love it, it'll drag you down. You'd end up selling it just to get out of it."

"Not so. I'd hire someone to do what I can't."

And spend the money the place rakes in, but never take pride in the job. Wayne's poor heart sank. He'd failed to instill a work ethic and dedication to doing a good job and the happiness and sense of accomplishment that comes with it into his sons. "Not can't do. Won't do. This place isn't for you."

Josh's silence on the matter proved he had no interest in getting his hands dirty either. The pair of them wanted the rewards without having to do the work.

"You barely spend time here as it is. First chance you got after high school to get out of here, you took it. I don't blame you. I always said to do what makes you happy. Seems to me you'd rather spend your time in Bozeman. City life is more your speed, and that's fine. I'm not disappointed neither of you has my cowboy heart. You've got other interests."

He didn't quite know what those interests included besides a new woman every week and living each day with nothing much to show for it.

"I'm late, I need to get going." Wayne walked forward.

"To see her," Josh said.

That stopped him in his tracks. "Dinner at the diner with good company. A man gets lonely living out here all alone. Another thing you'd both hate."

Simon held up a hand to stop Wayne from leaving. "We're not done talking about this."

Wayne put his hand on Simon's shoulder and squeezed. "Think on what we talked about. You change your mind about living my kind of life, I'm happy to discuss it further. You want to take an interest in the ranch, I'll put you to work, maybe you'll surprise me and actually do it instead of running off after an hour like you did when you were teens."

Simon's hesitation and Josh's gaze darting away spoke volumes.

"You can't give everything away," Josh snapped, his frustration showing in his words and the hard line of his mouth.

Wayne frowned and narrowed his gaze, locking his son in place with a look. "I can do whatever the hell I want. Which includes ending this conversation. You change your mind about working this place, you let me know. Otherwise, I've got all my affairs in order. When I'm gone, you'll get what I say you get."

Wayne walked past his fuming sons.

"Dad, Josh and I can take care of the ranch," Simon said.

"Empty promises, son. You got to want it to do it right." He'd worked damn hard his whole life to succeed where so many others failed. Not for lack of trying, but ranching was a tough business. He didn't want to see all he'd accomplished laid to waste.

Wayne walked out. Nothing he said would appease them.

He started his truck and rolled down the window. He took the driveway slow and easy, passing the front of the house. The boys slammed the front door and stood on the porch as he passed. He drove down the lane, the green fields on both sides filled with his beloved horses, feeling the cool breeze on his face. How many more simple pleasures would he experience before the countdown of his heart finally ended?

CHAPTER 2

Colt walked into the diner, spotted the only woman to take up residence in his head, and headed for a booth across the room, trying to ignore the tightness in his chest. He should have driven into Bozeman, found some yuppie bar, picked up an underpaid, overworked office girl who wanted to ride a cowboy and have some fun—he was always up for fun. But not tonight. Not most nights these days, because Luna stayed on his mind more than he liked to admit—to himself, never out loud—but she sure as hell wasn't getting into his heart despite the way it leaped every time he saw or thought about her. She wasn't for him. No way. She belonged to his buddy. At least she used to until that night at the bar when everything shifted and changed and became so confusing he was still trying to figure it out.

"Leave it alone," he warned himself under his breath. Easier said than done, especially now that his brother Rory was marrying Luna's best friend. Sadie kept at Colt, wanting to know what happened between him and the dark-haired beauty with the porcelain face and red lips he could still taste from that one searing kiss. Like now.

The damn woman branded him with that kiss.

He glanced over his shoulder as he continued on through the tables to the booth and caught her watching him from behind the counter. Those ice blue eyes with two brown specks in the right and three in the left darted away. The hint of embarrassment and shame in them matched his own feelings about what happened, but the flash of anger he always saw there tore him up. They'd been friends once. He'd ruined that and felt damn sorry about it, too.

"Hey you," Sadie called, walking out of the kitchen.

He ditched the booth idea and headed straight for her, taking a seat at the counter. Luna moved away to deliver her tray of drinks to a family at a nearby table.

"Hey, Mama, how's my niece or nephew doing?"

Sadie smiled and placed her hand over her slightly swollen pregnant belly. "Great." Her hand slid to her hip and she narrowed her eyes on him. The diamond ring his brother put on her finger last week winked in the light. "Did Rory send you after me? I can get home on my own, for God's sake."

He smiled at his soon-to-be sister. Yes, Rory tended to lean to the overprotective side of the line, but he had reason to where Sadie was concerned. At least before that trouble with her brother got settled. Now her brother spent his days locked up behind bars, and Sadie spent her time worry free and her nights in Rory's bed. Lucky bastard.

"I'm sure Rory's pacing the house waiting to get his hands on you, but he didn't send me to fetch you."

The starch went right out of her. "Okay then." She leaned over, planted her elbows on the counter, propped her chin in one hand, and stared right at him, a soft smile on her lips. "How are you, handsome?"

She wasn't flirting. Not really. His brother's girl had

become like a sister, filling their family with a feminine warmth that had long been lacking in a household of men. After her father died, he shared his sorrow over his own parents' deaths—he'd been barely old enough to understand they weren't coming home ever again—and they'd bonded.

"It's been one hell of a day. Thought I'd stop in here for something to eat, since you're working late and it's Ford's night to cook." Colt scrunched his face into a sour expression, mocking Ford's mediocre cooking skills.

"That's the only reason you're here?"

He planted his elbow on the counter and matched her gesture of putting his chin in his palm and staring right back at her. "Well, I have been trying to come up with a way to steal you away from Rory."

She put her hand on his cheek and gave him a soft smack. "Never going to happen, cowboy."

He gave her a mocking frown. "That's what I thought you'd say. Way to crush a guy's heart."

"You might stop guarding that heart like it's going to be crushed by pain and loss again . . ." A reference to losing his parents he didn't want to be reminded about. ". . . and consider making up with my maid of honor over there."

Colt sat back in his chair and tamped down the urge to look at Luna again. Urge, hell, it was a compulsion to stare at her pretty face, close the distance between them, both figuratively and literally, and kiss her again. Just one more time. One more moment when everything in his life felt so damn right—before it all went to hell again.

See, he had good reason to guard his heart. The one time the thing pulsed to life over a woman, he screwed it all up. One kiss messed everything up.

"Leave it alone, sis."

"Seems to me you and her have done that for a long time. Apologize."

"It's beyond a simple 'I'm sorry.' "

"You sure about that? Because from where I'm standing, you sneak a look at her. She sneaks a look at you. Both of you act like you've got something to say, but neither of you says anything."

"After what I did, there's nothing to say that can make things right. Sometimes, sis, you can't go back."

"Did you cheat on her?"

Colt shook his head, the thought so distasteful it made him purse his lips. "No. It's not like that."

"Did you purposefully hurt her? Call her a name? Insult her? Run over her puppy?"

He shook his head, smiling despite the seriousness of the conversation. "No. Nothing like that."

"Are you sorry?"

He let out a soft sigh that did nothing to untangle the ever-present knot in his gut. "More than I can say."

Sadie slapped her hands on the counter. "Then I don't know why you can't go over there and tell her so."

"It's not that simple. She was my friend's girl, and I crossed a line."

"Colt, honey, she's not a possession. He didn't own her."

He let his head fall forward and stared at the seam in the countertop. "Well, she sure as hell wasn't mine. I tried to help her out, but I messed it up instead."

"Let me ask you something. Did she cross this line with you, or did you pull her over it?"

Colt sat back and stared up at the ceiling. "What difference does it make?"

"If you both participated, maybe she's sorry and

you're sorry and this can be worked out, or at least put to rest, if you just talk to each other."

He gave her a look, putting all his resignation in his face. "Sis . . ."

"Colt, I love you like a brother, so I'm going to treat you like one. You're being an ass. She's helping me plan the wedding. She'll be at the house all the time. Are you going to keep walking away every time she shows up?"

"It's worked so far."

Sadie planted her hands on her hips. "Really? This is working for you? Pretending she doesn't exist and what happened between you didn't happen? Seems to me all it does is make you both miserable."

"She does the same exact thing," he shot back.

Sadie stood and planted her fists on her hips again. "Oh, grow up. You know what you need to do to make this right. Suck it up and get it done. I won't have you two glaring at each other in my wedding photos."

"I'd never do that."

"No. You'd stand next to your brother looking miserable because of the woman standing next to me."

He took a chance, hoping Luna gave Sadie some information, one glimmer of hope that he could make things right. "Has she said anything to you at all about me?"

"Only that she doesn't want to talk about it. The thing is, Colt, she doesn't seem angry."

He perked up at that bit of news. "No?"

"No. More embarrassed maybe. Like she doesn't want to admit what she did, to me, her best friend who would never judge her. Maybe it's because I know you now, and I'm marrying your brother."

"She didn't do anything. It was me."

"You take the blame. She takes the blame. Seems to me whatever happened, it was the two of you who did it together."

He didn't know what to say about that. When he thought back to that night, standing in the parking lot, one of her hands on his shoulder, the other touching the aching bruise blooming on his jaw that her ex, his best friend, gave him, he didn't know who moved first. Him? Her?

"Here's what I've learned from dealing with my brother. If you don't take responsibility for the choices you make, things only get worse. Own up to your part. Apologize for what *you* did. Maybe that's all that's needed to at least thaw the cold shoulder you both have for each other."

One tough chick, Sadie didn't back down.

"I see why Rory fell so hard for you."

"He sat across the diner, staring at me for the better part of two years, wishing he'd talked to me. Maybe if he had, we'd have found our way to each other a lot sooner. I'm not saying it's the same between you and Luna, but if you've carried this with you all this time and it's still this raw, maybe you need to settle it before it festers into something so much more than it ever was to begin with."

She had a point.

"I'm afraid it already has. She can't even look at me without me seeing it all in her eyes."

"Maybe because when she looks at you she sees it in your eyes as well. Exactly the way I do right now." Sadie reached out and laid her hand over Colt's. "Don't wait the way Rory did."

"I'm not looking for a wife and a family."

"Maybe not right now, but ask yourself, if you feel

this bad about things now, how will you feel if you never make it right and spend the rest of your life wondering what if she was the one?"

"It's not like that," he lied, remembering exactly how he felt when he kissed her. The connection he'd found with her in that moment tugged at him even now to close the gaping distance between him and the woman across the room.

A woman who couldn't stand the sight of him.

"You may not want to admit it, but I see the one thing you try to hide every time you look at her. Something I held on to myself for a long time."

Afraid to ask, but needing to know what she saw but he couldn't figure out, he spoke up. "What's that?"

"Hope."

Luna tucked her notepad back in her apron pocket, slid the pencil along the top of her ear, and turned toward Sadie, who tapped Luna's shoulder. "Hey you. Time to go home to that sexy cowboy of yours?"

"Yep." Sadie tilted her head toward Colt. "There's one waiting for you at the counter. He wants to talk to you."

Luna's eyes went wide on her friend. She'd been a ball of roiling emotions since Sadie started seeing Rory. One day, it would come to this. She and Colt would finally talk. She'd finally get her say.

"Did he tell you what I did?"

Sadie eyed her. "Funny, he refused to tell me what *he* did. He seems to think he's in the wrong. You think you're the one who did something. Could it be neither of you are to blame, because whatever it is, it's not that big a deal?"

Luna frowned, feeling the guilt rise up in her gut, and her face flushed.

"Did you cheat on his friend?"

Taken aback, Luna gasped. "What? No. Billy and I were broken up. And I didn't sleep with Colt."

"Could it be you did something you wanted to do but didn't expect and things got weird?"

Luna sucked in a surprised gasp and fought the urge to glare at Colt across the room. "He did tell you."

"No, he didn't. But I think the pair of you are perfect for each other. Go over there. He wants to talk to you as much as you want to talk to him." Sadie gave Luna a quick hug, then walked out the door just as Luna's favorite customer walked in for his Thursday-night dinner date with her. Wayne came in like clockwork. Tuesday and Thursday, eight o'clock sharp. She checked her watch. Twenty-two after the hour. Hmm. Something held him up. The strained look on his face told her his family, probably one of his sons, or both, were involved.

She went to him and gave the old guy a soft hug that she held an extra few seconds when he didn't let go. She felt his frailness and worried about his diminishing health. She stepped back but held him by the shoulders. "Everything okay tonight, Wayne? You're late."

"I'm old and slowing down. Everything seems to take me longer to do. Did you miss me?"

"Always. I have news. I got a job offer."

"That's great."

She tilted her mouth into a lopsided frown, not so sure. "I don't know. It's out of state."

"I thought you wanted to set up an equine therapy program for children with autism and disabilities."

"I do, but I need a job that will help me pay for the

program. The horses, gear, a place for the kids to ride. You know, all those pesky little details that mess up my dream."

That earned her a smile from Wayne. "Well, something better is coming your way. Let's sit. We'll talk about it."

She squeezed him tight again, spun out of his arms but kept one arm around his shoulders, and led him to his favorite booth. She already had it set up for him with his favorite iced tea with a splash of fresh lemonade.

Wayne scooted into his seat, took the dark brown Stetson from his silver head, set it beside him, and took a sip of his tea, letting out a satisfied sigh. "Exactly how I like my drinks and women—sweet and tart. Like you."

As predictable as the biscuits and gravy he ordered every week, he made the same comment about his preferred drink.

"You seem upset today."

His gaze dropped away. "Unsettled."

She slid into the seat across from him. "How so, Wayne? Your family giving you trouble again?"

Wayne's eyes darkened and rolled to the ceiling. "Again? Always. If it's not one of them, it's all of them."

"What are families for?"

"I thought by now I'd be settled down with grand-babies running around my ankles, riding the horses, eating all my food. Instead, I get nothing but a headache every time my sons show up. Don't even get me started on my sister and her husband." Wayne raised his gaze to the ceiling and shook his head like he was praying for mercy. "I do like their girls. My nieces are smart. Kind. Always taking care of more than their share. Like you."

She covered his hand on the table and gave it a squeeze. "Don't let them get you down." She didn't know what else to say. Wayne was a kind and generous man. He took care of his family, but they never thanked him. Instead, from all she'd heard, they expected it and wanted more.

"That's why I come to see my girl." He patted her hand over his. "You always put a smile on my face and lighten my heart."

"I love spending time with you, too."

"Let's talk about your job offer and something my sons brought up. It involves you."

"How so?"

Wayne didn't answer right away. She stopped staring at Colt and looked back at Wayne. He tilted his head and gave her a knowing smile. "Maybe we should talk about what's really bothering you. What's going on with your young man over there?"

Luna snuck another peek at Colt, who waited patiently for her to come over and take his order. "He's not mine. Never was. Never will be."

A twinkle shined in Wayne's eyes. "But you want him to be."

"What? No. I didn't mean that."

"I think you did, you just don't want to admit it."

"It's complicated."

"Well then, let's simplify it. Is he a good man?"

"One of the best." She didn't have a single hesitation in admitting that.

"Why?"

"Why? I don't know. He's kind. A little wild at heart, but steady. He's got principles and morals, even if he does like to shirk responsibility and have a little fun once in a while."

Wayne frowned a bit at that. "Everyone needs to cut loose now and again, I guess."

"He'd never leave someone in the lurch. Whatever he sets aside, he gets back to when it's time and makes up for it."

"So, a good man. Kind, as you said. A hard worker when he needs to be, but still knows how to have some fun. A loyal friend?"

"Always."

"To you?"

"Used to be, but I kind of did something and he took a huge step back."

Wayne's head bobbed. His lips pressed together in a line. "So that's why you two have spent the better part of too long avoiding each other."

Had it been that obvious to everyone?

"I'm not avoiding him," she lied right to his face. Just a little lie.

"You're a damn good waitress, yet you've let him sit there without a drink or taking his order for the better part of ten minutes. He's a patient man, but you got to ask yourself what he's waiting for. His food? Or you?"

"Wayne, what I did, I shouldn't have. I took what he believes in and disregarded it completely to take what I wanted."

"Say you're sorry."

"Why does everyone keep telling me to do that? It won't change what happened. I can't take it back. I don't really want to," she admitted softly.

"Did you ever ask yourself if he wants you to?"

She fell back against the booth seat and stared blankly, wondering if that could be true. What she felt from Colt that night for that one, all-too-brief-and-perfect moment felt so real, then he'd set her away from him with both hands firm on her shoulders and stared at her with this hard look in his eyes that she couldn't read. Mostly because he'd made her brain go haywire with that kiss.

"Take it from an old man, don't put things off. Time slips away so quickly, before you know it, it's gone."

She squeezed his hand again, noticing his pale face and weary eyes, the fine sheen of sweat across his pale brow. "Wayne, is everything all right?"

"Nothing you can do about me, sweet girl. But you can do something about him. Go. Do what you gotta do. A good man is hard to find. Believe me, I can't even find one in my own family."

"You're a good man, Wayne. You've always been kind and generous to me. I love our talks and spending time together. Your encouragement and understanding mean so much to me."

"You give me all those things and more, sweet girl. You're like a daughter to me, and I appreciate all our time together. Most people your age would dismiss an old man like me. Not you. You listen when I got something to say. You value the wisdom I've gained. Use some of it now and go make things right with your guy."

"He's not mine."

"He could be if you wanted him." Wayne reached over and cupped her cheek. "He'd be crazy not to want a beautiful, loving girl like you."

"Are you flirting with me, Wayne? It's true, isn't it? You have a mad crush on me." Most of the patrons teased about it. Even Wayne teased about it. But what they shared was nothing more than a deep friendship that meant more to her than anything.

"I'm not crazy." He tapped his finger to the tip of her

nose and smiled. "Go on now. I want you to be happy, so fix this and put the pretty smile back on your face. For me. I'll be right here waiting when you're done."

Colt stared at the shiny coffeemaker, lost in his own thoughts about the woman sitting in the booth behind him with Wayne Travers. The guy was rich. He owned one of the largest spreads in the state. And he had a thing for Luna. The whole town talked about their dates. Colt had to admit, they looked friendly. Too friendly for his mind, but he shut that line of thinking down quick. He wasn't jealous. Just . . . What? He didn't have a right to think anything about what Luna did, or who she saw. Not that he believed some of the racier rumors about the pair. If he was honest with himself, what he really saw between them was affection and a deep friendship. He hoped when he was in his sunset years he had a hot young thing doting on him and brightening his world, too.

Actually, he'd rather a woman like Luna by his side.

Maybe the old codger was trying to set her up with one of his sons. Colt smashed the paper napkin into his fist before he caught himself and tossed it aside.

He leaned forward and planted his head in his hands, elbows propped on the counter, rubbing his temples, telling himself he was not thinking about a wife and kids. That was for Rory. Not him. Not now. He had time to find the right woman—like Rory found Sadie.

"Headache?"

That voice made his belly quiver and his skin heat. She hadn't spoken to him directly since that long-ago night, but he'd never forget her soft, rich voice. It followed him into his dreams and called his name.

"Uh, no. Just . . ." He raised his head and looked at her. God, from a distance she caught his attention every damn time, but up close, she stopped his heart. "Hey."

"Hey yourself."

She set his favorite beer in front of him, along with a frosted glass. "Looks like you could use this."

"Thanks. Listen, Luna . . ."

Her eyes met his and something warm glowed there for a second before her gaze darted to the closed menu in front of him.

"What's it going to be? Steak, meat loaf, or burger?"

"Am I that predictable?"

"Not really. I like a man who knows what he likes and what he wants."

"Like Billy, right?" Colt regretted mentioning her ex the second before her eyes darkened and narrowed on him.

She planted her hands on the counter and leaned forward. "How can you say that to me?"

"He wanted you. Held on to you as long as he could, I guess."

She hung her head and shook it, her long midnight hair swaying. When her head came up and her pale blue eyes met his, he leaned forward, drawn into the pain in their depths. "I'm not the only one who didn't see it." Her lips drew into a quick frown. "If you didn't see it either, maybe I'm not as stupid as I thought."

"What are you talking about? *You* are not stupid." The words came out soft, but tinged with the dread building inside him. He didn't want to know that his best friend treated this amazing woman less than she deserved.

"That fight we had in the bar."

"He wanted you back."

"No. He wanted to keep me away from you." Her eyes stayed steady on his.

Colt couldn't breathe. He leaned in, needing to kiss her so damn bad he couldn't think a single other thought. Except, what the hell did she mean by that?

Her arms bent, bringing her closer, then her gaze shot past him and her eyes went wide. She leaped up onto the counter and jumped off past him on the run. He spun in his seat to see what put the terror in her eyes. Wayne fell to his knees beside the booth, clutching his chest, his face an unnatural, deep, dark red. He fell forward onto the scuffed wood floor, his shoulder knocking a chair out of his way and up and under the nearby table.

Luna slid to her bare knees beside him. She placed her shaking hand on his back and leaned down close to his ear. "Wayne, honey, what's wrong?"

Colt slid in beside her, took the old guy by his shoulders, and gently turned him over. "He's not breathing." He called over his shoulder to the few patrons in the restaurant who gathered close. "Call nine-one-one." He turned back to do what he could, but Luna had already unbuttoned the collar of his shirt and pumped Wayne's chest, her hands gripped tight over his heart.

"Give him mouth-to-mouth."

Colt didn't hesitate. He pinched Wayne's nose, tilted his head back, pushed down on his chin, leaned down, and breathed hard to fill the old guy's lungs.

Luna resumed chest compressions, her face a mask of concentration despite the tears slipping down her cheeks.

"Please, Wayne, come on. Don't do this to me. Please," she begged. "Don't you die on me."

Every break in Luna's hard work, Colt leaned down

and gave Wayne another breath, checking to be sure his chest rose and fell. He pressed his ear to Wayne's chest, heard nothing, and leaned back so Luna could continue.

"It's not looking good," someone whispered behind them.

Luna's tear-filled gaze held Colt's as she bounced up and down on Wayne's chest. He saw it in her eyes—she wouldn't give up, but deep down she knew the truth. He was gone.

Fire and rescue arrived, red and blue lights sweeping across the restaurant walls from the vehicles outside. Two guys dropped their packs beside Luna. She didn't stop compressions until they were set up and ready to take over. One put a plastic breathing resuscitator over Wayne's face and squeezed the balloon end to push air into Wayne's lungs. The other guy tore open Wayne's shirt, charged up the defibrillator, attached leads to Wayne's chest, and squirted gel on the pads.

Luna stared at the flat line running across the monitor.

Colt went with his gut. He stood, stepped over Wayne, hooked his hands under Luna's arms, and pulled her up and away so the paramedics had room to work. The hushed whispers from bystanders faded into the background. Luna's focus remained on the man on the floor even as Colt moved behind her, sat on the edge of a table, and pulled her between his legs. He wrapped his arms around her middle to hold her close, offer what comfort he could during this terrible time. Her hands pressed to his arms, her nails digging in with the first shot of electricity that went through Wayne's frail body, which jolted Luna's, too. She trembled, so Colt held her tighter to his chest. He propped his chin on her shoulder and watched the paramedics try to save Luna's friend and a man who'd been a pillar of the community and generous to those less fortunate.

The paramedics made quick work of loading Wayne onto the gurney, doing their best to bring him back.

"Will he make it?" The hope in Luna's soft voice tore at Colt's insides because he knew the truth that Luna didn't want to face.

The tall paramedic pressed his lips together and gave a subtle shake of his head. The flat line on the monitor didn't blip even once, no matter how many times they jolted poor Wayne with electricity.

"No. No. He's not gone. He can't be." She stomped her foot and tried to go after the paramedics to get to her friend. "You have to save him. You have to!"

Colt held tight to her. "Luna, honey, they'll take him to the hospital, but I'm sorry, he's gone." He buried his nose in her neck, smelled her sweet scent, and closed his eyes when a wracking sob tore through her. He kept his arms locked around her, holding her close, even when she tried to bust free again.

"No. No. It's not true. He'll be fine. The doctors will bring him back. They have to bring him back," she wailed.

Colt turned her in his arms and hugged her tight. She wrapped her arms around him, pressed her face to his shoulder and neck, and wept so hard he felt her pain rock through him.

With the paramedics gone and the commotion over, the other patrons quietly paid Tim at the register and walked out. Tim gave Colt a sad look, then ducked back into the kitchen. This late at night, it wasn't likely very many customers would come in for a late-night meal or snack. Colt settled into holding Luna through her tears and the quiet, somber way she leaned into him.

Settled in his arms, her fingers dug into his back, holding him close to her. He'd wanted her like this for so long, he'd actually forgotten what that nagging, insistent yearning inside of him was until now. That damn kiss started something between them, then turned into a curse that haunted him into his dreams, insisting for something he didn't understand until now. Such a simple answer he'd made complicated by staying away from her all this time, hiding behind the fact he thought he owed her an apology, an explanation. All he really had to do was admit one thing. He wanted her. She meant something to him.

Still, the pieces of him and her didn't quite line up. They still had unfinished business with the whole kiss and his friend, her ex, Billy.

Why did his friend want to keep her away from him?

For the reasons that seemed so obvious now, but he'd never seen in the past? What else had he missed back in the day when he'd avoided getting in between Billy and Luna, when he'd gone out of his way to hang with his friend, never acknowledging he really wanted a glimpse of her? A moment to see her smile at him when the smiles she'd given Billy dimmed and disappeared. A chance to have even a glimpse of the happiness his friend seemed to have had with her.

He always told himself, no, he'd never cross that line. But he did cross it, and he couldn't go back. He'd been stuck in a wasteland of wanting someone he shouldn't, but here she was, in his arms, but she still didn't belong there.

He held her shoulders and gently pushed her away, but not out of his grasp. She kept her hands gripped at his sides.

"He can't be gone." Her eyes were so filled with

sorrow he felt it in his soul, and his own eyes glassed over.

"I'm sorry, honey, he is."

Her hands gripped him tighter. She shook him, letting out her pent-up frustration. "I don't know what to do."

"The hospital will notify his family. They'll take care of him."

She deflated all at once, her shoulders going lax beneath his hands. "He was my friend."

"I know, honey."

Her tear-stained face tilted to the side. Those beautiful blue eyes stared at him with the question she whispered. "Are we still friends?"

He didn't know what to say.

"He told me to fix things with you, that I should do it now before it was too late. Take-it-from-an-old-guy, time-gets-away-from-you kind of thing. Too much time has passed without us saying what needs to be said."

He swiped his thumbs across her wet cheeks. "Luna, you're upset. This can wait."

"No, it can't. Not anymore."

"Then let me be the one to say it. I'm sorry. I shouldn't have kissed you."

"I kissed you, but I'm not sorry I did it. I'm sorry you stepped back and out of my life. I'm sorry that it's taken me this long to tell you that I never meant to push you to do something that went against the way you felt for me and your friend. I'm sorry that you were forced to stand up for me against your friend."

He pressed his thumb over her trembling lips to get her to stop. "I stood up for you because it was the right thing to do. I kissed you because I wanted to kiss you. I stepped back because I thought I took advantage, when

I knew you'd eventually make things up and go back to Billy."

Her hand wrapped around his, dragging his thumb over her plump lip and chin and down to her neck, where she held his hand against her soft skin. "You were wrong. I'd ended things with him weeks before that night, and I'm glad I did, because none of it was real."

"What are you talking about? He loved you."

She shook her head side to side, a fresh wave of tears sliding down her cheeks. "In the beginning, it seemed so genuine." Her voice cracked. "I loved the attention he showered on me. Then, he got bored. He'd pick fights, and we'd eventually break up."

"I told him what an idiot he was for letting you go."

"Yes, he told me that night at the bar that's exactly what you'd say. So he'd come crawling back with promises that he'd be nicer, we'd be better together. I fell for it over and over again. Until I couldn't do it anymore, because I finally saw what he tried so hard to hide. He didn't really want to be with me. He just didn't want me to be with you."

"Why would he think you wanted to be with me?"

"You were best friends. You two hung out together all the time. You kept a respectful distance from me. When the three of us were together, Billy went way overboard on the 'She's my girl. Look how lucky I am to have her' bullshit. I saw the way you were with other girls. You liked to have fun, but you treated the girls with respect even though you didn't want anything serious with them. When Billy got out of line, picked a fight for no reason, or generally acted like a jerk, I'd tell him to act more like you. You always treated me better than decent. You had manners. You worked hard with your brothers. You took things seriously when they counted.

"He didn't like me comparing him to you. In fact, it pissed him off."

"That's ridiculous. We were friends, not competitors."

"That's what you thought. But that night in the bar when you walked in, I got up from my friends and headed in your direction. I hadn't even seen Billy in the bar that night. But he'd been spying on me and intercepted me before I got to you. I didn't mean for him to see it, but I guess I couldn't hide it anymore."

"What?"

"The way I felt when I looked at you. All those times I told Billy he should be more like you, it finally dawned on me that's not what I wanted. Not him, acting like you. I just wanted you. So I got up when I saw you and thought I'd buy you a beer, say hi, and see what happened."

"Are you serious?"

"I know, long shot, right? I mean, you were his friend. You're not the kind of guy who does that to a buddy. But we were broken up, and I thought, Why the hell not? If I don't try, I'll always wonder." She pressed her hand to his chest. "I was tired of wondering."

Colt's mind did not compute. All this time, she wanted him. "What did Billy say to you?"

"Same thing he always said after we broke up and he wanted me back. The thing is, I didn't want to hear it anymore. I didn't want to hear it the time before, when we got back together, but I did because I thought maybe that time he'd be the right kind of guy. He wasn't ever going to change, but I had. I wanted something more.

Something better. Someone better. That night, he saw it. I didn't want him anymore. I wasn't going to take him back. I wanted to walk away from him and take a new path."

Still unable to believe the unbelievable, he asked, "One that led to me?"

"I'm sorry. I never thought my rejection would set him off like that."

"He grabbed you. Tried to drag you out the back door."

"Away from you. If he'd been sober, he probably would have laughed in my face and told me there was no chance in hell of you dating me, but he was drunk and acting stupid. You stepped in to make him let go of me and take him home to sober up."

"The next thing I know, he sucker-punched me."

"I'm really sorry." Her pale cheeks flamed pink. "It's so embarrassing to have to admit all this to you. I had no right to come between you and your friend. That was never my intention. Then I found you outside sitting against the bumper of your truck with your hand pressed to your swollen jaw. I only meant to apologize, but I saw your face and I felt so bad and then I . . ."

"You kissed me and proved what a colossal fool Billy was for letting you go."

"What?"

"You felt it. I felt it. My whole world rocked off center, but I thought you belonged to Billy, that you two would work it out again. I had no right to trespass in your relationship."

"You didn't. I walked out of that relationship long before that night."

"I didn't know that at the time, so I walked away. I guess you owe me that beer."

Her hands slid down his shoulders and over his arms. Her gaze dropped to the crescent moon cuts she'd left on him with her nails.

"Oh God, Colt, you're bleeding."

"Yeah, every time we're together, you leave your mark."

CHAPTER 3

Simon rushed into the Crystal Creek Clinic and stopped short when Josh stepped out of a room down the hallway. Aunt Bea and Uncle Harry followed Josh, hanging back several paces, whispering to each other. Simon ignored the woman behind the reception desk asking if she could help him, then headed for his brother. The anger in Josh's eyes didn't obscure the pain.

"He's dead." Josh's flat words didn't register at first.

Simon shook his head, unable to take it in. "No. We just saw him not even two hours ago."

"Heart attack. Dropped dead in the diner at his fucking too-young-to-be-decent girlfriend's feet."

Simon narrowed his gaze and drew his lips into a tight line. "What?"

"Paramedics told the doctor the waitress tried to save him, but no amount of CPR was going to fix his blown-out heart."

Simon raked his hand through his hair and stared at his brother, trying to figure out what the hell was with the anger-laced monotone. Josh could be brusque, but Simon had never heard him be this callous.

"We were too late." Josh didn't show an ounce of remorse about their father's passing.

Simon hung his head, overcome with sorrow, taking it in, feeling the pain enveloping his chest.

"We can't change whatever he put in his will. We'll have to work with whatever it says, try to swing things our way."

Simon's head snapped up. He shouldn't be surprised. Yep, that was Josh, always finding ways to turn everything to his advantage. Whenever they played good cop, bad cop, Josh always got the bad cop role. He excelled at it.

"So that's it. He's gone. Just like that?"

Josh stuffed his hands in the pockets of his gray slacks. "It's not surprising. We knew his health was failing."

Yeah, Simon knew, but he'd thought his stubborn, strong dad would somehow beat the odds. After all, he'd outlived his much younger wife. The fucking flu took her out five years back. In the back of Simon's mind, he'd half expected his father to remarry—maybe even the way-too-young waitress he was obsessed with—and live a long life into his nineties.

"Simon, we need to contact the lawyer and get the ball rolling," Josh pushed.

Simon rubbed his hand over his tight chest and blinked back tears. "Can I have five minutes to settle into the fact Dad is dead?"

"Take all the time you need, but I for one want to know what the hell that crazy old man put in his will."

"I'd like to know the same." Aunt Bea joined them, her white-blonde hair pulled back into a sleek knot, her ears, neck, and hands bedecked in dozens of sparkling jewels. She could probably add a new hospital wing with the amount of money she wore like she was going to a royal engagement.

Country Queen. The old nickname didn't bring a smile to Simon's face like it used to.

Uncle Harry, always Aunt Bea's backup and support in any situation, put his big hands on her shoulders. Bea was a tough old bird. Not a single tear gathered in her eyes. Simon choked his back so far, but Josh took after their taciturn aunt.

"Your father was a good man. He took care of you boys and me and my Harry."

Simon wondered if Aunt Bea wanted to plant the seeds for him and Josh to take care of her from now on. Really, didn't any of them miss Dad? Didn't any of them care?

"Your father could be generous when he wanted to be. These last years, he changed." The disappointment in Aunt Bea's eyes matched the regret in her voice. Where Simon's father was kind but stern, Aunt Bea was reserved and distant.

Simon shook his head, felt the well of pain and loss weighted down with his rising anger. "I'm going in to see him. This isn't the time to discuss the ranch and everything Dad left behind."

"He's gone. Now is the time to step up and take over." His aunt reminded Simon of what he thought was to be his duty although just hours ago his father had told them it wasn't going to happen.

"He's really gone?" The soft, sweet voice reminded Simon of his mother.

He turned to the woman he'd resented for a long time. The woman his father spent time with at the restaurant after his mother died. His dad talked about being lonely. Well, he should have gotten a dog, not a woman who could be Simon's little sister.

"What the hell are you doing here?" Josh's harsh

tone made the waitress flinch. The guy beside her narrowed his gaze, eyeing Josh and Simon up and down, taking their measure. He looked familiar. Simon might have gone to school with his older brother, but right now Simon couldn't place the family name.

Simon stepped forward and extended his hand. "I'm Simon, Wayne's youngest. That's my brother, Josh."

Luna took his hand in a brief shake.

"Luna. I was with your father when he passed." The words barely made it past her trembling lips. Tears gathered in her eyes. One rolled down her cheek. She didn't bother to wipe it away. "I'm so sorry for your loss."

Unlike his family, here was someone who grieved for his father.

"Thank you for coming, but this is a time for family." Aunt Bea looked down her nose at Luna, disapproval lighting her eyes.

"You're just here hoping to find out what he left you, his filthy, money-hungry whore." The words came out like a curse from Josh's lips, stunning Simon.

"Watch it," the guy beside Luna warned.

Luna gasped and took a step back, like she'd been struck. "No. No." She shook her head. "Not at all. He was my friend. I tried to save him. We both did." She took the hand of the guy beside her, linking her fingers with his.

Simon held out his hand to the man, still trying to place him. "Simon. Thank you for what you tried to do."

The guy had to release Luna to shake Simon's hand. "Colt Kendrick."

Ah, Simon vaguely remembered Rory Kendrick from school.

"No problem. I'm sorry about your dad. I didn't know him well, but he was a good guy. Smart. Always willing to lend a hand to others and give advice."

"Really?" Josh's surprise matched Simon's.

"He and my grandfather were friendly. They'd get to talking in town or out at one or the other's ranches. When I was around, I liked to listen to them exchange ideas, argue about crops and cattle, that kind of thing."

Luna turned to Colt. "I didn't know you knew him that well."

Colt shrugged. "Not that well. It's a small town. You run into people, exchange hellos and small talk. I don't do small talk, neither did Wayne. We mostly talked horses."

Simon studied the pair. These two were close, but not together. Interesting.

"So what you're trying to tell us is that you weren't sleeping with our dad?" Josh asked boldly.

Luna's bright blue eyes darkened with anger. "No. Like I said, he was a friend. We saw each other at the diner twice a week, and sometimes he had me out to the ranch."

"You expect us to believe you went out to the ranch and spent time with him, but you weren't sleeping with him?" Josh asked.

"We rode the horses. Talked. Had lunch together." She threw up her hands and let them fall. "You know, things friends do."

"Well, you're smarter than you look, I guess, if you got him wrapped around your little finger without so much as dropping to your knees for him."

Colt pointed his finger at Josh. "Shut your mouth, or I'll shut it for you."

Luna gave Josh a hard glare, her mouth set in a firm

line. "That's a vile thing to say, especially when a good and decent man just died. I don't know what is wrong with you people that you're more concerned with me than you are about Wayne's passing."

"Apologies. Grief has gotten the better of my nephew's good judgment. But if you're not here hoping to cash in on his death, then why are you here?" Aunt Bea pressed one glittering hand to her chest.

"I came to see if maybe the doctors had been able to save him." Tears filled Luna's eyes and clogged her throat. "I came to say goodbye."

"Yes, well, he's gone. We, as his family, need to say our goodbyes and make arrangements for what comes next. You should go." Aunt Bea waved Luna off, like shooing away a fly.

They'd drawn quite a few stares from the clinic staff, patients, and visitors. They'd kept their voices low, but everyone sensed the hostility as they faced off in the corridor.

"Colt," Dr. Bowden called from behind the group.

Colt stepped around everyone, pulling Luna along behind him. Embarrassed and angry, she ducked her head to hide the emotions playing out on her beautiful face. Simon had to admit, his father had great taste in women.

"Bell, would it be possible for Luna to see Mr. Travers for just a few minutes to say goodbye?"

"Of course. I don't see why not."

"She doesn't belong here," Aunt Bea snapped.

Simon shook his head and cocked up one side of his mouth. "Go ahead in, Luna. It's fine."

"Simon," Josh scoffed.

"What is the big deal?" Simon had a feeling this

wasn't the last they'd see of Luna. She may be saying goodbye to his dad, but he had a feeling she'd be a part of their lives. The way his father spoke about not leaving everything to him and Josh made Simon wonder what his father might have left to his "good friend" Luna, and how he would get it back.

CHAPTER 4

Luna stared down at Wayne's pale face. She'd never seen a dead person. She thought he'd look like he was sleeping. Instead, she got the sense he just wasn't there. His spirit had gone. Whatever it was that had made him the kind, vibrant, fun-loving man she'd known had disappeared with his last breath. The ache in her chest eased, knowing he was in a better place.

She already missed him. She'd miss their talks, visiting his ranch, the advice he doled out with a touch of humor and a gentle nudge. She had great parents, but Wayne had been like a second father to her.

She reached out and touched his hand through the sheet that covered him from neck to toes. With a soft squeeze, she silently said her final goodbye. "Soar, my old friend."

Head down, she turned for the door but snapped her head up when she spotted a pair of well-worn brown cowboy boots. She met Colt's hazel eyes, surprised to see the depth of sorrow in them.

"You knew Wayne better than I thought." She felt Wayne's presence, like a soft nudge between her shoulders, pushing her toward Colt.

"Not really. Not like you."

She narrowed her gaze, not liking his meaning at all.

"Dial down the outrage, honey. I mean I didn't share a close friendship with him like you did. I'm sorry for your loss."

She didn't expect the regret that he let show was for her. And she did mean he was letting it show, because Colt Kendrick could look at you without an ounce of emotion on his face or in those hazel depths. He'd done so with her for a long time. The talk they'd shared at the diner had changed things between them, but it hadn't really fixed anything. She didn't know if they were back to being friends, or if he was just helping out a girl he used to know who was in a bad spot.

He'd been sweet to ask her boss to let her out of her shift at the diner for the night after what happened. He'd gone above and beyond offering to drive her to the clinic to see if by some miracle Wayne had recovered.

"I can't believe he's gone."

"What you said to him was nice."

"Something he used to say to me all the time."

"He told you to soar."

"No. He told me I could. All I had to do was make up my mind and make it happen."

Colt cocked his head and studied her. "Yeah, you've got that in you. Determination. Guts. Given half a chance and setting your mind to it, you'd get just about anything done. When are you going to start using that special education degree you earned?"

"How did you . . . Sadie told you, right?"

"No."

She eyed him skeptically. "Very few people know about that."

"I guess that makes me one of the lucky few."

So, he'd made a point to learn things about her. A flutter of hope rose up in her heart.

"You worked hard to get it, why aren't you teaching?"

"There aren't a lot of opportunities for full-time positions out here. I do some part-time work at a place in Bozeman on the weekends with children and teens with autism."

"How's your brother doing?"

"Since Tanner has Asperger's, he's living mostly on his own in an apartment two doors down from my parents. They still spend most of their day with him. They're trying to give him his independence and find him a job."

Colt nodded. "He likes repetition, right?"

"Yes. He can work, so long as he does the same thing all the time. OCD is a major part of his life and mindset. Routine and structure allow him to have some freedom and independence from my parents, but finding him a job that suits his needs and skill set isn't easy."

"Is he any good with animals?"

"He loves them. My parents got him a dog when he was young. When everything else in the outside world became too much, that dog calmed him. We lost Burt a couple months back."

"You might think of getting him a job at a shelter feeding and grooming the animals. Maybe on a ranch if he's any good with horses. Even one of the places that has goats and makes those specialty cheeses."

"That's a great idea. I hadn't thought about that. I suggested a busboy at a restaurant, but too many people. Lots of noise with everyone talking and music playing. He'd be overwhelmed."

"If I think of anything else, I'll let you know when you buy me that beer."

That promising statement ignited a warm ache in her heart. Lord knows, she was grateful to have Colt here with her. "I could use a drink right now."

"Ready to go?"

She turned back and stared down at Wayne's placid face. Even now he looked like a good man. Just like the one standing behind her, distracting her with talk of her family. Something familiar for her to focus on besides her grief.

"Thank you. I appreciate you bringing me here, using your pull with the doctor to get me in to see him, and sticking around when you could have gone home a long time ago."

"First, there's no other place I need to be. The doc's a friend of the family, so it wasn't that hard to ask her a favor. If I'd stuck around the last time you and I had a crazy night, I might have gotten the real story of what happened and saved myself a hell of a lot of time avoiding you."

He held out his hand, indicating they should head back out and let Wayne's family come in to say their goodbyes. Luna wondered if all they wanted to do was pick Wayne's pockets for every bit of cash they could get their hands on. They really were something.

Luna walked out ahead of Colt. He stepped up beside her and laid his fingertips lightly on her lower back to guide her past Wayne's family, the tension so thick it nearly stopped her in her tracks. Colt's steady pressure on her back helped her ignore the stares and walk out with her head up.

Let them think whatever they wanted to think. She knew the truth. Friends like Wayne didn't come along often in one's life. She'd been blessed to know him.

Colt walked her to his truck and opened the door.

She sucked in a startled breath and grabbed the dark brown Stetson off the seat. "I forgot to take this in and give it to his sons."

"Keep it. They don't care about his hat. They want his ranch."

"But . . ."

"If they ask for it, give it back. Otherwise, keep it as a reminder of the man who meant something special to you."

"You don't think they'll want it?"

"I doubt they'll give a single thought about the man's hat when they're busy counting his money."

She frowned, climbed into the truck, and set the hat on her lap. He stared at her for a moment, pressed his lips together, thought better about speaking his mind, and closed the door, leaving her wondering what he might have said. He climbed behind the wheel, started the truck, and drove them out of the parking lot and down the road.

Luna lost herself in the stars and the quiet inside the truck cab. Colt drove with his left elbow propped on the window frame, his thumb hooked under his chin, his fingers pressed to his lips. He stared straight ahead down the dark road out of town.

"You missed the turnoff for my street."

Colt hit the brakes, jarring the truck before he let off the pedal and coasted to a stop. Luckily, no one followed behind them.

"Sorry. Autopilot."

Okay, so he wasn't in a hurry to get rid of her. That was good, right? Maybe. "You're tired. Ready to get home. I understand."

Colt managed the three-point turn and headed back toward the outskirts of town, where she had a tiny shoebox apartment above Mrs. Carroll's single-car garage. He took the turn for her street and deftly backed into the driveway in front of Mrs. Carroll's beloved rattle-trap Buick.

Luna's apartment stood empty and dark behind it. Another lonely night in her box and short one friend to look forward to seeing next week.

Colt's warm fingers touched her cheek. "Hey, where'd you go?"

She jumped and turned her gaze from the side mirror to Colt's hazel eyes. The automatic porch light from Mrs. Carroll's place highlighted the gold mist and brown flecks amidst the spattering of green in his eyes.

"Sorry. I guess I'm tired, too, though I shouldn't be. I usually work much later than this."

"It's been an unusual night. You lost your friend. It's understandable you're not yourself. I should have taken you back to the diner to get your Jeep."

"A good long walk tomorrow will do me good."

"It's across town. I'll come get you, or maybe Sadie can drive you over when she goes to work."

"It's no big deal, Colt. I got it."

Colt relented, pinching back one side of his mouth in a lopsided frown. He opened his door and slipped out.

"Hey, you don't have to walk me to the door."

He eyed her. "Yes, I do. My granddad would tan my hide if I didn't." He shut the door and rounded the hood to come to her side.

She'd forgotten about the manners. How something as simple as opening a door for her or saying please and thank you made her belly flutter like this. He'd done those things when she'd seen him out with friends or other women. Not going there. She erased the image from her mind. Billy teased about him trying to score points with women, but Colt didn't need to score points like that. Not with his sun-kissed good looks, sculpted muscles, and tall, lean frame. The gorgeous face and bod were something to behold, but the man knew how to have fun and make you laugh. Under all that was a guy who understood that simple kindnesses went a hell of a lot further in some people's minds than others.

Which is why the kiss they'd shared bothered him so much. He thought he'd crossed a line. She thought she'd overstepped, giving in to her need—the same need that resonated beneath her grief and exhaustion even now.

Colt opened her door and held out his hand to help her down. She took it but didn't move, except to turn and face him.

"Are you done avoiding me?"

"I'm sorry. You're sorry. At this point, I don't even know for what." He squeezed her hand, and tingles shot up her arm.

"Maybe because we both wanted that kiss and didn't know what to do when it felt like something more than we intended?"

Nothing. Not a single glimpse in his eyes or on his face that he felt that way.

"Or maybe that was all on my part," Luna added. "Billy is happily married. That's got to ease your mind."

"To Cheryl. They got together about ten minutes after your fight with him at the bar."

"Just goes to show that if he really cared about me, he wouldn't have met and married her so fast."

"I heard it was love at first sight." Colt rolled his eyes.

She could care less what Billy did and who he did it with. "So, not a romantic."

"I'm all for romance, but love isn't a lightning bolt kind of thing."

"I'm not sure Rory and Sadie would agree with you."

The muscle in Colt's square jaw flexed. He pulled her from the truck. She reached back at the last second and grabbed the hat off the seat. Colt stole it from her grasp and dropped it on her head.

"It suits you."

"Hardly. It's more your style." More rocker chick than cowgirl, she took the hat from her head, shook out her shaggy hair and bangs, and followed Colt to the stairs leading up to her apartment.

"Those bangs drive me crazy."

The odd admission made her smirk. "Why?"

"The black makes your eyes even bluer. The contrast drives me to distraction, but the way you sweep your finger along your brow to draw the hair back always gets to me."

She stared at his back as he walked up the stairs.

"Come on, Luna. You're almost home."

She shook herself out of her thoughts and staring at Colt's fine ass, snug in his Levi's, and hustled up the stairs behind him. He waited on the landing and held out his hand for the keys she dug out of her purse.

"You should leave the light on up here for when you come home late."

"I would if it worked."

"What's wrong with it?"

"Don't know. I put in a new bulb the last time it went out, but I think something broke, because it doesn't work anymore."

"How long ago was that?"

"Spring before last."

His mouth dipped into another dark frown. "Why don't you ask your landlord to fix it?"

"I have. Many times. But she's older and not inclined to make improvements."

"This is a safety issue, not an improvement."

"I'm young. I can see in the dark. Or so she tells me all the time."

Colt swore under his breath and pushed her door open. He reached in and flipped the switch, turning on the light in her living space.

"Holy wow!"

Luna laughed. "Holy wow. Really?"

"I don't know what else to say. This place is . . . not what I expected."

"It's the size of a closet, but it's home."

"No. It's like something out of a magazine."

Luna stood next to him in the doorway and stared in at her tiny place. The distressed whitewashed boards that she'd salvaged from her parents' old, run-down barn days before they sold the place to get the money to care for her brother covered the drywall the last tenant used as a punching bag, poking multiple holes in every wall. Her locker-size bathroom sat tucked in the corner at the left side, her collection of silver framed mirrors covering the door in all kinds of sizes and shapes. Her tiny kitchen sat beside it, with Formica countertops she'd resurfaced in a soft sand color, thanks to a kit from the hardware store. A short floating counter separated the kitchen from the rest of the living space, where she had her futon/bed, golden oak coffee table, TV stand, and an overstuffed tan chair. A gorgeous and bright turquoise rug anchored the living space and covered most of the scarred wood floor. She couldn't do anything about the ugly white/gold marbled linoleum in the kitchen and bathroom, but the rest of the place was clean and bright, just the way she liked it.

"That photograph above the sofa is gorgeous."

"Thanks. I took that last year. Cost a fortune to get it

enlarged like that, but I love the scale of it on the wall. Makes it seem like a huge picture window."

"I bet when it's snowing outside you look at that mountain covered in green grass and trees and wish for spring."

"I've tried to make this whole place feel like spring."

"Right down to the wildflowers in the vase on the coffee table."

"If you pick them yourself, they don't cost anything."

"Is that a picture of you and Wayne?" Colt cocked his head to the mantel shelf she'd hung below the front window with pictures of her family and friends in eclectic silver and black frames.

In the photo, she sat on Wayne's lap, her arms wrapped around his neck, his arms wrapped around her middle, lips pressed to her cheek as she smiled, facing the camera. Even now, she smiled softly despite her eyes glassing over, fondly remembering that special day. "My birthday last year. He came to the restaurant and brought me that pretty cake." The candle flames burned bright amidst the pretty pink roses decorating the top. "Raspberry filled vanilla cake with white chocolate frosting."

"What did he buy you for your birthday?"

She tilted her head and eyed him, wondering if he believed the rumors, if just a little bit. "A box of my favorite milk-chocolate-covered almond butter toffee from this specialty candy maker. You can't get it here. You have to order it."

"Nice. Thoughtful."

That's it. Nothing more.

"I like your place. You've taken living small to a whole new level. I like the boots on the shelf over the TV."

"A girl's gotta have her shoes." The rest were in the oversize wardrobe next to the window, along with her clothes.

"You might be the only girl I've ever met with this few possessions."

"I have what I need."

She finally stepped into her home and turned to Colt. "Coming in?"

"No. Dropping you off. Will you be okay here by yourself tonight?"

She thought of the long night they'd had and all that happened, which brought the sadness she tried to keep tucked away floating to the surface again. "I'll be okay. You were amazing tonight, jumping in to help me."

"I wish it turned out better."

She dropped the hat and her purse on the table beside the door where she kept her keys and mail. She propped her shoulder against the opposite side of the door frame, facing Colt on the other side. "I appreciate the effort and you sticking around to look after me."

He tipped his head to acknowledge her words, but he didn't say anything, just gave her a look that said so much about their unfinished business.

This close to him, her body heated, anticipated his touch, even though he'd made not one move to close the distance between them. The man wouldn't step foot inside her house. She wondered why he held back when she wanted to close the distance that had separated them for so long, when that kiss they'd shared proved a fire burned inside both of them for each other.

After the loss she'd suffered tonight, the emptiness building inside her, she wanted so bad to feel Colt's arms around her. For him to make her feel alive, when her insides and her mind wanted to turn numb and block out the pain and grief.

"Are you going to kiss me again?" She asked the bold question, but her stomach fluttered with nerves that maybe she'd been too forward yet again. She'd overstepped once, with disastrous consequences. She hoped she hadn't done the same again. She'd always been one to speak her mind, tell the truth, even when she should probably keep her mouth shut.

"Yes." Colt shifted his weight from the door, stood tall, looking down at her, then headed to the stairs, softly brushing his fingers over her hand as he passed and took his time stepping down each tread to the gravel drive below. He didn't look back, but she thought he hesitated for just a split second on the driveway. She stood on the dark landing, the light from her home spilling out and making it difficult to see him climb into the cab of his truck. He started the engine, and again there was that tense moment of hesitation before he pulled out of the drive and disappeared.

She closed the door and leaned her back against the wood, staring at her empty, quiet apartment, and she wondered if those small hesitations even existed or if they were just her imagination and hope that this time Colt noticed her as more than just his best friend's girlfriend. Ex-girlfriend. Heavy on the ex. Thank God. She'd dodged a bullet with Billy. Oh, she liked him well enough back in the day—for the most part. But she'd learned her lesson. He wasn't a forever kind of guy.

That one just drove away.

She walked into the kitchen to make herself a cup of tea, but stopped short with one word ringing in her head. Colt's simple reply to her bold question. *Yes.*

A soft smile spread across her lips. Anticipation fluttered the beat of her heart.

One question rattled around her head since the kiss they shared, and it moved to the front of her mind now, past all her grief and the worries about her life.

When will I see him again?

CHAPTER 5

Colt walked in the back door, smelled the cinnamon and coffee from the kitchen, and headed straight for both, but not before he wiped his feet on the mat. Sadie would kill him for tracking dirt into the house. Funny how he'd gotten used to her living with them. She really had become a part of the family.

Luna's comment about Sadie and Rory falling in love like lightning stuck with him since last night. So did the feel of her skin from when he'd touched her hand before he'd left. He'd nearly gone back up for that kiss the second his boots hit the gravel drive, and again when he'd sat in his truck about to pull out of her place. He'd ordered himself home and away from her, because . . . well, he'd had several reasons last night. None of which made a whole hell of a lot of sense this morning when he woke from one hell of a dream about her, his bed, his hands and mouth all over her naked body.

He poured himself a mug of coffee, snatched up one of the cinnamon muffins from the plate on the counter, and stuffed half of it in his mouth.

"Hey, Colt," Sadie said from the table behind him.

"Hey," he said around the muffin filling his mouth. "Whose car is outside?" He poured milk in his coffee.

"Mine."

Her voice jolted through his system like a California quake, making him stop and take notice. Colt turned with the milk jug in his hand and faced the owner of that soft voice, the one that followed him into his dreams and asked him outright if he planned to kiss her again. Hell yes—only not on the night her friend died and she was upset. Taking advantage of a vulnerable woman wasn't in his playbook. They'd gone about it all wrong the first time. If they tried this thing again, he wanted to do it right. Play by the rules. Ask her out on a proper date.

Lay her out on the kitchen table and kiss her senseless—the way she made him feel every time he saw her.

He shook off that thought and focused, but she went and swept her finger along her brow, drawing her hair away from those amazing eyes, and he lost all thought but one. Damn she's beautiful. And sexy. *And I'm losing my mind all over again.*

"Uh, where's your Jeep? I thought you were going to pick it up this morning at the diner."

"I did, but when I got there I discovered someone had thrown a brick into the windshield, so it's at the shop getting fixed."

Colt didn't like the sound of that, especially after the way Wayne's family treated her at the hospital last night. He couldn't quite put his finger on why they came to mind, but they seemed the type to knock people out of their way to get what they wanted. Still, the family stayed at the clinic after he took Luna home. They had enough on their plates to handle. He couldn't imagine they'd do something as petty and mean as wrecking Luna's car just because they didn't like her friendship with Wayne.

"What did the cops say?"

"Nothing. They took the report for the insurance company, but otherwise things like that happen all the time. The bar is only a couple blocks up. Some drunk and rowdy cowboys probably did it, thinking they were having fun."

"Colt, do you think it's something more?" Sadie asked.

He shook his head, having no reason to raise the red flag without any cause, despite the warning tingle at the back of his neck. "No. Unless something else like that happened to you recently, or around the diner."

"Cars get broken into all the time." Luna tilted her head, looking off and thinking. "Nothing stands out."

"Was anything taken from your car?"

"I don't keep anything in there worth taking."

"That's not what I asked."

"Nothing was taken. The doors were still locked. Nothing but a busted-up windshield."

Her response should have eased his mind. It didn't. Not all the way. "You're probably right. Just vandalism." He said the words but didn't quite believe them.

"Thanks for creeping me out anyway." Luna's body shook with a pretend, overdramatic shiver.

"Sorry. Just being cautious."

"When did you two start talking to each other again?" Sadie asked, eyeing him, then her friend.

"Last night." Luna kept her steady ice blue gaze on him.

"You didn't tell her about Wayne?" he asked.

"I just got here a couple of minutes ago."

"What happened to Wayne?" Sadie asked.

"He died," Luna whispered, her gaze dropping to her lap.

"Heart attack right there in the diner," Colt added. "Luna tried her best to save him, but he was already gone."

Sadie wrapped her arm around her friend and hugged her close. "Oh my God, Luna, why didn't you say anything?"

"It's just so terrible. One minute we're talking, then the next he's gone."

"He died during your dinner?"

"No. He sent me to talk to Colt. The next thing I know, he's dropping to his knees and he's gone."

"Why did he send you over to talk to me?" Colt found that interesting and strange. Maybe the old guy hadn't been trying to set her up with one of his sons.

"To apologize for what I'd done."

"You never owed me an apology."

"Is anybody ever going to tell me what actually happened between you two?" Sadie asked, staring him down.

"I broke up an argument between Luna and my best friend. She'd been dating Billy forever. I didn't want to see things turn ugly between them, and Billy was drunk enough to say or do something he didn't really mean."

"For all Colt's good intentions, Billy decked him. A couple of the guys Billy came into the bar with got him out of there. I found Colt in the parking lot and somehow during my thank-you, I kissed him."

"I kissed you back."

He'd never forget that kiss. In fact, he wanted more. If Sadie wasn't sitting next to Luna right now, he'd pull her up out of that seat and kiss her until the need finally eased. Which would probably be never, judging by how long that first kiss stayed with him.

Sadie hid a smile, watching the two of them stare at each other. Colt didn't care, because he saw the same desire reflected back in Luna's bright blue eyes. She wouldn't likely forget that kiss either.

"Are you working late at the diner again tonight?"

"No. My shift starts in a couple hours and runs through the dinner rush. I'm done at eight. I just came by to help Sadie pick out invitations."

"Not anymore," Sadie said. "We're going to have a cup of tea and reminisce about Wayne."

Tears gathered in Luna's eyes. He hated to see them there instead of the happiness and humor that danced in them most days.

"I'll leave you to it. I've got work." He snatched another muffin off the counter. "I'm taking this with me. Thanks, sis."

"Don't thank me, Luna baked those."

He stopped on his way to the door and turned to her. "You did?"

"Yeah. Is that so surprising?"

"No, not really. It's just, I like a woman who can cook."

Luna's mouth dropped open despite herself. Colt walked out the door, happily chewing the cinnamon pecan muffin she'd spent the morning baking because she couldn't sleep for thinking about Wayne. Oh, who was she kidding, she couldn't stop thinking about Colt, the way he touched her hand last night on his way down the stairs, and that "*Yes.*"

Now the man walked out after dropping that little comment about liking women who cook. Did he really mean he liked her? She wasn't sure, because he had yet to ask her out on a date.

"Should I get a bucket of ice water to cool you down after that scorching look he gave you?"

Luna laughed. "I truly don't understand that man."

"Take it from someone who fell hard for a Kendrick brother, what they say, they mean."

"He might mean what he says, but so far he's done nothing about it."

"Did I mention how stubborn they can be?"

Luna laughed again but caught herself.

Sadie's hand settled over hers. "You miss Wayne."

Such a great friend to understand that despite all this business with Colt, deep down Luna grieved, and everything else was a distraction to help her cope with the loss. "Yes. I feel like my grief over losing Wayne and my happiness that Colt and I finally resolved this whole kiss thing are at war inside of me. I'm lost in my memories of all I shared with Wayne, but the hope that what I feel for Colt will turn into something surges up, and I feel guilty."

"Wayne was your friend, not your husband or relative. You miss him, but his passing doesn't mean you stop living. He'd want you to go on, live your life to the fullest. You said he told you to talk to Colt. He wanted you to work things out with him and maybe have a chance at something more. He wanted you to be happy."

"I guess."

"You know I'm right." Sadie touched Luna's arm. "So tell me, what is going on with the two of you?"

"I'm not sure on his end."

"How do you feel about Colt?"

Luna tilted her head and stared out the window at Colt, who was walking into the stables. "I'm wondering that myself."

"What do you mean?"

"What's not to like? The guy is gorgeous. But he's so much more than that. He's funny, but never in a mean way. He's kind. He's the last person who'd pick on someone for any reason. He'd never start a fight, but he can sure as hell finish one. When Billy hit him, I thought Colt would slug him back, but he didn't. He kept his cool, even when Billy spouted off about Colt always getting whatever the hell he wanted. But that's not Colt at all."

"No, it's not. He's had kind of a rough life."

"Yeah, I imagine it's been difficult without his parents."

"He misses them and doesn't remember them at the same time."

Luna pressed her lips together and shook her head. "Which makes it all worse, right? You know what you're missing, but not precisely who you miss, which makes you wonder all the more. One of the reasons he's so close to his brothers. Anyway, I'm not sure where this thing with Colt is going, or if it's going anywhere. We resolved the past, but we don't seem to be doing much different than we've done the past couple years in the present."

"Give it time. After what you two went through last night, maybe he's just giving you time and space to grieve before he asks you out."

"Maybe. Or maybe he's just letting it go now that we don't have to avoid each other all the time. Oh, and we won't be scowling at each other in your wedding photos."

"He told you about that." Sadie laughed.

"Yes at the diner, right before . . ." The tears came again.

"I know. It's not going to be the same around the diner on Tuesday and Thursday without Wayne." Sadie dropped her voice and leaned into Luna. "Will you be okay without the special tips he left you?"

Not many people knew that Wayne left her a hundred-dollar tip those nights he came into the diner. She'd used that money to help pay for school. Sometimes that extra money meant she got to keep the heat on in the long winter months when the diner crowd thinned out and she made a hell of a lot less money.

"I'll be fine." Luna picked at an imaginary piece of lint on her jeans, afraid to tell Sadie her news, but needing to all the same. "I got a teaching job offer."

"That's great."

"Out of state."

"That sucks." Sadie gave her a halfhearted smile. "I really hate to think about you moving away. I'd miss you so much."

"I don't want to, not really, but I need a job that pays more than my rent, student loans, and food."

"The area's growing, expanding. Maybe they'll need another teacher here soon."

"We'll see. The school has more special needs children than the teacher and two aides can handle, but there isn't enough money in the budget for the district to hire another teacher."

"Maybe they can apply for more state and federal funding?"

"Until then, and they stop cutting education funding, I have to do what I have to do to get by. I've only got a week to make my decision."

"I really hope you stay, but I understand this is what you really want to do."

Was it?

Sadie frowned. "When is Wayne's funeral?"

"I'm not sure. His family was at the hospital last night. I was the unwelcome guest."

Sadie's eyes narrowed. "Everyone knows how close you two were. Why would they be upset if you paid your respects?"

"Because they think I was sleeping with him, trying to get his money."

Sadie rolled her eyes. "Nonsense."

Luna laughed without any real humor. "Even you can't pull that off when the grapevine grows every time Wayne and I are seen together. Uh, were seen together."

"The people who said such things don't know anything."

"No, they just had a grand time making stuff up. Anyway, that's over now."

"So you'll start tongues wagging over you and Colt."

"I don't know about that."

"Why not? Where there's a spark you can ignite a flame."

"I'm not sure if that bridge already burned." The disappointment and regret that might be true filled her up and deepened her sadness.

"I don't think so. The way he looks at you . . . He's definitely interested."

"But do we want the same thing?"

"What do you want?"

"Someone to have fun with, eat a meal with, talk to about my day. Someone who makes my heart race and makes me feel protected, like they care, because they really do. I want someone who can be honest even when it's hard." Luna sat back in her chair and stared up at the ceiling. "After what happened last night, seeing Wayne pass away and the way his family acted,

I want to wake up every morning in the arms of some-one I love and have that person by my side when times are tough. When it's my time to go, I want him to be the last person I see and the last words I hear to be him telling me he loves me."

Sadie squeezed her hand and held tight. "I'm sorry you're lonely."

Yes, that was the heart of it. Luna had never felt lonely, not really, until last night, when Wayne died and Colt left her in her tiny box with nothing but her thoughts and a loneliness that grew, filling up her aching heart.

"It's silly. I have my family. Friends. You most es-pecially. I see dozens of people at the diner every day. You're all a part of my life."

"It's not the same." Sadie spoke the words that echoed in Luna's head even now.

"No, it's not." Luna shook off her melancholy thoughts and mood. "Sorry. I'm just upset about losing my friend. I'm fine. Really."

Sadie pushed the open laptop back on the table. "We don't have to do this today."

"It's the perfect thing to distract me and lighten my mood." Luna turned the laptop and scanned the eight different invitations shown. "I think I like the white paper with silver foil script the best. It's elegant. What's your favorite?"

"Luna, it's okay to be sad and grieve."

"I am, but one thing overrides both those things. Something I think that hit you, too, after your father died."

"What's that?"

"Life is short. There's no time to waste. I need to stop waiting for things to happen. I need to make them happen. Like deciding if taking the teaching position for this coming September is better than being a waitress and waiting for something that may never come and wasting the education I worked so hard to earn."

"You'd really leave, move away?"

"I don't want to. I love living here. It's close to my family. Still, I need to stop getting through each day, hoping the things I want in my life will just happen."

"What about Colt?"

"I like him. A lot. I'd like to get to know him better and see if there's something there. But he hasn't even asked me out. Besides, even if he does, I can't build my life around him when I want so much more."

"What if he does ask you out and you two really have something?"

"I'd have to think about it then, but right now, my priority is figuring out what I really want and if staying here is actually holding me back."

CHAPTER 6

Simon arrived at his father's ranch late, judging by the fact that his brother and aunt and uncle arrived before him. He didn't recognize the man on the front steps. Josh was yelling, flapping his arms in the air, unable to stand still and speak reasonably with whoever blocked them from going into the house.

Simon got out of the car and walked toward the group. His aunt's face and eyes filled with haughty indignation as she stood in her black designer pantsuit, a bloodred handbag over her bent arm. His uncle kept his hands clamped on her shoulders, trying to comfort her.

"You can't fucking keep me out of my father's home," Josh spat out, taking a menacing step closer to the man dressed in a business suit. He stood his ground, briefcase in hand, power tie perfectly straight.

"I'm following your father's wishes. No one is allowed inside until the reading of the will tomorrow at eleven."

"Let's get it done now," Aunt Bea demanded.

"My instructions are clear. It's to be read directly after the funeral."

"Bullshit," Josh bit out. "What difference does it make?"

"All parties must be present at the reading. I've been unable to contact one of the people named in the will at this time."

"Let me guess, you're trying to reach that fucking waitress," Josh guessed.

Aunt Bea pointed her perfectly manicured, red-tipped index finger at the man. "You leave her out of this. She gets nothing."

"I'm sorry, ma'am, but Mr. Travers's will is specific. His wishes will be carried out to the letter."

Simon stepped in before Josh wound up again for another round of useless swearing and ranting. "Um, is it true the other person is Luna?"

Simon's gut tightened, knowing the truth and dreading what it meant and what needed to be done.

Josh would freak out.

Aunt Bea certainly didn't want Luna to get a dime.

The bulk of the estate would be split between Simon and Josh. Aunt Bea probably got a little something. She used to pester Wayne all the time for money. Most of the time he gave in, probably just to shut the woman up. Of course, he did the same with Simon and Josh.

Luna was a wild card. Simon didn't believe she'd been sleeping with his father. Not when she showed up with the Kendrick cowboy last night at the hospital. Why sleep with his old man when she had someone her own age? Unless she really was out to get his father's money. Maybe the two of them were in on the scam together.

Simon remembered Rory Kendrick as an intense, duty-bound guy who skipped out on fun for working his family's ranch. The exact opposite of the life Simon wanted. Colt seemed to take after his big brother, but maybe he just wanted an easy score and was using Luna to get it.

"You'll know everything tomorrow," the lawyer stated, not giving an inch. "Until then, no one goes into the house. Nothing is to be taken from the property. No one is to interfere in the ranch operations. If you do, I'll contact the authorities and have you arrested for trespassing." The lawyer held up his hand before Josh went off again. "Please, don't make me do that. It's just one day. Give yourself time to grieve. We'll lay Wayne to rest and sort out the rest tomorrow."

Josh waved off the lawyer, glared, and stalked off to his car.

Aunt Bea let out a frustrated huff, held her head high, spun on her high heels, and walked off to her car, Uncle Harry following along like her lapdog.

Simon had a feeling nothing would be sorted out tomorrow and they'd all be mired in some kind of muck, battling over the ranch, money, and everything else his father left behind. No one would be satisfied, because they each wanted it all.

CHAPTER 7

Colt screwed in the lightbulb and replaced the glass cover on the new outdoor motion-sensor light he'd bought and installed outside Luna's door. The thought of her coming home at night to a dark house tightened his gut with dread. What if she tripped on the slippery stairs in winter? What if some nutcase hid in the shadows and jumped her?

With a shake of his head, he dismissed the crazy, irrational thoughts that brought him here today. She'd likely call him out for overstepping, doing things for her he had no right to do. If he hurried and cleaned up, he could be out of here before she got home. He didn't though, because he wanted to see her. He thought about her a lot today. He wondered how she was doing. If her grief still fogged her every thought or slowly receded as time passed and she settled into her daily life once again. Would the memory of last night spring forth every time she walked into the diner to work? He hoped not.

She needed time.

Maybe he should take some, too, to think about what he was doing here and why he'd come.

Luna's Jeep pulled into the drive with a brand-new

windshield. A white pickup drove past his truck parked on the street. The guy driving slowed and stared at Luna as she got out of the car. Colt couldn't make out the dark figure, but he sure as hell didn't like the way the truck sped up abruptly and raced away.

Luna pulled her purse and two grocery bags from her Jeep. Ah, the reason she arrived home later than he'd anticipated.

The bright smile on her lips lit up his chest with a warmth that spread through him—and almost dimmed his concern about the brick through her windshield and the creepy drive-by moments ago.

"Hey," she called, making her way across the gravel drive to the steps.

"Hi." He bent and gathered up his tools, dumping them in the toolbox he kept in his truck. He picked up the discarded rubbish from the light and stuffed it into the box.

"What are you doing here?" Her words came out hesitant and unsure. He didn't like that one bit.

"Fixed your light. Can't have you coming home in the dark all the time."

She stopped on the stairs halfway up. He closed the lid on the toolbox, stood, and stared down at her, noting the surprise in her eyes. He thought about his words and what they revealed. Couldn't take them back. Didn't want to really, so he let it go.

"What's in the bags?"

"Mostly dinner. Some other stuff for the week." She walked up the rest of the steps. "Want to come in?"

"No. What's for dinner?"

Luna glanced at her closed door, then him. Confusion clouded her eyes, but he didn't explain his aversion to going into her house. If his last comment said too much, the reasons keeping him out of her house would tell her a hell of a lot more than he cared to admit right now. As it was, he barely held himself back from kissing her right here in the halo of light the new fixture cast over them as night swallowed day and the stars came to life overhead.

Luna set the bags down by the railing, leaned over, and pulled out two bottles of beer. His favorite brand. She handed one to him. "Thanks for fixing the light."

He twisted the top on the beer she handed him and gave it back to her, taking the other from her, popping the top, and clinking the neck to her bottle. He took a deep swallow, then let out his breath and some of the tension tightening his gut. "You're welcome." He fished the receipt from his pocket and handed it over. "Take the amount off your rent next month and give her that in its place."

The receipt disappeared into her purse, but she pulled out a wad of cash. Mostly fives and ones. Tips from tonight. She counted out some bills and held them out to him.

"I don't want that."

"Like you said, I'll take the amount off my rent."

"I don't want your money, Luna. Put it away."

She pinched her mouth into a lopsided frown, stuffed the bills back in her purse, and shook her head. She sat on the landing, her feet on the step below, and grabbed the bag behind her, setting it in front of her. He didn't expect a tug on his jeans, but he sat next to her when she didn't let go until he relented. They barely fit side by side on the steps, but he didn't make a move to give her even a little more space. His thigh pressed to hers, sending his system into overdrive. He just might overheat and do something stupid like kiss her again before he really got to know her. Before he had a chance to see if the girl he used to know, the one he couldn't stop thinking about, was the same woman sitting beside him. Did they have something? Or was the power of that kiss nothing more than them both giving in to something they thought was forbidden?

God, the woman was temptation times a million. The thing that really got to him, she didn't even know it. There she went, swiping her finger across her brow, sliding those strands back and over her ear.

Oblivious to his scrutiny, Luna set her beer next to his boot and pulled out a round plastic container and a foil package. She pulled out a plastic-wrapped fork and napkin and undid them. The scent of garlic bread made his stomach rumble. He hadn't eaten since lunch, having missed dinner two hours ago. As night had set in, he'd wondered what he'd pick up to eat on the way home. Maybe Sadie left him a plate in the fridge, as she often did when he didn't show up to the table on time.

Without warning, Luna shoved a huge bite of her salad into his mouth right before he took another sip of his beer. She pulled the foil open, took out a thick slice of garlic bread, and handed it to him while he chewed. "Damn, honey, that's good. What is that?"

She laughed and licked her pretty lips. "I call it Southwest Cole Slaw. I made the creamy cilantro dressing from scratch and added some shredded chicken to the cabbage, lettuce, carrots, and green onions. I sprinkled some crushed tortilla chips and pumpkin seeds to finish it off. It's one of my favorites."

"It's one of mine now, too. You really made that?"

She swallowed the bite she'd taken and cocked her head. "Yes. Is that so surprising?"

"Nothing and everything surprises me about you." He accepted the next bite from Luna and chewed, savoring the creamy, spicy concoction. While she ate beside him, he bit off a hunk of the garlic bread. "Man, that's good. Fresh garlic. Just the right amount of dripping butter."

Luna laughed again, setting off another flutter in his belly. She offered him another bite of the salad.

"You know, if we went inside I could put this on some plates and give you your own fork."

"This works." He tipped back his beer and stared up at the stars. All the better to see them now that the motion light went off.

"It's a nice night," she agreed.

"Did someone from work follow you home tonight?"

"No. Why would they do that?"

"Friday night. Maybe you had a date."

"Only with you, apparently."

"This isn't a date." He could do a hell of a lot better than this. The salad was outstanding, the company even better. But she deserved better than a starlit dinner on the stairs. It did have an air of intimacy he enjoyed.

"What is this?"

"I was heading home, you offered the beer and the food to thank me for the work."

"Ah." The soft smile didn't take anything away from the eye roll. She had his number, but he didn't give in and speak plain. He enjoyed teasing her. She didn't seem to mind.

"Did someone from the diner, maybe a friend, follow you home tonight?" he asked again. "A truck drove by right after you arrived."

She stuffed another bite into his mouth and gave him a sardonic look. "I don't have a boyfriend if that's what you're asking."

Good to know, but not why he'd asked. Still, he appreciated her offering up the information without him having to ask.

She bumped her shoulder into his. "Are you seeing anyone?"

"Nope." He took a deep pull on his beer, another bite of his garlic bread, and chewed beside her like he didn't have a care in the world. Actually, every cell in his being focused on the beautiful woman beside him. She'd stopped eating and sat still as stone, then she smiled softly and took another bite of the salad.

"What are we doing, then?"

He thought about it for a second and settled on the basics of what he wanted, why he'd come. "Working on being friends."

"So, you want to be my friend?"

"We are friends. Ones who have lost track of each other, so to speak."

Her head tilted. "A fresh start, then."

He tipped his beer and clinked hers. "Exactly."

"Okay. Still doesn't explain why you won't come into my house."

He laughed. "It's nice out here. Did you and Sadie pick out an invitation?"

"Changing the subject away from talking about us?"

"Starting with something we have in common and working up to getting more personal."

"White paper embossed with roses. Silver foil lettering. Very pretty."

"Sweet, like Sadie."

"I think I upset her before I left."

He'd avoided looking right at her while they ate. Too tempting to lean in and kiss her when they sat so close, their bodies pressed together, but not close enough. But he didn't like hearing she'd upset Sadie. "What happened?"

"We talked about Wayne and how his death made me think time is short."

He reached over, placed his hand on her opposite shoulder, and pulled her close in a soft hug. "I know you miss him, honey."

Her head pressed to his shoulder for a second, then she sat straight again. He released her, picked up his beer, and drained the rest.

"I want so much for my life, but I'm stuck here."

Colt stared straight ahead, not knowing what to do about the growing unease and sense of loss spreading through his system. "So, what, you're leaving?"

"I don't know. I received a job offer out of state. I can't find one here doing what I love. I'm stuck as a waitress, which pays crap. Look where I live and how. I'm barely getting by. My family is hours away. I have no—"

He hoped the word she cut off was "boyfriend." He'd like to think she wanted that to be him, but how could that happen if she left town?

"How long until you have to decide for sure?"

"A week. But the job doesn't start until September."

What kind of asshole was he that he hoped she didn't take this opportunity? He wanted time to get to know her. Not as his buddy's girlfriend but as a woman he liked and wanted to get to know better. A woman he didn't want to walk out of his life for good.

"I'm still on the fence about whether I want to leave at all."

"Really?" The band around his chest loosened at that bit of news.

"My family and friends are here. I wouldn't know anyone. I mean, it would be a great adventure, but what if I hated living in a city? How do I know that what I really want is out there, and not right here?"

"I guess you have to decide what will make you happy."

"Well, I haven't found it yet."

The admission made him think about what he wanted for his future. Sure, he loved working on the ranch with his brothers, but things were changing. Rory would marry Sadie soon. They'd want their privacy. A chance to live as husband and wife without two brothers around all the time. Once the baby arrived, they'd want to live in the house as a family. Hell, where would they put the kid, with him and Ford living in the other upstairs rooms and Granddad below?

He'd been thinking about getting his own place, but he didn't quite have the money to buy a house on a decent-size piece of land. He definitely didn't want to live in town. He'd heard whispers between Rory and Sadie about Ford taking over her property. The little green monster inside him peeked its head out but ducked back into its cave, because deep down, Colt agreed Ford deserved a shot at starting his own ranch. As the youngest brother, Colt was used to his big brothers getting what they wanted first. Didn't mean he liked it, but he got it. He planned to build a place of his own, work with horses, live on the land he loved with a family.

Whoa. Wait. Did he really just add in a family to what he wanted? Yep. Grandad and Rory had planted the seed. Well, he didn't have the means to water it, so he tucked it under the dirt in his mind to hibernate along with his green monster.

"I lost you, Colt. What are you thinking about?"

"Rory and Sadie."

She sighed and stared up at the stars. "Have you ever seen two people more in love?"

"No." An image of Luna with Billy came to mind, but they looked nothing like the happy couple Rory and Sadie made. He searched his memory for one moment where he'd seen the light shine in Luna the way it did in Sadie when she looked at Rory.

"Were you happy with Billy?" He couldn't believe he'd blurted those words out. Idiot.

"No." She said it just like that. No hesitation.

"I thought you two really had something."

"The illusion of a happy couple can't last. It breaks you down, wears you down until you don't look or feel like the person you used to be. You put so much of your time into pretending to be happy that you convince yourself you are, until one day you see someone smile and it comes from the inside out. You want to smile with them and feel even an ounce of the happiness you see in them because then you'll finally feel something real."

"Who was this mysterious person who pulled you out of the illusion?"

She propped her elbow on her knee and planted her chin in her hand and looked him in the eye. Her gaze went soft. She bit her bottom lip and studied his face. "You."

A single word that meant so much. More than he expected, judging by the way his heart raced in his chest and thumped against his ribs.

She leaned back and put her hands on her knees, stretching her back. "It's not just the job, you know? It's having something more. Something to build a life on."

"Are you looking for someone to build a life with?" Why did he keep saying things better left unsaid? Idiot. Like him, she was looking for a fulfilling job, a place of her own to call home that meant something to her. Something that was hers. But did she want it alone? Did he?

"Aren't we all?" She played off his question and gave him a way out. Somehow, her non-answer didn't sit well with him. "I want that illusion I thought was so great to be an even better reality with someone who is a true friend, partner, lover, keeper of secrets, and a man of romance and surprises. A man who leaves his mark, not just passes through my life."

Colt touched his fingertips to the half-moon cuts on his arm, the marks she'd left on his body. He thought of the mark she'd left on his life. He turned his head and stared at the woman who'd taken up residence in his head long ago. Someone who with one kiss woke something up inside of him he couldn't set aside or forget.

"You deserve that, Luna."

"So do you. We all do," she covered, because the air around them became charged. "So, my friend, you just came over tonight to fix my light?"

"Yes and no."

"What's the no?"

"Fixing the light gave me an excuse to come see you," he admitted. "I wanted to see for myself that you're okay after what happened last night."

"I didn't sleep well. I tried to get through my day, but it hits me all at once when I least expect it. I miss him."

"He left his mark. I guess, in the end, that's all we can hope we've done to the people who matter most to us."

Luna leaned into him and laid her head on his shoulder. To give her comfort and let her know he understood her grief, he leaned his head to hers and sat quietly with her in the night.

Everything felt right. Easy. Luna sighed, soaked up the heat of Colt's body pressed along the side of hers. She let the sense of belonging and connection work through her system and settle in, just like the night settled around them.

Jolted from the pleasant moment by her ringing phone, she held back a groan of regret, sat up, and pulled her phone from her purse.

"Who's that?"

He'd hinted enough about wanting to know if there was anyone in her life. A great indication that he was interested in taking their friendship to something more. It gave her hope that maybe they had something more than the flash of heat and lust they shared during that long-ago kiss. If they didn't, she'd still like another kiss and a whole lot more. She'd like to get her hands on the strong, lean cowboy beside her.

As the week to decide her life ticked down, she felt like she needed to rush. If she was ever going to discover what she and Colt might have, it had to be now.

Her phone rang again, bringing her out of her thoughts. She checked caller ID. "Same number as three other calls I missed at work. I don't recognize the number."

"Answer it. Find out who's trying to get in contact with you."

"It's kind of late for a social call. It can't be good." The sense of dread that came over her when she saw the missed calls earlier reared up again.

Colt swiped his finger across the screen and accepted the call before she could decide if she wanted to know who kept calling. He hit the speaker button and knocked his shoulder into hers.

"Hello," she said automatically.

"Miss Luna Hill?"

"Yes. Who's calling?"

"Dex Manning. Wayne Travers's attorney."

Luna glanced over at Colt. He raised an eyebrow in question, but she didn't know why Mr. Manning was calling her.

"What can I do for you?"

"I understand you and Mr. Travers were good friends. In fact, he told me on several occasions he thought of you as a daughter."

Choked up, Luna sputtered out, "Y-yes, he d-did."

"I'm sorry for your loss, Miss Hill."

She choked back her tears. "Luna, please."

"Call me Dex. We'll be working together closely unless you decide to hire another lawyer."

"Um, why do I need a lawyer?"

"You are named in Wayne's will. I'll go over the details tomorrow at the reading. Can you meet me at Wayne's home at eleven?"

"Can't you just tell me what Wayne said in the will?"

"All parties are required to be present. Can you make it?"

She thought of facing Wayne's family again. "Can I meet you at your office without the family present?"

"I understand your trepidation, but it would be best to take care of this with everyone present. I'll need to turn over some items to you at the ranch."

"Um, okay. I'll be there, but I start work at noon, so I can't stay long."

"You may rethink that after you hear what I have to say. See you tomorrow, Luna."

The attorney hung up without a clear explanation of what he meant by that statement, leaving Luna confused.

"You okay?" Colt's steady presence beside her helped ease her grief.

"I think so."

"You look a little shocked."

"I am. I never expected him to leave me something. I mean, we were close friends, but . . ."

"You're afraid people will talk and believe all those rumors about the two of you, since he left you something."

"I feel so guilty for thinking that. The thing is—was—he was generous with me. Yes, he liked to leave me huge tips."

"An easy way to help out a friend without handing you money and making it weird." Colt got it, and she appreciated that he expressed it to her.

She pressed her lips together. "Sometimes I really needed that money, but the sentiment behind it meant so much more."

"He saw that, so he didn't mind giving you a little extra here and there. You appreciated it."

"I tried so hard to make sure he knew I treasured our friendship more."

"Luna, you're a genuine person. You don't trick people or say things you don't mean. Take heart—in the end, he valued you so much he remembered you in his final wishes. That means something."

"His family is not going to like this." A warning shivered up her spine. She tried to dismiss it, but the chill trembling her nerves stayed with her, and so did her thoughts that if they'd be so bold as to accost her at the hospital right after Wayne died, what would they do if they didn't like Wayne's final wishes?

"Who cares? Wayne didn't."

"You're right. I'll go, collect whatever it is he left me, forget whatever his family spews at me, and go back to my life." She hoped it would be that easy, but she feared Wayne's spoiled sons would make trouble.

Colt set his hand on her knee and squeezed a second before he stood and stepped down several steps. He turned back and stared at her. "Then maybe you'll buy me that beer."

"We shared dinner and a beer tonight."

"That was a thank-you for the light, not the beer you owe me."

She laughed under her breath and smiled. "Okay. Fair enough."

Colt reached past her and picked up his toolbox, then started down the stairs. "Have a good night, honey."

"Have a good night, Colt."

"I'll try, but leaving you and going home alone isn't a great start."

"Is that so?"

"You know it is."

"But you're still leaving."

"Good night, Luna."

Colt walked down the drive and waved without looking back. Her eyes remained glued to his very fine, jean-clad ass.

The smile made her cheeks ache. She liked him. She'd thought that maybe whatever they'd had had gone away, faded with the days, weeks, and months they'd avoided each other. But it hadn't, at least not on her part: the flutter in her belly, the warmth that radiated through her when he was close, the anticipation that bubbled up every time she thought about him and the possibility of what they could have in the future. Only one week to decide her whole life. If only he'd spend a little more time with her. That's what really got her, how much she wanted to spend time with him.

CHAPTER 8

Luna pulled in behind all the cars in Wayne's driveway, veered to the left, and parked her car outside one of the barns. She hadn't been to the ranch in the last two months. Wayne hadn't invited her, saying he was having some construction done. She gawked at the massive covered arena he'd built in the unused portion of the front of the property. An unexpected thrill raced over her skin, making the fine hairs stand on end. Could it be? No. The idea was ludicrous.

"Only one way to find out what this is all about." She stepped out of the car and smoothed her black skirt down. She'd attended the funeral this morning, along with the family and other friends. She'd kept to the back of the small crowd so as not to draw the family's attention and instigate a scene.

No such luck avoiding that once she entered the house. Why the hostility? So Wayne left her something? They got all this. Thousands of acres of prime grassland and forest. The river and creeks. More cattle than she could count. And the horses. Beautiful horses. Some old, living out their lives in the pastures, fat and happy. The ranch hands used others to check the cattle, but for the most part, they used the trucks. She loved riding. Wayne knew that and invited her out often to ride one trail or another across his land. She loved it here. She'd miss her visits.

The house was something else. Large and sprawling with a wide porch out front and an even larger patio off the back. She and Wayne sat out back often under the huge tree that sprawled over the yard and shaded the house. In winter, those long and winding branches stood dark and bare against the soft blue sky with a thick layer of snow on top. She'd miss their cozy lunches on the back patio, watching the horses in the fields.

Seriously, they had all this, yet they begrudged her whatever little something Wayne left to her. She wondered what he'd left her. It nagged at her. She didn't want to take anything the family didn't want her to have, but she also didn't want to disregard Wayne's final wishes.

She held her hand up to knock on the door, but it flew open and Wayne's oldest son, Josh, stood blocking the entrance.

"You're late. You've kept us waiting."

Luna checked her watch. Three minutes after eleven. So she'd spent a couple of minutes admiring the property, tucking away a few more memories, since she wouldn't be coming back. "Sorry." She offered the apology, but she didn't really mean it. She didn't like Josh. He was brash and entitled and cared little for anyone but himself. And she'd just met him the other day, so that was saying something that she didn't even give him the benefit of the doubt.

"It's about damn time you showed up."

"If you let me in, we can get this over and I can get to work." She tried to keep her voice neutral, but the words came out with a bit of an edge. She sucked in a deep breath and let it out, reminding herself to remain calm and remember Josh had just lost his father. His grief left him with a short temper. She hoped he got over it soon.

Simon stepped out from behind his brother. "Luna, you're here. I saw you at the funeral. Thank you for coming."

Josh's eyes narrowed with anger. "You were there?"

"Just paying my respects, not to intrude."

"Give it a rest, Josh." Simon swept his arm out. "Please come in, Luna. You've been here before. We're in the library. Apparently no one is allowed in Dad's office until the end of the reading of the will." Simon rolled his eyes like that fact didn't bother him. He acted like none of this bothered him. Not like it affected Josh. She wanted to believe it was genuine, but she didn't quite take it at face value and didn't know why. Nothing about Simon put her off. In fact, he was a good-looking guy. They both were. She saw Wayne in their sturdy, lean builds, but where Wayne's skin tended toward a year-round tan from being outside all the time, these guys looked like they could use a few days in the sun. She didn't know a lot about them, just the tidbits Wayne dropped about them jumping from one job to the next. She guessed they worked in an office. Doing what, really, she didn't know. Sales. Something with computers. She thought Josh managed a car dealership. Or maybe that was Simon.

She stepped into the house, keeping Josh in her sights. She didn't necessarily think he'd harm her, but you never turned your back on a wild animal. The guy seemed on the verge of losing his temper and doing something stupid. Grief and greed did funny things to people.

"Since you probably only know the way to the bedroom, follow us." Josh turned and headed for the huge double pocket doors across the room.

She fumed with indignation that he'd say such a thing to her, but she followed him without a word. Asshole. Poor Wayne, that one probably gave him every gray hair on his head.

She loved the library. The wood doors, paneling, and massive bookshelves lining two tall walls made the room feel warm and welcoming.

Not today. She walked in, and the couple from the hospital turned and glared at her. The man standing beside them smiled. Two women about Luna's age sat in the dining room chairs brought in for the meeting. Their resemblance to the couple made Luna guess they were Simon and Josh's cousins. Three men stood by one of the bookshelves, talking among themselves. Toby, the ranch manager. Rich ran the cattle side of the business. Ed took care of the horses. She wondered why Artie wasn't in attendance. She liked to refer to him as head farmer.

All eyes turned to her the minute she walked into the room. The man standing with the couple came to her.

"Miss Hill, I'm Wayne's attorney, Dex Manning. Thank you for coming."

"Please call me Luna."

"Luna, we'll get started in a minute. I'll go over the will and what Wayne left to his trusted employees here at the ranch."

Artie rushed in at that moment, tipping his hat to Luna before he removed it and joined his friends by the bookcase.

"I'll go over everything for the immediate family. Wayne's sister, her husband, their children, and Simon and Josh. You will be last."

Why that didn't sound good she couldn't quite figure out, but it seemed an odd order. The ranch employees, the family, then her. The pecking order didn't seem quite right. As Wayne's friend, she should probably be first, or in between the family and ranch personnel.

"Are you sure you can't read the part about me first? I can't stay long. I'm sure the family would like me out of here immediately." She glanced over at the family on the other side of the room, Josh's head tilted toward his aunt, their matching death stares and grim frowns directed at her.

"It has to be this way," Mr. Manning said. "After I finish, I'd like a moment to speak with you about what happens next."

She tilted her head, staring up in question at the attorney. "I don't understand. Once this is done, I'm sure the family will want me as far away from this place as possible."

She wished she understood the strange look that came over the man.

"Did you love Wayne?"

The bold question surprised her, but she didn't hesitate to answer, despite tensing for the inevitable judgment. "Yes. I did."

"He loved you very much. He told me to tell you that he's sorry for putting you through this, but he had his reasons and knew you could take it."

"I don't understand what you mean. I know his family thinks the worst of me, but they're wrong."

"None of that matters now. You won't be able to convince them. Wayne believed in you. I hope you're ready for this."

Mr. Manning walked away and stood in front of the group. "Okay everyone, I'm ready to begin."

"About damn time," Josh said. "Did you warn her that we'll fight whatever our father left her? She doesn't deserve anything."

"We're his family," Josh's aunt added.

Luna sank into the club chair next to her. Rich, Artie, Ed, and Toby moved in behind her and stood, waiting for this to be over.

"The will is ironclad. Your father's wishes are specific, as you'll see. If anyone chooses to contest the will, they'll lose out on their inheritance in total. Believe me, ask any lawyer and they'll tell you it's futile to go against Wayne's wishes."

"Nothing is ever ironclad. Everything is negotiable," Josh snapped.

"No, it's not." Mr. Manning picked up the papers from the table next to him and pulled out a pair of reading glasses from the inside pocket of his suit jacket. They made the young man look distinguished. She hoped the family took him seriously, listened to Wayne's last wishes, and agreed to fulfill them without a fight. She hated that Wayne's passing had turned them all angry. They should be grieving, not bickering with her.

"If everyone is ready, I'll begin." Mr. Manning paused, allowing the family to take their seats.

It didn't escape Luna's notice that they gathered on one side of the room, while she sat with the ranch guys. The separation of "us" and "them" weighed heavy in the room.

"In Wayne's words, 'The legacy I leave behind is the sprawling ranch I loved. It gave me peace and a sense of purpose. I've seen success and failure, sometimes on the same day, but I never gave up and always worked hard to protect what is mine and provide for my family. That's not to say I did it alone. Everyone needs a helping hand, but I had valued friends who worked beside me. Toby, though you're not as long in years as I am, you've been a faithful employee more years than I can count. Whenever you should choose to retire, you should do so without a worry about your future. I leave you fifty thousand in cash and a retirement fund that will see you through your final years. Rich, Artie, and Ed, you've got a ways to go yet before you finally set aside the ranch life. You'll each receive twenty-five thousand dollars now, and should you choose to remain on the ranch into your golden years, you'll have retirement funds when you reach fifty-five or better.'" Mr. Manning looked up from the paper to the four men. "Toby, your retirement fund is available to you at any time now. The rest of you, the funds will grow over time. If you choose to wait until after fifty-five to collect, the fund will continue to be managed and grow over time until the time you choose to collect."

Mr. Manning gave the men an opportunity to ask questions, but all they did was give a solemn nod. They moved to walk out now that their portion was complete, but Mr. Manning held up a hand to stop them.

"Please, you'll want to stay to hear the information about the future of the ranch."

The men settled in behind her once again.

"Bea and Harry Murphy are to receive a lump sum payment of two hundred and fifty thousand dollars each. Their daughters, Anne and Kelly, will receive a lump sum payment of fifty thousand dollars, plus any outstanding student loans paid in full by the ranch owner. In addition, if Anne and Kelly have children, their children will receive school tuition by the ranch owner if times are good and the ranch can cover the cost."

"Wait," Aunt Bea interrupted. "What does that mean? If the ranch can't cover the cost of the tuition, the owner doesn't have to provide the money set by the terms of the will?"

"You've answered your question." Mr. Manning nodded. "Wayne's experience over the years taught him that ranching is a hard business. Though he had more good years than bad, the ones that were lean were hard to survive."

"The money is there now. Can't it be set aside to provide for the children?"

"At this time, there are no children. There may never be, or there could be an abundance of them. When the time comes, the ranch owner can determine if setting money aside is prudent, or if it's needed to maintain the ranch. Wayne's goal was to provide for his family, but also to protect the ranch."

"Family is more important than anything," Aunt Bea snapped.

"As the people in question are not born yet, there is no need for the money at this time. Who is to say that there won't be enough money years from now? Given the longevity of the ranch to date, the possibility is favorable."

Aunt Bea turned to Simon and Josh. "Don't think I'll let you run this place into the ground. We'll work together to keep this place making money to provide for the entire family."

"That takes care of the Murphy family."

"Not really," Aunt Bea chimed in, her back ramrod straight as she sat in her seat, eyes glued to the attorney. "There's still the matter of the ranch."

Clearly she wanted more.

"Simon and Josh. It's my understanding your father

had many discussions with you about running the ranch. Based on those conversations, he determined that neither of you desires the ranch life or being involved in the daily operations here."

"Just because we don't want to work here doesn't mean we don't want this place and can't manage it." Josh sat rigid in his chair, his fisted hands on his thighs.

"I won't continue the argument you had with your father on that point. He's settled it in his will. The terms are as follows: 'To my beloved sons, I leave the contents of my home, excluding the contents of my office and the library. You may decide what you'd like to keep and what you'd like to share with your aunt, uncle, and cousins. Anything you leave behind will remain the property of the ranch owner.' "

"What?" Josh rose from his seat. "Are you saying we don't own the ranch?"

"That can't be," Aunt Bea gasped, pressing her hand to her chest. "I helped him start this place. He can't not give part of it to me."

"Let me finish," Mr. Manning stated, remaining calm, despite the furious gleam in Josh and Bea's eyes.

" 'Josh and Simon, you will each receive the amount of one million dollars, or five hundred thousand dollars and a chance to own a fifty percent share in the ranch if you work on the ranch for a period no less than eighteen months with no more than fourteen days off during that period without sufficient reason and evidence to support your absence from work to satisfy the ranch owner that you've made a good-faith effort to fulfill your eighteen-month obligation and intend to commit yourself to the running of the ranch as your life's work. If both Simon and Josh fulfill this commitment, they will each receive twenty-five percent of the ranch. If only one fulfills this commitment, he will receive the full fifty percent share.' " Mr. Manning held up a paper. "I've got the details of how the ranch would be split here. At no time would you be allowed to sell any portion of the ranch without the other owner's consent. You have ten days from today to decide if you want to work on the ranch, or receive the one million payout and forfeit your chance to own a portion of the ranch."

"Who the fuck is this owner?" Josh demanded.

Mr. Manning pressed his lips together and turned his gaze on her. "Well, that only leaves one person in the room. Miss Luna Hill, you are the sole beneficiary of Rambling Range and everything else Wayne left behind. The cattle, horses, land, businesses, and the rest of his wealth. You, as ranch owner, will fulfill Wayne's final wishes. The house, minus whatever contents Josh and Simon take, is yours to live in even if either or both of them decide to work on the ranch and receive their fifty percent portion. If that comes to pass, Wayne designated two areas they will be allowed to build their own homes on with their own money."

"Are you fucking kidding me?" Josh leaped up and jabbed a finger out in the air, pointed straight at her. "She gets everything. No fucking way." His face turned red with rage.

"You have the opportunity to keep half," Mr. Manning pointed out.

Luna's gut soured and tightened. She didn't know what to do. This couldn't be real. He'd left it all to her.

"Luna, Wayne understood you may be overwhelmed with the daunting task he's set before you. While you are expected to manage the ranch, he's left you in very capable hands with the four gentlemen behind you.

Wayne also made sure that he didn't make you lead a life you may not want, so he built you your dream."

It hit her all at once. "The covered arena outside."

"Yes. And the equipment you'll need to run your very own equine therapy center for children with autism or with disabilities."

Ed placed his hand on her shoulder and leaned down. "You'll find everything in the new barn next to the arena. We have a couple of horses here that will work for your purposes, but you'll need to buy a few more, depending on how many people come to work with you."

Luna stared up at the man with the kind eyes and tried to process what just happened. She needed time to process everything, but one thing was clear. She couldn't do this on her own. "Thank you. If you're not too busy, maybe you can help me with that."

"Whatever you need. I work for you now."

"This is bullshit," Josh spat out.

"Utterly ridiculous," Aunt Bea agreed in her own dramatically dignified way.

"Those are the terms. They are Wayne's last wishes. Luna, Wayne has allowed five days for Josh and Simon to take the possessions they would like to keep from the house. Until then, you may come to the ranch to work with the ranch hands and managers and to go over the business information. You are free to move in after that. We'll need to meet to change over the accounts to your name. I suggest you meet me at my office tomorrow so we can get everything settled."

She nodded automatically but didn't really understand all she was agreeing to do. It really felt unreal.

"He left you a way out," Mr. Manning said. "If you feel you are unable to fulfill the terms of the will, there

is an alternative outcome if you don't want to take responsibility for the ranch."

"What is that?" Simon asked, speaking up for the
first time.

Mr. Manning kept his gaze on her. "You can choose
to sell the ranch. Simon and Josh will receive ten million each from the sale, and Bea and Harry Murphy
receive an additional one million. You will split the remaining amount with the charities listed in the will."

"Sell it," Josh demanded.

The men standing behind her, men who had worked
this ranch for years and put their blood, sweat, and
tears into doing so with a care and devotion she admired, gasped and cursed at the possibility.

Luna tried to keep up with the back and forth. She'd
inherited everything, but she could also give it all up.
Wayne had wanted her to keep it, oversee all he'd built,
but he'd given her a way out. He'd trusted her but allowed her to say she didn't want the responsibility.

Did she want it?

She wanted to do what her good friend asked of her.
Though saying no was an option, she couldn't bring
herself to turn down this opportunity—a chance for her
to do right by her friend and have her dream, too.

"No. That's not what Wayne wanted. He loved this
place. He cared about the land, the animals, the people
who worked for him. He wouldn't want to see it sold off
piece by piece, all he'd worked his whole life for lost."

"Sell it, or I'll make you wish you had." Josh strode
across the room, but Toby and Rich each grabbed him
by a shoulder and held him back.

Luna, feeling like a sitting duck in the chair with
Wayne's family all glaring down at her, stood and
faced them.

"Nothing you do or say will make me change my mind."

"Why would she? If she keeps the ranch, she's got more money than she'll ever be able to spend. She wins." Josh shook with rage.

"I didn't even know about this." Luna tried to defend herself, despite knowing nothing she said or did would change their minds.

Simon stood up and planted his hands on his hips. "We're not getting anywhere with this talk of selling the place. She said no. That leaves us our other options. So, I guess I work for you now, Luna. Josh and I will take care of the contents of the house, and in five days I'll start working here. You and I can go over the details then." Simon clamped his hand on Josh's shoulder. Though Josh refused to stop glaring at Luna, Simon asked him, "What do you say? You ready to earn your part of the ranch?"

"Hell no. I'll take the million and the ten when she can't hack it and decides to sell this place."

Luna never backed away from hard work or a challenge. She stood up for herself against bullies. Josh could kiss her ass.

"That's never going to happen," Luna said again, believing it in her heart. It all happened so fast, but one thing settled in for certain. She'd never sell the ranch. "If we're done here, I have to get to work."

"We'll walk you out," Toby said, falling in behind her as she left the library.

"I'll call you later to set up a time to meet," Mr. Manning called after her.

She needed to get out of there. She needed some air and time to think. Rich grabbed the front door for her. She walked out but stopped halfway across the front yard, then turned back to stare at the massive house, the arena off to her side, the massive amount of land that spread out around her and went on for miles that she could only imagine in her mind but not see from here.

"Holy shit."

Ed laughed. "Exactly. Never saw that one coming."

"Um, you know more than I do about the ranching business. You know your jobs. I won't interfere unless I think something isn't going right. Over the next few days, I guess, just keep doing what you do. When I come back, I'll spend time with each of you, going over what you do and how. I need to learn everything I can about this place and how it runs. We'll work together as a team. I hope that works for you."

They all nodded their agreement.

"Um, Toby, about you retiring soon."

"Don't worry about that now. I won't leave you in the lurch, but know that I hope to retire sooner rather than later."

"As in before this eighteen months is up with Simon, and possibly Josh, working here."

"Yes, ma'am."

"Oh, none of that. It's just Luna." She hated to lose Toby, but she had to face reality. Everything had changed for her and the ranch with Wayne's death. "I don't anticipate much will change in your day-to-day work, but we'll discuss the direction of the ranch and any changes that need to be made once I'm allowed back here."

"No worries until then," Artie assured her. "We've got this. How much damage can they do in a few short days?"

Luna didn't even want to think about it.

CHAPTER 9

Colt walked out of the barn and stopped short. Luna stood in the middle of the yard, staring out at the horses and cattle in the pastures. She didn't see him. At least he didn't think so. He hoped she wasn't ignoring him. He approached her slowly, wondering why she stood so still, with her arms wrapped around her middle. The wind blew her hair away from her face. He didn't like the sad, lost look in her eyes.

"Luna? Everything okay? What are you doing out here?"

She still wore her diner "uniform." Black skirt, diner T-shirt, and black cowboy boots. She looked damn good. The skirt hugged her curves and outlined her very fine ass. While he took in her curves, they didn't distract him from the fact that something about her felt off. Everything in him went on alert. Nerves tightened his belly and made him want to reach out and touch her, pull her close and hold her until she smiled again.

"How do you do it?"

"Do what, honey?"

"Run this massive place?"

"With a lot of help," he admitted. "It's routine. It's my life." What more could he say? This was all he knew.

"I don't know if I can do it. It's so much."

He didn't understand. "Honey, you're not making sense. What can't you do?"

"Run a ranch."

He narrowed his gaze, studying her, wondering what she meant. His heart beat faster, hope rising in his chest that she'd decided to stay here instead of taking the teaching job out of state. "Did you buy one since the last time I saw you?"

"No. I inherited one. Rambling Range is mine."

He gasped. "Holy shit." She owned more land, cattle, and horses than he and his brothers shared.

"That would be, 'holy fucking shit.' " She raked her hand through her hair and held it away from her pale face.

"Start at the beginning. What happened at your meeting with the lawyer today?"

"I thought maybe Wayne left me a trinket, some kind of show of affection and friendship. Maybe a piece of jewelry that belonged to his beloved wife. One of his prize horses. A treasured book from his collection. I thought I'd go there, collect whatever it was, and move on with my life with a reminder of my good friend."

"But he left you the ranch? So, what, you're partners with his sons?"

She pressed her lips into a tight line and shook her head. "Nope." She went on for five minutes without taking a breath, detailing the terms of the will. "Now I'm in charge of everything."

"Holy fucking shit."

She laughed, a smile finally brightening her too-serious face. "Told you."

"How did the family take it?" Colt certainly wouldn't have taken it well if his parents hadn't left the ranch to him and his brothers. He could only imagine how Wayne's sons felt losing out on so much.

"They want me to sell. If I do, it's the best deal they get out of the terms."

"Is that what you want to do?"

"Hell no. Wayne worked his whole life for that place. It was everything to him. I can't just sell it."

"Are you ready to make that place your whole life?" *Please stay.*

"I don't know. It's still kind of rattling around my head like a dream I can't shake. It doesn't feel real."

He hated to ask, but did so anyway, because in the end, he wanted her to be happy. "What about teaching?"

"More than I wanted to teach, I had another dream. Wayne set it all up so I can have the ranch and the equine therapy program I wanted to start."

"Seriously?"

She faced him for the first time and glared. "Yes. Why? You think it's stupid?"

"No. I think it's fantastic. You'd be great and provide a wonderful service and experience for people with special needs."

The starch went right out of her.

He drew back one side of his mouth in a half frown, disappointed she'd think so little of him. "Why would you think I wouldn't approve?"

"Because of all of this." She spread her arms wide to encompass the ranch.

"What about it?"

"I thought maybe you'd think the ranching business is enough and what I should focus on."

"Honey, you can do both. You can do anything you want."

Luna's eyes went wide, like it surprised her he believed in her. Easy to believe in someone who worked as hard as Luna and who cared. About her job. People. Those things she considered important. Like helping others.

"You've got the men to help you on the ranch. Wayne's guys work hard. They know their stuff. They've been with him for years."

She stared up at the sky. "Toby wants to retire."

"He's the ranch manager, right?"

"Yes. Which means I either need one of the others to step up and take his place and replace one of them, or I need to hire a new manager. Either way, I don't know what I'm doing, and I could mess it all up."

"First, if you need help, all you have to do is ask. Second, Wayne's guys aren't going to let you mess anything up. They'll teach you what you need to know. If they're dicks about it, you let me know, and I'll take care of it."

"No. They seem like nice guys." She bit her lip, and her eyes clouded with an even deeper concern. "It's not them I'm worried about."

"Simon seemed to have his head screwed on straight. The other one, Josh, is a hothead. Watch out for him."

"He is not happy about what happened. Neither is Wayne's sister."

Colt gave her a sardonic smirk. "Were they that surprised?"

"That the woman they think slept her way into the ranch got it?" Luna shook her head. "Not so much."

The rage inside Colt burst in his chest, but he held it contained inside of him with no outlet, not one of those assholes in reach to punch for thinking such a thing.

"The guys were surprised their father left them so little."

"They got some big-time cash. If they want the rest, he gave them a means to get it."

"Josh is all for the sale. In fact, he pretty much said he'd make sure I wanted to sell."

Colt read between the lines and the dismay in Luna's eyes, the defensive way she wrapped her arms around her middle again. "He threatened you."

Her pretty lips compressed together. She gave him a soft nod, fear filling her blue eyes.

"Bastard. He does anything, I want to know about it."

One side of her mouth quirked up into a half grin. "You're sweet."

Colt tensed, his hands fisting. "Sweet, hell, I'll fuck up the asshole if he touches you."

Luna threw up her hands and let them fall. "What's the point? There's nothing he can do. I won't sell. If he wants any part of the land and the money the ranch makes, he's got to meet the terms." She said the words, but her tone said she didn't quite believe them. Josh scared her.

Colt didn't want to argue that Josh could make her life hell to the point where she would want to turn her back on the ranch and that family just to be done with the whole business. Hadn't Wayne thought about that? He'd practically dared his family to make her life a misery to get her to sell. Of course, Wayne had probably thought they'd take the knock on the chin and slink away, because they were lazy as hell. He hadn't accounted for their greed.

Colt vowed he'd watch over Luna. One of those assholes frightened her again, he'd bash their faces in. One of them touched her, he'd kill them.

"It's just so much." Luna sighed and stared up at the darkening sky.

"Start with the simple stuff. You need to quit your job."

"I already did. Tonight was my last shift."

"I'm surprised they let you go so fast."

"Well, since Sadie put in her notice, they'd interviewed several people. They already hired one new girl and had a couple more they planned to bring on within the next month. They had no problem letting me go and calling them to start work immediately."

"Then you'll need to move into the house."

"I don't have much to pack."

"I noticed."

"I'm surprised you did, since you refuse to come into my house," she teased.

He didn't answer that loaded statement with an explanation. "What day do you want to move in?"

"I can't for five days. The family will move out Wayne's things, except for the office and library. I guess I'll move in then."

"We'll be at your place with the trucks next week."

"Wait, what?"

"Three trucks ought to do it. If we need to make more than one trip, no problem."

"You can't be serious. You're going to help me move? And you volunteer your brothers, too?"

"You're Sadie's best friend." He tried to play it off, but he hated the slight frown and disappointment in her eyes. "Besides, I want to do it." That put some of the spark back in her eyes. "Rory will do it for Sadie and because he likes you. Ford won't mind pitching in. My brothers and I will check in with your crews, see how things are going, and let you know what you need to focus on first."

"You'd do that for me?"

He'd do anything for her, but didn't say so. They were still working their way through this are-we-friends-or-something-more stage. Maybe he needed to stop feeling her out and just kiss her again. He didn't, because the attraction was obvious and all-encompassing, judging by how hard he had to work to keep his hands to himself. What he couldn't afford to do was go all out and take her to bed, risking fucking it all up and still having to see her all the time because she was Sadie's best friend. Rory would kill him for messing with his soon-to-be-bride's best friend. Not to mention if he did go down that path, it better be for real, because Luna was a forever kind of girl. Maybe a once-in-a-lifetime kind of girl. Was he ready for that kind of commitment? He wasn't quite sure, but it was growing on him. Or maybe that was just the need gnawing at his insides to get her naked and pressed up against his aching body.

"We'll be there. Since you're not working at the diner anymore, you've got time to get everything packed. Until then, come up to the house and have dinner with us. I'm starving."

Colt took her hand and tugged her gently to get her to follow him.

"I don't want to intrude."

"You came here for a reason, right? To talk to Sadie about what happened. Here's your chance."

A soft smile spread across her lips, and she gave his hand a squeeze. "I don't really need to unload on her now. You set my mind at ease. I can do this. Wayne's guys will help me. And if I need help, I'll call you."

"There you go."

"You might regret it if I end up counting on you for every little thing I don't know about ranching."

"Won't bother me a bit, unless you don't call when you need me."

He felt her stare, but didn't look down at her. Instead, he walked into the house with her hand firmly in his and led her into the kitchen, where his family had already gathered at the table to eat. The house smelled of roast pork and cheesy potatoes.

"Hey everyone, look who I found outside." Colt led Luna to his place at the table, pulled out the chair for her, and waited for her to sit before he finally released her hand. She stared up at him with that dazed, overwhelmed look in her eyes he'd seen when she'd stood out in the yard, staring at the ranch spread out before her. He liked that he surprised her.

"Luna, how did it go today?" Sadie asked, starting the conversation about Wayne's family and the will.

Colt washed up at the sink, then grabbed a plate and silverware from the kitchen. Ford had pulled a spare chair to the table. Since Luna was too busy answering his family's questions, Colt took her plate and filled it with food before he made himself a plate. He sat across from her, listening to her tell the tale again and making plans for what he needed to do to help her. First, take Simon's measure. If the man really did want to work on the ranch with Sadie for the next eighteen months, Colt needed to be damn sure he wasn't a threat. Or turned into a rival for Luna's affections. Colt really hadn't thought about that until this moment, staring at the beautiful woman across from him, eating dinner with his family like she belonged. Because she did.

His grandfather eyed him from across the table. Colt kept his features blank and tried not to glance over at Luna and fuel his grandfather's enthusiasm that he might get another of his grandsons to propose.

Not going to happen. Not now. No way. No how. He needed to stop this train of thought before it went off the rails he thought the path of his life was headed down. That particular matrimonial stop was way in the future.

So why did he think about that future when he looked at Luna at the family table? Why did he spend hours each day wondering what she wanted for her future? Why did he worry endlessly through the night that she might actually take that teaching job out of state at any moment?

Well, he didn't have to worry about that anymore. She had a massive ranch to run. An equine therapy program to start. A new life ahead of her full of possibilities. Did one of those possibilities include him? He'd make sure it did, because holding back how he felt about her had to stop. He wanted to take things slow, get to know her better, but there was taking things slow and making very little progress. Toward what, he didn't really know. Or at least wasn't ready to acknowledge. What he did know was that he wanted to spend more time with her. Helping her with Rambling Range would be a great way to do that.

The daunting task overwhelmed her. He'd make it easier by overseeing the guys who worked for her, watching her back with Wayne's family, and teaching her everything he knew about ranching.

He pulled himself out of his thoughts long enough to get back into the thread of conversation. "Tell Sadie about the equine therapy program you're going to start."

Luna cocked her head. "You really are interested in that, aren't you?"

"I'll even help you pick the horses and train them for what you need."

"You will?"

"Colt is great with horses. You won't find better than him." Granddad couldn't help boasting about Colt, especially when it made Colt look good and advanced Granddad's agenda.

Colt didn't miss the knowing glances Ford and Rory shot his way, or the smirks they tried to hide for Luna's sake. Sadie planted her chin in her hand, elbow propped on the table, and stared at him with a certain gleam in her eyes. He shot her a *You better not be planning a double wedding* look.

Sadie cocked up one eyebrow and smiled softly at him, like she knew exactly where this was going. So did he. He just didn't want to think about it too much. Instead, he was ready to make something happen.

"Like I said, I'll help you with anything you need." He let the innuendo hang, especially since he'd dropped his voice to make his point.

Luna spent the rest of the evening filling in Sadie and working on some of the wedding plans. Colt gave the ladies space to do their thing, but when it came time for Luna to head home, he rose from his chair in the office where he'd been checking out the online horse auctions coming up. He'd found a couple of candidates for Luna's new endeavor.

"Hey, heading out?" He stood in the office doorway.

Luna turned to him after hugging Sadie goodbye. "Yeah. It's been a long day. I'm wiped out."

"I'll walk you to your car."

Luna waved him off. "You don't have to."

"Let him. He won't take no for an answer." Sadie turned to leave, winking at him as she passed through the living room on her way to find Rory waiting for her upstairs.

Colt followed Luna out the door to her Jeep. She didn't say anything but turned back to him before she opened the door and got in. He didn't expect her to close the distance between them, but his arms opened and wrapped around her without a coherent thought coming to mind. He held her close, her arms wrapped around his shoulders.

"Thanks."

"For what? I didn't do anything."

"Yes, you did. You made it easier to breathe when it felt like the enormity of what I'm about to take on closed in on me."

His heart beat faster just having her close, but her words sank in and a warmth spread through him. He hugged her closer and kissed the side of her head. She settled into his chest and sighed.

He indulged holding her close for a few minutes, letting the quiet night settle around them. She didn't seem inclined to release him, but he couldn't hold on to her all night in the driveway. He hated to send her away, but she needed time to settle into her new life and decide what her new future looked like. He hoped it included him.

With a reluctance that stunned him, he leaned back, cupping her soft cheek in his hand. He leaned in and kissed her forehead, then gently set her away.

"Go home before I can't let you go at all." His aversion to sending her home made his voice gruff.

A soft smile spread on her too-tempting lips. "I'm kind of hoping you won't let me go."

"Trust me, I'll see you soon."

The smile brightened and made her eyes sparkle. "I'm counting on it."

He watched her drive away, anxious to see her again, wanting to call her back. If that didn't tell him how deeply he wanted her, the tightening band around his chest reminded him. So did the dreams and mounting urge to go see her over the next few days. Five days turned out to be far too long to go without a glimpse of the woman he couldn't stop thinking about.

CHAPTER 10

Luna walked into Mr. Manning's spacious office feeling like she should have dressed for the occasion. The handsome blonde lawyer with the light green eyes wore an expensive-looking suit that definitely made him look like the successful attorney several people told her about when she subtly asked about him to those in the know in town who dropped by the diner.

"Luna."

"Good morning, Dex."

He shook her hand, waved her into the seat in front of his desk, and went around to his seat and picked up a stack of folders in front of him. "So, first things first. I represented Wayne in all personal and business matters for the ranch. Do you plan to hire your own attorney? Or would you like me to continue and represent you and the ranch going forward?"

"I'd like you to stay on. You know the players, the businesses, and I hope you will be an asset as I figure out how to fill Wayne's shoes."

"I don't think Wayne intended you to do that, but protect what he built."

"I plan to do that. The how of it eludes me, but I'm up for the challenge and learning what I need to know."

"Wayne trusted the men working for him. The ranch is a well-oiled machine."

"Except I'm losing Toby. I'll need a new manager."

Dex patted the folder beneath his hand, picked up his glasses from the desk, and slid them on. The tortoiseshell frames made the green in his eyes stand out. Striking. But not as nice as Colt's hazel eyes when he looked at her.

"That leads me to the will and some items Wayne included that I didn't share with the family."

She held her hands tightly in her lap. "Okay. Do I have to meet some other terms to keep the ranch?"

"What I'm about to tell you stays between us. You are not allowed to share it with anyone. Not your friends or family. No one. Clear?"

Butterflies fluttered in her belly. "Perfectly. But why?"

"Because if you tell anyone and try to invoke the terms I'm about to outline and it's a lie, you'll lose everything and the Traverses will be allowed to sell the property."

A stone dropped in her gut. "Well, I definitely don't want that to happen."

"Good. I hoped you'd say that. Yesterday we went over the terms of Simon and Josh inheriting fifty per cent of the ranch. What I didn't tell them, or you, is that at any time you can give them that portion if you feel they want it and deserve it. You can also pay out more than their cash inheritance if you feel they deserve it."

"Really?"

"Yes. But it must be based on the fact they want to be a part of the ranch business and contribute in a meaningful way."

"Does that meaningful way have to include working there every day?"

Derek smiled. "No. Maybe they decide the business

side of things is more in their comfort zone. They want to help you set up your nonprofit and raise funds and that makes you happy and satisfied, you can pay them or give them a portion of the ranch. They want to take over buying and selling the cattle, horses, or crops, fine. They want to take over the books for the businesses and do the financials, no problem."

"But that's not how it sounded in the will."

"People hear what they want to hear. Simon and Josh don't want to play cowboy, but they are good at other things. They've been businessmen for years. They're college educated. They could have worked with their father in any number of ways. They chose not to."

Luna nodded, understanding dawning. "They don't see the value in the land or ranching. That's what Wayne wanted. For them to see that what he does matters."

Dex smiled softly and gave her a firm nod.

"Okay, so I have the option of compensating them if they do a good job in any area of the ranch. That might come in handy if they need an incentive."

"You can give them money as a bonus, but giving them a piece of the ranch requires they prove they're dedicated to maintaining it for a lifetime."

"Got it."

"Now about you."

"Oh God, what else do I have to do?"

One side of Dex's mouth pulled back in a half smile. "Decide between you and them."

That got her attention. "How so?"

"Wayne added a provision in the event you decide to get married. If that happens before the eighteen months is up, you can choose to keep the entire ranch no matter what."

"Wait, what?"

"Wayne wanted you to be able to run the ranch

with your husband if that's what you and your husband wanted for your life."

"Well, that's not going to happen." But Colt did come to mind. She shut that train of thought down before it left the station.

"The thing is, you can't tell your prospective husband about this at all. He cannot know that you can keep the ranch in its entirety. If you tell him and try to defraud the estate, you lose everything."

Never going to happen, because she didn't have a prospective husband. She mentally swiped Colt's image from her mind like switching screens on her phone.

"Okay. So that's it?"

"One more thing. If you marry and decide that you want another life, you can also choose to sell the ranch. You will get half and the other half will go to the charities Wayne designates."

"I don't know what to say."

"Wayne left you options. He wanted you to take care of all he left behind, but he didn't want to bind you to that place if it's not what you wanted. He knew you'd be fair and conscious of your decisions."

"And the consequences of selling the land. The jobs that would be lost. The potential for the land to be developed and not preserved for future generations."

"It's more than money at stake," Dex confirmed.

He might have said those words, but she spent the next half hour going over bank statements, investments, and signing new signature cards for everything to be in her name. By the time she left, those facts and figures circled her head. She couldn't believe she owned so much, had more money than she ever thought she'd earn in a lifetime, more than a top CEO made, and held the power to hold on to a legacy, let it go, and change people's lives. Hers included.

CHAPTER 11

Simon and Josh stood in the living room, looking around at their father's home, the house they grew up in, wondering what the hell they wanted to keep and toss, when what they really wanted was everything.

"I can't believe she gets the house and ranch and we've got to jump through fucking hoops for a place that's been ours since the day we were born." Josh picked up a crystal vase their mother used to keep fresh flowers in but which had stood empty since her death years ago. He tossed it against the wall, shattering it into tiny bits across the tile entryway.

"You're cleaning that up," Simon bit out, irritated that Josh's instincts always went to destruction and taking what he wanted without any thought to anyone but himself. The guy didn't know how to be subtle. Simon did. Luna would never see him coming.

Josh shook his head. "I can't believe you gave up your job to work here. You hate this place as much as I do."

"Not enough to let her take the whole damn thing. I can do it for a year and a half and then coast." He had a plan. He just needed some time to settle in on the ranch and with Luna so he could get close enough to his target and get what he really wanted.

Aunt Bea and Uncle Harry pushed the front door open wide and walked in, their shoes crunching on the shattered crystal all over the floor. Aunt Bea glanced down at the mess, then looked up and frowned at both of them.

"Why are the movers standing outside doing nothing?"

"We're looking around to see what we want to take." Josh rubbed his hand over the old sofa and frowned.

"We are not leaving anything for that girl. Take what you can load. I've already got an appointment with an auction house to sell whatever you boys don't take to save you the trouble of having to dispose of it yourself."

Simon and Josh exchanged surprised looks. They already had furnished houses. Most of this stuff they'd have to store, sell, or donate. This would save them time and a hell of a lot of work. Her plan made better sense.

Josh nodded to their aunt. "Good idea. Give Simon and me some time to go through the house and pick what we want." Translation, Josh wanted to get his hands on everything worth the most amount of money.

Simon fell in line because he really only had a few sentimental things he wanted to keep. Mostly pictures of his dad and mom, him and Josh as kids. As he sorted through pictures, Josh took a few as well.

His aunt held the office door handle and rattled the door. "Why is this locked?"

"We can't go in there. *She* gets that room and the library." Josh's face contorted into another mask of pure rage, the same one he wore every time *she* came up.

"Is that so?" Aunt Bea scoffed.

"Yep," Josh bit out.

"What are you boys going to do about this?" she demanded.

"Show her that she's not welcome here and that selling is her only choice if she wants a peaceful life."

Aunt Bea smiled at Josh with approval. "That is the only prudent option."

Josh nodded. "Damn straight."

Simon didn't think they'd actually convince Luna to sell this place and give up all that money. She wasn't stupid. Neither was he. He'd get what he wanted and none of them would be the wiser about how he did it right under their noses.

CHAPTER 12

Luna wrapped the last coffee mug and tucked it into the box at her feet. She stared around her shoebox apartment, happy to be moving to a new, much bigger place, but feeling a bit sentimental. This had been her first home away from home. Everything in it, she'd done herself. From the wood walls to the updated countertops. It might not have been much, but it had been hers. And thanks to Colt, she'd come home the last few nights to her brand-new light. Why that simple little thing touched her so much, she didn't know, but it did. Probably because he'd been looking out for her. It had been a long time since someone looked out for her. As a child, she'd always come second to her older brother. She understood why. His disability, outbursts, and needs came first for a reason. Still, little girls, children, wanted to be the most important thing in the world to their parents. Too often, she felt forgotten, or at least an afterthought.

Her cell rang. She picked it up and smiled. "Are your ears burning?" she asked her mother.

"Talking about me?"

"No. Thinking about the past, giving up my place, and moving on to something I'm not quite sure about yet."

"You're going to do great. I still can't believe he left it all to you."

"Believe it. I have all the papers and bank statements to prove it." She placed her hand on the six-inch stack of files Mr. Manning gave her at their meeting a few days ago. A meeting that lasted three hours. Way more time than she ever thought she'd need to put all of Wayne's assets into her name and sign checks for the inheritance owed to each of the family members and employees at the ranch. Checks so big, she'd never thought she'd write one that large, let alone have the funds to back it up.

Being overwhelmed at the reading of the will turned to outright terror when she went through the papers and saw the accounts, the amount of money left to her, the overwhelming task running a ranch the size and scope of Rambling Range would be. Unprepared didn't begin to describe how she felt. It left a stone in her gut the size of a cannonball.

"I still can't fathom why." Her mother's voice held an edge of suspicion. "I mean, you aren't family. You're not a rancher. It seems so odd."

"Mom, I told you, he was a close friend. And no, I wasn't sleeping with him, for God's sake."

"I never thought that, sweetheart."

She said the words, but Luna still heard her mother's *Maybe just a little* in there.

"Goodness. I'm just saying, things like this don't happen," her mom continued.

"Believe me, that phrase has been rattling around my head for days. It did happen. It is happening. What time will you be here to help me move in?"

"Well, that's why I'm calling. Your brother—"

"Enough said," Luna snapped, not meaning to.

The stress was getting to her. She softened her voice. "Sorry, Mom. I know he needs you."

"You need me, too, and I'm sorrier than I can say that I can't be there right now to help you with this transition in your life. I really do want to see your new place, help you pick out paint colors and new furniture."

She'd always known she was loved, admired for her independence, and appreciated for her unwavering help with her brother. But sometimes, she'd like to come first. She'd like her parents to see that although she could do it on her own, she'd like their help, if for no other reason than they wanted to be a part of what she was doing. Witness it firsthand so she didn't have to fill them in later. Some things lacked the proper description, depth, and emotion when told. Sometimes she felt that if they weren't there, it didn't matter if she told them about it later.

"You'll come soon, right?" That *"right?"* was the little girl inside of her hoping for her mother's attention.

"As soon as I can."

"I want to find something for Tanner to do at the ranch. Once I'm settled in, I hope to make a place for him there."

"Your father and I talked about it last night. We hoped you'd try to do something. He misses you so much. Your father and I could use a break."

"You'll get one. Give me some time to get settled and see what works."

"Um, we got the check you overnighted to us." The hesitation in her mother's voice made Luna's shoulders tense. As if they didn't ache enough with all the stress she was under.

"Yeah."

"Thank you," her mother whispered, her voice choked up and filled with tears.

"Mom, don't cry. It's not that much. Only what I could send without you having to pay taxes on it."

"It's not the money, Luna, it's that it makes things easier." Yes, and nothing had been easy for her parents since their little boy turned two and his developmental delays took on a whole new meaning for him and her parents' lives.

"If you need more . . ."

"No."

"If you've got specific bills that need to be paid, you can send them to me. I'll pay them. I can pay them." Yes, she could afford to do anything she wanted now. Buy anything she wanted. She knew that, but at this moment, it really hit her. She could do something for someone and make their life better.

She'd do it with the equine therapy program, too.

"We'll talk about it later when you've had time to settle into your new life. Like you said, maybe there will be a place for Tanner at the ranch that will give him what he needs without interfering in what you want to do with your life."

"Mom . . ."

"I understand, Luna. You love him, but he makes your life harder sometimes."

"He makes it better, too, Mom. He makes me a better person. At least, I want to be."

"You are, Luna. You're kind. You care. You love with your whole heart."

Tears gathered in Luna's eyes and spilled over. The last few days had been too much—losing her friend, inheriting a future she couldn't quite see yet, stumbling through all the details of taking on Wayne's life, and now her mother not coming to help her move but still finding a way to tell her she was loved and make her feel it even through the phone.

"Hey, honey, where do you want us to start?"

Luna turned to the cowboy with the deep voice that resonated through her like a homing beacon. Drawn to him, she took a step closer, but stopped herself when his eyes narrowed on her face and his mouth set in a grim line.

"Mom, I have to go. My friends just showed up to help me move. I'll call you later."

"Love you."

"Love you, too, Mom. Say hi to Dad and Tanner."

Colt closed the distance between them, coming into her home for the first time. He cupped her face, swiped his thumbs over her wet cheeks, and pulled her into a hug, wrapping his strong arms around her like he did last week when he escorted her to her car.

"What's wrong, honey?"

"Nothing. I'm fine." Better than fine with her cheek pressed to his chest, his heart thumping against her ear.

"People who are fine don't cry."

"Uh, we'll come back in a few minutes," Ford said from behind Colt. "But I'm taking the muffins with me." Ford grabbed the platter off the counter and headed back out the door, pushing Sadie out on his way.

Luna leaned back and stared up at Colt. His hazel eyes remained narrowed on her. "Hey."

"Hi. Why the tears?" he demanded.

"I got a little sentimental with my mom on the phone. Really, it's nothing." She swept her bangs away from her eyes.

Colt caught his breath and held it. His body tensed beneath her hand still pressed to his side. She set her other hand on his shoulder and simply stared into his eyes, searching for some magical answer to what it was between them that seemed so familiar, right, and too much to put into words.

"You're in my house," she blurted out.

Colt's gaze scanned the room with all the boxes and stacks of wood planks she'd taken down from the walls.

"It's not yours for much longer." He stepped away, releasing her all at once.

Luna felt his absence all the way to her bones. She wanted to be wrapped in all that strength again. She wanted the heat that pulsed through her when he touched her. He must feel it, too. Right?

The second she questioned it, his gaze roamed over her face, down her chest and navy blue T-shirt to her hip-hugging jeans with the frays and tears on her thighs and calves put there by the manufacturer and made even more well-worn by her. His gaze stopped on her bare feet, and a soft smile touched his lips and brightened his eyes.

"Nice toes. Never seen ladybugs."

She'd finished packing yesterday afternoon. With nothing to do, she'd painted her toes with red and black polish.

"I got bored yesterday."

"You should have come up to the house. To visit Sadie," he added, though he made it sound more like he wanted to see her.

"No, I should have called you to see if you wanted to go out for that beer. Lord knows, you won't ever want to see me again once you have to move that huge armoire down the stairs."

"Saturday. I'll pick you up at eight."

"All right, you two, let's get a move on. Time's a wastin'." Sadie walked right into Luna's kitchen and grabbed one of the boxes on the counter.

"Drop it." Luna pointed at her until Sadie did as commanded.

"What?"

"My pregnant friend is not lifting boxes and carrying them down the stairs."

"But . . ."

"No buts. Sit." Luna pointed to the chair she left next to the counter. She went to the microwave and set it for one minute to heat the tea she'd made for Sadie just a little while ago.

"What's with all the wood?" Rory stepped into the room, Ford hot on his trail, with only three muffins left on the plate.

"Luna salvaged it from her dad's old place. It goes with us." Colt took a muffin from the plate and bit into it a split second after he pulled the wrapper free.

"Good Lord, Colt, get the paper all the way off before you inhale it," Luna scolded.

"If I don't eat it fast, these two will eat them all." Colt nodded toward his brothers.

Luna took the plate from Ford, handed a second muffin to Colt and the last to Sadie. She pulled the cup of tea from the microwave and set it in front of her. "Now you have everything you need to supervise."

Sadie smiled and eyed Rory. "Oh, I love watching him work."

Luna shook her head, laughing a little under her breath at the way Sadie openly adored the big man standing in front of her.

"First, let me thank you guys for coming and helping

me out. I really appreciate it. Everything is packed and marked. If you brought all three trucks, we can probably do this in one run."

"Where's the rest of your stuff?" Ford asked.

Colt smacked his brother on the shoulder. "This is it."

"No shit?"

Luna had to admit how sad it was to realize her whole life came down to fifteen boxes stacked against the wall, an armoire, TV stand, futon, and a couple of armchairs. It had taken her two full days to pack. Half of that time she'd spent going through her things, organizing them, and discarding anything she didn't want or need anymore.

"This is it," she confirmed. "Oh, be very careful of that wrapped-up picture. It's my favorite thing."

"Since you have so few favorite things, we'll try not to break any of them," Ford teased, but she caught a trace of concern in his voice that she didn't have more.

Colt stepped forward, the two muffins she'd given him long gone. "You take the boxes to Ford's truck, honey. We'll get the furniture in mine and Rory's. You'll be all settled at Rambling Range by the end of the afternoon."

"Hell, we'll have her set up by lunch," Rory teased.

"Luna, what is all of this?" Sadie asked, flipping through the folders on the counter beside her.

"My new life in print. Everything of Wayne's transferred to my name."

"Wow." Sadie put her hand on the stack of files. "That's quite a pile of stuff you own."

"You have no idea. I have eleven pickup trucks. Eleven. A Cadillac. Three separate businesses, soon to be four if I go forward with the equine therapy program."

"Why wouldn't you?" Colt asked.

"I need to learn ranching, farming, and horses before I can take on something new."

"You've got some of the best land and cattle in the state," Rory praised. "You'll have no trouble keeping the business running well. Colt said he'd check in with your men. He'll make sure everything is as it should be."

Luna turned to Sadie. "Did you hear that? I have men." She shared a laugh with Sadie while all the guys groaned. Colt gave her a menacing look that quickly changed to a smirk when she poked him in the gut and said, "Just kidding."

"Are you two finally seeing each other?" Sadie asked, earning her a head shake from Rory to keep her mouth shut.

Luna didn't mind their interest. Sadie would get all the details. It was in the best friend agreement. "We have a date on Saturday night. I'm taking Colt out for a beer."

"We have plans that day, too," he added, picking up the rolled-up rug and hoisting it over his shoulder to carry down to the truck.

"We do?"

"Big horse sale." He turned his back and nearly knocked Ford down when he swung the rug around.

"Watch it."

"Sorry." Colt glanced over his shoulder at Luna. "Pull the papers from my pocket."

Luna took a minute to stare at his very fine Levi's-covered ass.

"Are you going to take them or what?"

"Just taking a moment to admire the view."

Ford and Rory groaned even louder this time. Each

took a side of the couch and lifted it. They headed for the door. She grabbed the papers and unfolded them.

"These are horses for sale."

"Exactly. I picked them out based on their age and training. We'll go look at them on Saturday and you can decide if you want to buy them."

"All of them?" She sorted through the ten or so pages.

"However many you want for your program that turn out to suit your needs. They have to be gentle and not spook easily by sudden movements. We'll test them out, talk to the owners, and see if we can't find some therapy horses to start training."

"You're serious?"

"Uh, yeah."

"Okay."

"Good. I'll pick you up at your ranch. We'll take a look today at your horse trailers and see if you've got what we need, otherwise, I'll bring one from my place." Colt walked out with the rug, following Ford and Rory after they maneuvered the couch through the door and onto the small landing outside. She didn't know how they managed it, but she left it to the strong men to get the job done.

"He's asked me a dozen times over the last few days if I've talked to you and if you were coming over to go over wedding stuff," Sadie said.

"I'm sorry I've been AWOL the last few days."

Sadie waved that away. "The point is, he couldn't wait to see you again."

"All he had to do was call me."

"Things haven't exactly been normal since Wayne died and turned your life upside down. He's giving you time to settle."

"Maybe I don't need time. Maybe all I need is a hug and an 'Everything will be fine, so let's move on.' "

Strong arms wrapped around her middle and squeezed her tight to a long, lean body. The heat, the familiarity settled into her body, and she relaxed against Colt. He kissed her on the head. He released her and gave her a smack on the ass. "Everything will be fine. Get a move on, honey. You can't expect me to do all the work."

She turned and stared at him.

His open gaze locked with hers. "Want something?"

"You to stop being so confusing."

"It's simple, Luna. I'm here and not planning on going anywhere but out with you on Saturday."

"So we start there?"

Colt glanced at Sadie, who pretended to be immensely interested in her tea. "*We* started with a kiss. Don't you think it's about time we see where that takes us?"

Rory and Ford walked in and stopped short, feeling the gathering tension in the room.

"Let's get that big dresser thing next," Colt said, breaking eye contact with her. He turned to get the job done, giving her a way out of answering the question after she'd hesitated a second too long because he'd stunned her with how boldly he'd put it. He'd laid it out right in front of Sadie like he didn't care if she overheard what felt like a private conversation.

But them seeing each other wasn't private. She wanted everyone to know she and Colt were a . . . thing. More than that, it felt like.

"Colt." She waited for him to stop shimmying the huge piece of furniture away from the wall with Rory on the other side. "Thanks for the hug and telling me everything is going to be all right even though it all feels so out of sorts."

He held his hand up with his index finger pointed up and circled it to encompass the room. "You like things simple and orderly. I can see where all this would over-whelm you."

She had to admit he was right. Even with her place packed up and ready to move, she'd kept things orga-nized. She liked her life that way, too.

"You and me on Saturday."

"You and me, right here, right now." He gripped the side of the cabinet and nodded to Rory to lift his side. Rory wiped the smile off his face right after throwing Ford an *I told you so* look.

She changed the subject, hoping to get everyone to stop looking at her. "I like the palomino the best." She held up the papers Colt gave her on the potential therapy horses.

"I knew you would, that's why I put her on top."

"You two done flirting?" Rory let out a huge sigh under the weight of the armoire. "This thing is heavy."

Colt pushed on his end, sending Rory stumbling backward toward the door.

"Hey, you two be careful with that," Sadie called, worried about her man.

Luna set the horse papers on top of the files next to Sadie and grabbed a box off the stack against the wall. Ford followed her out the door with a load of her old lumber balanced on his shoulder.

They spent the next two hours loading the trucks and tying everything down. When her tiny shoebox stood empty, she stood in the center, looking around, feeling a little nostalgic.

"Did you leave anything behind?" Colt asked from the doorway.

"Back to not coming into my place."

He stepped in and closed the distance between them. Ford and Rory's trucks started up outside and drove away.

"This isn't your place anymore."

"I know, but am I ready to take over that new place?"

"Yes."

"You seem so sure about that."

"I am. You're smart. You work hard. I have no doubt you'll make your mark on Rambling Range. Wayne thought so, too, otherwise he wouldn't have left it to you."

"I think he set me up as a babysitter to his two sons."

"They'll never stick out eighteen months."

Luna tilted her head. "But you think I can hack it the rest of my life?"

"I know you'll make that place yours the way you made this place into the home you wanted to come back to each and every day." Colt looked around at the patched-up holes in the walls she'd uncovered now that she'd taken down the barn boards. All her landlord had to do was paint and move in her next renter.

"Still, it's a lot to take on, especially when his family will be pressuring me to sell."

"It only takes one word to get them to back off. 'No.' "

"I can say that until I'm blue in the face, but they're going to keep coming back at me to sell."

"They'll get it once you settle into the house and start working on the ranch."

"We'll see."

"Yes, we will. Don't worry, honey, I'll look out for you."

"Why would you do that?"

He tilted his head and eyed her. "Why do you think?"

"Because you're my friend," she guessed.

He shrugged. "Sure. Let's start there and see what happens."

"Is that what we're doing?"

"We gotta start somewhere, right?"

She took the two steps toward him and stared up into his hazel eyes, filled with anticipation, need, and patience. The man had been driving her nuts the last couple of hours lifting all her heavy stuff, his muscles flexing beneath his tight black T-shirt.

She shook her head and scanned his big body from head to foot. "You drive me crazy, you know that?"

"You drive me crazy."

She didn't even hide her smile. "Why?"

"Because all I want to do is kiss you."

"More things we agree on." She placed her hand on the back of his neck, went up on tiptoe, and brushed her lips over his. Like a match swiped across the rough edge of the box, a fire lit inside of them. Colt's arms banded around her. One big hand held her lower back. He planted the other right on her ass, his long fingers laying over the curve, inches from the tingling heat building between her legs. He pulled her closer and took the kiss deeper. His tongue glided along hers. She moaned. He growled, tilted his head for a better angle, and kissed her socks off.

Luna lost herself in Colt's arms. The first kiss they shared rocked her world off center and left her wondering if what she felt that night in the parking lot was real or just her imagination. Now that she knew the passion and need were real, something opened inside her and everything within her settled. She let loose the tight hold she had around his neck and combed her fingers through his sun-kissed golden hair. His hand on her ass contracted and squeezed, pulling her closer to him. He might have made everything inside her focus on him, but she still had enough wits to know they couldn't take this any further here in her empty apartment. Plus, everyone was waiting for them at her new place.

She hated to end the mind-blowing kiss. The man's mouth was soft, supple, and he put just the right amount of pressure, demanding, but also giving. God, the man could kiss.

Her hand settled on his cheek. She gave in to one more long kiss, her tongue sliding along his, exploring his mouth and the thrill that raced through her. She broke the kiss, leaned her forehead to his, and tried to catch her breath. To keep him from kissing her again, she pressed her thumb to his parted lips. He took it into his mouth and sucked softly, releasing her just as a wave of heat rocketed through her system and made her legs tremble. Good thing he kept a tight hold on her. His lips pressed to the pad of her thumb. She fell back on her heels and whispered, "Damn."

"I must be king of the idiots for letting you get away the last time we did that."

She smiled and laughed, and just like that she could look at him again, knowing he felt exactly what she felt when they lost themselves in each other.

As if he couldn't bear to stop touching her, his hands smoothed up her hips and back before they slid along her sides and he released her.

"We need to get going. We pull in more than fifteen minutes behind the others and they'll be thinking we . . ."

"Yeah. You're right." All of a sudden, she didn't know what to do with her hands. She smoothed one down her still-fluttering stomach. She used the other to brush the hair from her eyes. Nervous and off balance, she looked everywhere but at him.

"Luna."

"Yeah," she said to his chest.

"You ever going to look at me again?"

She tried to fight the smile but failed miserably.

"What is it?" he asked, his voice filled with patience and concern.

She managed to look up and sighed when his hazel gaze met hers. "You are so much. I don't know what to do with it all. Does that make sense?"

"If you're feeling half as much as what I'm feeling, then yeah, that makes perfect sense." His fingers caressed her arm down to her hand. He linked his fingers with hers. "Ready to move into your new place?"

"Ready to move into a house where my bedroom isn't also my living room and kitchen? Uh, yeah."

Colt smiled and melted her insides again. "Let's go, honey. I can't wait to see the house."

"You mean you're actually going to go inside?"

"Yes, because I won't be sitting on your bed, fighting tooth and nail not to strip you naked and have my way with you."

The laugh burst out of her gut. "Is that why you didn't come in?"

"Damn straight."

"And you think I would have just fallen into bed with you?"

He tugged on her hand and she fell into his chest. His mouth claimed hers in another searing kiss. His big hand brushed down her hair and settled on her jaw. His thumb swept over her chin as he broke the kiss and held her away. He squeezed their joined hands and stared down at her. She'd never seen anyone look at her with that much hunger and need in their eyes. All of that for her.

"Damn straight."

It took her a minute to figure out what he meant. Oh yeah, she'd have fallen into bed with him without a thought to consequences or the outcome. When Colt touched her, she wanted him. She'd never felt this way about anyone. Not even her ex, who she once-upon-a-time thought she could love.

What she felt for Colt went beyond simple lust. He truly had opened something inside of her. A dream. A hope that what they shared could be real and true and lasting.

CHAPTER 13

Colt drove down the long driveway behind Luna's Jeep, passing under the Rambling Range sign. Fence lines spread out. A herd of horses grazed to his right. On the left he spotted the brand-new covered arena. Everything, from the land, the animals, the house that loomed large in front of them, to the massive stables and barns on the property, belonged to Luna. A spread this size was worth more than he could possibly imagine.

The spread he shared with his brothers was only half the size of this place. While he'd been thinking of building his own house, he could never afford something this massive. Luna owned all this, had more money than she'd likely spend in a lifetime, and the possibility to do anything she wanted now. What the hell could he offer her? All of a sudden, she didn't seem like the woman he used to know. Who she was and what she had took on a whole new meaning in his mind.

He thought of the kiss they shared back at her old place. Now that was the woman he remembered. The one who lit him up and made him burn. The same woman who stopped her car in front of him, stepped out, and stared at everything in front of her with a look of wonder on her face. He caught the flash of fear and hesitation in her eyes. She'd talked about how this place intimidated and overwhelmed her. She'd barely spoken of the money. She'd lived with only what she'd truly needed in her tiny little space. Sentimental, she'd torn the boards she'd salvaged from her family's place and brought them with her here. Luna cared, but not about the money. Not in a way that made her greedy or look down on those who didn't have what she had. He hoped that never changed about her.

Sadie approached Luna, pointing up to the house, and hugged Luna close. They had a deep friendship. If he messed this up with Luna, he'd have hell to pay with Sadie. Rory would be pissed if he upset his soon-to-be-wife, especially in her delicate condition. Hell, he'd be pissed at himself if this thing with Luna went south. He liked her. They had a connection he'd never felt with any other woman. If kissing her sent his system into overdrive, sleeping with her just might kill him. He'd die happy though, because being with a woman like Luna was worth it.

Luna turned and stared at him, her eyes filled with anger.

Great, what did I do now?

He opened his truck door and slipped out, calling, "What's wrong?"

Luna swept her arm out to indicate the front of the house. He looked past her, spotted Rory and Ford walking over with a wheelbarrow and shovels, and followed the path up to the front door and a huge pile of manure.

Luna quirked up one side of her mouth, but it didn't hold any humor. "So what the family is trying to say is that my moving in here is a pile of horse shit."

He couldn't help himself; he laughed. "I guess so."

He liked that she had a sense of humor about this stupid prank, but it pissed him off that someone in the family did this to her. They had to know she understood their upset. Nothing would change the fact that Wayne, not Luna, set all this in motion, but they still believed she'd manipulated Wayne—and slept her way into all that money and this ranch.

Bullshit. He didn't believe that for a second. Luna was kind. Generous to a fault sometimes. Look how long she'd put up with Billy.

Sadie let loose a giggle, too, at Luna's sarcastic comment, pulling him from his thoughts about punching whoever pulled this prank. He might have laughed, but he didn't think it was all that funny. "We'll get this cleaned up and hose down the porch before we start moving things in."

"I wonder what we'll find inside." The worry in Luna's eyes bothered Colt.

He began to wonder if she'd be safe here alone. Would the family's resentment turn from a stupid prank to something much more direct and threatening? They wanted her to sell. How hard would they push to persuade her to do it?

"That's a very dark look." Luna touched his arm to get his attention. "What are you thinking?"

"Nothing." He traced his fingers over her soft cheek. "I don't like they've upset and worried you."

"I kind of expected worse."

Her admission didn't ease his mind or the knot in his gut.

"Let's hope we don't find worse inside."

Sadie shoved his shoulder. "Go help your brothers clean up so we can get in and help Luna put her things away."

Colt touched his finger to his forehead in a salute. "Yes, ma'am."

Sadie smacked him again, sending him off to help Rory and Ford shovel shit. Just another day on a ranch.

Ford kept shoveling when he approached.

Rory stopped and propped his arm on top of the shovel, wiping his brow with the back of his hand. "I don't like this shit."

"Literal or figurative?" Colt's smart-ass remark earned him a glare from both his big brothers. "I don't like it either. Once this is cleaned up and we can get inside, we go in first. They had five days to clear out the house. Let's make sure they didn't leave any other surprises."

"Worse than this?" Ford asked, pulling his T-shirt up and over his nose and mouth to help minimize the stench.

"I hope not, but I'm not taking any chances with her."

Rory and Ford smiled, eyeing him.

"Shut the fuck up and get to work."

"We didn't say anything." Rory took on the look of an innocent child, but he couldn't quite hide the smile that came much easier now that Sadie had come into his life.

"Yes. You did. With one look. Now come on. Let's get this done."

"Touchy, touchy, little brother." Ford smacked the back of his hand on Colt's shoulder.

"Can we not do this now." He cocked his head toward Luna and Sadie, who were leaning against the front of the Jeep. "In front of them."

"You mean in front of her," Rory pointed out. "How serious is this thing with her?"

"Look, man, I know your girl is her best friend and fucking this up will affect Sadie and you."

Rory held up his hand to stop him. "Don't do that. Don't add Sadie and me to whatever relationship you have with Luna. If it works, great. I'm happy for you. If it turns out you two split down the road, that's your business. Sadie and I want you both to be happy. Together or apart."

"Me, too," Ford added. "You seem to have gotten past what happened with her ex. You're friends again. If it's more than that, or that's what you hope it will be, then good for you."

"Plus, Sadie and her already act like sisters. If you marry her, you can make it official." Rory smacked him on the back, picked up his shovel, and started in on the pile again, kicking up dust.

Colt knew when to quit. He pulled his T-shirt up over his nose and mouth, took the third shovel from the wheelbarrow, and helped out. Like all the other times they worked together, they got the job done quickly. Colt handed off his shovel to Rory. Ford hoisted the wheelbarrow handles and steered the load back to the stables, Rory following him to put the tools away. Colt unwound the hose by the garage and dragged it over to the porch.

"Hey honey, can you turn the water on," he called to Luna.

"I wish I had some flowers to plant in those beds, seeing as how we're about to fertilize them so well."

"The bushes aren't so bad."

"No. But some color would be nice. It's spring."

"Let's at least get you moved in before you start gardening."

Luna turned on the water, and Colt made quick work

of spraying down the front door and porch. Once done, the entrance remained wet, and a bit slippery, but they'd make do and get Luna into her home before dark set in.

"So, were you guys taking bets on what the inside of the house looks like?" Luna fished the keys from her tight jeans.

"Hand over the keys. We're going in first, just in case."

"Seriously, Colt, it's my house."

"I'm still not letting you in first." He held out his hand. She plunked the keys into his palm and tried to pull her hand back, but he captured it with his fingers. He gave her a little tug and she fell forward. He met her in the middle and gave her a quick kiss. "You're real pretty when you're pissed."

The anger simmering in her eyes softened with the surprise of the kiss. In front of everyone. Sadie, his brothers, and a couple of guys from the stables, who walked back with Rory and Ford.

"Colt, it's no big deal. A pile of crap isn't going to make me change my mind."

"Which is why I'm wondering what they might have done inside to push you along to seeing things their way."

"Miss Hill," one of the men from the stables called.

"Toby, it's just Luna." She looked at the other man. "Hello, Ed."

"Nice to see you again, Luna. Sorry about the trouble. We had no idea they'd done such a thing."

Luna waved it off. "Any other trouble here while they moved things out that I should know about?"

Toby frowned. "They came in with three moving trucks and packed up everything. I wanted to check the house after they left, but Josh wouldn't let me in.

He locked up and took off, along with Simon and their aunt."

"Has Simon started working here?"

"He walked through the stables, checking out the horses. Took a look around the property, especially the new covered arena. Nothing more than that."

"Okay. He'll probably start sometime in the next few days if he's going to start at all."

"What do you want us to have him do?"

"Well, he's not the boss or the owner, so don't let him boss you around. He's to learn to run this place if he wants to get his fifty percent. I suggest he starts as a ranch hand doing what the others do to keep this place running as smoothly as you make it run. Put him to work."

"Yes, ma'am," Toby agreed.

"Luna."

"Luna." Toby nodded.

"If he doesn't pull his weight, or refuses to do what's asked of him, I want to know about it. I'm okay if there's one area of the operation he's better at than the others and he wants to focus on that, but he should get a feel for everything that goes on here. I'll be doing the same."

Toby and Ed glanced at each other, surprised she'd show an interest in the daily operations, then stared back at her.

"Okay, then, let's see about the house." She took a step forward but stopped and stared down at their joined hands, the keys locked in their combined grip. Her lips tilted in a soft smile. She headed for the stairs with Colt beside her. When he got to the door, he released her hand and unlocked the door. He pushed it open. The sickening stench hit him first. Worse than the manure. The sickening, acrid scent of rotting food. He stared at the wall across from him and the big bold letters scrawled in ketchup. BITCH.

Sadie retched behind him.

"Rory, get her away from the smell," Colt warned.

Colt stepped into the house, kicking a plastic bottle across the entryway. Luna came in behind him. "Stay outside until I look around," he told her.

"There's no one here, Colt. Aside from the atrocious smell, nothing is going to hurt me."

"Stay outside and call the cops. They can't get away with this."

Luna shook her head. "It's not worth getting into it with them over petty vandalism. Hopefully they got it out of their system. I can't really blame them. Though I wouldn't do this, I would be really pissed if I lost my family home and most of my inheritance to someone else."

"You might change your mind about that once I check things out and see what other surprises they left."

"I'm coming in with you."

Colt let out an exasperated sigh. "Stay behind me." He gave Ford a look. He moved in behind Luna. Between the two of them, they could protect her from any threat they might find. Right now, Colt searched for the source of the gut-souring smell, keeping an eye out for any more damage to the huge, amazing house.

"Damn, Luna, this place is beyond great," Ford said, bringing up the rear with Toby and Ed.

"It's bigger than any place I've ever lived, including my parents' old ranch house." Luna stopped behind Colt and put her hands on his sides and cursed under her breath. "Damn, that rug is ruined. That is no way to use a perfectly good bottle of red wine."

Colt stared down at the spray of wine across the almost white carpet in the living room. "You might be able to have a cleaning crew get that out."

"I don't think so. Guess I get to pick out new carpeting. It's going to cost a fortune."

"Good thing you've got one." Ford pointed out exactly what Colt was thinking, too.

"Oh yeah, right. New carpet!" She forced the enthusiasm because of why she needed new carpet, but she'd bounce back. Who didn't like to shop? The excitement would be real when she started looking at samples. Especially once she embraced the fact she could pay the bill and didn't have to worry about her next paycheck to cover it.

"What color do you think, Colt?"

Surprised she'd ask him, he looked around the spacious living room, taking in the massive stone fireplace and wood mantel. "Pull one of the darker tans from the stones. Maybe something that's a few mottled colors to help keep it looking clean."

"Exactly what I was thinking." She glanced around the room. "Those are the doors to the library. They should still be locked. I have the key. Same for the office on the other side of the entry. The bedrooms are down that hall and another hall past the office."

"How many rooms?" Colt asked.

"Two next to the office that share a bathroom. Two master suites down that hall."

"Damn, this place is big." Colt started toward the back and headed for the kitchen, following his nose toward the smell he wanted to get away from more than he wanted his next stench-filled breath.

Everyone covered their mouths and noses when they entered the back kitchen and breakfast room.

"Well that explains it." Luna stared at the rotten food sitting on the counters and dumped on the kitchen floor. "I guess I can't offer you anything to eat," she teased.

"Toby, you guys got some heavy-duty garbage bags out in the stables?"

"I'm on it," Ed volunteered, rushing to the front door and fresh air.

Colt and Toby went to the breakfast nook and opened the windows. Luna unlocked the back door and pulled it open. They got a soft cross breeze, but it wasn't enough to sweep the stench out.

"I'll head down the hall and open up the windows in the bedrooms. We'll air this place out while we move my things in." Luna tiptoed around the mess on the floor, hitting cabinet doors shut on her way through the massive kitchen. She stopped by the sink and looked in. "Yuck. I don't think I'll be eating leftover lasagna any time soon." She turned on the tap and hit the switch on the wall. The first switch turned on a light over the sink. The second turned the garbage disposal on.

She drew her lips into a tight line and washed down the sink. She glanced at Colt but turned away quickly. Not fast enough for him to miss the shine of tears in her eyes.

Colt braved the debris field on the floor and rubbed his hand back and forth across her shoulders, her soft hair brushing the back of his hand. "We'll get this place cleaned up in no time, honey."

"I guess I have to buy a new refrigerator, too, since they took it with them. At least they left the microwave and dishwasher."

"That's because they're bolted down." Toby finished closing the empty cabinets on the island but swore when he got to a set of drawers by the stove. "We'll need something to wash out the drawers over here."

Colt swore, too. "I get they're pissed, but this is just . . ."

"Shit."

Colt turned to the man standing in the kitchen entryway. An overwhelming urge to tackle him and beat the living shit out of him washed through Colt's body. Luna shut the sink and disposal off and clamped her hand over Colt's forearm, holding him still.

"We already cleaned that up on our way in." Colt glared at Simon Travers, trying to see past the disgust in Simon's eyes for the horrible scene in the kitchen. Colt actually couldn't tell if the guy was a good actor or really had no idea his family had wrecked the place.

"What?"

"Load of horse shit someone left on the porch, blocking the door." Colt couldn't quite believe this guy had nothing to do with it, or at the very least knew his family did it.

"Are you serious? Who would do something like this?"

"Someone whose inheritance went to Luna and not him," Colt suggested.

Simon pointed at his chest. "You think I did this?"

Colt had to give the guy credit. He almost sounded believable. Colt didn't buy it.

"Simon, what are you doing here?" Luna asked, still holding on to Colt's arm.

"I came by to talk to you about working here. Since you're moving in today, I thought I'd start tomorrow with you."

Colt fumed. "Let's get something straight, you aren't working with her. She owns this place. You work for her. You earn your place here."

"But you move right in on her right after my father dies, she gets this place, and you get everything?"

Colt's muscles bunched, ready to go after the guy for saying such a thing, but Luna moved faster, stepping in front of him and blocking him from moving without shoving her out of the way.

"Get out."

"What?" Simon narrowed his gaze on Luna. "I came to talk to you, not listen to him tell me what's not mine and what I have to earn."

"Instead, you've accused me of sleeping my way in here, then you do the same to my friend. You and I will work out a schedule and what your role will be on this ranch tomorrow at seven, when we meet with Toby in the stables. Until then, I've got work to do to clean up this mess and get myself settled in the house."

Simon sucked in a deep breath and let it out, his nose scrunched from the atrocious smell. "We've gotten off to a bad start."

"A real shitty one," Luna agreed, playing off the whole horse shit welcome. Colt had to give her credit, the woman had a good sense of humor even when she was pissed. He didn't doubt that under all that anger simmering in her tense body was also hurt that Wayne's family treated her this way and thought the worst of her when she'd done nothing wrong.

Simon softened his tone. "I never said you slept with my father."

"Saying it and thinking it are two different things. Right?"

"I didn't think it either." Simon raked a hand through his blonde hair, his frustration clear. "Listen, Luna, I didn't have anything to do with this. Yes, my family wants what should have gone to them. I want what my father should have left me. That's why I'm here, to get back at least half of what is mine. I don't like that I have to do it. I don't want to do it. But I will, because this place means something to me. This is my home."

"This was your home," Colt reminded him. "Even if you get half the ranch, this is her house to keep."

Simon raised his gaze to the ceiling. "I know that. Believe me, it's all I've thought about since he died and left everything to her. But that doesn't mean I don't want to be a part of this place, of what he built, of the place he held so dear."

"Then you'll show up for work tomorrow at seven and earn it like your father wanted." Luna held her ground, not giving Simon an inch to wiggle out of doing what his father demanded. Colt admired Luna's tenacity and guts to hold true to Wayne's last wishes.

"He loved this place," Luna said, a touch of sadness in her voice. "I won't let you destroy it. I won't be persuaded to sell it and watch someone else carve it up and turn it into a bunch of overpriced mansions, so if that's what you think you and your brother will do if you get your fifty percent, you're wrong. I won't sign off on that."

Simon huffed out a frustrated breath and turned to leave, but he faced Rory and Ford standing behind him like a wall.

Colt let a smile touch his mouth when Simon turned back and glared at him. "You were right about one thing."

"What's that?" Simon asked.

"I will be here watching over her and this ranch. I may not have known your father well, but I did call him friend. He looked out for Luna, and so will I."

"You won't have to protect her from me. I'm here to do the work, that's all. Who knows? Maybe Luna and I will become great friends."

Colt simmered. *Not going to happen, asshole.*

This time Simon turned and walked out, looking smug for riling Colt's green monster.

Ford and Rory let him pass.

"You didn't have to say that." Luna broke the remaining tension in the room. "I can handle him and the rest of the family."

"Never said you couldn't, but it doesn't hurt to let them know you're not alone here. You have people who will back you up. People you can call on if you need help."

"Or someone to intimidate them."

"I'm good for a lot of things besides kissing you, honey." He tried to tease her out of her anger and frustration.

It took a second for her to suck in a breath and let loose the smile she tried to keep from creeping across her face.

"Oh yeah? What else are you good at?"

"Now, darlin', that's a loaded question to ask a man in front of everyone." He leaned into her ear and whispered, "If you think I like kissing your sweet, tempting lips, wait until I kiss every inch of you. Down your neck, over your mouthwatering, I-can't-wait-to-get-my-hands-on-them breasts, down the soft slope of your belly, until I taste you on my tongue." He swept the tip of his tongue along her earlobe. She shivered. The grip she clamped onto his side when he leaned into her became painful as her hand contracted again.

He kissed the side of her head. "Let me loose, honey."

She did all at once and whipped her gaze to his. "You're diabolical."

"You're cute when you blush."

She jabbed him in the gut with her small fist. "Let's get this place cleaned up."

When they both turned to the living room, everyone was gone. They'd all disappeared to give Colt and Luna their privacy.

Luna snagged the bucket of cleaning supplies off the counter. Colt took the roll of plastic garbage bags and pulled one off. The two of them scrubbed down the kitchen and the "un" welcome sign on the wall by the front door. Nothing could be done about the ruined carpet. Rory measured the space in the kitchen for a new refrigerator. Since they refused to let Sadie do any heavy lifting in her condition, she drove into town to buy a new fridge and groceries. The rest of the house needed a good cleaning, but they managed to move Luna's things in without any further incident.

Colt breathed a huge sigh of relief when Ford finished grilling up the hot dogs and hamburgers on the outdoor grill. They stood around Luna's kitchen eating at the counter and helping Luna make a list of things she needed to buy for the house.

"I'll leave the spare rooms empty for now. The most important thing to get is . . ."

"Chairs," Rory pointed out.

"Big-screen TV and a sofa," Ford added.

Luna laughed. The sound tightened Colt's gut. He loved to hear the sound, but more so now, since Wayne's family turned a day that should have been exciting for Luna—moving into this big new place—into something disheartening.

The kitchen gleamed bright and clean. The sickening smell had long since dissipated with fresh breezes wafting through the open windows. Luna stood beside him, beautiful and relaxed after the meal they'd shared. He hooked his arm around her shoulders and pulled her close, kissing the side of her head. She giggled and stared up at him, a wide, open grin on her pretty face.

"Thanks for all your help today." She tapped her beer bottle to his near-empty one. They drank together.

Colt smiled back at her, the light feeling inside of him when he was with her expanding. The long day wore him down, but she renewed him in a way he didn't expect.

Sadie yawned again.

Rory hugged her close to his side. "I need to get this one home and into bed before she falls over."

Luna broke away from Colt, rounded the counter, and hugged Sadie. "Thank you for the emergency refrigerator and food run. This dinner was made possible by you alone."

"What are friends for but spending your money?"

Luna laughed. "We'll spend some more together when you help me pick out carpet, draperies, furniture, dishes . . ."

"A TV," Ford requested.

"Anything else you'd like for the next time you come over?"

"A woman of my own," Ford shot back. "I'm tired of watching these two have all the fun."

Luna and Sadie both laughed. Rory wore the same prideful expression Colt felt, knowing he had a woman like Luna by his side. They might have just begun this relationship, but the way he felt about her went deeper than anything he'd ever felt for another woman. She belonged to him. A hard thing to admit for a guy who'd sworn he wasn't looking for anything more than fun. Now, setting up house for her here, thinking about what this place would be like once she got it furnished, what it would be like to live here with her and make it their home, well, it sank in and took hold. He didn't even try to fight it. He didn't want to. As much as he told himself to stop dreaming of a life with her here for reasons that didn't make much sense anymore, he let those dreams sprout and take root. It might take time for them to get there, but he wanted it. He wanted her to be a real and lasting part of his life. He wanted what Rory found with Sadie. What he imagined his parents shared and lost way too soon. He never thought he'd want that, let alone find it, but he had a chance with Luna. A second chance he would do anything within his power to hold on to and make her happy.

"Colt?"

"Huh. Yeah?"

"You must be tired, too." Luna touched his arm and squeezed. The heat raced through his system, making him want more. "Everyone is leaving."

Rory and Ford gave him one of those looks, like he'd lost his mind and gotten drunk on the woman beside him. True. On both counts.

"Right. It's late. Long day. You must be ready for bed."

Rory and Ford both snickered, turned, and walked out of the kitchen, Sadie shoving Rory along to get him to shut up.

Luna tried to hide her own sweet smile. "Thank you for helping today. You went above and beyond with what those guys did to this place." Luna walked beside him to the front door, where the other three waited to say goodbye. "You guys are the very best of friends.

Thanks for moving me and taking time off work to do it in the middle of the week. I can't thank you enough."

Rory patted her shoulder. "You're welcome. See you soon."

Sadie hugged Luna again. "Call me in the morning. We'll make plans."

"Definitely."

Ford hugged Luna. "Be careful tomorrow when you meet Simon."

"I will. Toby will be with me. I start being a rancher tomorrow."

Rory and Sadie walked down the porch steps. Rory called back, "You'll be great at it."

Ford gave them a wave and headed for his truck, too.

Alone on the porch with Luna, Colt held back until his brothers drove away.

"What's the matter, Colt? Something has been weighing on your mind since Simon left."

"What he said about my using you for this place . . ."

Luna placed her hand on his chest. "Stop right there. I know how things went down between the two of us before Wayne died. I know how I felt about you then. I know how I feel about you now. I do not think, nor have I ever thought, you are the type of person to use anyone to get something you want."

"You mean that."

She really did. She recognized it wasn't a question, so she didn't respond with anything more than a simple nod.

"Will you be all right here alone?"

She leaned up and kissed him softly. That was the first time she'd done so without him kissing her first since they resolved their past.

"You're sweet, but I'll be fine. After the day we've

had, I'm going to crash and get an early start tomorrow. Big day at my new job."

"I'll be by sometime tomorrow to check on you."

"You don't need to do that."

"Yes, I do. As much as I hate to leave you now, I won't make it through a whole day without seeing you."

She smiled up at him, her hand still on his chest. She must feel his pounding heart after he said that to her. He hadn't meant to reveal so much, but it was God's honest truth.

"Okay, so long as it's not because you don't think I can run this place without you."

Colt fell back a step, completely shocked. Luna's hand fell to her side.

"Why would you think such a thing?"

"It's a daunting task. You know what I'm facing. If you think I can't do it, well, I've got to wonder if I can."

Colt went to her, cupped her face in his hands, and tilted her head so he could look straight down into her eyes. "You can do this. It's hard work, but nothing you can't handle. When you put your mind to something, you get it done. You've got me to back you up if you need me, but I don't think you will. I know you can do this on your own." Colt took a breath and let his heart speak. "I'm just hoping that maybe we'll get to that point where you don't want to do it alone."

Her eyes went wide with that admission, then softened and filled with dawning understanding that he meant it. He leaned down and kissed her softly, brushing his lips against hers. One taste of her and he sank in to tempt her into giving him everything. He wanted to take her inside and make love to her, but it was still too soon. Too new. Besides, he liked this thrill and the anticipation building between them. She'd go willingly, but Colt wanted more time to solidify the foundation of their friendship and the deeper part of their relationship. If the way she kissed him told him anything, it was that the physical part of their relationship would be explosive. That part had always come easy to him. The part about getting to know her, building something deeper and more meaningful took time. Patience he hoped he had, because when her tongue slid along his and her body pressed against him, all he wanted to do was sink into her and burn in the fire they created.

Colt kissed her one last time, long and deep, hoping she understood how much he hated to leave her. When he softened the kiss and laid his lips against hers and held it, her grip on his back let loose. Her hands swept up his shoulder and down to his hips. Only then did he break the kiss and stare down at her.

"I'll see you tomorrow." He kissed her on the forehead and let her go. He made himself walk down the stairs and across the yard to his truck. He got in, started it, but stared at her standing on the porch in the soft pool of light, shiny on her dark hair and casting shadows over her beautiful face.

I'll keep you safe. A promise to her, one he intended to keep.

Home, Rory and Ford waited on the porch for Colt to join them. He fell into the chair beside theirs.

"Did you tell her about the dead rats in her bathtub and the 'Sell' message in their blood on the tiles?" Rory asked.

The rage came back in a wave through Colt's body, making him tense and ready to punch the asshole who did that bit of nasty business. "No. And I'm not going to."

"What are you going to do?" Rory's hard gaze bore into him.

"Spend as much time as I can over there without her getting suspicious that I'm guarding her."

"This is some fucked-up shit." Ford leaned forward and planted his forearms on his knees.

"Did you talk to Toby, Rich, Artie, and Ed about what happened and watching out for her when I can't?"

Ford nodded. "They'll try to make sure she's never alone. They'll talk to the other men about keeping a close eye on everything, including her."

"Good."

"Let's hope now that she's there, and the family is out, they'll settle down and let this thing go." Rory didn't make that optimistic statement sound plausible in the least.

"What did you guys think of Simon?"

"He's an asshole," Ford said.

"He's got his sights set on Luna." Rory's assessment surprised Colt.

"Why do you say that? He and the whole family think she slept with Wayne."

"I'm not sure he actually thinks that, but it wouldn't surprise me if he made a play for her. Cozy up to her, get her to trust him, then get her to hand over what he wants," Rory added.

"No way. Luna won't fall for that crap."

"He tried to make you look bad to Luna so he'd have a chance with her. Watch your back. I wouldn't be surprised if he kept trying to undermine you with her. If they can separate her from you, her friends, and get her alone and vulnerable, they'll use it to their advantage to pressure her into doing what they want."

"Man, Rory, you really know how to make a guy

feel good about leaving her there alone. Thanks. I'll never sleep again."

"Sure you will. Go back and sleep with her," Ford suggested.

Colt raked his hand through his hair, contemplating that very thing. "We're not there yet."

"You two looked real close today," Rory said. "Sadie even commented about how happy Luna seemed with you."

"Well, that's something." And great news that Sadie and Rory both didn't mind his relationship with Luna. At least for now, when things were good. "Still, I'm not going back there to sleep with her just to keep her safe. It's gotta be more. It's gotta be right."

"Reeeally," Ford said, one eyebrow cocked up nearly to his hairline. "Since when do you need a good reason to sleep with a beautiful woman?"

"She's not some girl I picked up in a bar or met at a party."

"So, she's special?" Rory asked, genuine interest in his voice.

Shit. Now they wanted to know everything Colt was still trying to figure out for himself.

"She's something." Special yes, but more. Hell, he didn't know how to explain her, them.

"Well, the fact that you want more than to just sleep with her should tell you something." Ford chimed in with that bit of wisdom.

"I want her, okay? But please don't get any ideas about planning a double wedding. And for God's sake, don't tell Granddad that Luna's anything more than . . ."

"What?" Ford asked, smiling like a crocodile. "Your girlfriend?"

"Don't tell Granddad that you love her?" Rory asked.

"What? No." He didn't love her. She wasn't his girl-friend. Wait, that didn't sit well.

Colt didn't do relationships. He had friends with lots of benefits. But Luna felt like more than a friend. He went out with those other women. Dinner. Movies. Drinks at the bar, but he'd never taken the time to re-place a light, or move them into a new place. Some-thing deeper connected him to Luna. He wanted to share the pieces of himself he didn't share with anyone but his family. His need to protect her, to be with her was unlike anything he'd ever felt.

His insides knotted. His heart jackhammered in his chest. He found it hard to breathe beneath the band squeezing his ribs. What the hell was she? He'd never put a label on what he had with a woman, so why did he feel the need to put one on what he had with Luna?

Oh hell no. He wasn't going to sit here analyzing how he felt about Luna with his brothers. "I'm going to bed." He rose and went through the front door with Rory and Ford sharing a laugh at his expense.

He didn't sleep for hours that night, too worried about Luna alone at Rambling Range. One horrible nightmare after another kept him tossing and turning in his bed until he forced himself to think about her in another way. He focused on the kisses they shared and fell into a dream so filled with passion and need that he reached for her in the night, believing it was real. He woke at dawn with her taste on his tongue, the feel of her body against his, the memory of her wrapped around him, and Rory's question ringing in his head. *Do you love her?*

CHAPTER 14

Simon slammed the door to his house and headed for his car. He set his second mug of coffee on the roof and fished his keys from his jeans. He'd given up a perfectly good job as a district rep, which paid a decent salary and consisted of him mostly taking clients out to lunch, bullshitting his way through a meal, talking up the company and their lame products, and collecting on the commission when the sales rep closed the deal. The sales rep did most of the work, he reaped the benefits. His kind of job.

Now he found himself falling into his car half asleep at dawn to head over to a ranch he didn't own, to do dirty, hard work he didn't want to do or care about, all so he could schmooze some waitress who probably didn't know the first thing about running a business, let alone a ranch the size and scope as the one his father had the audacity to leave her.

Simon slammed his palm into the steering wheel. Pain shot up his arm and his palm tingled like a thousand tiny pin pricks. "What the fuck, Dad? How could you leave it all to her?"

"We'd all like to know that."

Simon jumped and pressed his hand over his thrashing heart. "Damnit, Josh, you scared the shit out of me."

Josh didn't apologize or care. He stood next to the open car door staring down at Simon. "Don't you look like Farmer John this morning in your jeans, boots, and button-up plaid? I guess if you're going to make her believe you like working there and ranching is your life, you need to look the part."

Simon let the Farmer John comment go with a resigned sigh, knowing that he wasn't getting out of this talk with his brother. "What do you want?"

"I want to know what the hell you're up to, little brother."

"Getting my fifty percent."

"You really think she's going to let that happen? Hell, son, you've lost your ever-loving mind." Josh added some extra twang to his words.

"Who sounds like a farmer now?"

"Get your head out of your ass and think. The terms say she decides if you get that fifty percent. She says if she thinks you've worked hard enough, loved that place enough to have any of it. We need her to sell. Ten million is a hell of a lot better than eighteen months of hell to get nothing."

"With what that place earns a year and over a lifetime, hell, I can sit back and let others do the work and collect. I'll never have to work again."

"You're not listening. She's never going to let that happen."

"She's sappy and sentimental. She's not a rancher. So long as I do better than her, it'll be enough."

Josh shook his head, a deep frown drawing lines on his rugged face. His eyes were bloodshot from another night of too much drinking. At this hour of the morning, Josh probably hadn't even been to bed.

"Whose idea was it to mess up the house? Yours? Aunt Bea's?"

Josh's face softened. He placed his hand over his chest and declared, "I have no idea what you're talking about."

"Yeah, well, knock that shit off. She knows it's you, or at least us. You're lucky she didn't call the cops. All you did is piss her off and that cowboy she was with at the hospital."

"You don't want to mess with him," Josh warned, shaking his head. "He's a Kendrick. Colt. The youngest. Word is, they're some badass brothers. The oldest, Rory, got into it with some drug dealers recently. He shot one dead."

"Great. Do me a favor, stop doing whatever it is you're doing."

"I'm not doing anything." The innocence Josh put into the words didn't ring true. "I got my million bucks. I'm counting on you to convince her to sell."

"That's not my goal. I want that fifty percent share."

"You won't be saying that in a week. You prefer a cushy leather chair to a saddle every day of the week and a job where everyone else does the work. You and me, we're cut from the same cloth, and it ain't plaid." Josh sneered at Simon's shirt again.

"I've always been good at getting others to do the work while I still get the credit. This time won't be any different."

"That's what you think. You and I both know there's no getting out of shoveling shit, branding those damn smelly cattle, or winding your way across a field in a tractor. You better rethink your plan and your priorities. Ten million is on the line. I'm already up double what you got, taking this stupid deal to work there. Make sure you don't end up with nothing."

That half mil got him out from under his debt and gave him a nice cushion, but it wasn't enough. Not by a long shot. He'd have to make it last over the next year and a half, longer if she didn't give him what was his by right. By birth.

He'd play things straight for now, but if he even thought she was out to fuck him over, he'd set his other plan in motion.

Simon slammed the car door on his brother. He started the engine and revved it, making Josh back up. Simon backed out of the driveway, hit the brakes, and cursed when his coffee mug thumped across the roof and down the back window, spilling coffee all down the glass and dropping with a metal clink on the pavement.

"Fuck."

This day couldn't get any worse.

CHAPTER 15

Luna stood in the kitchen, finishing her second cup of coffee. She bit off the corner of a piece of toast with raspberry jelly, licking off the dollop that landed on her finger. She leaned over the counter, studying the list of items she needed to buy, which included stools to go on the other side of the island so she had someplace to sit in the kitchen. A cute little table for the alcove by the windows. New pots and pans, suitable for her amazing kitchen. Her one pot and two pans weren't going to cut it. With the means to buy anything she wanted, she planned to have all the things she'd done without for so long. Goodbye shoebox apartment living. Hello custom kitchen, walk-in closets bigger than her car, and spacious rooms she could fill with things she loved.

Like books.

Which she already had in abundance. Anxious to unpack the two boxes she'd left next to the closed and locked library doors, she pulled the keys from her purse and headed for the library. She stared at the array of keys on the ring Mr. Manning gave her. She tried one, then another, and finally got it on the third try. She slid the heavy carved wood pocket doors open and stared at the mess inside.

"Damnit, that's not funny."

The floor-to-ceiling bookshelves had been wiped clean, the books and decorative objects literally swiped off the shelves and dumped in piles on the floor. Most of the books survived with little to no damage, but some of the older, leather-bound books were worth a lot of money, and any damage to them would decrease their value.

"Damn. Damn. Damn."

"Do you always start your day off swearing?"

Luna spun around with her hands up to ward off the man standing directly behind her. "What are you doing here?"

"We have a meeting. Seven a.m., you said." Simon glanced at his watch. "I'm five minutes early."

"I mean, what are you doing in *my* house?"

"It used to be *my* house," he said matter-of-factly. "I have a key. Old habit, I guess. I let myself in. I thought we could talk before we meet with Toby and the others to go over the ranch business." Simon stared past her into the library. "What happened in here?"

"Like you don't already know. You have a key to the house. I assume you have one for the library, too."

Simon reached past her and pulled the right side door out several inches. "The lock is nothing more than a latch. Stick something in here, and you can work the lock without the key. Josh and I did it a dozen times when we played hide-and-seek as kids."

She didn't acknowledge the fact he was right. The lock could be picked by a precocious ten-year-old.

"You ever walk into my house again without my permission to enter, I'll have you arrested for trespassing."

Simon held up his hands in front of her in a gesture of surrender. "I'm sorry." His voice was smooth.

"Chalk it up to autopilot. I missed my second cup of coffee because it flew off the roof of my car." He let loose a self-deprecating chuckle. "I'm not used to getting up at the crack of dawn, and the last thing I want to do is fight with you. Can we call a truce?"

"Maybe. Depends on what I find in the office." She walked away, not ready to give him the benefit of the doubt. The explanation he gave seemed genuine on the surface, but he had reason and motive to want to mess with her.

"I didn't do anything to the office. I don't have a key. None of us did. Dad didn't trust anyone to be in there alone."

She spun around and faced him, making him stop short before he slammed into her. "Why?"

"I don't know. It's where he kept all his important papers, bank information, all the stuff he needed to run the ranch. He didn't want us messing around with his things."

"Do you have any idea how much your father was worth?" She didn't think he had any idea.

"The lawyer made it very clear without saying anything that Dad didn't want anyone but you to know that. The term 'assets' isn't that specific, now, is it?"

She pressed her lips together and shook her head. "No. It's not."

"I'll just bet you're going to keep that information to yourself, too, aren't you?"

"Yes. I am. For eighteen months. At that time, if you've earned it, I'll give you your fifty percent, and then you'll know."

"Tell me this, is that fifty percent worth all the shit I'm going to have to endure to get it?"

She kept her face blank, not wanting to give anything away, because what Wayne wanted most was for Simon and Josh to want to be here. He wanted them to want to take care of this place not because of the money but because they loved it like Wayne loved it.

"We'll see."

Yes, we'll see if you find something here you love more than the money. She wanted that for Simon, because she cared about Wayne and the hope he'd held on to for his sons.

"That's not an answer."

"You know what your father wanted from you. You work hard enough at anything, you'll find success."

"How successful was my father? Because believe me, that man worked harder than anyone I know."

"Very successful." She gave that much up because success wasn't always measured in how much money you made.

Simon pinched up one side of his mouth in a sardonic grin. "You're a wealth of information."

Luna unlocked the office on the fourth try. She really needed to label the keys until she got used to using them. She pushed the wood-paneled door open, thankful this room hadn't been touched.

"It's not so easy to pick a dead bolt." Simon stuffed his hands in his front pockets and rocked back on his heels.

Luna closed the door and locked it again. She'd go through the files and computer later. Right now she had a wannabe cowboy to put through his paces to see what kind of metal the man had for sticking it out eighteen months with her. If he thought she'd be a pushover, he had another think coming.

"Ready to ride?"

"Ride?"

"Yep. You know, that thing you do atop a horse."

One of his eyebrows shot up. "You're kidding."

"This is a working cattle and horse ranch. You used to live here. I thought you could show me around this morning. We'll talk."

"Whatever you say."

She swept her arm out to indicate that he lead the way to the door. "You know the way out."

They made their way to the stables in tense silence. Ed walked out, leading two horses. He tied them off at one of the fences. "Here you go, Luna, just like you asked."

"Thank you, Ed. We'll take it from here." She turned to Simon. "How long's it been since you rode a horse?"

"Fifteen years. Maybe more."

"Well, this should be fun. Nostalgic, right?"

"Sure." Simon followed her into the stables.

They each grabbed a blanket and saddle and walked back out to the horses. She'd grown up on a ranch and rode horses every day of her young life. She missed the horses most. Now she could use her knowledge about horses and riding to watch Simon. Wayne said his sons were never interested in the ranch, but that didn't mean Simon wasn't a capable rider. It didn't mean he hadn't paid attention to what they did here on the ranch. For all she knew, he'd make a great partner. Maybe he didn't love it, but he'd settle in and be happy.

Simon tightened the synch on the saddle around the horse's chest. The horse danced sideways and rubbed against the fence. Luna ran over and steadied the horse. "Whoa now. Okay," she crooned. "Undo that synch and loosen it up."

"Sorry. It's been a long time."

"You want to be pissed, fine, take your frustration

out on me, but you harm one of the animals on this ranch, you might as well call it quits now because I'll throw you off this property so fast your head will spin. I didn't call the cops about the passive-aggressive mess you all left at the house."

"I didn't do that," he bit out.

She kinda believed him, but held on to her reservations just in case he proved her instincts wrong.

"I will make you, or anyone in your family, pay if you hurt the animals."

"You don't have anything to worry about from me." Simon loosened the synch and the horse relaxed.

Luna let go of the horse's rope and walked back to finish her horse. Simon finished with his, even getting the bridle on without incident. Either he took her threat seriously, or he'd made a mistake putting the saddle on too tight. Either way, they were finally ready to ride out, so she saddled up and kicked her horse into a nice walk down the gravel road to the dirt road that wound through the pastures. Simon caught up quickly, bouncing in his saddle.

"It has been a long time since you rode. Relax," she coaxed.

"Where are we going?"

"You tell me. What's your favorite spot on the ranch?"

"Follow me. I'll show you what everyone wants."

The ride took about half an hour for them to wind their way across the property and up into the hills. By the time they crested the hill overlooking the property for miles, she'd relaxed and so had Simon. He'd still be sore as hell later, but his riding style improved.

The wind blew into her face, sweeping her hair out behind her back. She sucked in a deep breath, tinged with the scent of pine, grass, horses, and just good, clean, crisp air. She closed her eyes for a moment and savored everything about being here.

"You're really beautiful, you know that?"

She automatically laughed under her breath, dismissing his words. "I love it up here."

"Changing the subject doesn't change the truth about what I said."

"I don't know why you said it at all."

"Because I looked at you lost in the sun and wind and the quiet up here and I forgot everything about my father passing, what he did, and what it means, and I saw you."

"Not what I represent."

"I suppose so. I'm angry about what my father did. It makes it hard to mourn." Simon stared out at the land, the house, stables, and barns standing off in the distance to their left. Fields and pastures spread out to the right. She spotted the twisting river farther off, creeks branching off in several directions. "Up here, I remember him like I'm a boy again. He brought Josh and me up here all the time. He'd spread his arms out and say, 'All this is our land. Our home.' "

"It must be really hard to sit up here now and look at it all with me beside you."

"Why did he give it to you?"

"There's no simple answer. It's not because he didn't want you to have it. It wasn't to punish you in any way. Knowing your father the way I did, I imagine him sitting up here, overlooking all this land, his home, and I believe he felt as if he was its keeper. The land, the animals, they provided for him and his family. I believe he felt a true kinship for this place. Not as an owner but as a caretaker. That's what he wants for this place."

"And that's you?"

She stared out at the land and couldn't imagine selling to anyone, knowing they might not appreciate the natural beauty all this land had to offer that you couldn't put a price tag on. This wasn't just Wayne's home, this was his legacy to be passed down to the next caretaker. Her. One day, she'd have to pass it on to the next. She hoped to one of her own children. If not, someone like her who felt something like this needed to be preserved, when so many people bought and sold, stripped the land, took what they could get, and moved on without a thought to what they left behind.

"Yes, Simon. I am that kind of person. I don't want to take anything from you. I want to make sure this place is here long after I'm gone."

"But you did take this from us."

"It was given into my safekeeping. What do you want with it? The money it makes? Your dad left you half a million dollars outright. Wasn't that enough? You can take the other half million and be done. How much will be enough? What's it worth to you?"

Simon didn't answer her.

"Just wanting it isn't enough."

"You sound just like my dad."

"We were kindred spirits, I guess. We understood each other." For the first time, she turned and looked at Simon. "Are you really going to stick out the next eighteen months?"

"I'm going to try."

"Why? To what end? Even if you get the fifty percent, you can't sell it. You'll still have to work here. We both know you don't want that."

"Maybe all I want is for you not to get everything."

"You holding fifty percent share doesn't change that.

I'll still have the final say on everything. I still live in the house. I control everything that happens here."

"I know."

"And still you want to put yourself through this?"

Simon nodded. "I guess so."

Which in Luna's mind meant he wanted something else. What? She couldn't guess, but she'd watch him, because anyone who'd do something they hate for that long had a plan to get out of doing it for the rest of his life.

"Well, all you have to do is show me you've earned it."

"Do you really intend to fork over half this place even if I do a good job?"

"Yes. It's what your father would have wanted."

"What the hell do you care what he wanted? He's dead. He'd never know."

"I would. The attorney would."

"Like he's not on your side, too."

"His job is to make sure I do mine."

"You're paying his salary. He'll do what you want."

"Maybe so, but it'll have to hold up in court, now, won't it? I mean, you do a good job, you'll have proof to present to a judge. Everyone here will see you've met the terms. I can't buy off everyone."

"Yes, I imagine you can."

She shook her head. "You'll just have to trust me like your father did."

"We'll see."

"Come on, let's get going. Rich is waiting in the west pasture for us."

"Uh, why?"

"We're putting in a new fence line to separate out a new bull."

"Fun." Nothing in his tone or expression said he thought the next few hours of hard labor would be fun. Sinking posts and stringing barbed wire was no easy task.

"I thought you'd like that," she teased.

She turned her horse and headed out, wondering if he'd change his mind and just go home. No such luck. He caught up in a matter of minutes, his face tight with pain from sitting in the saddle so long. He'd be happy to be on the ground again, digging post holes if she guessed right.

"Can we bury the hatchet and start over?" Simon asked.

"Depends on if you're planning to bury that hatchet in my back."

He laughed. "I didn't peg you as a tough chick when I met you."

She relaxed and let loose a soft laugh. "I'll dial down the bitch. You dial down the asshole. We'll get along fine."

"Deal. How does your boyfriend feel about us working together?"

She didn't confirm or deny the "boyfriend" term. Mostly because it wasn't his business. Partly because she wasn't sure she could actually call him that. "Colt has no say about this place." Not now. But maybe one day they'd build a life together. It seemed they were well on their way to starting down that road. "This place is mine. Most of the people, actually all of them, are men. I'll hire on a few horsewomen once I start the equine therapy program, but that's still a ways off for now."

"So that's why he built the arena. Josh and I thought he might be doing some horse training or showing."

"Nope. He built it for me." Pent-up tears clogged her throat just thinking about it. He'd planned for her to be here. It meant so much to her that he'd thought of her dreams and helped make part of them a reality. He'd given her a place to put her schooling and her passion to good use.

"So that will be your focus?"

"Soon. Right now, I'll be focused on learning everything I can about the three businesses this place supports."

"And today is cattle ranching."

"Yep."

"I hate to ask what's in store for tomorrow."

"The wonders of hay bailing."

"Boring as hell, but I can probably do it in my sleep. Dad used to punish me with that particular chore."

"Great, then it shouldn't be hard to get up to speed and get the job done."

"Such a hardass. How does your boyfriend put up with you?"

Luna didn't fall for his teasing tone. Not when it sounded like he was gathering information. "Leave Colt out of this."

"Hard to do when we're being followed, probably on his orders. Right?"

Again, she didn't confirm or deny, though she knew Colt set this up. She'd spotted the rider not long after they'd left the stables. He kept his distance but always kept them in sight. She also noticed the rifle strapped next to his saddle. "After what I came home to yesterday, it's wise to be cautious." She couldn't decide if she wanted to kill Colt for thinking she couldn't take care of herself or thank him for being sweet.

Ugh. Men. *"Can't live with them. Can't poison them*

with pot roast," her mother used to say. Considering her mother was the worst cook in the world and had given her father food poisoning on many occasions— the brave soul—her mother might not have made her point.

"I'm not here to hurt you."

"No? So just to get me to sell?"

"Neither. I'm here to earn my half and that's all. Relax, Luna. I'm not the one out to get you."

"Oh good, one family member down, a handful to go."

"I really don't know who did all that stuff to the house, though I suspect, as I'm sure you do, too, that it was Josh. Although, he's more the direct threat kind of person, so who knows. Then again, I can't really see my aunt and uncle doing that stuff either."

"Thanks, you're a lot of help." She smiled to let him know she was teasing. If he knew who did it but wasn't saying, so be it. Right now, they needed to find a way to work together, so she dialed down the hostility and tucked her suspicions at the back of her mind.

They rode up to Rich's truck. He already had two guys working on a post hole. Rich carried a bundle of barbed wire over to the pile of posts they had on the ground. He dumped the wire and came to greet her.

"Hey there."

"Hey yourself. How's it going this morning?"

"Everything is on schedule. The new bull should arrive in a couple of hours. We need to get this fencing up and secure before he gets here."

"I brought you some help. I'm sure you two know each other."

"In passing," Simon confirmed. He nodded to Rich. "Good to see you again."

"My condolences on your father. He was a good and generous man."

Simon graciously accepted Rich's sentiments. "Thank you." He dismounted his horse, shaking out his legs one by one.

Luna hid her smile. "Well, you guys have fun. I'm off."

"Wait. What? You're leaving?" The surprise and anger in Simon's voice nearly made her laugh.

She gave Simon a look. "Yes. I have other things to do today."

"But you said you need to learn the business, too."

"I do, but I'm still trying to get settled in the house. I need to run to town to buy new carpet." She also needed some furniture.

"So I do all the work and you spend all the money," Simon snapped.

Rich and the other two men stopped what they were doing and stared at them.

"I got the place free and clear. You have to earn it. But that doesn't mean I don't take my responsibilities seriously. I am, however, the boss. I can do whatever the hell I want, including replacing the carpet your family ruined. You had five days to clean out the house. I've had half a day to move in. I'd like to finish, if you don't mind?"

He seemed to catch himself and plastered on a contrite grin. "I'm sorry. You're right."

She pulled the reins around and kicked her horse into a tight turn, leaving Simon at her back, no doubt pissed off and thinking of ways to make her pay for leaving him to work while she went shopping with Sadie.

Her tag-along met her a quarter mile up the dirt road and fell in beside her.

He tipped his Stetson. "John, Miss Hill."

"Tell everyone on the ranch, it's just Luna."

"Yes, ma'am." He caught her frown and added, "Luna."

"Did Colt send you?"

"I work in the stables with Ed. He asked me to keep an eye on you and Simon. Word's spread the family is giving you some trouble."

"That they are, but nothing I can't handle."

"Until you can't," he pointed out.

She hoped it didn't escalate to the point she actually needed an armed guard. For now, she'd stop balking at the necessary caution and let it go. Until she had Colt in her sights.

CHAPTER 16

Colt hung up from his call and stuffed his cell into his back pocket. He walked out of the mare's stall and closed the gate on her. He reached over and gave her a pat down her nose. "Not long now, mama."

"She still hasn't dropped that foal?" his grandfather asked from down the aisle.

"Not yet. She likes to hold on to them as long as possible."

"She makes pretty babies."

Colt let that one pass because he didn't want yet another lecture about settling down and having a family, especially when his grandfather got an earful this morning at the breakfast table from Rory, Ford, and Sadie about him and Luna.

"It won't be long before we've got a baby in the house. Sadie looked good at breakfast. The morning sickness is tapering off." His grandfather nodded, satisfied Sadie was doing better.

"Her belly is starting to round, but don't tell her I said that."

His grandfather laughed. "Not if I want to keep my own head."

Colt nodded his agreement.

"Everything good with your girl? Any trouble this morning?"

Of course his grandfather knew everything. "She's fine, so far as I know."

"It's a good thing you're doing looking after her."

"Fishing for information?"

"Telling you I'm proud you stepped up to help her. The two of you worked through that rough patch."

"We didn't have a rough patch. We were never together."

"Not until now," his grandfather guessed.

"Granddad, can't you be happy and satisfied Rory is getting married and having a baby. Give me some space to breathe."

"No one is crowding you, son. I'm happy for you, is all. She's a great girl."

"She is. She's also a whole lot of other things that complicate the situation. So give me some time to figure it out."

"Do you like her?"

"Yes. I like her a lot."

"Does she make you happy?"

"Every time I see her," Colt admitted, though the smile on his grandfather's face told him he should shut the hell up before his granddad called the preacher.

"Okay then."

Colt didn't question Granddad's abrupt end to the conversation, or the fact that he walked out of the stables without prodding Colt for more answers about his feelings. Colt didn't want to talk about his feelings. Mostly because they were all jumbled up inside of him, because he'd spent the morning worried about Luna and talking himself out of going over there every other minute until he'd driven himself nuts wondering what she was doing and how everything went this morning.

"Hello, Luna. How's the day treating you?" his grandfather asked.

"Not bad," her voice carried to Colt on the wind. He bolted from the stables, trying to get to her before his grandfather really embarrassed him and started asking her how she felt about him.

"Luna. You're here."

"Standing right in your yard," she teased. "Is Sadie around? We're supposed to go shopping."

"She's inside working on her book. I'll go get her. You just wait right here." Granddad made a beeline for the house.

"Subtle," Luna teased Colt again. Of course she'd heard from Sadie about his grandfather's obsession about marrying off all three of them. "Has he called the preacher to schedule a double wedding yet?"

"Don't encourage him, please."

"Okay." The word held a defensive tone he didn't like.

"Luna, I didn't mean I wouldn't marry you."

She laughed. "Um, okay."

Colt raised his face to the sky and sighed. "Have mercy." He faced her again. "You know what I mean."

"Relax. I was just joking. Besides, I have a bone to pick with you."

He narrowed his eyes. "What?" he asked cautiously.

"Did you order the men who work for *me* to guard me?"

"Um . . ."

"So that's a yes. I'll bet Toby or Ed or one of the others already called you to let you know everything went well with Simon this morning."

"Uh . . ."

"I can check your phone and find out."

"Only if you can get it off me."

"You'd like that, wouldn't you?"

"Uh, yeah." He held his hands out wide, silently daring her to take her best shot.

She closed the distance between them. Without touching him, she went up on tiptoe and planted a kiss on him that made him stop thinking and pull her in close. He dove in for more, sliding his tongue along hers. Setting aside the fact he probably needed to wash his hands, he slid them down her back to her hips. Her hands slid across his sides to his back and smoothed up his spine to his shoulders. He kissed her again and again, lost in her taste and the feel of her pressed against him. Her hands slid down his back. He gripped her hips tighter and pulled her closer. She planted one hand on his chest and shoved him away, breaking the kiss and his hold on her.

Lost in the lust running through his veins, it took him a second to register what she held up in front of him. His cell phone. He made a grab for it, but she spun away and swiped her finger across the screen.

"Last call came from Ed. Right after I dropped my horse back at the stables." She turned to face him with a *tsk, tsk* spilling from her kiss-swollen lips. Lips he wanted to kiss again.

"How was your ride?" He tried to pull off the question without admitting guilt, but she didn't buy it.

"Don't you trust me, Colt?"

"Yes. Why wouldn't I?"

"Because you seem to think I'd do something stupid to put my life in danger."

"No, I don't. I think the Travers family will do anything to get you to sell the ranch, including trying to hurt you to intimidate you into doing it."

"So you did it solely to protect me, not because you think I'm an idiot and wouldn't have taken my own precautions?"

"Were you really going to protect yourself?"

She frowned and tossed his phone back at him. He caught it, but not before she turned and started walking back to the Rambling Range truck she drove over.

"Hey, wait."

"Why?"

"I did it so I'd know you were safe. Because I spent the better part of every second after I left you last night crazy worried something might happen to you. Remember what happened to Sadie with her brother and that drug dealer who wanted to get her out of the way so he could get what he wanted? It still gives me nightmares, and I can't even think for a second about anything happening to you."

She stopped in her tracks and stood for a few seconds before she turned around to face him again.

"I can't let anything happen to you," he admitted.

She tilted her head and brushed the bangs from her face, driving him crazy to kiss her again. "Wanna make it up to me?"

"You think I need to make it up to you that I want to keep you safe?"

"The sentiment is sweet. The way you went about it behind my back, kind of annoying."

"What do you want?" He hadn't meant to sound so beleaguered about it.

She laughed anyway at his annoyance. "Come over tonight. I'll feed you dinner, then you'll help me clean up the mess we missed yesterday."

He closed the distance between them and held her by the shoulders, searching her face for any sign that she'd been hurt or upset. "What are you talking about? Did something else happen after I left?"

"No. It happened at the same time as the other stuff, by my guess. We never unlocked the library."

Colt thought about the dead rats in the tub and the message written in blood on the tile. "What did they do in the library?"

"Nothing too terrible. They pulled all the books and knickknacks from the shelves and dumped them on the floor."

He let loose the breath he'd been holding and raked his hand through his hair. "Okay. That's not so bad."

Her eyes narrowed with suspicions. "What did you think they did?"

Since she only knew about the garbage and rotten food, he played off his concern. "Nothing. Maybe ruin more walls and furniture."

"Thank God they left the furniture in there alone. It's my favorite room."

"Is that why Wayne didn't allow them to take anything from there?"

"Yes. And some of the books are worth a small fortune. He didn't want them to sell them off for quick cash or toss them out, not knowing they're special."

"You and Sadie have that in common, huh? Books."

"Yes. Here she comes. So are you coming over tonight, or what?"

"Sure."

"Well, that's a resounding 'Can't wait to see you.'" Her voice rose with false cheer.

He slid his hand to the back of her neck and kissed her again. His mouth fit to hers in a searing kiss that should tell her everything she needed to know. He held her close, broke the kiss, rubbed his nose against hers, and pressed his forehead to hers. "I can't wait to see you tonight."

Her hand rested against his cheek. She closed her eyes and let out a heavy sigh. "I know I'm acting like a crazy woman. You kind of scramble my insides whenever I see you. And when you kiss me, I can't think of anything but more."

"Good to know." Colt loosened his hold on her and stood tall in front of her, but missed being a breath away. "Have fun shopping. I'll see you later."

"Okay. Um . . ."

"What is it, honey? Sadie's waiting in your truck."

Luna spun around, surprised Sadie had already climbed into the passenger seat. She waved from inside the truck, smiling at them.

Luna spun back to face him. "What's your favorite color?"

He didn't expect that question. "Green. Why?"

"Things I should know, right?"

"Sure, I guess. What's yours?" He should know hers, too. Why? He didn't know.

"Purple."

"Which explains why you have so many purple shirts and scarves." He tugged the purple-and-white gauzy fabric circling her neck over her lavender T-shirt.

"Right. Uh, gotta go." She spun to head to the truck, but he grabbed her arm and spun her back again.

"What time do you want me to come over tonight?"

"Six. Five-thirty."

"God, I really do scramble your brain. Which one?"

"Five. We'll clean up the library while the chicken is in the oven, then we'll eat and stuff."

"I'm all for stuff." He pulled her in for a quick kiss while she giggled at his stupid joke. "Go. Buy things to sit on and eat off of. Four plates, bowls, and sets of utensils is not enough."

"Anything else you want?"

"Looking forward to dinner with you."

"Ah, there's that sweet side again."

"Done being pissed about me watching out for you?"

"That's sweet, too. Next time, keep me in the loop."

"The tank arrives tomorrow," he teased, heading back to the barn, waving goodbye over his shoulder. Her laugh followed him and kept him wanting her the rest of the day while he counted down the seconds he worried about her and until he saw her again.

CHAPTER 17

Colt pounded on the front door but got no answer. He fished the key out of his pocket. In another of the awkward moments they shared, fighting their growing attraction to each other, he'd kissed her good night after they cleaned the library and had dinner together last night, and she'd handed him a key to her house. "For Sadie," she'd added after a few tense seconds. "Just in case."

Thank God she'd remembered to change all the locks.

He'd meant to give the key hanging from the horse-charm key ring to Sadie, but hadn't found the opportunity. Avoided the opportunity, one might say. And for exactly this reason. He had to get in there to see why she didn't answer the damn door.

He'd knocked once before and gotten no response, so he'd gone down to see if Luna was still in the stables working with the horses she adored. Ed had told him she'd been up at the house all day, taking one delivery after the next after the carpet installers put in the new carpet this morning.

So where the hell was she? Her Jeep sat in the driveway, along with the truck she'd driven to his house yesterday to pick up Sadie to go shopping.

He pounded his fist against the door again, wishing his stomach didn't feel like he'd swallowed acid. His heart thumped as hard as his fist on the door. Nothing. Not a damn sound from inside.

He slid the key in the new lock and jiggled it to get it to work. Key copies never worked as smooth as the original. He unlocked the dead bolt and pushed the door open. She'd put the old barn wood from her apartment up on the foyer wall. Wayne's old hat hung on a hook next to the display of silver and black framed mirrors Luna used to have on her bathroom door surrounding the photo of her and Wayne. A slim, brand-new table sat opposite the door, holding a plant in an antiqued mirrored glass pot on each end. Nice.

The house smelled like chemicals from the brand-new carpet. She'd gone with a medium shade of tan that complemented the stone fireplace. A dark brown leather sofa and two club chairs filled the living room, along with a wood coffee table and side tables. Silver lamps with white shades flanked the couch. A purple blanket lay over the back. White and deep green pillows sat on the sofa and chairs for added comfort. He liked the look.

"Luna," he yelled, walking past the new furniture toward the library and hallway to her room beyond. He peeked into the now organized and perfectly neat library. No Luna.

Alarms went off in his head. Adrenaline pumped through his system and pounded though his heart. She had to be here.

He walked down the hall past the empty spare room and stopped just inside her bedroom. She'd bought a brand-new, king-size bed and covered it in a white-and-purple vine-patterned quilt that reminded him of the scarf she wore yesterday. A huge plum-colored rug covered the hardwood floor beneath the bed. A wooden chest sat at the end of the bed. Luna's jeans and a pink T-shirt were tossed across the top of it. The huge photograph of the mountain hung across from the bed. When she woke up in the morning, it'd be the first thing she'd see.

She'd converted the wardrobe thing she'd used at her other place for clothes into a TV cabinet. A new wood dresser and night tables had been added to fill up the massive room.

He took this all in but still didn't find Luna.

The door beside him opened, and Luna walked out in a cloud of steam. She held a towel against her hair and wore nothing at all. His eyes nearly popped out of his head at his first glimpse at all that creamy skin and pink-tipped breasts.

"Luna," he croaked out around the lump that formed in his throat.

"Colt!" She draped the towel in front of her, holding it at her breasts.

"Is that a butterfly tattoo on your belly near your hip?"

She held the towel tighter against her. "What are you doing in here?"

"Looking for you."

"How did you get in?"

He held up the horse key chain. "The key you gave me last night."

"I gave you that key to give to Sadie."

"I forgot. And it's a good thing, too. You didn't answer the door."

"I was in the shower."

He tilted his head. "I see that." In fact, he hadn't taken his eyes off her.

She raked one hand through her wet hair. "Do you mind?"

"Not at all, honey. I'm so damn glad to see you're okay." So much so that the relief swept through him in a wave. Maybe that was the heat exploding through him.

"What? Why wouldn't I be?"

"You didn't answer the door. I got worried."

"Well, as you can see, I'm fine."

He nodded, not even trying to hide the grin he couldn't help. "Oh, I can see you just fine and you're beautiful."

She blushed all the way from her chest up to her black hair. The embarrassed smile brightened her eyes and softened them after he'd scared her half to death. Fair enough, she'd scared him just as bad not answering the door.

"What's in the bag?" She cocked her chin, indicating the bag he still carried.

"Since our plans changed and you made dinner last night. I thought I'd throw a couple of steaks on the grill for you tonight."

"Really?"

"Yeah. That okay?"

"No one's ever cooked for me."

"That's because you're such a damn good cook they want you to cook for them."

Shy again, her gaze dropped to her ladybug-painted toes. "I'm not that good."

"I'm still craving more of that Mexican fried rice chicken thing you made last night."

That turned her smile up a few more notches. "Okay, well, go cook and I'll get dressed."

"Any way I can talk you out of that?"

She bit her lip and eyed him. Nerves made her hold

the towel a bit tighter. Okay, not fair of him to catch her off guard like this and say something like that.

"Dinner in about half hour." He spun and walked back down the hall, giving her an easy way out of answering his bold question.

Last night, they'd shared a good meal, talked about their day and lives past and present, and worked side by side putting the library back together. He loved that being with her seemed easy. Relaxed. No rush to see if he could get her into bed, when it seemed more important to get to know her better.

Now he'd seen her naked and called himself a damn fool for waiting for things to move forward to some point in time that made sense. Nothing made sense anymore, except being with her in every possible way that made him closer to her.

He walked into the kitchen and dropped the grocery bag on the counter. He pulled the items out and set them aside to prepare for the grill. He went to the cabinet to get a plate and found a whole new white set, including a platter, which he grabbed for the steaks. He went to the pullout spice rack by the stove and grabbed the salt, pepper, and garlic powder. He prepared the steaks and washed his hands in the sink. The towel he used last night wasn't hanging on the oven door bar, so he pulled out the drawer two below the silverware and found a bunch of new dark green and purple dish towels. He dried his hands and stopped in the middle of the kitchen, completely taken off guard.

Everywhere in the house, she'd decorated in dark green and purples. The living room pillows. The bedroom comforter and rug with the photograph of the mountain all in spring greens. The kitchen towels. He looked around the room and realized he knew where practically everything was because he'd helped her unpack. Yes, she'd added more, but he could still find everything.

Just to test it, he opened the cupboard next to him, expecting to see the only pot and two pans she owned. Instead, he found them along with a new set of dark green pots and pans.

"Why are you making that face?" Luna asked from the other side of the counter.

"Nice pots and pans."

She smoothed her hand over her now dry hair. "Thanks. I got them today."

"Furniture is awesome. Living room and your bedroom are really nice."

"Did you like that rug under my bed? I totally scored on that one. It's the perfect size, and the color . . . so amazing."

"It's you."

"You didn't mention the new stools." She put her hand on the back of one.

He walked around the counter and checked out the black leather seats with curved wood backs and legs. "Those are nice."

"They cost a fortune, but I fell in love with them. Aren't they perfect for right here? They tuck under the counter and don't overpower the space."

"Everything you picked is really great." He held up the towel to include it.

"Yeah, those match the pots and the tiles in the backsplash." She pointed to the wall behind him.

Sure enough, set into the tan tiles were tiny, square, deep green glass accent tiles. He felt like such an idiot for thinking she'd bought the green items because of him.

"I knew you'd like them because it's your favorite color."

That comment gave him hope. For what? He didn't live here. But the more time he spent with her, the more he wanted to be here with her all the time.

"Those are some thick steaks. What can I do to help?"

"Stop fidgeting and thinking that every time I look at you all I do is see you naked."

She shifted from one foot to the other again. "It's kind of hard to forget you walked in on me."

"You walked out and I was standing there."

Her cheeks flamed pink again. "Can we stop talking about it?"

"Won't stop me from thinking about it." She tried to turn away, but he caught her by the shoulder and gently turned her back to face him. "You are a beautiful woman. There's no reason to be embarrassed. After all, I will see you naked again."

"Oh God, that just makes me even more nervous."

He arched one eyebrow, concerned. "Why?"

"It's just weird the first time. Then you'll start picking out all the things you don't like."

Colt held up a hand. "Whoa. Why the hell would I do that?"

Her head fell forward and she avoided looking at him. "Never mind. Forget I said anything." She tried to pull away, but he held her still.

"Maybe I should have asked who the fuck did that to you?"

"Really, forget I said anything. Let's have dinner."

"No, not until you tell me who the hell would take you to bed and do of all the boneheaded, fucked-up things anyone can do, complain."

Her chin came up and she looked him in the eye. "Who do you think?"

Billy. "That fucker. I should have punched his lights out that night instead of letting him get away with shit like that."

"I told you he didn't want you and me to be together. Now I know why he said all those things. If I thought I wasn't good enough for you . . ."

Colt covered her mouth with his fingers. "Please stop talking before I really lose it." He took a minute to let the rage in his gut settle so he could speak without gritting his teeth. He slipped his hands beneath her arms and lifted her up onto the counter in front of him so she was pretty much eye level with him. "Listen to what I'm about to say, and even though you believe it already, hear how much I mean this. There is nothing, not one tiny little thing, about you that isn't beautiful and perfect."

Her head fell to the side. "Colt . . ."

He kissed her to shut her up again. But this time he poured every ounce of what he felt inside for her into the kiss. His hands cupped her face. He pressed his lips softly to hers because he didn't need to take, but give her everything. Her arms came up and wrapped around his neck, holding him close, telling him how much she wanted this, him. He slid his hands down her sleek neck, over her chest until he cupped her breasts and weighed them in his hands. He smoothed his hands down her trim stomach and waist to her hips. He kept his fingers out to her sides and his thumbs sliding over her sweet center, but he didn't linger and quickly moved on to rub his hands down her toned thighs and calves to her small bare feet. He brought his hands up in one long sweep again to her hips and around to cup her bottom, squeeze, and pull her closer to him.

He broke the kiss long enough to growl out, "Perfect. Every inch of you." He dove in for another kiss and couldn't help reaching for her soft breasts again. They fit his palms, and he squeezed, swiping his thumbs over her tight nipples.

Luna leaned into Colt's touch, wanting more and savoring the feel of his big hands on her body. He'd been right. She didn't really think there was anything wrong with the way she looked, but old wounds scarred over still held the faded memory and emotion of how it felt when someone made her feel less than. Some people could be just plain mean. Not Colt. He had a deep sense of right and wrong. A protective instinct that drove him to ask the guys who worked for her to watch her back when he wasn't here doing it himself. An honesty that went bone deep and made him speak his mind even when she didn't like what he had to say.

Colt's mouth pressed to her neck, his hand kneaded her breast. She wrapped her legs around his waist and pulled him close, his hard length pressed to her aching center.

"Dinner or bed." His voice rumbled against her throat.

She didn't need to think. Couldn't really. "You." She gave him the honest truth, because the only choice was being with him.

Colt went still and lifted his head from the top of her breast. His gaze locked with hers. "Yeah?"

She nodded and gave him a soft smile, the flutter in her belly intensifying with his hungry gaze on her. "Yes."

Colt swept his gaze over the groceries on the counter, then turned it back to her. "Don't move." He pulled her legs off his waist, rounded the counter, picked up the platter of steaks, and shoved it into her new fridge.

The rest he left in the shopping bag, came back to her, gripped her hips, and pulled her right off the counter and back into his arms. He took her mouth in a searing kiss and walked out and down the hall. Lost in each other, he bounced off the wall once and set off down the center of the hall once again.

She giggled against his lips and he smiled against hers.

"You drive me crazy," he said, kissing her again.

They finally reached her bed. She expected him to lay her down and cover her. She wanted his weight on her, his hands trailing heat over her body, his mouth soft and wet on her skin. Instead, he leaned over, took the bedcovers in hand, and tossed them back. He turned and sat on the bed with her straddling his lap. She reached up, sliding her fingers into the back of his soft hair, her thumbs swept over his cheeks. She stared into his hazel eyes and saw nothing but raw hunger and infinite patience.

"I've never wanted to be with someone the way I need to be with you. I think about you all the time. You're a distraction I crave. The friend I want to share my days with. The woman who's gotten under my skin and I like it." He slipped his hands beneath her shirt and slowly slid them up her sides, bringing the soft material with them, and pulling it up and over her head. His gaze swept down her face and chest and landed on her breasts encased in white satin and lace. He sighed. "You're so damn beautiful. Every time I look at you, you take my breath away."

Sweet words from a man who knew how to make her feel special. Not a practiced line, but God's honest truth as he knew it. She felt the openness in him. The total focus on her, them, in this moment.

His hands went around her back. He unhooked her bra and drew the straps down her shoulders, trailing his fingers down her arms. Shivers danced across her skin. Bare to the waist, she sighed. He traced her collarbone with his fingertips, his eyes following his fingers down her chest to the soft slope of her breast and over the mound and peaked tip. His fingers brushed over her hard nipple. She sucked in a desperate breath, longing for more. He gave it to her with his mouth covering the pink bud, his tongue sweeping over her skin, heating her body, and sending a bolt of lust blazing through her system.

She raked her fingers through his golden hair, letting the strands slide through her fingers. She held him to her as he lavished one breast and then the other with sweet, warm kisses that made her rock against Colt, wanting more, but savoring all he gave from one tempting moment to the next.

He rolled to the side, laying her out on the cool sheet. His mouth worked her breast, one big hand molding the other to his palm, her nipple caught between his long fingers. She smoothed her hands down his neck and back, grabbed his shirt, and pulled it up and over his head. Finally free to touch his warm skin, she slid her hands over all those tight muscles down his back and up.

He kissed a path down her belly to the waistband of her black yoga pants. His fingers hooked in the waistband. He pulled them down her legs, leaning back and standing at the edge of the bed, then he pulled the pants off her bare feet and stared down at her in nothing but a pair of black lace panties. Heat and need gathered in his eyes, but he still took his time, sweeping his gaze over her body, his hand up her thigh, over her hip and belly, then back down her center, hooking his fingers in the lace and drawing them down her legs as she lifted her hips to help him. She settled back on the mattress. He didn't come to her then, just stared at her laid out naked before him.

"Colt."

"Yeah, honey."

She leaned up, scooted to the edge of the bed, and pressed her mouth to his bare stomach over all those tight abs. His fingers combed through her dark hair. She looked up at him, his hazel eyes dark and intent on her upturned face.

"You drive me crazy."

She smiled softly, then undid the button and zipper on his jeans. She gripped the sides and pulled them down his corded thighs. She reached up, planted her hand in the center of his wide chest and dragged it down over all those muscles, mapping his eight-pack abs to his hard cock pressed up the length of his black boxer briefs. She smoothed her hand down his rigid length then back up. His head fell back and he let loose a ragged curse. Driven on by his desire feeding hers, she worked her hand up and down the length of him, her mouth pressed to his hard stomach, planting open-mouthed kisses against his warm skin. She swept her other hand around his hip to his tight ass. She gripped one buttock in her hand and squeezed. His breath whooshed out on a sigh.

Smiling against his skin, emboldened by his response to her touch, she grabbed the briefs in the front and back and pulled them down to his knees where his jeans remained tangled around his legs. She glanced up at him watching her, and with her gaze locked with his, she moved ever so slowly close to him again and licked her way from the base of his dick to the thick head in one long sweep of her wet tongue. His eyes went wide, then half closed when the sheer pleasure hit him. Both hands on his very nice ass, she pulled him close and took him into her mouth all at once. His hands gripped her head, his palms covering her ears, but not enough to cover the sound of another soft curse escaping his lips. She swept her mouth down over him again, and when she came back up, he gently lifted her lips from his swollen flesh and pushed her to lay back on the bed. She scooted back. He quickly dragged his clothes and boots off his legs, pulled the folded packets of condoms out of his pocket, tossed them toward the pillows, and crawled toward her, his mouth planting kisses up her thighs. First one side, then the other, back and forth to her hips, where he planted his mouth over the blue-and-black butterfly tattoo.

"I love this thing. It's sexy as hell."

"You haven't found the surprise on my back."

His eyes lit with fire. He slipped his hand beneath her bottom and rolled her over. She lay on her stomach, her arm braced by her chest. She glanced over her shoulder as Colt leaned over her on his hands and knees, staring down at the crescent moon with an owl sitting at the bottom slope at the base of her neck and the spattering of stars spilling down her spine and spreading out at her waist. Some of the stars were just outlines, other filled in with blue ink. She loved it, but couldn't tell if Colt approved, or hated her marked-up back.

One big hand palmed her ass. He squeezed, leaned down, and kissed one of the stars at her waist. He kissed every single one of them, then started up her back. She melted into the mattress and turned molten when his fingers slid over the slope of her bottom and down to her tingling center. He slid his fingers over her slick folds, back and forth. She moved her hips, wanting more. He gave it to her, sliding one finger into her wet center, his lips still kissing a heated path up her spine. When he reached the moon at her neck, his big body lay down the length of hers. She turned on her side and scooted closer. He pulled her close with his hand still hooked around her hips, his finger still working in and out of her throbbing center. She moved her leg over his thigh and pressed her body against him. His thick length pressed to her belly and she rocked against his hard cock and hand, kissing him, her arm wrapped around his neck.

"Colt," she whispered against his mouth.

He gave her another soft kiss, then released her long enough to grab the packets of condoms. He tore one off and opened it with his teeth. While he sheathed himself, she mapped his body with her hands and mouth, keeping the intimacy between them strong. He took her mouth again in a searing kiss and used his body to roll her back onto the bed. He shifted over her and settled between her legs. She drew her legs up his thighs. He pulled himself up on his hands, stared down at her, and nudged her entrance, the thick head rubbing her soft folds. She gripped his hips and pulled him close. He filled her in one smooth glide. She sighed, her eyes locked on him.

Colt pulled out, nearly leaving her, but thrust back in at the last second and filled her again. He closed his eyes on the pleasure and lost himself making love to her. She gripped his ass, pulled him close, then softened her hands and swept them up his back. She gave herself over to him, making love, enjoying what they created in each other's arms. Everything about him appealed to her, but making love to him solidified the connection she'd felt for him all this time into something that became a permanent part of her. She didn't know how. She didn't know why. But she felt it like a physical part of her now deep in her chest.

He must feel it, too, because something in him shifted, making something build inside of her. Not the pleasure, that took on a life of its own. Something deeper, more meaningful and life changing. Her heart swelled with it, made her hold on to him, pull him closer, let everything else fall away but the two of them locked in this lovers' embrace.

Colt thrust deep again. Luna circled her hips against his, finding that sweet spot that made the fire in her belly flash and burn brighter. Colt caught on and did it again, matching her moves and creating that sweet friction she needed. Her body tensed around his. He groaned and picked up the pace. She followed and let herself go as that fire burst inside of her like a star. Colt shuddered and fell on top of her, his weight sinking her into the mattress. His breath sawed in and out as fast as hers. Relaxed. Happy to have this man in her arms, she rubbed her hands up and down his back, then hugged him close. He pressed soft kisses to her neck and levered himself up on his forearms. He traced his finger over her head and swept her bangs aside. Something she did often that drove him crazy.

She stared up at him with a soft smile on her lips. She couldn't help it, she'd never felt quite like this. Her whole body hummed, like Colt's energy vibrated through her. She felt that close to him.

"You have the most gorgeous eyes."

"All the better to stare at your gorgeous face." She reached up and laid her palm to his rough jaw.

"And that mouth." He swept his thumb across her lips. She pressed a kiss to the pad of his thumb.

She thought of how they started making love, her taking his hard length into her mouth. "You just like that thing I did," she teased, smiling because it made her a bit embarrassed.

"I like everything you do to me."

"Is that right?"

"Yes. Especially the way you make me feel." He leaned down and kissed her softly on the lips. He pressed back up and gave her an intent look, making sure she understood he meant those words.

"I really can't explain the way you make me feel, except to say that I don't want to lose it."

Colt rolled to her side and fell on his back, hooking his arm around her and pulling her close. She settled against his big, warm body with her leg draped over his and her head nestled on his chest at his shoulder.

She reached out and traced the scar along his forearm resting on his stomach. "What happened here?"

"Barbed wire broke and snapped back at me. Doc Bell at the clinic sewed me up."

"Looks like it hurt like hell."

"That about covers it." Colt kissed the top of her head. "Are you hungry?"

"You're staying?"

Colt tilted his head up and looked down at her. She stared back at the disgruntled frown on his handsome face.

"Don't you want me to?"

"Um, yeah, I do. I just thought . . ."

"What? That I'd just walk out now that I got what I wanted?"

"Something like that."

Colt laid his free hand over his forehead, stared at the ceiling, and swore. He looked down at her again and squeezed her to his side with the arm down her back, his hand on her hip.

"What I most want is to spend time with you, Luna. Don't you get that? Haven't I shown you that?"

"Yes. I'm sorry. I'm using my past mistakes to anticipate how this will go."

"I really should have punched some sense into Billy when I had the chance."

Colt was nothing like Billy. He might have been the good-time-guy with other women in the past, but he'd shown her a different side of himself. She didn't think he shared his serious, protective side with many others outside his family. He truly cared about her. He'd just shown her how much. He made love to her like she was special, precious, not just a good time, though they'd had that, but it was so much more. She needed to trust it. Him. After all, he didn't back away because her life had become a whole lot of drama. He stayed and tried so hard to keep her safe.

She leaned up and nipped his chin. "I would love for you to stay and have dinner with me."

"Good, because I'm not done having you either." He gave her a soft kiss, then rolled away and sat on the edge of the bed. He leaned down and picked up his jeans, dragging them up his legs as he stood and pulled them over his lean hips and very nice ass.

"Such a shame to cover up all that yummy goodness."

Colt turned with a mischievous grin. He leaned down over her and swept his gaze over her naked body. "You get to unwrap it again later." He pressed down on his hands and laid a kiss over the butterfly tattoo on her hip again. Pleasure tingles fluttered out from the spot and made her giggle. "Get dressed, honey. I'll go light the fire in the grill."

Colt turned and went to the bathroom before giving her one last hot glance and walking out of her room. She took a minute to lie in the bed they'd made love in and think about the fire he'd started in her. Even now, it smoldered in her chest. His staying for dinner, maybe even the night, made her happy, but she wanted more. She wanted him here with her always. She didn't want to think of spending another night without him. She . . . nope, not going to go there. It was too soon for her to think her feelings went deep enough to that L word she'd used with another man, which had turned out to be nothing more than lust and wanting attention from someone who only gave it when it was convenient for him.

Colt wasn't like that. But she didn't trust her feelings. She trusted him, but not herself. She'd grown up the child who'd always come second but had wanted to be first. That deep need drove her as an adult to find that someone who thought her special enough to put her first in his life. Someone who thought of her happiness. Someone who wanted to be with her because he loved her. She wanted something like that. Something that lasted a lifetime.

CHAPTER 18

Luna smiled up at Colt from her seat at the table. He set the platter of mouthwatering steaks in front of her, forked one up, and dropped it on her plate. He put the other on his and sat beside her, reaching out to place his big hand on her bare leg beneath the simple black cotton tank dress she put on after they made love. He squeezed her leg, sending a shot of heat up her thigh.

"Hungry, honey?"

"Starving." She put a helping of salad on his plate, then hers, tore a hunk of bread from the loaf for her and him and spread the garlic butter she'd whipped up in the kitchen on her piece. She slid the bowl to him and handed him the butter knife. "I'd eat some of that, otherwise I'm going to stink like garlic and you'll never kiss me again tonight."

Colt hooked his hand around the back of her neck and drew her close. "Never going to happen." He kissed her softly, keeping the heat between them at a simmer. She loved the dancing trills in her belly, the anticipation of being with him again. More than anything, she liked the easy way she felt being with him.

She bit into a perfectly cooked piece of medium rare steak and hummed with satisfaction.

"Good?"

"Fantastic. Thanks for cooking."

"My pleasure. Grilling is one of the few things I do well when it comes to cooking a meal."

"You don't like to cook?"

"I've got cooking duty twice a week, though Sadie does most of the cooking these days. I don't mind cooking, it's just I tend to stick to what I know, so it gets boring after a while."

"You should experiment. Try new things."

"I'm willing to try anything you cook, honey. And bake. I'm addicted to those muffins you make."

"You're a sucker for sweets."

"You're sweet. I'm definitely a sucker for you." God, his grin might just kill her.

She giggled. "Good for me, then."

"Oh, honey, it was good for me, too," he teased about them making love.

The blush rose up her cheeks, but instead of shying away like she used to, she reached out and rubbed her fingers along his rough jaw and smiled, enjoying being able to touch him and play like this.

"Just good, huh? I'll have to try harder next time."

Colt chuckled. "Driving me crazy again will only land you in hot water."

"I'm counting on it."

Her cell phone rang back in the house. Wondering who'd call this late, she frowned at Colt. "Maybe that's Sadie wondering where you are."

"Doubt it. She and the rest of the family probably assume I'm with you."

"I'll be right back." She rose and ran for her phone on the kitchen counter. She didn't recognize the number but swiped the screen to accept the call anyway. After eight at night, it couldn't be a telemarketer trying to sell her car insurance or siding for her house, right?

"Hello."

"You two look real cozy sitting out on the patio, eating dinner together."

Her heart stopped. She didn't recognize the voice. Couldn't, since their gravely whispers made it even harder to decipher if it was a man or woman.

"Who is this?" she asked, stepping back to the kitchen doorway, staring out at the darkness that lay beyond the halo of light surrounding the patio. Her sharp tone drew Colt's questioning gaze.

"He's using you, you stupid bitch. He only wants you because he wants Rambling Range. He's tired of taking the scraps his brothers leave behind, and he wants what you stole."

"Who is this?" The tremble in her voice made Colt stand up and search the area behind him because she kept doing the same, looking for any sign of the person who watched them.

"Sell the ranch. I've got your cowboy lover in my sights. I could kill him right now."

Luna didn't think. She ran to Colt and put herself between him and the darkness, shoving at his chest to get him to move back into the house.

"Luna, what is it?" He stumbled back and got moving, because she kept pushing him.

"Move. Now. Hurry."

"That's right, you want to save him, but is he worth it?"

"Shut up. You don't know what you're talking about. I don't know which Travers you are, but hear me when I say this. I won't sell, so leave us alone."

"Sell, or Colt may not be around much longer to kiss the stars up your back."

The caller hung up and Luna dropped her phone on the kitchen floor. She sucked in a horrified gasp and covered her mouth with both hands.

Colt nearly lost his shit watching her on the call, but seeing her face pale and her eyes go wide as saucers made his insides go cold.

Her phone slid across the hardwood floor and thumped against the wall. They stood away from the windows, tucked in the alcove that opened up into the walk-in pantry. He grabbed her shoulders and gave her a soft shake to make her see him. "Luna, honey, what is it? What happened?"

"Th-they saw us."

"Who?"

"I . . . I don't know. I'm not sure who it was. One of the Traverses. They watched us . . . in the bedroom . . . while we . . ."

"Christ." Colt pulled her against his chest, wrapped his arms around her, and held her trembling body. "It's okay, honey, I won't let anything happen to you." The thought of someone peeking through the windows, watching her, them, creeped him out and pissed him off. That went beyond someone messing up the house in the heat of the moment. Whoever the fuck thought they could come here and scare Luna like this needed to be taken down.

Luna pressed closer, burying her face in his chest, gripping his sides so tight, her nails bit into his bare skin. "They threatened to shoot you."

Colt jolted with the news and glared down at her. "Is that why you pushed me into the house? You put yourself in front of me?"

"Yes. I couldn't let them hurt you."

"But you'd take a bullet for me?"

She wrapped her arms around him and held on for all she was worth. "I couldn't let them hurt you."

It hit him all at once. She really would have taken a bullet for him. He could count the three people who loved him that much they'd stand between him and danger without a thought for themselves. His two brothers and his granddad. Add to that small list: Luna.

Holy fucking shit. Did she love him?

His chest went tight, cutting off his oxygen supply and making him dizzy. Did he love her?

He cared about her a lot. Enough that the thought of someone hurting her pissed him off more than he'd ever been in his life. He didn't want anyone messing with his woman. And there you go. He did think of her as his.

Not one to be possessive about any one woman, he'd kept his relationships in the past low-key, nothing but fun. This thing with Luna was as serious as he'd ever gotten about a woman, a relationship, the possibility they'd actually have a future together.

He couldn't think about all that right now. He needed to take care of the woman still shaking in his arms, desperate to hold on to him and keep *him* safe.

With a gentleness he had to work to find within the rage coiling his gut, he set Luna away. She gripped his arms, not letting him go.

He cupped her face and stared down into her big blue eyes, hating the fear and desperation he saw in their depths. "It's okay, honey. I'm just going to call the cops."

He tried to step away to grab her phone off the floor, but she tugged his arms to get him to stay. "No. They'll shoot you."

"I'm not going near the windows. We'll let the cops check things out."

He wasn't stupid enough to go out there searching in the dark and leaving her inside the house, vulnerable and alone, a sitting duck for whoever wanted to hurt her. She'd be a perfect target while he searched the yard. He didn't have a gun, or any idea how many of them were out there. Probably just one, maybe both of Wayne's sons. It had to be one or both of them.

He kissed Luna, trying to ease her mind with the soft touch of his lips to hers.

"Please, Colt, stay here."

"I'll stay with you, honey, I promise."

Colt let her go, but it took Luna an extra few seconds to release his arms. He carefully made his way the five feet to her phone and picked it up, making sure he didn't put himself in the line of sight from any of the massive windows surrounding the kitchen. Luna had made a smart choice when she'd shoved him through the huge room to the back alcove.

He went back to her, leaned against the wall, held her down the length of him, and called the cops. He put the phone on speaker so she could listen while he explained the situation to the dispatcher. They stayed on the line while the cops drove out to the house. He wanted to call his brothers, but he'd left his phone and wallet on the bedside table in Luna's room.

It seemed to be taking forever for the cops to arrive. Colt and Luna waited in the tense silence, listening for any sound that someone tried to get into the house, and the intermittent check-in and relayed instructions and updates from the dispatcher.

Colt and Luna let loose a sigh of relief when the dispatcher came back on the line.

"Mr. Kendrick, Deputy Foster just entered the

property. He should pull up in front of the house in a minute."

The siren grew louder. "We hear him."

"Wait until he knocks on the front door before you leave the kitchen and answer it. More officers have been dispatched to the house and are en route. They will assist Deputy Foster in searching the property for the suspect."

Luna jumped at the knock on the door. "Are we sure it's him?"

"Stay here. I'll go let him in."

"No. I'm going with you."

"Deputy Foster is at the door," the dispatcher confirmed.

Colt took Luna's hand and led her from the kitchen, through the living room to the front door. He shoved her behind him and opened the door, keeping a firm grip on it in case someone tried to kick it in. An over-abundance of caution, yes, but he wasn't taking any chances.

Deputy Foster stood with his back to the door, his hand on his weapon, and turned his head side to side, sweeping the yard with his gaze. He glanced quickly over his shoulder, then backed into the house and slammed the door.

"Mr. Kendrick. Miss Hill. We have a report that someone threatened to shoot you."

"They were watching us. He called on my phone." Luna pointed to the phone in Colt's hand. He ended the call with the dispatcher now that the cops had arrived.

Deputy Foster held out his hand, indicating they should move into the living room. He went to the shutters on the windows and pushed them all closed.

"What exactly did he say?" The deputy pulled out a notebook and pen, ready to write down Luna's statement.

"That Colt and I looked cozy having dinner together. We were out on the back patio."

"Did you see anyone? Hear anything that made you suspect someone was out there watching you?"

"No. Nothing."

Colt shook his head, agreeing with Luna. They'd been oblivious to the danger.

"What did the caller say next?"

Luna hesitated and looked away from Colt.

"Luna, whatever the bastard said you can tell me."

Luna still didn't look at him but answered the officer. "He said that Colt was using me the way I used Wayne. That Colt was tired of the leftover scraps from his brothers and looking to use me to get Rambling Range."

"Fuck." Colt raked his fingers through his hair. He tried to walk away to pace off the anger roiling in his gut, but Luna hooked her finger in his belt loop and held him still.

"I don't believe one word of that, Colt."

"But it sounds about right, doesn't it?"

"No. I never used my friendship with Wayne to get anything from him. You don't believe I'd do something like that, right?"

"No. Never." She was too kind and softhearted to do anything of the sort.

"You don't see your place with your brothers as anything less than a true partnership. You work that ranch together. You share in its successes and failures as one. Maybe you do want more. But not from them. You want something of your very own. Who wouldn't?

But that doesn't mean you'd use someone else to get it. You're just not that guy, Colt."

"Simon tried this same thing on you the day you moved in here," he pointed out. "He said just about the same thing that fuck said on the phone tonight."

"Did you recognize the voice on the phone?" Deputy Foster asked. "Could it have been Simon?"

"They kept their voice very low, gravelly. I couldn't tell if it was a man or a woman."

"Are you sure they were watching the two of you and not just saying something about you having dinner together and guessing right that you did?"

Luna shook her head. "He told me to sell or Colt wouldn't be around to kiss the stars up my back."

"What does that mean?" The officer narrowed his gaze.

Colt swore again. "The bastard watched through the bedroom window while Luna and I made love. He saw her tattoos."

Luna stood with her arms wrapped around her middle, her gaze on the floor. Colt hooked his arm around her shoulders and turned her body into his. He held her close and kissed the top of her head.

"Are you sure he hadn't seen the tattoo before and made a reference to it now?"

"I'm telling you, he was outside the house watching us. That statement is very specific to exactly what I did tonight," Colt snapped, losing his patience. "You can't see the tattoo when she's dressed." Colt indicated Luna's back, brushing his hand over the tank dress she wore.

Sure enough, the deputy stared at her back. Luna held herself tighter under the scrutiny.

"I specifically positioned the tattoo so that it isn't

obvious when I'm dressed. Sure, in a swimsuit you'd see it all, but not when I'm wearing a shirt or dress or whatever."

"I've known Luna for years. I had no idea she had the tattoo," Colt told the officer.

"How long have you had it?"

"It started with the moon when I was eighteen. I added the owl and stars when I was twenty. Another tattoo on the front of my hip when I was twenty-one."

"Could it be an ex who wants to make trouble for you now that you're seeing someone else?" the deputy asked.

"No."

"Has there been anyone since Billy?" Colt asked.

"No one serious. No one for a long time."

"Who's Billy?"

"My ex-best friend. Her ex-boyfriend. I didn't know it back in the day, but he had a real thing for keeping her close and away from me."

"You tried to take her from Billy."

"No. Never," Luna spoke up, defending him again. "It's not Billy. The caller said I had to sell or they'd hurt you. It has to be one of the Traverses. Billy wouldn't care about me selling this place, and he wouldn't know that it's one of the stipulations in the will for the Traverses to get more money."

"Tell me about that." Deputy Foster pointed his pen at Luna.

She sighed and pushed away from Colt. "Wayne left each family member a cash settlement, but the bulk of the estate went to me. Namely Rambling Range and the rest of his assets. A lot of money included. His sons can earn back half the ranch by working here for eighteen months. Or, if I decide that I do not want to uphold my portion of the inheritance, namely keeping the ranch running and protecting the land, then I can sell the property to a suitable party and his sons get ten million each, their aunt and uncle receive one million, and the rest is split fifty-fifty between me and several charities." Luna took a deep breath. "They want me to sell so they'll get the money."

"You seem to be holding something back."

Luna eyed Colt, then looked away again. "There are other stipulations in the will that I can invoke if I meet certain requirements or I choose to use them. But the family doesn't know about them," she quickly added.

"What are these other stipulations?"

"I can't say. Only Mr. Manning, my attorney, and myself know about these added alternatives to the will that was read to the family. It has to stay that way, or I could forfeit my right to invoke them."

"This isn't the first time they threatened her. When she moved in, my brother and I found several dead rats in her bathtub with the word 'sell' written on the tiles in their blood."

Luna gasped and covered her mouth, her eyes narrowed with disgust and fear. "Why didn't you tell me?"

"I didn't want to frighten you. I hoped they'd back off."

"Looks like this situation is escalating," Deputy Foster added.

"We need a restraining order against the family," Colt demanded.

"You'll need proof showing who did this and the other acts of vandalism. Let us investigate this latest incident, pinpoint the perpetrator, and you'll get your restraining order against that person." Deputy Foster turned away when his radio squawked. He stepped away and quietly spoke into his radio to the men searching the property.

Luna faced Colt and finally looked him in the eye again with eyes glassed over and filled with worry. "I'm sorry. I don't want to keep things from you, but I really can't tell you what it says."

"I'm sorry I didn't tell you about the rats. But Luna, honey, I don't need to know what it says. Rambling Range is your business. Not mine."

"I don't want secrets between us. I want to be able to tell you anything."

"I hope you feel you can, even if you have to keep this one thing from me to protect yourself and fulfill Wayne's last wishes."

She pressed her lips together, holding back whatever she wanted to say. She gave him a quick nod but still looked wrecked about not telling him.

"The other officers have made a complete sweep of the outside. They didn't find anything or anyone out there. They checked in with some of the men living on the property in the cabins. They didn't hear or see anything."

"I'm not surprised. They're too far away from the house." Luna fell onto the sofa and stared straight ahead. "This is useless. What am I supposed to do? Wait around for them to do something else?"

"You've got it on record that someone threatened Mr. Kendrick. If something else happens, let us know. Meanwhile, give me the names of all the players. I'll pay them a visit and see what they have to say."

"Simon is at the top of the list," Colt said. "He's the logical suspect. He works here, so he could have stayed behind when everyone got off work. He accused me once about seeing Luna because of her inheritance."

"Josh is a hothead," Luna pointed out. "He threatened to make me pay if I didn't sell."

Deputy Foster glanced up and eyed her, then wrote down what she said. "Anyone else involved?"

"Bea and Harry Murphy. Wayne's sister and her husband. They received a payout but expected a hell of a lot more. Their daughters, Anne and Kelly, received some money and school tuition. I've paid them and set up a payment plan for Kelly. She's decided to take this opportunity and go back to school and change careers."

"You'll pay for her to attend college?" The deputy sounded skeptical.

"Yes. It's part of the will. So long as the ranch has the money to pay, I'm required to do so."

"And the ranch makes enough money for college?"

"More than," she confirmed without giving any details.

The deputy flipped his notepad closed. "Okay. I'll speak to the parties involved and get back to you. I doubt any of them will confess, but I'll do my best to get one of them to dig their own hole. Anything else happens, give us a call. I'll have an officer posted outside for the night, not that I think anyone is coming back now that they've probably seen us here. I'll ask for regular patrols for the next few days to dissuade anyone from coming back. Most likely this was just a prank to see if they can rattle you. They did. Let's hope they got what they wanted and give up."

Luna shook her head and spoke to her joined hands in her lap. "They won't give up. It's too much to give up."

Colt shook the officer's hand and saw him to the door.

"Don't go playing hero and running around this place with a gun thinking you'll shoot the bastard who spied on you. Don't want you shooting the wrong person by accident."

"Don't worry about it. I got this covered."

"How is Sadie?"

Colt eyed the cop.

"She and I go way back with her brother. Rory helped take down that drug lab, and we're grateful to him."

"Sadie's good. Expecting their first baby. The wedding is a few weeks away."

"Good to hear it. That girl deserves every happiness after what she's been through."

"Yes, she does. She and my brother are very happy."

"Looks like you're heading down the same path. Let's hope it doesn't end with you shooting someone to save your girl."

"I will if I have to, but I'm hoping you'll sort this out for me and I can go back to being with her."

"Smart man."

"Just so we're clear, anyone touches her, I will kill them."

"I never heard you say that." Deputy Foster walked down the path to his patrol car.

Colt closed the door, locked it up tight, and went back to the kitchen and out the back door. He tried not to think about someone out there with a gun pointed at him, so he ignored the chill racing up his spine. He gathered up the plates and glasses from their meal and took them inside, dumping everything in the sink. He locked up the back door, went to the freezer, found the tub of rocky road ice cream, grabbed two spoons from the strainer, and went back to Luna and plopped down on the sofa beside her. He picked up the remote and turned on the huge big-screen TV she bought to go along with the furniture.

"I see the satellite guys got you all hooked up today."

"Yeah. Ford will be very happy the next time we have him over."

He popped the top on the ice cream container but went still when her words hit him square in the chest. *"The next time we have him over."* Like this was their place. He tilted his head and stared at her staring at the TV. She glanced at him, nothing but worry and wonder in her eyes that he'd looked at her.

"What?" she asked, completely oblivious about what she'd said and how she'd phrased it.

"Nothing. Did you get the sports package?"

"No. Do you watch a lot of sports?"

"Football and hockey."

She nodded. "I'll call tomorrow and set it up."

"You don't have to if you don't want it."

"I don't mind. I was so focused on the movie channels, I didn't think about anything else. I only had basic cable at my other place. I love watching movies."

"Great, let's find one and have dinner."

"That's dessert."

"Tonight, it's dinner, since we didn't get to finish our steaks. You pick the movie." He handed over the remote, mostly to get her out of her head and do something else.

She took the remote but didn't scroll through the channels or even pull up the guide.

"Don't you even want to ask me what the will says?"

He shook his head and cocked up one side of his mouth into a derisive frown. "Wayne's put a lot of pressure on you. See if you can make ranchers out of his too-good-to-get-their-hands-dirty sons, who could care less about this place and what it represents. Oversee his niece going to college. Deal with his greedy sister.

Keep this place running the way he did when you've got to learn how to do that at the same time. You've got a lot on your shoulders, honey. I won't add my weight to that burden. Whatever else Wayne put in that will, I'm sure you'll share it with me when and if it becomes relevant. Whatever it is, it doesn't have anything to do with the way I feel about you, the way you feel about me, or our relationship. I'm here because I want to be with you. Not for a piece of land, money, or anything else. If that's good enough for you, then I don't care what anyone else has to say about it."

"I'm so glad you're here, but I'm worried your being with me has put a target on your back."

"Nothing and no one is going to keep me away from you. Anyone tries to hurt you, they'll have to go through me."

Luna took her spoon from him, dipped it in the ice cream, ate a bite, and leaned into his side.

"Tom Cruise or Jason Statham?"

"How about the Jason Bateman comedy?"

"Even better." Luna turned on the movie and sat quietly beside him. It took her nearly half an hour to settle down and stop checking the windows and jumping at every little sound.

By the time he took her to bed, she was wound so tight he figured she'd never fall asleep. The second they entered her room, she went to the windows, slammed the shutters shut, and pulled the deep purple drapes closed tight.

"Luna, honey, come here." He opened his arms and she flew into them, hugging him close, her face buried in his neck.

"This place was just starting to feel like mine, especially after you and I made love in that awesome new bed."

"If the bed was awesome, what was I?" He tried to tease her out of this dark mood.

"Everything I want."

He didn't know what to say to something that rang true, hit him right in the chest, and echoed in the dark.

He slid his hands down her sides, gathered her dress in his fingers, and pulled it up her thighs and over her hips into his hands. He pulled the soft material up her sides and right off her raised arms. Naked, she stood before him and smiled softly, reaching out to place her hand on his bare chest. Her fingers slid down his belly. He sucked in a breath and tightened his abs when she tickled him. The seductive smile on her lips grew. She undid the button and zipper on his jeans, leaned in, kissed his chest, her open mouth driving him crazy. Her hand dipped down his jeans and worked over his swelling flesh until he was hard and heavy in her small hand.

He cupped her face, dipped his head, and kissed her softly, drawing her back with him as he sat on the bed. He broke the kiss, slid his hands down her body to her hips, and pulled her onto his lap to straddle his thighs.

"God, honey, you are so beautiful." He traced his fingers over her shoulders, down her chest and pink-tipped breasts to her slender belly. His gaze swept over all that creamy skin to where his suntanned hands gripped her waist.

Unable to resist the sweet temptation in front of him, he leaned forward and took one tight nipple into his mouth. He sucked and licked the small bead, loving the taste of her on his tongue.

Her fingers combed through his hair. She held him to her breasts, one and then the other, but it still took her longer than he liked to relax and enjoy the attention he lavished on her.

He wanted her to forget, at least for a little while, and let go. He wanted what they'd shared hours ago before it had all gotten ruined by some asshole who thought tormenting her would change anything. She wouldn't back down. She wouldn't give in. Not for anything. Not Luna.

So Colt set out to make it all go away and draw her back to him.

It took some time, but when he had her sighing and moaning and laid out beneath him, he joined their bodies once again and pressed his heart to hers. He showed her with his body the connection they shared. Lost in him, she responded, her fingers gripped tight at his hips, pulling him in, holding him close as her body moved against his in the night. He kept the pace slow and steady, taking his time to love her, enjoy what they shared so easily, and languish in the warm feelings she evoked inside of him. He didn't want to look too closely at what those feelings meant, but one thought refused to leave his mind. If something happened to her, what would he do then?

The thought tightened his chest and built into a need to be close to her that he couldn't contain or control. He thrust into her hard and deep and moved over her in a desperate need that built until the desperation gripping both of them came to an explosive crescendo. He'd never felt this kind of overwhelming emotion after making love to a woman. Maybe because that wasn't what he'd been doing with those other women.

Luna was different.

Everything about her called to him in a way he couldn't define. He needed more of this intense feeling and her in his life.

Knowing exactly where his thoughts wanted to lead him, he tucked them away again, because no way did he fall for Luna in such a short time. He wasn't ready for something permanent. He also wasn't about to give her up, or let anyone ruin what they had and take her away.

CHAPTER 19

Luna woke up warm and tingling with Colt's big hand on her breast, his other hand cradling her head, and his sensual mouth pressing kisses all over the stars on her back. It felt like a dream and reality mixed into one lovely wake-up call.

"Good morning," Colt's deep voice rumbled. Still not quite awake himself, he pressed more kisses to her skin.

"It is now."

"You have to give me back my hands. I've got work to do."

"No." She leaned over, pressing her breast into his palm even more, then took his hand from under her cheek and moved it to her other breast. She giggled and lay down on both of them.

Colt smiled against her skin. His chuckle vibrated across her nerves. He rolled her to her side, his big body pressed along her back, one hand pressed to her chest over her heart, the other laid against her belly, holding her close to him. "You're dangerous," he whispered in her ear. "All I want to do is stay in this bed with you."

"Mmm. Sounds like a great plan."

"I've got work to do."

She rubbed her backside into his hard length. "Uh-huh, yes you do."

His hand dipped between her legs, one long finger stroking her soft folds. She sighed and rubbed her bottom against him, catching his rhythm. He pressed soft kisses to her neck. She reached back and rubbed her hand over his hard thigh.

One hand at her breast, the other heating her body, he bit her shoulder in a soft love bite that shot electricity through her whole body, making her breasts tingle and her insides melt. "I like waking up with you."

She had no complaints about the strong body wrapped around hers, or the man who held her during the night when she couldn't sleep and made her feel safe and protected. She reached back to touch his face.

Someone pounded on the front door, jolting her out of the sweet cocoon they'd created this morning and making her insides go cold. She latched onto Colt's arms around her and stiffened in his embrace.

"Stay here. I'll see who it is." Colt rolled out of bed behind her, dragging on the jeans he picked up from the floor.

She shimmied out of bed and grabbed the dress he'd tossed aside last night. Feeling exposed and vulnerable, she ran for the closet and pulled out her robe. Colt left the room ahead of her, but as he reached the front door, she caught up, saw their early-morning visitor through the glass side panel, and swore. Colt glanced at her, then opened the door, blocking her with his body.

"What the hell do you want?"

Simon pushed past Colt when he spotted Luna over Colt's shoulder. "You sent the cops to my house last night," he yelled at her.

Colt planted his hand on Simon's chest and shoved

him back against the wall, not letting him get close to Luna.

"No one invited you in."

"To my fucking house," Simon shouted.

"Not yours. Hers. Accept that simple fact. You'd save yourself a lot of anger and the ass kicking that's coming your way if you don't calm down."

"Not her place. You mean yours. You just can't wait to take over this spread, can you?"

Colt narrowed his gaze. "That sounds an awful lot like what the caller said last night about me using her for this place."

"The cops said someone got an eyeful of you with her."

Colt held his hand firm against Simon's chest. "Was that someone you? Were you the one lurking in the bushes?" Colt shoved Simon, thumping his head against the wall again.

Simon pushed back. "I'm not some perv." He reached up and rubbed the back of his head where he'd hit the wall. "Not my style. I want her to do the right thing and give back what doesn't belong to her because she knows it's the right thing to do."

"Your father left it to her for a reason."

Simon tilted his mouth into a half frown, his eyes filled with hope that she'd see things his way. "He left her a way out for all of us."

She got the anger. Part of his grief over losing his father. Spoiled and arrogant, it upset him things didn't go his way, but she didn't think he was the type to lurk in the shadows and outright threaten her. "Colt, he didn't do it."

Simon seemed stealthier, more calculating. He was too smart to do all the things that outright pointed to the family. Too obvious. While she was trying to hope for the best for Wayne's sake, she had no doubt Simon had a plan to get her to sell. The fact he'd agreed to work here for the next eighteen months indicated he had an endgame, and getting half the ranch wasn't it. She didn't know if the sale and the ten million he'd receive was really what he wanted ultimately, but he'd settle for that or half the ranch if he didn't get what he really wanted. She hoped that didn't include payback on her.

Colt released Simon. The guy wasn't a threat. Not a direct, imminent one anyway.

Simon kept his steady gaze on her. "You know what I want, but since you won't give it to me, I'm here to do the work."

Fair enough. She really did want him to succeed. She wanted him to prove that he wanted it for the right reasons. At least he was trying. She couldn't say the same about the rest of the Travers family. Well, except maybe his cousins. They were great girls.

"You're expected down at the stables this morning. Get to work."

"Right, I put in the work, you can't deny me what's mine. That's what you said. That's what you'll have to do."

"Eighteen months is a long time. Longer than most of the jobs you've held," she pointed out. "You're the type of guy who gives up when things get tough." She pushed, hoping he'd find his way past his grief and look toward his future.

"Not this time." His words were filled with conviction. She hoped he stuck to it.

She gave him a firm nod, hoping to encourage him. "Prove me wrong. Prove your father wrong. That's what this is about. He wanted you to work for it. He wanted you to want it."

Simon raised his head to the ceiling, then looked back at her with a disheartened bleakness in his eyes. "Nothing I ever did was good enough. Why the hell would he think I'd go through all this to live up to his expectations when he was gone and it doesn't matter anymore?"

"You still don't get it."

"Enlighten me."

"Hope."

His eyes narrowed with skepticism. "What?"

"A parent's eternal hope for their children. Hope that they will find something in their lives that gives them the kind of satisfaction you can't get with money. Your father found that for himself on this ranch. The one thing he loved to do that he'd have done even without all the money. This place never felt like work to him, but a labor of love. It's how Colt feels about working with his brothers. Wayne wanted that for you and Josh. He didn't actually think you'd find it here, but he left you the opportunity to try in whatever capacity suited you. Otherwise, he left you the money and another opportunity to find your own path to happiness. Your cousin Kelly starts school in the fall."

"I'm too old to go back to school and start over."

She shook her head. "You're never too old to learn something new and start over. That's what I'm doing."

"You've got the money to do anything you want."

"So do you."

"Not the kind of money my father left you."

"Maybe not, but he didn't leave you without options, a roof over your head, and an example of what life could be."

"I'm not like my father."

"Truer words," Colt said under his breath.

"You're not your father," Luna agreed. "But that doesn't mean you can't be the same kind of man."

"Stupid enough to leave a woman everything I ever built and made." Again, Simon's anger got the better of him.

She didn't have the patience for it this morning. "Get out. I'm not going to sit here and lecture you about something you've got no concept of and could care less about. Either get to work, or get off my property. I'm done trying to make you see what your father did, what he really left behind, and the opportunities you squander away thinking of ways to steal back what your father didn't want you to have in the first place.

"You tell your family, I will not sell. Not ever. Not for any reason. Certainly not to see you get another dime from this place. You tell Josh, he steps foot on this property again, I'll have him arrested for trespassing."

"If I don't shoot him first," Colt warned.

Simon glared at her for a full ten seconds, the tension in the room growing thick. She let out her breath when he turned and stormed out the front door, slamming it so hard the windows shook.

Colt wrapped her in his arms. "Are you okay?"

"Fine. Pissed. I get that he's angry, but I'm so tired of defending the choices Wayne made."

"But you do it so well," Colt teased. "You two really were close. You know exactly what he meant by doing what he did."

"We were a lot alike. You remind me of him."

Colt tipped his head. "How so?"

She bit the side of her lip and let her gaze fall to his chest. He cupped her face and made her look at him.

"Tell me."

"Being happy isn't about a thing, or a place, or having what you want and need. It's like you said last night. You're here for me. Not this place, the money, what this place would mean for your future."

"You really mean that? You believe it?"

"If I didn't, you wouldn't still be here. I'm not that stupid, naïve girl I used to be. You're not the kind of guy who uses someone to get what they want."

"I'd never do that to you, honey. But if this thing between us keeps building to something permanent, we will have to face that my life with you here and my life with my brothers will have to change in some way. It's already getting to that point for me with Sadie pregnant and marrying my brother. They've started a life together, and I don't know how long I can stay there and not feel like I'm intruding in their life."

"Are you thinking of moving out?"

"Yes. Sadie plans to surprise Ford with her old house and ranch any day now. Maybe I'll move in with him. Maybe I'll finally build my own place so that I'm not insinuating myself into the new life he starts there."

"Everything is changing." For both of them. Their lives were being altered by the people around them. "I don't think Sadie expects you to move out." She tried to reassure him.

"I don't think she or Rory do either. But we can't all keep living there when it's clear they want to build their family and their life on the ranch."

"But part of that ranch belongs to you."

"It always will, but that doesn't mean I need to be underfoot all the time. Besides, I'm tired of walking in on them when they're making out in the kitchen, or the stables, or on the porch. Those two are all over each other all the time."

Luna laughed and looked down between them. Colt held her close while they talked.

"Don't get me wrong, I get it." He squeezed her close and kissed her softly. "Doesn't mean I like seeing my brother kissing his girl all the time."

"I get what you mean."

"I need to get dressed and get back there. I'll be back later today. Promise me you'll stay here until Ed comes from the stables to get you. I'll have a talk with the crew about what happened last night, Simon's outburst this morning, and make sure you are never left alone."

"Colt, I don't think it was Simon."

"Neither do I, but I'm not taking the chance he's just a damn good liar."

"I don't need to be guarded."

"Either you agree to this, or you're coming with me. I won't get anything done if all I do is worry about you."

"Colt . . ."

"I mean it, Luna. You agree and mean it, or I'm not letting you out of my sight."

"For how long? I can't live my life like that."

"Until I know for sure you're safe."

"I'm not the one they threatened last night."

CHAPTER 20

Luna plucked a four-pack of her favorite raspberry Greek yogurt from the refrigerated shelf and moved down the aisle to get a new container of sour cream, trying not to resent the fact that one of her ranch hands had followed her everywhere she'd gone for the past ten days. Seriously, PJ was a nice guy, but she hated the necessity of his constant presence.

She shifted her thinking, remembering that Colt implored her to keep someone with her for her protection. He wanted to keep her safe. It made her smile that he cared that much, that deeply.

Small hands clasped together at her waist as a child hugged her from behind, bringing her abruptly out of her thoughts of spending the night with Colt again.

"Angie, honey, you can't run off like that."

"Luna," Angie said, hugging her tighter as Mrs. Krolick rushed over.

Luna turned in the girl's arms and hugged her close. Angie looked up at her, smiling so big it lit Luna's heart and made her sad at the same time. She missed being with the kids.

"How are you, sweetheart?"

"School."

"Yes. It's been a while since I've been to the school." Luna glanced up at Mrs. Krolick. "How is she doing?"

"Working hard on her reading."

Born with Down syndrome, nine-year-old Angie had intellectual and developmental disabilities that made learning a challenge. She didn't like letters, but numbers fascinated her.

Luna held the sweet girl close and ran her hand over her soft golden hair. She stared down into Angie's bright face. "Do you have a favorite book?"

"Twinkle."

The one-word answer made it easy to figure out she meant the nursery rhyme. "One of my favorites, too."

"Miss Christy told me you're opening an equine therapy program soon." Mrs. Krolick's eyes filled with interest.

"Yes. I hope to open the school in the next few months. I let Miss Christy know, hoping we could work together to identify kids most in need of the program and what type of skills to focus on for each."

"Well, I for one would love to sign Angie up for the program. I think it would be a great confidence builder if nothing else."

"Horse." Angie pulled on Luna's shirt. "Horse."

Luna cupped the girl's soft cheek. "Yes, honey, you can come and ride the horse." Luna glanced back up at Mrs. Krolick. "I'll get the information to you soon. I've got some personal matters to work out, but I really do want to make the school a priority."

Saying it solidified the conviction in her heart, but she couldn't start the program and bring children to the ranch with the Traverses still causing trouble. Plus, two of the horses she wanted to use in the program came up sick over the last week. Worrisome on its own, but suspicious when she factored in Simon working at the ranch. She didn't want to think he, or anyone in his family, would hurt the horses. She couldn't rule it out either.

"Let me know as soon as you're ready."

"I will. Maybe Angie would like to come over and be my helper as I set up and work out the routines."

"Luna," Angie said, squeezing her tight.

"Well, you are her favorite person. Give me a call. We'll set it up." Mrs. Krolick stared down at her daughter with indulgent eyes. "Come on, Angie, we need to find your favorite cereal."

"Chex!" Angie released Luna all at once and dashed off down the aisle. Mrs. Krolick touched Luna's shoulder in goodbye and rushed after her daughter.

More than ever, Luna wanted to get her project up and running, despite all her other responsibilities. But how could she when the Traverses kept threatening her? She couldn't bring children to the ranch not knowing what the Traverses would do next.

She pulled her phone from her purse and called Dex. "Hi, this is Luna Hill. Is Dex available?"

Luna waited for his assistant to put him on the line.

"Dex, do you have time to set up a meeting between me and the Traverses this afternoon?"

"Sure. What's this about? Did something else happen?"

"No. I think it's time I put my foot down and let them know they keep pushing me, I'll push back."

"I'll set it up and call you back."

Luna tucked her phone in her bag and rushed to finish her shopping, anxious to talk with the Traverses and end this dirty business.

So far, she'd been on the defensive, waiting for the next thing to happen. Time to go on the offensive and make them back down before someone really did get hurt.

CHAPTER 21

Colt stared at the computer screen, lost in thought, with no real answer coming to mind for his dilemma. His plan had been to talk to his brothers about adding his own house to the property and building up the small but lucrative horse business on the ranch. The part of the business he enjoyed the most. A piece of the business he'd excel at and make his mark.

But what did he do with his life now that Luna had become such a big part of his? How that happened so lightning fast, he didn't know. But he couldn't decide what to do on his own because he always started factoring her in.

He spent every night with her now. They'd fallen into a pattern. He arrived at her place around four and checked in with her guys, making sure the ranch ran smoothly. He made decisions with her men on the best thing to do for whatever came up. Luna listened, learned, and weighed in. Each and every day, she worked hard to earn her place on the ranch and the respect of those who worked for her. Even Simon had shed his hostility, put his head down, and worked at whatever task they'd assigned him, though he always had a dark glare to shoot Colt's way.

Each night Colt and Luna shared their day over a
meal they made together, though she did the heavy lifting on that front. He loved sitting across the table, talking to her about anything, everything, and seeing her
face light up when he told her about a new colt or calf,
or hearing her laugh when he joked or teased with her.

He made love to her every night and woke with her in
his arms. He'd never been one to spend the night with a
woman, let alone have her draped over him while he slept,
but he couldn't seem to fall asleep without Luna anymore.

Every morning he left at dawn to shower and change
at home, then spend his day working the ranch with
his brothers when all he wanted to do was be at Luna's
place. Yes, because he worried about her safety despite
the Traverses backing off after that menacing phone
call, but mostly because he just liked being with her.

He stared at his bank balance again, wondering what
to do. Build a house and buy a bunch of horses here on
the Kendrick spread, or build a life with Luna on hers?
This was his home. The place he always thought he'd
live and work. He couldn't ask Luna to give up Rambling Range. He wanted to be with Luna, but did he
want to give up his place here to be with her there? Did
she even want him there?

"Why the long face, son?" His granddad stood in
front of the office desk, looking down at him.

Colt let out a heavy sigh and swiped his hand across
his mouth.

"Did something more happen with Luna?" Grandpa
Sammy plopped down in the chair in front of Colt,
ready for a good long talk. Colt had always found it
easy to spill his guts to his grandfather. Mostly because
talking to his brothers involved a lot of razzing that
Colt didn't really need right now.

"No. She's fine as far as I know. Toby texted me the all clear a couple hours ago."

One of Grandpa Sammy's eyebrows shot up. "Is that right? How often does he do that?"

"At least twice a day."

"Sounds to me like you're keeping a close watch on your girl."

"I'm trying, but I'm needed here, and I can't really be there as much as I'd like."

His granddad's head tilted to the side and his eyes narrowed.

Colt waited, wondering what he'd said that made his grandfather study him so hard.

"Maybe you should tell me what you're trying to figure out."

"Rory and Sadie are getting married any minute." At least that's what it felt like to him. A clock ticking down on the time he had left here before the newly-weds took over the house.

"It won't be long now. Soon after, we'll have a baby in the house. So?"

"There's the thing with Ford tomorrow." Sadie and Rory planned to hand over the keys to her old place to Ford. They'd asked Colt to come and lend his support.

"You feeling left out of that?"

"No. He's been talking about his own place for a long time. The plans he's got stored up in his mind . . ." Colt shook his head in wonder. "He'll be excited and happy and exactly where he's supposed to be."

Especially since Ford had once thought to go off on his own to start his own place with the girl he fell hard and fast for long ago. But he'd given that and her up to save the ranch when they hit hard times. Rory and Grandpa Sammy didn't know that, but Ford got drunk one night and unwillingly spilled his guts to Colt. Sometimes, Colt still saw the haunting heartbreak in Ford's eyes.

"Ah, so where does that leave you? Is that it?"

Colt didn't like change. He liked things the way they were. He was happy for his brothers, but he wanted things between them to stay the same, too. Then again, he was thinking of making his own changes.

"I'm still needed here. Ford will need me at his new place."

"But all of a sudden, it feels very much like theirs and not yours anymore. Or at least not the three of you anymore."

"We're going in separate directions."

His brothers had great new things in their lives. So did he. But it wasn't easy for him to grab hold of it and believe it would all work out.

"That's life, Colt."

"I guess I'm wondering, if Rory is staying put, Ford is moving on, do I find a new place here, or somewhere else?"

"Seems you've made a good start with Luna. I thought the two of you were getting real close. You haven't slept in your bed in a long time. It's not like you to be gone more than a night."

His grandfather's diplomatic way of saying he'd been a hound dog out chasing tail, but always coming home alone. Well, Colt was damn tired of being alone, living his life each day on this ranch with his brothers, working his ass off, only to see them moving forward in their lives while he felt adrift in his own. He thought the tether he had to this place would never be broken, but it sure did feel like he'd become the odd man out.

"Everything between Luna and me is great. I don't

like her being in that house alone at night after what happened."

"Do you prefer being with her than being here?"

Colt couldn't hide the grin. "I prefer sleeping with a beautiful woman than without."

"That's not true. You prefer sleeping with her than without her. That's different."

That did sound about right. The knot in Colt's gut that came from thinking about not having her in his life agreed with his granddad, too. "She's different," he admitted. "I'm different with her. Better. I want something different between us than I've ever wanted with anyone else. But what am I supposed to do? This doesn't feel like my place anymore. It feels like Sadie and Rory's. Even Ford will be moving on. I thought I'd build a new house here, but Luna's got her place there."

His grandfather's eyes narrowed. "So you want your place to be with her?"

"It's not that simple."

"Why? You just said you wanted something different with her."

"I do. Luna and I are just getting started, but sometimes it feels like I've known her every day of my life. I don't want to rush things, and I want to hurry up all at once."

It made his gut tighten to think of leaving this place, his parents' legacy, because it felt like another loss of the connection he had to them, but he admitted, "I've been thinking of ditching my plans to expand the horse business here and go to work for Luna."

"She talked about Toby retiring the other night when she came by to help Sadie pick out things for the registry. I think you were still out in the barn. Anyway, she said Toby's been talking to her about a good time for him to leave."

"So soon?"

"He wants to move to where his daughter and grand-children live in Arizona. He's tired of the long winters here."

"I knew he wanted to retire, but I thought he'd wait until Luna was ready to run the place."

"Does she really want to be a full-time rancher?"

Colt shrugged—he didn't really know. The equine therapy program was important to her. She'd probably like to spend more of her time doing that than actually running the ranch.

Grandpa Sammy held up a hand, palm up. "You know everything there is to know about the business. More than Rory and Ford about the horses. You could really do well at Rambling Range if you ran things."

"And leave Rory high and dry?" More than losing his connection to his parents and this ranch, he didn't want to disappoint or be disloyal to his brother. Rory had sacrificed to keep this place and a roof over their heads, allowing Colt the chance to grow up and repay him by working hard next to his big brothers when he was old enough to pull his own weight. It felt like a betrayal to leave their ranch to work another, even if it meant he got to be with Luna.

"Rory wants you to be happy."

True. Colt fell back in his seat. "I don't even know if she'll hire me." They'd only been seeing each other a short time. This would be a huge leap forward. Were they ready for that kind of commitment? He was. But what about her?

"Why wouldn't she hire you?"

"Because how will that look?"

"Like she hired the right man for the job," his grand-father suggested, deadpan. "You've never cared what anyone thought about what you did. Not even your family really. So why do you care now what anyone thinks?"

Colt threw up his hands. "I don't care what anyone thinks." He pointed past his grandfather. "I care what she thinks."

His grandfather sat back, completely relaxed. "Then why don't you ask her what she thinks."

Because as much fun as they'd had over the last few weeks, and no matter how close he felt to her or how much he saw that she felt the same way, she'd never actually asked him to stay or take the lead with the ranch. He'd stepped in to do both and she'd gone along, grateful for his presence at night, when she was the most nervous about something happening, and his making sure the ranch didn't fall apart around her. Not once had she asked him if he'd be interested in taking over for Toby.

"I'm sending him to you right now," Sadie spoke into his phone and walked into the office. She disconnected the call and held the phone out to him. "She's been calling you for the last half hour." Colt didn't need to be scolded. He mentally kicked his own ass for forgetting to pick up his phone from the counter after he came in and washed his hands. He'd been so diligent about keeping his phone close and charged just in case something happened or Luna needed him. "Luna's on her way to Mr. Manning's office for a sit-down about the will with the Travers family. She wants you to meet her there."

Colt closed the laptop and stood, pulling his truck keys from his pocket. "The terms of the will are set. What's there to talk about?"

"She's tired of being on the defensive. Easy enough

to look past the petty vandalism, but spying on you guys, another horse falling ill is way over the line."

"Another one?" Colt swore under his breath, hoping the Traverses had nothing to do with hurting the horses, that it was just an illness and not something more sinister.

"She's going to put them on notice that she won't put up with any more of their threats."

His grandfather slapped him on the shoulder as he headed for the door. "Talk to your girl. Straighten things out."

"What's going on with you and Luna?" Sadie asked.

"Nothing. We're fine," Colt bit out, pulling the front door open, more interested in getting to Luna before the Traverses arrived than explaining his ever-changing life and mind.

He hoped his grandfather kept quiet about Colt's feelings about Rory and Sadie getting married and what that meant for Colt. He knew they'd never ask him to leave, but that didn't mean they wanted him to stay either.

How would Rory really feel if he went to work for Luna?

He leaped into his truck and gunned the engine, tearing down the driveway, desperate to get to the woman who turned his world upside down and righted it all at the same time. He didn't know how she did that, or why he didn't mind, but he'd be damned if he let the Traverses mess with her again.

CHAPTER 22

Luna stood in Dex's conference room confronted by a wall of Traverses, minus Bea and Harry's daughters, standing outside the interior glass windows, glaring at her. Her gut went tight and fluttered with nerves. Time to put them on notice. She wasn't going to take any more and let them get away with it.

Simon walked in first. They'd avoided each other for the most part since Simon had come to the house about the cop's late-night wake-up call. Mostly because she'd been stuck in the stables watching over her sick horses.

Josh followed Simon, sweeping a dirty leer up her body to her face. She tried to ignore him, but couldn't fight off the creepy feeling dancing over her nerves, or the way her stomach pitched and soured just thinking about him standing outside her window, watching her and Colt make love.

Bea and Harry walked in together. They seemed to be a tight couple, though Harry tended to look to his wife for direction.

Bea stood just inside the entry, her head high, her silvery blonde hair swept back in a sleek style. Her gaze settled on her nephews, and for a moment her eyes filled with sadness.

"I see so much of Wayne in them," Luna said, hoping to connect with this woman on some level so they could speak amicably.

"Stupid fool." The words held a wealth of anger overlying the deep hurt Bea tried to hide, but which showed in her eyes when she looked at Simon and Josh.

So, amicable is out the door. Actually, it never arrived, judging by the thick hostility in the air they'd all brought with them.

"Please everyone, have a seat. My attorney will be here shortly. May I get you something to drink?" Luna swept her arm toward the counter behind her and the coffee and water Dex's assistant brought in for the meeting. Her mother taught her to always mind her manners, even when people were rude.

"We want you to do the right thing," Bea snapped, plopping her ass in the chair at the head of the conference table.

"My guess is that what I think is right differs greatly from your interpretation." Luna tilted her head and scrunched up her mouth. "Like I don't think it's right to vandalize someone's home."

Bea didn't even flinch. But her husband's eyes shifted to his wife, and his lips pressed together just enough to tell Luna that Bea, in all her snobbish ways, might not be above petty pranks.

With her head high, shoulders tight and straight, Bea kept her steely gaze locked on Luna. "Taking what doesn't belong to you isn't right."

Luna kept her head up, gaze locked with Bea's. "Wayne left the ranch to me. It is mine. It will remain mine."

"Because you have no intention of turning over half to Simon when he completes his father's outrageous demands."

"If Simon meets the terms, he'll get what's coming to him."

"So you'll do as my brother asked, despite how it is tearing this family apart."

Overdramatic, but Luna tried to make Bea understand where she was coming from. "Wayne and I were very much alike in certain ways . . ."

"He liked looking at the stars with you?" The innocent tone in Josh's words only made the statement that much more disturbing. A shiver danced up her spine. He'd made that threatening and creepy call to her. If she could prove it, she'd have the asshole arrested.

"Shut your mouth, or I will shut it for you," Colt said from the doorway.

Just to piss off the Traverses, Luna plastered on a bright smile for Colt and said, "Honey, you made it."

"He doesn't belong here," Bea scoffed, her outrage building to the point her ears turned red.

To prove he did, Colt walked past the Traverses and straight to her. He leaned down and kissed her, holding it for just a few second longer than was suitable in front of others to let them know their relationship was solid.

Josh grabbed Colt by the shoulder and spun him around. "The both of you are fucking in on this together." Josh planted both hands on Colt's chest and shoved him.

Colt stepped back on one foot but came back swinging. He punched Josh right in the jaw, snapping his head sideways and sending the man to the carpet. "You start a fight, I'll finish it."

Luna grabbed Colt's arm to stop him from going after Josh again. Completely unnecessary. Colt remained in complete control.

Josh jumped up from the floor, shook his head like a

wet dog, then tried to rush Colt. Simon jumped in front of him and held him back.

Josh held one hand to his bright red face and used his other to point a finger over Simon's shoulder straight at Colt. "Asshole. I won't let you take everything just because you're screwing her and she's too stupid to see you're using her."

"I'd be careful what you say about her." The tension in Colt radiated off him, but he didn't move, just vibrated with pent-up anger.

Simon gripped Josh's shirt and shook him. "Shut the fuck up. You're only making things worse." Simon ushered Josh across the room and shoved him into a chair two down from their aunt, putting distance between Josh and Colt.

Josh glared at Colt and worked his bruised jaw.

Luna sighed out her relief that the two didn't go at it again. She held her hand against Colt's face and stared up at him in a silent conversation, letting him know she appreciated his restraint and hated that he'd had to resort to punching the idiot.

Colt took her hand and kissed her palm.

Bea rose from her seat and held her hands fisted at her sides, her arms rigid. Apparently, the fight wasn't over. "You can't live with her at the ranch."

Colt stepped to Luna's side and hooked his arm around her shoulders, pulling her close to his side. He gave Bea one of his good ol' boy charming smiles and winked. "Are you sure about that? Because I've got a bed with my name on it and a woman who wants me in it every night. Now, I'm a smart man, and I do what she wants. Am I right, Harry?"

The congenial tone set Bea's teeth to grinding.

A trickle of sweat ran down the side of Harry's face. He eyed his wife, not saying a word.

"You called us here. Why, if not to discuss the will?" Bea bit out, even more frustrated Colt turned all easy-going instead of arguing with her.

Luna stepped out of Colt's embrace and faced off with Bea. "I will not tolerate any more vandalism, tres-passing, or threats. If you don't stop, I'll have no choice but to get a restraining order and file charges against you."

"You can't prove that we did anything that's hap-pened at the ranch," Simon spoke up for the first time.

True enough. She had nothing but bluster at this point, because the cops couldn't prove that any one of them had done one or all the stupid things they'd done, each of which pointed to them collectively but not one of them directly.

She wanted to punch Simon in his smug face.

"You haven't been that subtle about it." Luna glanced at all the Traverses, her gaze settling back on Bea. "Why are you still involved in any of this?"

"To protect my nephews and stand up for them and their rights."

Sounded reasonable, except Luna didn't buy it. Not one word. "They're big boys. They can stick up for themselves. Their father left them quite a sum of money. Their houses are paid off, they've only got their living expenses. They've received more than enough to cover them and not have to work too hard. Simon is working at the ranch. He earns a good salary and has the opportunity to earn half the ranch. What more do you want?"

"Sell the ranch and pay out the ten million," Josh snapped.

Luna turned to Simon and pinned him with her gaze. "Is that what you really want?"

Simon planted his hands on the back of the empty chair beside Josh's and leaned over, but turned his steady gaze on her. "This is where I differ with my family. While I don't object to you selling if that's what you choose, I see more . . . benefit in getting my half of the ranch."

"Even when that leaves your brother out of getting anything more?"

"He's made up his mind on what he wants. I've made up mine."

Dex walked in and came around the table to stand by Luna and Colt. "What have I missed?"

"Colt decked me," Josh spat out.

Dex looked back at Colt, standing there without a care in the world.

Colt actually shrugged off Josh's implied accusation that he'd done something wrong. "He thought he could push me around."

Dex looked Colt up and down, then turned to Josh. "Good luck with that." Dex studied Josh's dark red jaw. "You got off lucky."

"Fuck off." Josh continued with his brooding glare but didn't make a move to start the fight all over again.

"I want to see the missing pages from the copy of the will you sent to all of us," Bea demanded.

Luna shared a look with Dex.

"No."

"No," Bea spat out, her outrage getting the better of her again. She wasn't used to being told no. She almost stomped her foot, making Luna hold back a laugh, though nothing about this situation struck her as truly funny. "We are entitled to see the entire will."

"No, you're not. The portion of the will that pertains to you has been provided. The other pages are specific to Luna and the terms of her keeping the ranch."

"Are you saying there's a chance she won't get to keep it?" Simon asked.

Josh eyed the lawyer, eager to hear what he had to say.

"Luna is fully aware of all her options, the stipulations, and the benefits and consequences. As things pertain to you all, you've been made aware of what you receive, how, and that some of it is based on Luna's discretion."

"This is the part of the will you're not allowed to talk about?" Colt asked.

Luna's gaze shot to Dex's, the silent exchange a reminder that she couldn't tell Colt anything about what was on those missing pages.

"Yes. They have nothing to do with the Travers family, but everything to do with the decisions I make." She glanced at Dex, who nodded that her answer was okay and not too revealing.

"There you have it," Colt said. "Now get out."

"We aren't done here." Bea turned to Dex and addressed him directly. "Can we force her to sell?"

Dex shook his head. "No. That is her decision alone, though it goes against everything Wayne wanted."

"The man is dead, who cares what he wanted." Bea's cold tone made even Simon and Josh wince. A trace of desperation flitted through Bea's eyes. Why?

"You're talking about their father." Luna waved her hand toward the two men who reminded her so much of Wayne in looks, but not in personality. She caught glimpses of Wayne in Simon sometimes, but those moments were few and far between, lost under the illusion he created that he wanted to be at the ranch. He still hadn't convinced her. She wasn't sure he ever could, but she held out hope that he would prove her, and Wayne, wrong.

"Yes, their father. Not yours. The ranch is their home. It's their birthright. Not yours. You don't deserve any of it," Bea retorted.

"And you do?" Luna shot back.

"Wayne wouldn't have the ranch if it hadn't been for me letting him use my half of our inheritance from our parents to buy the land."

"He left you quite a bit of money. More money than I'm sure you've ever seen."

"It's not enough," Bea shouted, the desperation coming back into her eyes. Just greed? It seemed like something more, something deeper?

Luna spread her arms wide. "Here is your chance. Tell me why you need more. Make me understand why the half a million you and your husband received and the money that went to your girls isn't enough."

"You don't deserve it."

"Believe me, sometimes I feel the same way, but that is no reason for me to give it to you when Wayne wanted me to have it. So give me a valid reason. One that tells me you deserve it."

"You're not going to give us anything." The barely restrained rage in Bea's voice told Luna the woman's anger clouded her judgment and made it impossible for her to reason. She didn't see the opportunity in front of her.

Luna glanced at Dex, who remained passive beside her. He knew Luna had the power to pay out more money, though no one else in the room did.

"One reason," Luna prompted, giving Bea another chance to make her case.

"Because it's the right thing to do," Josh spoke up when his aunt remained silent. "You don't want the ranch. Not really. So sell it and pay us."

"Just because you want it doesn't make it the right thing to do."

"So you refuse?" Bea asked.

"I won't sell. I've told you why. Wayne told you why the survival of the ranch meant so much to him. This is the last time I discuss this subject with any of you. Keep coming after me, I will hold you accountable by every means at my disposal, including having you arrested. It ends now. Stay away from me and the ranch."

Colt glared at each and every one of them, backing up her words with the threat of having to deal with him if they did anything to her again.

Bea snatched her designer bag off the table, the strap swinging out and hitting her husband across the arm. She didn't even apologize by word or a look to the poor man.

Simon and Josh followed their aunt and uncle out.

"Well that was fun," Colt said, pulling Luna into a hug.

She held him tight, taking in his strength and comfort. She didn't like that this meeting had been necessary, but she hoped the Traverses understood now that she wasn't going to put up with their shit anymore.

Colt released her and stepped away to introduce himself to Dex. The men exchanged handshakes behind her. She stared out the window as the Traverses stood in the parking lot, talking among themselves. She hoped they weren't plotting more mischief, or worse.

"So, let me guess, those missing pages say Luna can pay out more money to the family if she wants. That's why she asked them to give her a good reason, right?" Colt asked.

Luna caught Dex's reflection in the window as he gave a noncommittal shrug.

Luna turned to face the two gentlemen, not surprised

Colt understood her motives for pushing the Traverses.
If they'd only see she didn't intend to keep everything.

Colt turned to her. "So, are you going to give them
more money?"

"No." She turned to Dex. "What did you think of
all that?"

"I hope they got the message that any more threats
or mischief will come with serious consequences.
They've gotten away with it so far, but the cops come
up with actionable evidence and they'll have to answer.
They're desperate to get you to sell, but you made your
point that they've gotten quite a bit of money, so why
do they need more?"

"It's not about needing more, they just want it," Colt
summed up what the whole mess boiled down to. "So
tell me, Dex, is it really possible for Luna to lose the
ranch?"

"Does it matter?"

"Not to me, but it mattered to Wayne. He entrusted
the ranch to her. She's the perfect person to oversee it."

"Why?" Dex asked, taking as much of an interest in
Colt's take on things as she did.

"Because she cares about the ranch, and even those
self-centered, greedy Traverses. If they'd given her
one good reason for more money, she'd have given it
to them. They're so obsessed with getting everything
they can, they don't see that she's willing to work with
them, not against them. Wayne would have been just
as generous and understanding, but like her, he didn't
want to feed their greed."

"Wayne entrusted Luna to make sound decisions."

"She oversees the ranch. You oversee her, is that it?"

"It's my job to remain objective and ensure she up-
holds the terms of the will."

"Especially the terms she's not allowed to talk about. The family finds out about those, they'll cause more trouble, maybe even make her forfeit the ranch, is that it?"

"I've said all I can on the matter." Dex walked to Luna and laid his hand on her shoulder. "You handled that very well."

"Thank you for doing this on such short notice."

"I'll see you next week." Dex left, leaving her standing in the middle of the conference room with Colt.

"Why are you seeing him next week?"

"Huh? Oh, we have an appointment every Wednesday."

"To discuss ranch business?" Colt eyed her, not acting like himself at all.

She held up her hands. "What else would we discuss?"

"Dinner plans?"

"Why would you say that? He's my lawyer."

"He'd like to be more, judging by the way he looked at you and touched your arm."

"You're being ridiculous."

"Am I?"

Luna closed the distance between them physically, hoping to do so emotionally as well. "Yes." She went up on tiptoe, wrapped her arms around his neck, and kissed him softly. "I have a thing for a certain sexy cowboy."

"Good, because I've got a thing for you. Want to go out to dinner? You still owe me that beer," he teased, because they'd never actually gone and done that, though they'd shared dozens of meals together.

"Actually, I need you to do something for me that can't wait. Will you check on Rocco? Ed says we don't need to call the vet, but I think that horse is getting worse."

"Ed knows what he's doing."

"He takes care of the horses very well. You've given him advice for doing things better and turned Ed on to some new innovations for their care and feeding. All I'm saying is that maybe you have a different opinion than him on Rocco. I trust your judgment and want to be sure we're doing everything we can to keep Rocco healthy. I don't like that he's the fourth horse to come up sick since I took over."

"Do you think Simon has something to do with it?"

"I'm not sure. Ed assures me that it's not unusual for something to spread through a stable. Maybe I'm being overprotective of them, but with everything else that's happened, my suspicions are piqued."

"You're doing what you should do. Questioning why the herd is taking ill before it becomes a bigger problem is smart. I'll check things out. Did you make any changes to the food supply? Go with a different kind of grain or grass? Get it from a different supplier?"

"We grow a lot of it on the ranch, as you know. Other than that, nothing has changed. Why? Do you think they need something different?"

"Not necessarily. We do things a bit differently at our place. Nothing you do at Rambling Range would make the horses sick."

"If you have suggestions that will improve the overall health of the horses, please, speak up."

"I don't want to step on Ed or Toby's toes. They run your place. Not me."

"I run the ranch. I'm asking for your help and your expertise. The men go about their business and do it well, but they're stuck in routine and doing what they've always done. Things change, and so should the running of the ranch and how we care for the animals and land.

I've already talked to Artie about trying out some new organic fertilizers and looking into some new irrigation systems."

"You did?"

"I think I'm turning into a farm girl. At least, I understand that business a lot better. It's easier than the horses and cattle."

Colt chuckled. "You probably make more on the farming side of things than the cattle."

"That's a fact. What do you think about bringing Tanner to the ranch and putting him to work with the horses?"

"I'd start him with the orphaned calves. He'd probably like to baby them."

Luna smiled, thinking of her brother with the fuzzy little cows. "You're right. He'd like that."

"You need to get him a dog."

"It's on my list, but first I need to see if he can live and thrive at Rambling Range."

"Where are you going to put him?"

"The little cabin across the way from the stables. Ed said he used to live in it before he and his wife got their own place years ago. I need to clean it out and get it ready to be lived in again, but I think it could work. Why?"

"No reason. The cabin is perfect if he can live on his own."

"You don't want him in the house with us?" The edge to her voice made one side of Colt's mouth dip in a half frown.

"I don't want you to take on more than you've already got on your plate with the ranch. You haven't even begun to put together the equine therapy program."

"I'm sorry. I know you picked out all those horses for us to go look at, and we never got the chance."

"Several of them are still available."

"You checked?"

"Yes, because I want to see you have what you want, too."

She wrapped her arms around his neck and hugged him close. "That's really sweet. I actually contacted several families today. So far, I've got confirmation from four families that will send their kids once I have the program up and running."

"That's fantastic. And honey, I don't care if your brother moves into the house. That's not the issue. You're so overwhelmed with the Traverses breathing down your neck, the ranch, and us."

"Us?" She leaned back in his arms. "Nothing about us overwhelms me. Us is what I hold on to when things get crazy."

Colt leaned down and pressed his forehead to hers. "Good answer."

CHAPTER 23

Luna arrived back at the ranch ahead of Colt. He had to stop off in town at the feed store to pick up some supplies for his ranch. She needed to finish her work from this morning, so she headed for the stables and the office there, where she'd spent the morning going over accounts and supplies with Ed. She'd take her laptop back to the house and finish while Colt checked on Rocco, then they could have dinner together and maybe watch a movie and cuddle on the couch.

She spotted Simon's car parked under a tree to the left of the stables. So he'd come back to work after their meeting at Dex's office. She hoped that meant he planned to see things through to the end. At least one of the Traverses meant to earn his place here. She hoped that thought wasn't all wishful thinking.

The stables were quiet and empty. She stopped by Rocco's stall before heading to the back office to retrieve her laptop.

"Hey, baby. Colt's on his way to check on you." Rocco stood in the middle of the stall, legs spread wide, looking miserable. "He'll take good care of you, baby." *The way he takes such good care of me.*

A strange rustling came from the office down the

way. She turned and headed down the aisle, calling out, "Ed? Are you in there?"

Simon burst through the doorway and stared at her. "You're back."

"I just got here." She narrowed her eyes. "What are you doing?"

"Ed asked me to grab Bailey's bridle. He said he left it in the office."

Luna eyed Simon and closed the distance between them. She snagged the bridle off the table outside the office door and held it out. "Here it is."

"Hey, look at that." Simon played it off, but she didn't quite believe he'd only been in the office looking for a bridle.

Luna glanced at the desk and noted her laptop had been shifted slightly so the screen pointed to the back wall and not toward the chair. He might have bumped it by accident, or turned it so whatever he'd been doing couldn't be seen by anyone passing the doorway.

She'd spent the morning going over the bills and accounts. Who knew a ranch generated so many spreadsheets? Crop reports, breeding information for the cows and horses, and supplies. It went on and on.

What was he up to? What could he possibly want to see on her laptop? Most of the information was innocuous. If anything interested Simon at all, it would be the money side of things. But how could knowing how much money the ranch generated help him in any way? If anything, it only proved that his working the next eighteen months and getting half was more lucrative in the long run than taking a payout.

She looked Simon right in the eye. He didn't flinch or look guilty about anything. While Josh let his feelings show on his face, in his eyes, and the words he spewed, Simon played things close to the vest. She wouldn't want to play poker with him.

"Looks like you got what you wanted." She wished she knew exactly what that was besides the bridle he used to cover his reason for being here.

His gaze hardened on her, but he quickly dismissed whatever thought darkened his gaze. With one eyebrow raised and a smirk on his lips, he said, "I always do in the end." He headed for the door, his arrogance on full display in his confident stride.

"Not this time," she muttered to herself.

"What's that, honey?" Colt asked from behind her.

She stopped glaring at the door Simon left through and turned to Colt. "Nothing. Thanks for coming over."

"Sure thing. Want to check out Rocco with me?"

"No. I'll leave him to you. I've got something else I need to check out." She went into the office and grabbed the laptop off the desk, scolding herself for leaving it out here in the first place and not shutting it down. She'd left herself wide open, and Simon took advantage. What he wanted to exploit, she didn't know, but she aimed to find out.

"Come up to the house after you check on my babies." She kissed Colt, then walked down the aisle with him to Rocco's stall door. "I'm worried about him."

"I'm worried about you. Everything okay? You look upset."

"I'm fine. I just have a lot on my mind."

"You handled yourself really well today. I'm proud of you for standing up for yourself and this place."

It meant so much to her to hear him say that. She appreciated him coming over and helping her with the horses and checking on her crews. She hoped they worked together for a long time to come. She hoped they forged a true partnership in every way. She wished she knew how to make that happen and work for the rest of their lives.

Colt stared over the stall gate at the poor, listless sorrel quarter horse standing with his front and back legs stretched out, indicating pain in his abdomen. Poor Rocco. At least he wasn't laid out on the floor in the straw, but still, all his symptoms indicated he wasn't feeling that great. His dull coat and labored breathing bothered Colt. Rocco's ears perked up when he spotted Colt, though his eyes weren't alert and clear, and he kept his head down. The poor guy appeared tired, though he'd been kept in his stall all day.

"You don't look so good, my friend."

Colt unlatched the gate and stepped inside. He ran his hand over Rocco's sweaty shoulder. "Got a fever, huh, big guy." Colt placed his hand over Rocco's thumping heart and counted out the beats. He didn't need to count the full minute to determine Rocco's racing heart indicated the animal was sick and in distress.

"Okay, Rocco, what's the deal. You've got my girl worried."

Daisy, two stalls down, banged on her gate and whinnied.

"Your girl is worried about you, too. She hasn't seen you in the pasture in a while, and that's just not like you to stay away from your mares."

Rocco's ears didn't even twitch.

"How's it going, Colt?" Ed asked from the open gate.

"Not good, judging by the way this guy is acting."

"He seemed better this morning, but after he ate . . ." Ed shook his head.

"What did you feed him?"

"Same as always, though he only ate about a quarter of his usual amount. He drank some water. He's just not right."

"Does he eat the same feed as the other sick horses?"

"Yeah. Some of the horses get a different mix, depending on their needs and likes. More or less grain and the same with the grasses, depending."

Colt walked over to the bin of grain. Out in the open, anyone could get to it. Great for convenience when feeding the horses, but it also meant anyone could tamper with the food. Colt pulled the lid off the bucket and stared in, not noticing anything out of the ordinary in the appearance of the food. No visible mold.

"What are you thinking?" Ed asked, eying him.

Colt pulled out a scoop of the grains and set it on the shelf next to the stall. "Dump this whole bin. Wash it out with soap and water real good before you put new food in it. Change over Rocco to nothing but oats and rice bran. Change out his water every two hours. Bag up some fresh manure and urine if you can collect it. Call the vet. I think someone poisoned Rocco and the other horses who got sick."

"You don't think it's just some illness or a bad batch of grain?"

"That's why I want the vet to check the stool, urine, and take some blood from Rocco. I want it all tested for poison. I'm going to send the food to the sheriff and have them test it, too."

"Man, I suspected this was something more than an illness that needed to run its course, but I blew it off because I didn't want to believe they'd hurt the animals. I mean, what does that change? Nothing. It's senseless."

"Just goes to show whoever did this has no conscience." Colt shook his head, stared in at Rocco, read the discomfort and pain in the horse's sad eyes, and swore. "We'll get you better, buddy." He turned back to Ed. "Throw out any food that's open. Send someone to buy new stuff if any of the bags of grain even look like they've been opened or tampered with. I'll call Deputy Foster and let him know we're sending in a sample of the grain. Have one of the guys drive it down there."

"On it." Ed's gaze fell to his boots. He shuffled his feet, then looked back up. "I'm sorry, Colt. I should have tossed out the food the minute I even suspected it caused the horses to get sick."

"You thought they caught a bug. We all did. Maybe that's what it is and I'm just being overly wary. Until we know for sure, we side with caution. Get Rocco started on that rice bran. Let's see if we can't clear his system. If you can't get him to eat, see if you can entice him with some apples." Colt studied the inside of the stables. "Until this is over and settled with the Travers family, let's get someone to stay overnight in the stables and watch over the horses. I don't want anyone sneaking in here, contaminating the food again."

"On it."

"I'm headed back up to the house to tell Luna about what we suspect. Let me know when the vet arrives. I'd like to be here while he examines Rocco. If Rocco gets any worse, I want to know about it."

"You will. Please tell Luna I'm sorry."

"Nothing to be sorry about, Ed. You take real good care of these animals. Not your fault someone *might* have tried to hurt them."

"Still, I don't like all this seedy, underhanded business."

"Neither do I." Colt vowed to put a stop to it.

CHAPTER 24

Colt walked in the front door and shouted, "Luna!"

"In here," she called from the office.

He turned right and walked through the entry and stood in the open office doorway, staring at the beautiful woman sitting behind the desk, a huge window behind her, the light making her dark hair shine. She held the phone to her ear with one hand and pecked at the laptop keyboard with the other.

"Okay, got it. Do you see that on your end?"

Colt moved closer, standing at the side of the desk. He looked down at the screen. The cursor moved and someone typed in several lines of code that looked completely alien to him. "Did you let someone into your computer?"

"Hold on," Luna said to the person on her phone. "Hey, how's Rocco?"

"I called the vet. You were right, he's not getting better fast enough. I also ordered the guys to throw out all the open grains."

"Why?"

"That's all Ed's been feeding Rocco."

"You think the food is spoiled?"

"Tainted might be more accurate."

Luna drew her lips into a tight line, anger flashing in her eyes. "I wouldn't doubt it."

He couldn't believe she agreed so easily.

"Did you keep some of the food? I'd like to send it to be tested. There must be a lab or something that can tell us if someone put something in the food."

"I kept a small amount. One of the guys will take it to the sheriff's office and see if they can help us out."

"Great. I'm almost done here."

"What are you doing?"

Luna sighed. "Giving in to my suspicious nature."

That didn't really answer his question.

"Yes, Amal? Are we all set?" Luna listened, watching Amal type in several more lines of code, run it, and close out the screen. "Thank you. You'll let me know if anything comes of this."

Luna said her goodbye to Amal, her bank's IT girl, who'd just put an alarm on Luna's accounts, and stared up at him. "Why do you look like you've just run a mile?"

He swiped his hand across his brow. "Because I had to jack up my truck and change the tire."

"What? Did you run over something?"

"One might think I ran over the nail and it started a slow leak. Judging by the angle, I'd say someone hammered it into the tire, but that's just my guess, my own suspicious nature."

"Probably Josh. He's a menace."

"I peg Simon for poisoning the horses."

"I've got one or both of them for the rotten food, ruined carpet, and the load of horse shit."

"But which of them is responsible for the dead rats? That's the guy we need to worry about, because whoever would do something like that is dangerous."

"I still can't believe you didn't tell me about that." Luna tried to guess who did what, but really any one of them could have done any one thing. She didn't believe only one person was responsible for all of it. It seemed they were all involved, even if they weren't working together. "I think Aunt Bea is hiding something."

"Yeah? You think Aunt Bea is hiding a mean streak and might pull a knife out of her overpriced handbag and go all gangland slaying on you?"

Luna wanted to laugh it off, but shook in her seat with a fake shiver instead. "It seems implausible that dignified, designer Aunt Bea would get her hands dirty, but she seems angry enough to push Simon and Josh to do these things."

Colt didn't look the least convinced. "I don't know if we'll ever know who did what. The cops can't seem to pin anything on any of them." He pinched the front of his shirt and pulled it out, peeling it from his wet skin. "We have to stay here for dinner. I'm all sweaty. I need a shower and a change of clothes, which I don't have here."

"Yes, you do." She leaned over to check out his legs. "The jeans are clean. You'll find that black thermal you left here the other night hanging in the closet along with a Led Zeppelin T-shirt you left on the bathroom floor the other morning. I washed both."

"You did?"

"Now what kind of girlfriend would I be if I didn't pick up after my man and wash his clothes?" The irony in her voice made Colt smile.

"Well, since you did, that makes you the best girlfriend I've ever had."

"Well, at least I stand out against the many."

Colt didn't miss the wry tone. He spun her chair so

she faced him, then planted his hands on the armrests and leaned down close as she sank back into the chair and stared up at him. "You don't compare to anyone, because I've never met anyone like you. Until you called yourself my girlfriend a moment ago, I never thought of you as that."

"I'm sorry. That was presumptuous."

"No it wasn't. We've been sleeping together for weeks, sharing our lives together." He pressed down on his hands then back up again, shaking her chair, frustrated she didn't get it, and in fact had backtracked on the status of their relationship.

"I haven't labeled you my girlfriend because you mean more to me than that. It doesn't seem enough. Do you understand what I mean?" He really needed her to get it, because he was having a hard time putting it into words.

Her hand came up and rested on his cheek. "Yes. I understand. We've woven our lives together so easily." She held up her hand, palm up. He pressed his palm to hers and they linked fingers. She squeezed his hand. "Our lives have come together just like this. It works without us having to really try. I like being with you."

"I like being here with you." He stood in front of her, pulled a box out of his back pocket with his free hand, let loose the hand he held, and turned it over. He set the box on her palm. "I meant to give you this tonight at dinner, but it only seems right I give it to you right now."

Tears glistened in her eyes. "You bought me a present?"

"I'm not great at the present thing. Ask my brothers. But I saw this in a shop in town and thought of you." He'd never bought a gift for a woman. Sure, he'd sent flowers, or bought them at the store and given them to a date. But a real gift. That meant something.

His gut tightened and his heart thrashed in his chest with anticipation of her opening the box. He wished she'd hurry up. He watched her face, hoping she'd like it.

The tears spilled over her eyes and rolled down her cheeks. She pulled a bracelet from the box and held it up, draped over her fingers. The light blue stones sparkled in the light.

"They're aquamarines. The same color as your eyes."

"Colt, it's beautiful. The butterflies are perfect."

Each blue stone was separated by a sterling silver disk with a butterfly stamped into the metal.

"You like them, right? You've got the tattoo."

"I love them. I love this. Thank you."

"Okay, then stop crying." He didn't know what to do to make her stop. He hated seeing the tears even if she did seem happy about the gift.

He slipped the bracelet from her fingers, unhooked the catch, wrapped it around her wrist, and secured the clasp again. "You may think I have a wild, reckless heart, maybe I do, but all I know is, it belongs to you." He brought her hand to his mouth and kissed the back of it.

Luna's eyes shined and filled with emotion. She stood and walked past him, pulling him around to follow her by his hand. She looked over her shoulder and gave him a sexy grin. "You know we're not going to dinner, right?"

"We're not?"

"No. I have to thank you properly for my gift and those sweet words."

"Oh, well, if you insist."

She turned, grabbed him by the front of the shirt, kept

walking backward, that sweet, seductive smile on her lips, dragging him down the hall to their room. "I do."

He smiled back at her, enjoying seeing her this carefree and happy. If it took her mind off everything weighing her down, he'd bring her a gift every damn day.

"You still owe me that beer, you know?"

"I'll pay up one day. Swear."

"You keep saying that."

They entered the bedroom. She backed up until her legs hit the bed. She fell backward, pulling him down on top of her by his shirt. They bounced on the mattress. She wrapped one arm around his neck. Her other hand rested on his face. She smiled up at him lying atop her. "First things first." Her lips pressed to his, her tongue sliding along his bottom lip before slipping inside to slide along his. He kissed her back and lost himself in her flowery scent and sweet taste. By the time they tossed aside the last of their clothes, he was desperate to have her. Cradled between her thighs, he stared down into her sparkling blue eyes and thrust into her. Her body gripped his, and it was all he could do not to lose himself in her right then and there, but he held back the need gnawing at his insides and gave himself over to loving her as the sun sank outside and his heart brightened with the light she lit in him.

Her eyes fell closed as his body moved over hers and her nails bit into his back. Her face softened. The sigh she let loose when her body tightened around his rippled through him, calling him to join her in that blissful high. He followed eagerly, thrusting deep and letting go of everything but one thought. *She's mine.*

He meant it in so many ways. His woman. His partner. The woman he wanted beside him to live and laugh and work and play.

They headed for the shower, where he took his time worshipping all those curves, which led them back to the bed, where he made love to her slow and easy into the night. They missed dinner and didn't eat until they shared an omelet and coffee at the breakfast table, watching the sun come up over the trees.

"I gotta get back, but I'll see you later tonight."

"You better."

He leaned down and kissed her long and soft, lingering over her lips, taking his time saying goodbye because he didn't want to leave her.

She reached up and held her hand to his rough jaw. "Thank you, Colt. For my gift. Last night. You being here with me."

The sweet sentiment in her eyes touched him. "I love being here with you." He took her hand and kissed her palm, then held her hand to his chest over his heart. "Let's talk tonight about me, you, this place, my place, and the fact I hate leaving you each morning."

"I don't want you to go."

"Me either. I'd like to apply for Toby's job if one of the others hasn't already talked to you about taking his place."

"They all talk about you taking his place."

"What?" Surprised, he stood and held her hand in front of him. "You're serious."

"You are the most qualified. You've been running a ranch since you were a kid."

"Rory runs that place."

She tilted her head and eyed him.

"Okay, well, we run it together," he amended.

"You could run that place on your own with your eyes closed. You three are interchangeable at that place. You each have your strengths, but you can do anything on that spread."

"I guess. But doesn't Rich or Artie or Ed want to move up into Toby's position?"

"I talked to each of them about it privately. They're all happy doing what they're doing and don't want the responsibility of taking on overseeing the whole operation. It's a big job. While they're all experts at their own areas, none of them knows enough about all the ranch businesses to oversee it the way Toby has all these years with Wayne. So, if you're interested, I can give you a glowing recommendation to the owner. Toby will back you, too. She's tough though. She wants the right person. Someone who's in it for the long haul."

"So, a lifetime kind of thing, is that it?"

All joking aside, she turned serious. "Think about it, Colt. I'm not playing around with this place. It's not a phase, or some hobby. I'm dedicated to being the caretaker of this ranch for the rest of my life. It's business. I'm learning, but I need someone I can rely on and trust. Someone who wants to build their life here, too. Our relationship may complicate your decision and whether you really want to work here or not. I don't need someone for a few months or a couple of years. I need someone who's in it for the long haul, good times and bad.

"If things don't work out for us . . . working together may not be wise if you're not sure."

"I just don't want to be one more person in your life who you think only wants something from you."

"I don't believe that's true. Not at all." Her gaze fell away, but she mustered her courage and looked back at him. "I am concerned that while this place will always appeal to you, I may not."

He tried to reassure her, but she held up a hand to stop him before he said a word.

"Things are great right now, but let's face it, you've never had a meaningful long-term relationship. Neither have I really, if you consider that my relationship with Billy was built on a lot of wishful thinking and not a lot of reality.

"Take your time to think about what I'm offering, considering the fact there's a lot at stake. It's a big change for you, leaving your family ranch to work here, taking on a hell of a lot more responsibility."

"If you don't think I'm up to it—"

"I think you'd be fantastic at it. I think you want it but you're afraid to ask for it. Maybe you even think it's more than you can handle. I don't believe that. I believe in you. I trust you. I guess you have to decide if you're ready to change your whole life to take it."

CHAPTER 25

Colt stood on the porch of Sadie's old house next to her and Rory. Their grandfather stood next to him. Ford should arrive any moment for his surprise, but all Colt thought about was the conversation he had with Luna. Like everything in life, he felt as if he stood at a fork in the road. Make one decision, his life went one way. Make another and it went down the other path. Which one did he want?

"You got home a little later than usual this morning," Sadie commented, breaking up the silence.

"Luna and I got caught up in a talk about something." Their conversation played on repeat in his head.

"Everything all right?" His grandfather turned to him.

"Fine. She offered me the ranch manager job. Toby's leaving next month."

"What?" Rory eyed him, giving Colt no sense of how he really felt about the news. "You didn't tell me you were thinking of leaving the ranch to work for her."

The guilt rose up in Colt. He hated to betray his brother and all he'd done for Colt since their parents died.

"When she inherited the ranch and I found out Toby wanted to retire, I considered it, but dismissed it when things between Luna and me got more serious, complicating things."

"Well, I'd say it's damn serious if you're thinking of working for her," Rory commented.

Sadie remained conspicuously quiet.

Colt sucked it up and spit out the truth, because he owed that much to Rory and a hell of a lot more he couldn't repay. He could at least be straight and hope Rory understood. "I'm not thinking about it—I'm taking the job. I hope I figure out a way to keep it and her, because I wouldn't be able to work there and see her, knowing I fucked it all up."

Rory held up a hand. "Wait a second. Why are you the one to blame for this imaginary breakup?"

"Of course it will be me. She's an amazing woman. I'd be a fool to walk away from her."

Sadie's whole face lit up with a huge smile. She turned away, trying to hide it. Rory laughed outright.

His grandfather smacked Colt on the back. "Well, son, don't be a damn fool. Marry that girl."

"Oh please. Right. Just ask her to marry me after we've been together for what, a few weeks."

"You've known her a good long time," his grandfather pointed out.

"If you love her and it's what you want, why not?" Rory asked. "Sadie and I hadn't known each other long when I asked her."

"Sadie, help me out here. She's not going to marry me."

Sadie tilted her head and stared at him, all humor gone from her face. "Why not?"

"Because it's ludicrous. She just inherited a fortune and a ranch she's still learning how to run. She doesn't want to get married. Not right now."

"How do you know unless you ask her?" Sadie's eyes turned serious and direct on him. "Yes, she's got a bunch of stuff, but it doesn't make her smile or light up the way she does when she sees you, or when someone mentions your name. She went after you all those years ago. She kissed you. She felt like she pushed you away, until you finally cleared the air. She wanted you then. She wants you now. She offered you a job, but what she was really asking you for was so much more. Wasn't it?"

Luna's words echoed in his head. *I don't need someone for a few months or a couple of years. I need someone who's in it for the long haul, good times and bad.* "Yes," he admitted.

"It's a brave thing she did, laying her heart out there for you to see, asking if you want the same thing she wants. If you're not sure, I suggest you take the time you need before you make any decisions or changes," Sadie advised. "She's always had to do things for herself and stand on her own. Look at her standing up to the Traverses. She's taken on that huge ranch and a life she didn't ask for or expect. She will do it on her own because that's who she is. But I admire her strength and courage to ask you to be her partner in that. Not because she can't do it but because having you beside her to support her means she's not standing all alone anymore."

Colt imagined that growing up with a brother with special needs meant that Luna had to take care of herself most of the time.

"Her parents love her like crazy, but they sacrificed putting her first for Tanner's sake. Luna deserves to be first in your relationship, Colt. If the job is more important to you than she is, walk away from her, take

the job, and keep your friendship with her. Give her a
chance to find someone who—"

"That's never going to fucking happen," he snapped,
letting his anger show at the very thought of someone
else with Luna. "I'm sorry, sis. I didn't mean to talk to
you that way."

"She's my best friend, Colt. I want the best for her. I
think that's you, but if you don't . . ."

"The job is second," he assured her. "I want it because I want to be with her."

"Since you're clear on that, let the rest happen when
it will," his grandfather said, giving him a break for
once.

"We need to talk about you transitioning to Rambling Range." Rory stuck his hands in his pockets and
stared at the ground.

"If you want me to stay . . ."

Rory shook his head. "No. That's not it. You have a
chance to have what I found with Sadie. I want you to
take it. I want you to be happy. It's just that with you
and Ford gone, the ranch won't be the same." Rory's
words echoed the thoughts running through Colt's
mind. Nothing was the same since Rory had met Sadie
and Colt had fallen for Luna. That's life. You grow
up and discover that the family you've always known
changes, expands, and people go their separate ways
but are still tied by family bonds. Colt held on to that
because he didn't want to, wouldn't, lose his connection to his brothers.

"No, it won't be, but we'll still see each other all the
time. Besides, you're going to be so busy with your new
wife and baby, you won't miss us at all." It took Colt
off guard to realize he'd made his decision. He'd said it
out loud already, but it really had taken hold and solidi-

fied in his mind. He wanted to be with Luna, work at her place, and make a life with her. He couldn't wait. Didn't want to wait another minute.

"Yes, I will." Rory's admission came as a surprise. His brother wasn't one for sharing his feelings. Ever since he and Sadie got together, Rory had softened. He enjoyed life more. He even smiled.

Colt wondered how he'd changed since meeting Luna. He'd settled into his life. He used to run wild, now he ran to her. Nights at the bar, drinking and picking up women, playing cards and pool with his buddies used to be a good time. Now, an evening at home with Luna, watching a movie, going horseback riding, talking about their days and work fulfilled him in a way all that other stuff never did.

"Ford's here," his grandfather announced.

Ford closed his truck door and stared up at the sign they'd hung over the porch.

"Welcome home," Sadie said, echoing the words on the sign.

"What are you talking about?" Ford asked.

Sadie walked down the steps and met Ford on the path. "Well, you're always talking about getting your own place, starting your own ranch. I have this big place and no one working it. So, Ford, you and I are partnering up. You take over this place and run it. I get a small percentage."

Ford looked past Sadie and addressed Rory. "Is she serious?"

"Yes, she is. Tell him, sweetheart."

"I don't want to sell this place, but Rory and I don't want to live here either. His place is at your ranch. So I, we, thought you'd want to move here and start your own ranch."

"You're serious. What about Colt? You're moving in here, too, right? Then Rory and Sadie will have the house to themselves."

"Hey," Granddad said.

"Don't worry, Sammy, you're not going anywhere," Sadie assured him, then turned back to Ford. "This place is just yours. Colt has other plans."

"Moving in with Luna, huh?"

"If she'll have me," he said, waiting for the nerves and his stomach to pitch, his mind to shout, *No!*

Nothing. Not even a single second thought. Just that same sense of ease and need to see her that he got whenever he thought about her. *Yep, it's a done deal.*

"Well, I'll be damned. When you asked me to come over, I thought you needed help fixing something," Ford said.

"Rory, Luna, and I have the house all in order. I hope you like what we've done, but you've got a hell of a lot to fix around here before you really start working this place."

"I can't wait." Ford picked Sadie up and spun her around. "Thank you, sis."

"Hey now, careful with her, she's got precious cargo on board," Rory scolded.

Ford set her down gently, took her hand, and pulled her up the stairs behind him. "Show me what you've done."

Colt stood in the kitchen for the next hour listening to Ford and Rory work out the details of starting a new ranch at Sadie's place. He had to change that in his mind to Ford's place. Ford thrived on a challenge like this. His enthusiasm showed in the smile that hadn't faltered since he arrived.

"Colt, you're too quiet." Ford drew his attention. "Are you sure you don't want in on this?"

"I've made my decision. All I have to do is work out the details with Luna."

"I'm sure you will, but if something changes, I could use your help here."

Colt appreciated the offer, but he'd made up his mind about the job, Luna, and what he wanted for his future.

CHAPTER 26

Colt took the turnoff and sped down the road leading him straight to Luna's place. It had taken some time to drive into Bozeman, find what he wanted, and head home, but the excitement building in his gut and the rapid beat of his heart the closer he got to her told him he'd done the right thing. The only logical thing.

He'd asked her this morning to have a talk tonight. He never expected to have it this late, but he didn't want to go one more night without making her a promise he'd keep the rest of his life.

The stars sparkled overhead. He flipped the black velvet box open again and let the diamond catch the moonlight. It sparkled more brightly than any star in the sky. He wanted to surprise her. Well, asking her to marry him would certainly come as a surprise.

He wondered if she wanted a big or small wedding. What about a long or short engagement? Definitely short. Now that he'd made up his mind to marry her, he wanted her to be his wife immediately. Rory and Sadie's wedding was only two weeks away. Maybe he and Luna could plan something for the month after that. Enough time for her to get a dress and make arrangements, but not too long for him to wait to make her his bride.

Did she really mean it when she said she wanted someone for the long haul—in life and as a partner for the ranch? Maybe she didn't mean for them to make it permanent immediately, but she wanted a life with him.

"Mrs. Kendrick," he said, just as headlights blinded him through the passenger window and a truck slammed into the side of him, T-boning his truck and sending him off the road, down a ditch, and pitching him sideways. The truck rolled and skidded through the dirt, slamming his shoulder and head into the side window. The air bag slammed into his face. Pain exploded through his body and split his head. Blood gushed down his face, turning his vision red before the lights went out.

Luna's cell phone rang, breaking her focus. She rubbed her tired eyes. The computer screen in front of her went blurry after hours of working on the ranch books. She hoped to finish the paperwork, so she could spend all day tomorrow with Colt. They had a lot to discuss, plans to make, things to face if they planned to make a life together here on the ranch.

She smiled at Colt's name on her caller ID and answered. "Hey, honey, where are you?"

"Bleeding in a ditch on a deserted road."

Oh God! All alone.

The rough, whispered voice sent a chill up her spine. The person sounded like some creeper from a horror movie. Not Colt's deep, rich voice that whispered to her in the night.

"What did you do? Where is Colt?"

"Not far. Sell the ranch, or the next time he won't be so lucky."

"You leave him alone," she screamed into the phone, her chest tight with terror. Tears clogged her throat so tightly that she barely sucked in her next breath.

"If you'd done the right thing to begin with, no one would have gotten hurt. His blood is on you."

The caller clicked off and Luna was already on the run for her purse and keys in the kitchen. She dialed 911 on her way out the door to her Jeep.

"Nine-one-one. What is your emergency?"

Luna jumped in her car, stuck the key in the ignition, and slammed her foot on the gas pedal. The car lurched and sped up. "My name is Luna Hill. I need an ambulance out on Round Rock Road."

"Do you have a cross street?"

"Not yet. There's been a car accident. I think someone ran my boyfriend off the road. A white Chevy truck with 'Kendrick Brothers Ranch' on the side. I'm heading out there now. I'll let you know when I find the truck."

"Sending emergency personnel now. Stay on the line."

Luna raced down the long driveway and took the turn onto the road far too quick, her tires squealing on the pavement. Colt had mentioned driving into town, so instead of heading the other way toward his ranch, she went in the opposite direction, hoping she didn't guess wrong. She didn't know how badly he'd been hurt. Her imagination took care of scaring her even more than that ominous call did.

"Please, Colt, hold on. I'm coming."

Her hands shook, so she gripped the steering wheel tighter. The constricting band around her chest made it impossible to breathe. If she lost him . . . It didn't bear thinking about, because the future they talked about earlier was everything she wanted, but only with him.

"Come on," she prayed, slamming her hand on the steering wheel as she drove, searching both sides of the road and finding nothing. Part of her hoped the call was just a joke, but the call came in from Colt's phone, so it had to be real. How else would they have gotten his phone?

She couldn't have missed the accident. One of her Rambling Range trucks blocked both lanes, the front end completely smashed and facing the side of Colt's overturned truck in the ditch.

"Nine-one-one, are you there?" Her voice cracked. "I found him."

"Where is he, ma'am?"

Luna slammed on the brakes and brought her Jeep to a jarring stop, ten feet of rubber skids on the asphalt. She leaped out of the car and ran for Colt's truck but stopped short when she saw the flicker of flames under the hood.

"The truck is on fire. Hurry. Round Rock and Cherry Creek. His truck is on its side in the ditch. Someone hit him and forced him over the edge."

She ran for the back of her Jeep and opened the door. She dragged a canvas bag forward, unzipped it, silently thanked her father for being a bit overprotective and outfitting her car with jumper cables, flares, and, yes, a small fire extinguisher.

"How many people are in the truck?"

"One. I think. I've got a fire extinguisher. I'm going to try to put the fire out before I check on Colt." She stuffed the phone down her front pocket and pulled the safety pin on the nozzle. With the truck hood down, she couldn't get to the fire effectively, so she stuck her fingers through the grill to find the latch. She yanked her fingers back when they burned on the hot metal.

"Shit. Colt! Colt! Can you hear me?"

Nothing. Not even a whimper or moan. She didn't have time to check on him. She needed to put this fire out before it consumed the car and she lost her chance to get him out.

If she could get him out.

The fear built inside of her, but she did what she had to do and tore her shirt off over her head, wrapped it around her fingers, and used it as protection as she un-latched the hood. Extinguisher at the ready, she pushed the hood up. Flames rose in a wave of heat that hit her in the face. She pressed the nozzle and pointed the stream of white stuff directly at the flames. Lucky for her they went out quickly, because the canister emptied way too fast.

"Colt!" she screamed, coughing from the smoke blowing in her face and filling her lungs.

She dropped the canister and climbed up the hot grill, working her way over the front fender to the broken passenger window. She stared in and found Colt crumpled and unconscious on the other side of the truck, his face covered in blood. A big, black duffel bag obscured the rest of his body.

"Colt, honey, can you hear me?" Her voice shook.

He didn't answer. She placed her hands on the window frame and dipped her legs into the truck cab, bracing her feet on a headrest and the steering column. She sank down into the truck cab, tossed the duffel bag into the back extended cab, and reached for Colt's neck with trembling fingers. She touched his warm skin, felt his pulse, and sighed with relief, knowing that his being alive didn't take away from the direness of the situation.

A muffled voice came from the phone in her pocket. She pulled it out.

"Yes, I'm here. I found him. He's unconscious with a very large gash on the side of his head. He's got another bad cut on his shoulder and down his arm. He's lost a lot of blood, but he's got a steady pulse. Um, h-he's n-not w-waking up," she choked out.

"Put pressure on the wounds," the operator advised.

She unwound the shirt from her hand and leaned down, pressing the soft material to Colt's head without moving him. "Come on, Colt. Wake up for me."

"Is he awake?" the operator asked.

"N-no." Tears cascaded down her face and dripped on Colt's cheek. "I can't stop the bleeding."

"Paramedics are on the way. Six minutes out. Keep steady, firm pressure on the wound."

She did and prayed that what little she could do for Colt helped. The scent of roses mixed with the metallic scent of Colt's blood. She didn't understand why until she spotted the dozen red roses stuffed under his legs in the wheel well.

"I'm so sorry. This is all my fault. You have to be okay. You have to. I love you. I'd do anything to keep you safe."

Colt stirred. "Lu-Lu . . . na," he mumbled, then fell back into unconsciousness.

Luna brushed her fingers through Colt's hair. "I'm here, Colt. Help is coming."

Six minutes felt like a lifetime. The quiet in the cab felt like a tomb. The sirens she finally heard in the distance drawing near gave her hope that this ordeal would finally be over. For Colt's sake, she hoped they got him out of the truck quickly and to the hospital where he'd be fine. He had to be fine.

"They're almost here, honey. Hold on. They're coming."

The sirens went off and lights flashed overhead. A man stuck his head over the side of the smashed truck door and stared in the broken window.

"Hey, I'm Scott. How is he?"

"Unconscious. Still bleeding."

"I need to get you out of there so we can help him."

"If I let go of the pressure on his head, it bleeds more."

"Okay. Hold on." Scott disappeared from view, but came back, leaned over the door, and stuck his hand down to her.

She grabbed the thick pad and roll of gauze.

"Change out what you're using with the pad. Wrap the gauze around his head tight to hold it in place and keep pressure on the wound. Do not move his head."

"Got it."

Luna's legs hurt like hell from holding herself in the odd crouched position. She ignored the pain, leaned forward, and pulled her blood-soaked shirt away from Colt's head. The blood still oozed, but not as fast. "The bleeding is slowing down."

"Good."

She did as the paramedic instructed, wrapping Colt's head the best she could in the small space she had to do the job without moving him.

"Great job. Now, I need you to climb out of there so I can get in and put a neck and back brace on him so we can move him."

Luna raised her hands to Scott. "My legs are kinda locked in this position. Can you give me a hand?"

"Sure thing. Hold on." Scott gripped her hands and pulled her up.

Her thighs, calves, and knees burned, but she managed to stand on her feet and grab hold of the window frame and lift herself out. Scott helped her down off the truck and jumped up to take her place inside.

Police arrived just as the other fire paramedic nudged her aside and began helping Scott, sending equipment down to him as Scott called up for it. Their methodical way of doing things eased her mind. They knew what they were doing. They'd get Colt out.

A sheriff's deputy pulled her aside and peppered her with questions she automatically answered, even though her focus remained on the truck and the man she loved more than anything or anyone.

The firemen shut the hood and used a tool to pry the windshield off. They pulled Colt from the truck through the gaping hole, strapped to the backboard, his arms crossed over his chest and bloody shirt. They'd bandaged his left arm and shoulder, but they'd kept the bandages she'd put on his head in place. Blood seeped through the white gauze, making her stomach sour and pitch. She fought back the urge to hurl and held herself tighter, fighting off the shivers that had everything to do with her fear of losing Colt and not the brisk night.

"Miss Hill. We found this in the cab of your Rambling Range truck. Is it yours?"

She stared down at the plastic bag containing Colt's cell phone. "No. It's Colt's. That's how they called me."

"But you don't know for sure who made the call?"

"No. I've given you all their names. Check with Deputy Foster. He'll have the report on the last time they threatened Colt's life." She held her hand out toward the truck. "Look at what they did. They even used my truck to make their point."

"How did they get the keys?"

"We keep them in the office in the stables. We lock

it up at night, but during the day, we're all in and out of there. Anyone could sneak in and take a set."

"You need to be more careful."

She needed to protect Colt from something like this ever happening again.

The paramedics gave her a look when she ran to the back of the ambulance and jumped in. Scott pulled a blanket from a drawer and draped it over her shoulders. For the first time, she realized she didn't have a shirt on and had stood there all this time in nothing but her bra. She gripped the sides of the blanket and held it closed, noticing the blood on her hands. Colt's blood.

She stared down at him strapped to the gurney. A fresh wave of tears filled her eyes and spilled over. Scott took Colt's vitals again. Afraid to ask, but needing to know, she whispered, "How is he?"

"Vitals are stable. He's lost a lot of blood. He's in and out of consciousness, but nonresponsive. We'll have to do a CT scan at the hospital to check for intracranial hemorrhage. Do you know if he's allergic to any medications?"

"I-I don't know. I need to call his brothers."

"Do that," Scott encouraged.

She placed one hand over Colt's and squeezed. She pulled the phone from her pocket and realized she didn't have Rory or Ford's cell numbers, so she called Sadie.

"Hey, Luna, have you talked to Colt?" Sadie answered.

"Sadie, put Rory on the phone right now."

The urgency in her voice made Sadie hesitant. "Luna?"

"Now. Hurry."

"What's up?" Rory's deep voice sounded so much like Colt's.

"First, Colt is alive. We are on the way to the hospital right now. Does he have any allergies to medication?"

"No. What happened?"

"Someone ran him off the road. He's got a major head injury. H-he's unconscious."

"We're on the way. What else do you need to know now?"

She asked Scott.

"Has he had any recent illnesses or injury?"

"No," Rory answered after she put him on speaker.

"Does he take any medications or recreational drugs?" Scott asked, still monitoring Colt.

"No," Rory snapped.

"Has he been drinking tonight?"

"No," Luna answered. "He'd never drink then drive."

"He left here to go do some shopping or something in Bozeman, then he said he was staying at Luna's place. I doubt he stopped off for a beer or anything."

"R-Rory," Colt mumbled, responding to his brother's voice.

"I'm on my way, Colt. You hang in there. I'll be there soon. Luna is with you."

Luna squeezed Colt's hand, a wave of relief washing through her. He held tight back but never opened his eyes. The small show of strength gave her hope he'd be okay.

"I'm here, Colt. You're going to be okay. I'm here."

Colt squeezed her hand tighter. "Stay," he whispered.

She wished she could make that promise and mean it.

CHAPTER 27

Luna sat in the waiting room, her mind and heart in the emergency room with Colt. They wouldn't tell her anything. She wasn't family. She wasn't his wife. She'd filled out as much of the admitting paperwork as she could, but his family would have to complete all the little details she didn't know. The things she hadn't had a chance to learn yet and might not get the chance to if he didn't pull through this.

"Do you know when the truck was stolen?"

She'd almost forgotten the deputy was still standing there, waiting for her to answer another round of questions.

"No."

"And you're sure you can't identify the person who contacted you?"

"I wish I could." The information she believed to be true didn't help her prove a single thing. One of the Traverses tried to kill Colt.

"All this to get you to sell the ranch."

Not really a question, but she nodded just the same, her gaze locked on the doorway, waiting for a doctor or nurse to come and tell her about Colt. She sat on the edge of the chair. Hoping. Waiting. She really needed to hear something soon, or she just might lose her mind sitting in this drab room that smelled of stale coffee and her own desperation.

The Kendricks filed in the doorway, led by a very angry-looking Rory.

"Deputy Foster. You again."

"Nice to see you, too."

Rory crouched in front of Luna, pulled the blanket draped over her back closed, and touched her face. "Luna, what happened?" He kept his voice soft like he spoke to a child. She had to look really bad, to make the gruff man treat her so gently.

Tears gathered in her eyes. "They said they'd hurt him if I didn't sell. I didn't sell, so they hurt him. They hurt him really bad." The tears streamed down her face again, but she didn't care. Her heart throbbed with a piercing pain she thought would never stop. "They hurt him because they knew it would hurt me." She looked Rory in the eye. "I'm sorry."

He took her hand, but she snatched it back, hissing in a swift breath to ease the sting. Rory took her wrist and gently drew her hand back and turned it over, swearing when he saw the raw, blistered skin.

"How did you burn yourself?"

"Truck was on fire. I had to put it out."

Rory and Ford both swore. Sadie took the seat beside her and wrapped an arm around Luna's back. "What happened to your shirt?"

Rory had let go of the blanket. Luna stared down at her light blue bra and the blood smeared across her middle. "I'm covered in Colt's blood," she whispered.

"It's okay. We'll clean you up."

Remembering what Sadie really asked her, she said, "I used my shirt to open the hood and put out the fire, then I used it to stop the bleeding on Colt's head." She turned to Sadie. "It wouldn't stop."

"I think you're in shock." Sadie stood and pulled Luna up by the arm. The blanket fell to the floor at her feet. Rory and Ford and even the detective looked everywhere but directly at her. "Let's go find a nurse to look at your hand. We'll find you something to wear. Ford, go look in the car and see if Rory left a shirt in there or something."

"On it." Ford rushed out ahead of them.

Before Sadie took Luna out of the room, Luna turned back to Rory. "If the doctor comes, you tell him I have to see Colt. Okay? I have to see him."

"You will, Luna. I'll make sure of it."

Luna walked down the hall with Sadie, but not before she heard Deputy Foster say, "She's messed up."

"Sounds like she saved Colt's life."

"She did."

A shiver raced up Luna's spine, thinking of Colt bleeding in that ditch. Luna had only one thought in response to their conversation: Colt wouldn't have needed to be saved if the Traverses had heeded her warning. Now she'd make them pay and keep Colt safe, no matter how much it hurt her to do it.

Colt woke up by degrees, the many aches and pains in his body throbbing along with the beat of his heart. Nothing hurt more than his head. He opened his eyes and blinked against the soft light coming through the mostly closed blinds. Rory sat next to his hospital bed, his arms crossed over his chest, his head bowed, sound asleep. Ford sat on the floor by the windows behind him, back against the wall, in pretty much the same crossed arms pose as Rory. Sadie lay asleep on a cot in front of Ford.

Colt's head felt like someone struck him with an axe and left it lodged in his brain. He tried to think about what happened and how he got here, but nothing shook loose from his throbbing brain except the pain. He raised his hand to his forehead and rubbed at the headache, making it hard to keep his eyes open. He pulled his hand away, making sure he didn't pull the IV line out of his hand, and spotted Luna standing with her back against the wall, staring straight at him.

"Luna." Her name came out on a relieved sigh. When he hadn't seen her right away, he'd thought she wasn't here. But there she was, standing there staring at him with those beautiful blue eyes, though they were filled with worry and a sadness he didn't understand.

She swept her bangs away from her face. He loved it when she did that, but he didn't like the bandage circling her fingers and palm.

Why the hell was she wearing a man's shirt?

"Honey, what happened to your hand?"

Rory leaned forward and put his hand on Colt's arm. "Man, you're awake. How do you feel?"

"Like shit. Everything hurts."

"You took a pretty good beating to your left side."

Colt hadn't even tried to move his left arm, his shoulder hurt so badly. He felt the bruising across his chest where the seat belt caught him.

It all came back to him. "Shit. Someone hit me with their truck. I don't know how they didn't see me."

"They did it on purpose." Luna didn't move from where she propped herself against the wall.

"What?"

"We'll talk about it later," Rory said, pulling a sleepy

Sadie into his lap. "Right now, you need to rest. You've got a concussion to go with the nasty cut on your head. Your arm's been stitched up in several places. The bruised ribs from the seat belt will take the longest to heal. Meanwhile, enjoy the pain meds."

While the pain encompassed most of Colt's body, the distance Luna kept from him hurt the most. He held his right hand out to her. "Luna, honey, come here. What happened to your hand?"

She pressed her lips together and closed her eyes, fighting off tears that came anyway. She bounced off the wall and finally came to him, taking his left hand gently in her right one, pressing something against his palm.

He didn't understand the pain in her eyes or the tremble in her lips, but it made his chest tight and his own eyes water. Something was terribly wrong.

"I love you."

The softly spoken words stunned him. She actually loved him. Until that moment, he hadn't understood how much he wanted to hear her say it. How much he wanted her to mean it.

"I am so sorry this happened. More sorry than I can possibly say." She bent her head, fighting off her emotions, then raised it and looked him right in the eye. "They won't stop. But I'm going to find a way to make them pay for what they've done. Until then, do not call me. Do not come to the ranch. Stay away from me," she choked out, squeezing his hand closed around whatever she put inside of it. "I'm going to finish this on my own, and you are going to let me, because I can't live each and every day knowing they're coming after you to get to me. I hope when this is over, we find our way back to each other again, but I can't take the chance I lose you forever. Please, Colt, for me, do as I ask. Stay away." She turned to Rory. "Keep him home. Keep him safe. Please." She walked right out of the room.

"Luna," Colt called after her, but she didn't even turn back, and the door automatically closed. He opened his hand and stared at the butterfly bracelet he gave her. "Luna!"

Rory stood and pressed a hand on his shoulder to keep him from sitting up. "Try not to move too much. You'll only hurt yourself more."

"How can I possibly hurt more than I already do watching her walk out of here like that? What the fuck is going on?" He turned to his family and saw nothing but regret. "Sadie, go get her. Bring her back here."

Tears ran down Sadie's face. She pressed her lips together. "I'm sorry. I can't."

"Please," he begged, but no one moved to run after the woman who showed him he had a heart, then ripped it right out of his chest. "What the hell is wrong with you guys? Go get her." No one moved. "Fine. I'll go get her." He tried to sit up, winced against the pain and wave of dizziness, and gave up way too easily when Rory held him down again.

"Stop. You're in no shape to go anywhere."

"Goddamnit, Rory, I can't just let her walk out of here like that. I need to fix this."

"She did this for your own damn good, and I agree with her."

That took the starch right out of Colt. He fell back on the bed, stunned his brother would say such a thing when he had to know how much Luna meant to him. Why wasn't Rory backing him up on this?

"Why is Luna running across the parking lot crying?" Granddad asked, walking into the room.

"I'd like an answer to that very question." Colt

pinned Rory with a sharp gaze, feeling every bit as dev-
astated as Sadie looked, with her arms wrapped around
her middle, her brows drawn together in deep concern
for her friend. Him. The situation he didn't understand.
"Start talking," he ordered Rory.

"The car accident wasn't an accident at all. She didn't
do what they wanted. They threatened you before, and
they made good on it this time."

"What?"

"They tried to kill you to make her sell the ranch. If
she refuses, they'll come after you again."

"So, what? She's going to sell?"

"No. She won't let them win. So she's going back
to the ranch. You will stay clear of her from now on,"
Rory ordered.

"The hell I will."

"Do you want to die?" Rory shouted, his anger getting the better of him. "Do you want to give them another shot at killing you?"

"I want my life with her."

"She made up her mind. She wants you out of the
picture until the cops arrest them."

"I'm not leaving her there a sitting duck. I'll change
her mind."

"No, you won't."

Colt opened his mouth to convince Rory, but Rory
stopped him with his next words. "They called her
from the accident. They told her what they'd done and
that if she didn't sell, they'd kill you next time."

Colt couldn't imagine how she felt receiving that
call. She must have been so scared. The bastards terror-
ized and threatened her. He'd kill them for that alone.

"She found you on the side of the road. She saved
your life."

"Is that how she hurt her hand?"

"The truck was on fire. She put it out, burned herself in the process."

"You tell me all this so matter-of-fact. Do you not get that she is what I want?"

Rory's gaze grew even darker. "Your family wants you alive. Not living with the threat of death hanging over your head every time you're with her."

"I might as well be dead if I'm not with her," Colt shouted. He pressed his hand to his splitting head, mentally scolding himself for yelling and tensing up every sore muscle. "Fuck."

"Feel the pain, brother. Remember this all happened because you were with her."

"Sadie, how can you possibly marry such an asshole?"

"He's worried about you, Colt. Luna is doing what she thinks is best."

"What is she going to do, stay out on that ranch all alone until God knows when the cops finally get some actual evidence to arrest them?"

Sadie looked away.

"That's what you want for your best friend? For her to hide away out there all alone and vulnerable, all to protect something they'll never stop coming after her to get?" Neither Sadie nor his brothers said anything. "You guys are unbelievable." He turned to his grandfather. "Go get the truck. You're taking me to her place."

"No can do, son. Doc says you're here until day after tomorrow at least."

"You've got to be fucking kidding me."

"You can't even sit up," Rory pointed out.

"No, but as soon as I can kick your ass, I'm going to."

"Try it, brother. You need someone to knock some sense into you."

"Damnit, I love her. You think I'm going to let some spoiled, self-centered, entitled assholes keep me away from her all for a piece of land? Fuck that."

The smile that erased every ominous line on Rory's face did not compute. Colt couldn't figure out why Rory was being such a hardass about this when he should be saying, *Let's take those fuckers down.*

"Mr. Kendrick, you need to settle down," a nurse said, coming into the room.

"I need to get out of here," he shot back.

She shot a syringe full of meds into his IV after checking the band on his wrist. "I'd like to see you try."

The pain meds hit his system in a whoosh that made him lose his breath. "Damn."

"They've got some kick to them. Now, get some rest. The rest of you, keep him calm." She wrapped the blood pressure cuff around Colt's arm and pumped it up, letting it out slowly. "It's high. One forty-seven over ninety-one. You need to relax and bring this down before you make your head worse." The nurse left, still frowning at him.

"If none of you is going to get Luna back here, then get the hell out. You're of no use to me."

"Colt," Sadie said, giving him another of those sad looks.

Rory held up the black velvet box, nothing but understanding filling his eyes. "Is this for real?"

Sadie gasped and covered her mouth. "Where did you get that?"

"Tow truck driver found it in the ditch along with a dozen red roses after he dragged Colt's truck out."

"Oh Colt." Sadie reached forward and laid her hand on his arm.

"It's as real as it gets," Colt answered Rory's question. "As soon as I get out of here, I'm putting that on her finger and getting her promise. I don't care what any of you think about it either. She's mine. You say one word to her about it, Sadie, and I'll never forgive you." The drugs kicked in and his eyes drooped, his mind began to numb. "Did you see the sadness in her eyes? I can't stand it when she cries. I have to get to her before they try to hurt her again." He tried to roll out of bed but only fell back, closing his eyes, giving up the fight. For now.

"Looks like we're dropping him off at her place on the way home," Rory said.

"Why did you put him through that?" Sadie smacked Rory's shoulder.

"If he's going to risk his life, I needed to know it's for the right reasons, not just because he thinks he's some invincible superhero and trying to impress her."

"I'm not twelve," Colt mumbled, trying to stay awake. "I love her. That's all the reason I need to protect her."

"Relax, the cops are looking after her right now. So get some sleep. You'll need to figure out a way to get her to change her mind about keeping you away for your own good. Something I agree with but wouldn't do myself if we were talking about Sadie."

"Glad you see my point. And you're holding the reason she'll want me back. She loves me. She said that, right?"

Rory squeezed his hand. "Yeah, man, she said it. And we are behind you all the way. Whatever you need, we're in."

"Good. Then I'll get her back."

He had to get her back. Then he'd find a way to stop the bastards who tried to tear them apart.

CHAPTER 28

Luna's cell vibrated against her desk, startling her. She picked it up, checked caller ID, saw that it was Sadie yet again, and set it down.

"Is he ever going to give up?" Dex asked from the sofa across the room, where he sat with the FBI cyber-crimes expert.

"It wasn't him." This time. Colt had called her several times over the last two days he'd been in the hospital. She'd checked on him twice, begging the nurse to have mercy and at least tell her that his condition was improving and there'd be no lasting effects from the car accident, though he'd have a few more scars to add to his collection.

The voice mails he left ranged from him asking her to please come back and see him in the hospital, to sweeter ones, telling her to remember some wonderful moment they shared together. A walk under the stars in the pasture, laughs they shared over dinner, the joy they shared seeing the new foal stand on shaky legs in the stables.

She told him to stay away to keep him safe. He reminded her why they should be together. Each one of those calls eroded her resolve that what she was doing was for his own good and her peace of mind. If something happened to him, she couldn't live with herself. She didn't want to live without him.

Judging by how late those calls came in, he'd gotten very little sleep. Guilt sat in her gut like a lead stone. She hated leaving him that way. She hated even more that things had to be this way to keep him safe.

She hoped his family stood by her decision and kept the stubborn cowboy home with them, where his brothers could protect him if the Traverses tried to go after him there.

She stifled another yawn.

"You need to get some sleep."

"I need this to finally be over so I can have my life back."

"Does it include him?" Dex asked, eyeing her from across the room.

She swiveled her chair around and stared out the window at the land she'd been entrusted to protect. Horses ran in a cluster across the green grass in one of the pastures. Rocco took the lead, better now that Colt had thrown out all the food, tainted with arsenic, according to the lab the sheriff's office sent it to for testing.

She'd banned Simon from the property since Colt's accident. Only people who worked here were allowed on the property. She tried to be patient while the cops did their investigation, which involved several crimes committed by several different people. From what she could tell, they weren't really in on it together. So who did what? She was having a hard time figuring it out, so no wonder the cops were having such a hard time proving it, too.

The why was easy. The how not so difficult to figure

out. Nailing them for it seemed infinitely harder and a lot more costly. Colt paid the price. So had she. Every time he called, she forced herself not to answer, reminding herself that the consequences of letting him close had almost cost his life.

Colt sat in the front seat of Rory's truck beside Sadie and cursed every bump in the road that jarred his aching ribs and sore shoulder.

Sadie put her phone back on her thigh and sighed.

"She won't even answer for you." He shook his head, trying to hold back a fresh wave of anger.

"Colt, she thinks she's doing the right thing. If they were after her to get you to do something, wouldn't you send her away to protect her?"

"I get it, doesn't mean it doesn't piss me off."

Rory turned down Round Rock Road and Colt's stomach tightened, thinking about the last time he drove down this stretch of road, all his hopes and dreams about to come true. Until someone slammed into his truck and busted up his life.

"Slow down." Colt leaned forward as they approached the Cherry Creek turnoff.

Rory stopped the truck on the shoulder. Colt scanned the road just ahead.

"From what I saw when we drove up on the way to the hospital that night, they drove the truck down Cherry Creek and straight into your truck. The timing was incredible. They hit the passenger door dead center and pushed the car across the street and right into the ditch."

Colt saw the deep ruts and gouges in the dirt where his truck went over the side and skidded to a stop. Glass speckles covered the dirt, twinkling in the sunlight. A small portion of the earth turned black from the fire.

"They had to rip your windshield off to get you out. The truck's a total loss, but I got your gear."

Who gave a fuck about his truck or his stuff? He lived. And now he was going to have a life with Luna. God, he missed her.

"They planned this. They waited for me to drive down this road. They knew I'd be coming from this way."

"Who at the ranch knew you'd be going into Bozeman?" Rory pulled back onto the road and drove toward Luna's place.

"I called Luna to let her know I'd be late. She was in the stables, checking on one of the sick horses. Anyone could have overheard her talking to me. She might have mentioned it to one of the ranch hands."

"Do you think Simon ran you off the road?"

"If he did, he's bolder than I believed. It doesn't make sense that it would be him. Using the Rambling Range truck to do it, that points right to him, but I think someone wants us to think it was him."

Rory turned onto the road leading in to Rambling Range and stopped at the closed gates. "She's locked the place up tight."

"Yeah, as if that is going to stop me." Colt opened the truck door and got out, turning back to the cab. "Thanks for the ride."

"You might need this." Rory held out his hand.

Colt put his out, palm up. Rory pressed the black velvet box into Colt's palm and held on to Colt's hand. "Good luck, man."

"I'm not settling for anything less than a yes." Colt stuffed the box in the front pocket of his jeans.

Ford handed his bag forward from the back. "Go get her."

Colt looked over his shoulder at the tall fence he had to climb over to get onto the property. "This is going to hurt like hell."

" 'Love hurts,' " Ford quoted the Nazareth song.

"Maybe you can get Luna to kiss it all better," Rory suggested, teasing him.

"Count on it. She owes me big time for this stunt."

"Colt, let me use the call box. She'll open the gate for me."

Colt shook his head. "She's got this place locked down because she's scared. If she won't let me near her, she's not going to let her pregnant best friend anywhere near her either." Colt gave Sadie's hand a pat. "I got this, sis. Don't worry. She can't keep me out."

"If she has you arrested for trespassing, we'll bail you out," Ford offered.

"Thanks." Colt rolled his eyes, grabbed his bag off the seat, and stepped back, closing the door.

Colt hefted the bag in his good hand and tossed it over the eight-foot fence. He could walk down the fence line to where it dropped to a split rail along the pastures, but that would take time and make him have to backtrack a hell of a ways. He might think it a better plan, once he landed on the other side.

Sucking it up, he grabbed hold of the stone pillar and the gate bar. He hooked his foot in between two stones as high up as he could get and hoisted himself up, hoping his boot didn't come loose.

"The woman's got me scaling walls to get to her." He must love her, otherwise why would he put himself through this?

He planted his free foot up higher, grabbed the bars

and stones, and pulled himself up to the top of the pillar. Great. Now all he had to do was get his legs up and over the pillar, which meant he had to support his weight on both arms. He groaned through the pain, swung his legs over, sat on the pillar, and jumped down, bracing for the impact and the jolt to every sore muscle and bone.

"Shit," he bit out, holding his hurt arm against his stomach and crouching over to ease the pain in his ribs and shoulder.

Rory honked twice behind him, pulling out of the drive. All Colt managed was a wave with his good hand to see them off. He still had a half-mile walk to the house. Plenty of time to think about what to say to her.

He picked up his bag and tossed it over his good shoulder. It wasn't all his stuff, but enough for him to get by until he packed up the rest at Rory and Sadie's place and moved in here.

It might take some convincing, but he was moving in right now.

He came around the bend and stopped, staring at the vehicles in her driveway. With the gate locked, he expected to find her alone. Well, he didn't care who the hell was here, she was going to hear him out.

He walked to the front door, waving off Ed and Toby as they stepped out of the stables. Several other men showed their faces in the field and out by the barn.

"Good girl. Keep the men close to the house."

He limped to the steps, his side aching, the bruise on his hip where he slammed into the door during the accident throbbing from all the walking and probably that eight-foot drop from the stone pillar.

He tried the door but found it locked. "I've got the key to your tower, honey. You can't hide away from me."

He unlocked the top and bottom lock and pushed the door open, confronted by Wayne's hat hanging on the wall, along with the picture of Wayne and Luna. He thought it a sweet gesture she hung them there. A nice reminder of all Wayne had given to her and the friendship they'd shared. Right now, Colt wanted to punch Wayne's lights out for putting her in harm's way with his deranged family.

"Luna," he bellowed, wondering where she was when he didn't spot her in the living room.

"Colt." Her surprised voice carried out of the office.

He headed straight for her, blind to everything but the woman coming around the desk to head him off.

"Colt, what are you doing here?"

"Did you really think you could tell me you love me and then order me to stay away?"

"They're trying to kill you."

Colt held up his bandaged arm, though it cost him to move his shoulder. "Yeah, I got the memo on that one."

"You can't be here. You have to leave."

"No." He tossed his bag down. "I'm staying here with you. Not just for today. Not just until this thing is over. I'm staying here with you because you said you love me."

"I do, Colt, but you have to understand. I couldn't live with myself if something happened to you. Do you have any idea what it did to me to see you lying motionless in that wreck, bleeding?" Her voice cracked, tears welled in her eyes and fell down her cheeks.

"Do you really think I'll leave you here alone? Do you think I can live without you?"

That took her off guard. She opened her mouth, then closed it.

"I can't. Do you have any idea how hard it was to

lie in that hospital bed, needing you there with me so badly I could barely breathe? Do you have any idea how worried I was that they'd come after you and I wouldn't be here to stop them?"

"I . . ."

"No. I get to talk now. You had your say at the hospital, now I get mine. I want to be here with you. I want us to make a life together. I want you to know that you can count on me when things turn to shit. That I'm not going to run out on you just because some asshole tries to kill me. You do not have to face this on your own. You do not have to do this on your own."

"Colt."

"I'm not done talking."

She clamped her mouth shut.

He tried to find the right words. "I get this place is important to you, that what Wayne wanted is important to you. He was your friend and you want to do right by him. I love that about you. Your dedication. Your loyalty. The way you care about the people in your life. The way you love me so much that you'd push me away to keep me safe. I can't imagine how hard that was for you. So hard that I can't do it myself. I can't let go. I can't stay away. I won't." He pulled the ring from his pocket, opened the lid, and showed it to her. "I love you, Luna. Make a life with me. Marry me. Please."

She nodded before any words came out of her mouth. "Yes." She finally found her smile, and it spread across her beautiful face and lit her tear-filled eyes. "I probably should say no because of everything that's happened and what might happen," she rambled. "You shouldn't be here."

"Stick with yes. You said yes."

"It's the manners. They get me every time."

"Well, then, please come here and kiss me."

She flew into his arms and nearly sent him to the ground, but he caught her and crushed his mouth to hers. His aches and pains disappeared beneath the wave of joy that filled him up and made him laugh against her lips. He kissed her again and again, then pressed his forehead to hers and looked into her bright blue eyes. "I love you so damn much."

"I love you, too." She gave him another quick kiss. "I don't want anything to happen to you."

"We'll find a way to keep both of us safe." He held her tighter, putting his worries aside and letting the happiness he felt rise up. "You said yes."

"I did." The smile on her lips got even bigger.

He set her on her feet and pulled the ring from the box. He held her hand in his but turned it over and stared at the healing burns on her fingertips. "Are you okay?"

"They're much better. I got some medicated salve from the hospital."

He gently slid the ring on her finger.

"Colt, it's beautiful."

"Only half as beautiful as you. Rory and Sadie told me how you found and saved me. Thank you, honey. I don't know what I'd do without you."

"You may change your mind about this if they come after you again." Luna pressed her hand to her stomach like even the thought made her ill.

"Nothing will change my mind."

"What about the fact that Luna loses everything if she marries you?"

Colt turned and faced Luna's attorney. "Dex, what are you doing here? And who are you?" Colt asked the other tied-up-in-a-suit man standing next to the lawyer.

"Agent Montrose. FBI cybercrimes."

"Uh, okay. Why are you here?"

"Luna's computer caught a virus."

Not understanding why that required the FBI or believing the FBI's presence was that simple, Colt focused back on the attorney. "Why would Luna lose everything if she marries me?"

"It's part of the terms of the will. So if you think marrying her will gain you this place, you're wrong."

Colt turned to Luna. "You said you'd marry me, even though you lose this place?"

"I want to," she confirmed.

"Okay, then I guess we'll live at my place. I've got some money. We can build a house on the property. You'll want to make sure whatever happens to this place is the right thing. That the people who work here are taken care of properly.

"I've got a few horses you can work with to start your equine therapy program. Rory and Ford will help me fix up a small arena on the property. It's not as nice as the one Wayne built you, but it'll suit until I can build you a better one."

"You'd do that for me?"

"I'd do anything for you, including pulling that barn wood off the wall out there and putting it up in our new house."

Luna turned to Dex. "Good enough for you?"

He turned to the FBI agent. "Do you believe he loves her and doesn't want the ranch or money?"

"I believe him. No one is that good of a liar. Believe me, I catch liars for a living."

"What are you guys talking about? I'm not lying."

Dex turned back to Luna. "It would solve a lot of

problems if you invoke the terms of the will now before they get away with this."

"They won't get away with anything," Colt vowed.

"Colt, honey?"

"Yes, darlin'." He played along with her teasing tone. "Did you want a long or short engagement?"

"I would marry you this second if it made you happy. Otherwise I leave it to you to tell me what to wear and when to show up."

"I can have a judge here tomorrow," Dex said.

"Wait. What?"

Luna smiled. "Works for me." She turned to Colt. "You in a suit. Tomorrow night under the stars."

"What are you talking about?"

"What to wear and when to show up. You, me, a judge, married for life."

"Luna, don't you want to plan the wedding of your dreams? Don't you want to do the flowers, the food, the dress, the . . . whatever else girls dream about for their wedding?"

"The only thing I want is to be your wife."

"Don't you want to take your time to think about what you're giving up here? You may change your mind." He hated to say those words.

"I'm not giving up anything."

"But Dex said if you marry, you lose this place."

"A test," she said, smiling.

"Did I pass?" he asked, still not understanding how everyone got involved with their wedding plans.

Instead of answering, she glanced at Dex again.

"Yes," he answered. "The terms of the will are very specific if Luna marries. Those terms had to be kept absolutely secret from any man she dated. He, you, couldn't know that if she marries, she can override Wayne's bequeath to his family and keep the ranch for herself."

"What?"

Luna wrapped her arms around his neck. "Wayne knew his children didn't want this place. He wanted me to have it, but like any good friend, he was looking out for my well-being. He didn't want some man looking at this place, wanting it without wanting me more. You are a man of integrity."

"No. I'm the man who wants you more than anything else in this world."

"Good. But I come with a really big ranch for you to run."

"*We* run this place, but working and living here is not why I asked you to marry me."

"You don't even need to say it, Colt. I know it. They know it," she said, waving her hand at the suits. "Everyone knows it. So stop worrying."

"The Traverses are going to be even more dangerous when they find out you're keeping this place," Colt warned.

"Maybe, but we're on to them," Luna told Colt. "The cops are closing in on gathering enough evidence to arrest them for their many misdeeds. Until then, you need to call your family. Invite them to dinner, here, tomorrow night at seven. Don't tell them we're getting married. We'll keep it a secret so word doesn't get out to the Traverses."

"You want to have a surprise wedding?"

"Why not?" She pressed her hand to his chest. "You don't want to. You want to wait."

"No." He cupped her face in his hands and stared down into her lovely eyes. "I want you to be sure this is what you want, that we have the wedding you want."

"Colt, honey, I already see it in my mind. I know what I want. You. Me. Under the stars. Candles and stringed white lights."

"You're sure?"

She nodded at him again.

"Make a list of what you want. We'll send a few of the guys out to get everything."

Her whole face lit with delight. "You mean it."

"I can't say no to that smile."

"You don't need more time to decide, to settle in here and see how it goes?"

"I made up my mind when I made the decision to marry you and bought you that ring. Whether we get married tomorrow night or a year from now, I won't change my mind." Colt turned back to Dex. "I guess you can bring whatever I need to sign tomorrow before the wedding."

"I'll draw up the prenup."

"Is that necessary?" Luna asked. "The will is clear that if I get married, the ranch becomes mine."

Colt took Luna's hands. "Of course it's yours. But we need to put some things in writing. What if something happens to you? What if we have children, what will happen to the ranch if you pass before me? If you decide to divorce me, you don't want me to be able to take so much of what we build together it puts the ranch in jeopardy. Besides, I've still got my stake in the Kendrick spread."

"But Colt, it should be ours."

"It will be ours. The ranch will pay me a salary, maybe a nice bonus when things go our way. I don't need my name on the deed to know that we're partners in this, but you need to answer those questions and more to protect yourself and this place. Most of it we'll never need to use, but it'll be there if you need it." Colt turned to Dex. "You and Luna work out the terms. I'll sign whatever she wants."

"It will include that I have no claim to the Kendrick property or business."

"Fair enough," Colt agreed. "You do understand this is only going to incite the Traverses more."

"Unfortunately, yes. But I want this, Colt. I don't want to give you up and our life together. I want to put an end to this. It's taking longer than I expected for the cops to build their case and put together enough evidence to make it all stick."

"Of course they didn't make it easy, right?"

She smiled, but it didn't touch the regret fogging over her earlier joy. "No. In fact, because they're all doing one thing or another, it's hard to sort out who did what, when, and if the others knew about it."

"Marrying me and taking away their chance at a piece of this place will only make things worse. I'm concerned they'll come after you next time."

"There's something else you don't know."

Afraid to ask, he did so anyway. "What?"

"I have the ability to override Wayne's original bequeaths and pay them more money. Perhaps I can pay them to go away."

"No."

"No?" Dex asked. "You'd prefer to keep everything?"

"So suspicious." Colt eyed the lawyer, then turned his gaze back to Luna. "You pay them now, they'll come back for more, knowing you can give it to them. If you don't, they'll do exactly what they're doing now and try to force you to pay more. If you do, they'll do it again. You give in now, you'll only feed their greed and make them more dangerous. We will not reward them for their bad behavior. That's not what Wayne wanted, right? That's why he didn't leave everything to them."

Luna glanced at Dex. "He's got a point."

"Yes, he does," Dex grudgingly admitted.

"We marry tomorrow night in a quiet family ceremony. Dex notifies the Travers family the next day that Luna has invoked her right to claim the ranch in whole. Then we wait."

"That might speed things up," the FBI agent said. "It'll also make things a hell of a lot more dangerous."

"Desperate people make mistakes," Colt pointed out. "They come after me or Luna again, we won't be easy targets."

"What's your plan?" Luna asked.

"To start, we lock this place down and make it real hard for anyone to get close to us."

"I'll notify the sheriff's department and ask for added protection over the next few days and weeks," Dex added.

"Call your family," Luna coaxed. "They're probably dying to hear from you."

"I swore Sadie to secrecy when Rory gave me back the ring the tow truck driver found in the accident."

"You were on your way here to ask me to marry you?"

"Bought the ring. Had the flowers. All I needed was a yes. It took me a couple extra days to get it, thanks to those Traverses. They try to stop me from marrying you, they'll have hell to pay."

"Relax. Nothing will go wrong. Tell Sadie to wear the purple dress I love and spiff up the guys."

"What are you going to do?" He touched her soft cheek and the dark circle beneath her eye with the pad of his thumb. "You look tired."

"I can't sleep without you."

"You won't have that problem for the rest of your life," he promised.

"I'm going to call my mother, then finish up with Agent Montrose and Dex."

"What are you guys doing?"

"We set a trap. We're waiting to spring it."

"On who?"

"As with all the other things that happened, it looks like one person, but it could be more."

CHAPTER 29

Luna woke up with Colt completely wrapped around her back and side, with his leg thrown over both of hers, his bandaged arm draped over her side, his hand covering her breasts. Her head rested on his right arm. She tried not to move and hurt his left shoulder. He'd tossed and turned most of the night, trying to get comfortable with his many injuries paining him nonstop. He refused to take any more pain meds, opting instead for a clear head, ready to face their wedding day and tackle the mile-long list of things they needed to do to prepare for their perfect night.

"Morning, honey," Colt's deep, groggy voice rumbled at her ear.

"Did you ask me to marry you, or was that just a dream?"

Colt scooted back and pulled her over to face him. He stared down at her and traced a finger over her forehead, drawing her long bangs away from her eyes. "Please marry me. I want a life with you." He leaned down and kissed her lips softly. "I need you."

She trailed her fingers over the long bruise that crossed his chest from the seat belt that helped save his life in the accident.

"You don't need the danger I brought into your life." She met his steady gaze. "Are you okay? I mean, really okay?"

"I'll prove it to you." He leaned down and kissed her again, but in a whole different way. Not good morning, but let's start a fire. Colt did, right in her heart. It spread through her body long before he ended the sweet, tempting kiss and moved down her neck to stroke her skin, lick her hard nipple, and take it into his warm mouth. She combed her fingers through his sun-streaked hair and held him to her, his body partly covering hers.

He shifted again, kissing her chest, but sucked in a breath and hissed in pain when he hurt his sore shoulder by pressing on his left hand to hold his weight.

"Colt, honey, you don't have to do this."

"I want to do this." The grin he gave her made her smile. The way he thrust forward, his hard length rubbing against her center, sent a flash of heat burning through her body.

Yeah, she wanted him, too. But she didn't want to hurt him more in the process.

She leaned up on her elbow, laid her hand on his hurt shoulder, and gently pushed to get him to roll over onto his back. She followed him, rising up and straddling his hips. She pulled the sheet up to cover her breasts and glanced at the windows.

Colt's hands covered hers. "We're alone, sweetheart. There's no one there. They can't see in."

No, because he'd made sure to pull the drapes closed.

She reached out and traced the long stitched gash on his head. Dark bruises spread around it. "Look what they did to you."

"The headache's gone, but it still hurts."

She leaned down and pressed a kiss close, but not on the worst of the wound. He sighed, his warm breath feathering over her cheek. She smiled and pressed a kiss to his temple, his cheek, his chin, and kept moving lower to his chest and the nasty bruises there. She avoided the stitched cuts on his arm.

His big hands clamped onto her thighs and smoothed up her skin to her hips. She rocked against his hard length, grinding against him, pleasing him and her at the same time. Colt suffered the sweet torture along with her, but it only took moments before they both wanted more.

Colt reached for the strip of condoms hanging out of the side table drawer. He pulled one free and tore it open with his teeth. She took it from him, leaned back, and rolled it down his hard length. Colt reached for her, drawing her down for a long kiss, his tongue gliding along hers. She rose up, then sank down, taking Colt in, filling herself up with him and the feeling that overcame her every time they were together like this.

"I love you," she whispered against his lips.

Colt wrapped his arms around her back, whispered, "I love you," and thrust deep, rocking against her, holding her body close to his.

They made love, clinging to each other and the closeness they both felt and needed. The desperation that gathered in them exploded with an intensity she'd never felt herself or with him. She lay atop him, his arms banded around her like he couldn't bear to let her go. She hoped it didn't foretell more danger in the future. She shivered with the thought.

"Nothing is going to happen today. Today is for us."

She hoped Colt was right.

"Sun's up, honey. We need to get out of this bed and get everything ready for tonight."

"I really just want to stay here with you."

His big hands rubbed softly up and down her back and over her bottom. He pressed her hips down on his again, setting off a new round of thrilling aftershocks that made her smile against his shoulder.

"I want that more than anything, except making you my wife. Come on, lazy."

He rolled to his side, knocking her off him. She held on to his side and squeezed. "What did your family say about coming over tonight?"

"They're excited. Happy for us, just like your family. They think it's an engagement celebration."

"It's kind of fun to keep everyone in the dark about the wedding."

"I can't wait to see my granddad's face."

She laughed with him. "Did you ever think you'd get married before your big brother?"

Colt chuckled. "No. I didn't think I'd get married for a long time."

"Are you sure you want to do this now?"

"I already told you, now, a year from now, doesn't matter. My life is with you, here, wherever you are, that's where I want to be."

"You mean that?"

"Yes. Absolutely. Why? Are you having second thoughts?"

"None. I just don't want you to ever regret marrying me, especially after what happened, what might still happen."

"None of which is your fault. You are kind and generous and sexy and beautiful. You have such a good heart." His warm hand pressed to the side of her face as he stared down at her. "It started with a kiss, Luna, but what we share is so much more than I ever thought I'd have in my life. I always thought the missing piece I felt inside myself was because of the loss of my parents. Maybe it was, but you filled it up with the love you show me and the love I feel for you. Don't you get it? I need you, Luna. You are the one thing that makes my life better and worth living."

"Everything happened so fast."

"Maybe, but if it feels this right, why question it, or look for reasons or excuses to slow things down, wait longer, when all we both want is to be together? Let's just be together, Luna."

She hooked her arm around his neck and pulled him close in a tight hug. "You're everything I ever wanted."

"Good, because you said yes and I'm not letting you out of that promise, or the one you'll make me tonight."

"I will always love you," she vowed, knowing that would always be true no matter what came next.

CHAPTER 30

Luna held a garment bag over her shoulder in one hand. Several shopping bags weighed down her other. She walked around the house, her ever-present sheriff's deputy on her trail, to the back, where Toby and several ranch hands were setting up chairs around the white-draped tables on the patio. Luna stopped short and stared as her father adjusted a gerbera daisy in a purple painted pot with a white satin bow tied around it in the center of one table. A string of tiny white lights surrounded it. Her mother stood behind another table, potted plants of all kinds and more purple pots before her.

"Mom." Luna didn't expect to see them this early. No one was supposed to arrive for at least two more hours.

Her mother looked up and smiled so bright it touched Luna, making her realize it had been too long since she'd seen her parents.

"Luna, you're back. Oh, I hoped to have this all done before you got here."

Luna looked at the other potted plants on the tables her mother had finished. "You did all this?" Luna had asked Colt to send one of the guys to the nursery to see if there were any flowering plants they could use for the tables. This went beyond what she'd expected. Such lovely centerpieces her mother had created.

"Well, if you'd given me a bit more time to plan your wedding, I might have ordered some centerpieces from the florist."

"You know?"

"Colt called. He asked me to help give you the wedding of your dreams. In one day."

Tears gathered in Luna's eyes. Her mother was annoyed, but under that a wealth of love came through loud and clear.

"I didn't know things between you were so serious," her father said, coming to her and planting a kiss on her forehead like he always did when he saw her. He held her shoulders and stared down at her. "Are you sure you want to do this? It's very fast and sudden."

"I'm sure, Dad. He's a good man. He loves me. I love him."

"You're happy?" Her father searched her face. She'd never been able to lie to him. He read her so well.

"Yes, Dad. I'm very happy, most especially when I'm with him."

"Okay. Then what do you think of the lights?" He held out his hand to indicate the star-shaped lights strung over a path flanked on both sides by the garden, which ended at a wide patio area with a bench.

Luna smiled. She'd asked Colt to marry her under the stars. He'd found the perfect lights to complement the stars that would be out later. "They're perfect."

"Colt insisted they had to be those."

"Where is Colt?"

Her mother smiled again. That alone told Luna she liked Colt. "He took Tanner over to see the horses and to feed a calf."

"He did?" Luna worried that Tanner would be too much for Colt to handle. Tanner didn't take to strangers easily. A lot of people worked on the ranch. It might overwhelm her brother.

"We explained to Tanner on the way over that Colt will be his brother. The minute they met, Tanner took to him. He even shook his hand," her father said, giving Luna a satisfied look.

Tanner had a way of sizing someone up.

"He touched Colt." Luna couldn't believe it. "Wow. Okay, that's good."

"We'll see if Colt thinks so after they've spent some time together." Her mother gave her a knowing look. Tanner could try the patience of a saint.

So, her mother still held some reservations about Colt. Not so surprising. They'd spend time with him and see what an amazing guy he was in no time.

"Colt suggested we put Tanner to work on the ranch," Luna told her parents. "He thought it best to start Tanner out with the abandoned calves. They're sweet and gentle. Not too big for Tanner to handle."

"He did?" both her parents asked.

"We plan to get Tanner a dog once he's settled here."

Her mother gave her father a look, which he returned.

"Why are you two so surprised?"

Her mother pressed her lips together, then sighed. "We thought you might change your mind now that you're getting married. We thought you might like to have time alone with your new husband."

"Colt and I would like to take a honeymoon in the next couple of months, but right now we need to be here. Colt is taking over as manager on the ranch. I want to learn the businesses so I feel comfortable with all this place does. I want to work on setting up the equine therapy program. Those things will take time, and I'd love to include settling Tanner in here, too."

"We never expected you to take responsibility for him now. Later, when we're gone, yes."

"This is a good place for him, Mom. Don't you think so, too?" she asked both her parents.

"Yes. We'd have liked to keep the ranch, but the bills . . ." Her father's voice trailed off.

"You did what you had to do, Dad. I have the means to give him the life you wanted for him. If something happens to you, to me, he'll be taken care of no matter what. Dex Manning will be here later. He's got some papers for you to sign."

"Luna." Her mother teared up. "You didn't have to go through all this trouble."

"You've taken care of me my whole life. Wayne left me so much. What I'm doing for you seems so small and so big at the same time. You are responsible for Tanner for the rest of your life. Most parents raise their kids and watch them go off and lead their own lives. Tanner will always need looking after, but that doesn't mean you don't need a break, a chance to be responsible only for you for a little while."

Her father glanced at her mother. "We have an amazing daughter."

"Yes, you do," Colt said, stepping out of the house with Tanner right behind him.

"Luna!" Tanner ran to her and enveloped her in an awkward hug, mostly because she still held all her packages, but also because as much as Tanner loved her, he found it weird to touch people.

"How are you, Tanner?"

"You got me a brother. I like him. We fed the cow."

Luna laughed under her breath. "I'm glad you like Colt."

"He's named after a horse." Tanner said it deadpan.

Luna tried to hide the smile. "I don't think his mother actually named him after a horse. It's a good, strong name."

"He gave me his hat." Tanner touched the brim of Colt's black Stetson on his head.

"I let you borrow it," Colt amended Tanner's statement.

"You're lucky, Tanner. That's Colt's favorite hat. He doesn't let just anyone wear it."

"I can't wear the one in the house. It's special."

Luna felt the grief rise up for her old friend. "It belonged to the man who used to live here. He was a very good friend."

"Colt's my friend. Tonight he'll be my brother. He's got more brothers."

She gave him an indulgent smile. "Rory and Ford will be here tonight. So will Sadie."

Tanner's face lit up. He loved Sadie dearly.

"She's growing a person in her uterus." Tanner's face flushed red.

Luna smiled. "She's having a baby."

"Colt showed me my new cabin," Tanner said, changing the subject. "I don't like the color. My stuff isn't there."

"We'll take care of everything," her father said. "Your mom and I will help you make it just the way you want it."

"Tanner, do you think you'd like to live here with Colt and me?" Luna asked, hoping a change didn't overwhelm him.

"I'm in charge of the calves. I have to feed them and

clean their pen. When they're older, I have to let them go with the herd. Colt said. But I get to keep Cloud. Colt said."

Luna turned to Colt and raised an eyebrow in question.

"The calf he fed has a huge white patch on its side."

"Looks like a cloud," Tanner added.

Colt nodded and grinned. "She's a sweet girl and took to Tanner. He wants to keep her."

"You're okay with this?" she asked Colt.

"It's one cow, honey. We've got about two thousand."

Pleased he finally felt like this place was theirs, this life would be theirs and they'd share everything, she smiled at him, happy he'd said "we."

Colt closed the distance, leaned down, and kissed her softly. "You found a dress." He nodded toward the hanger gripped in her fingers at her shoulder.

"I found the perfect dress."

He smiled indulgently at her. "Great. We need to get a move on if we're going to have everything ready by tonight. The caterers just arrived. They're in the kitchen."

"Perfect. Looks like things are moving along out here. I bought you a tie to wear with your suit to match my dress. Is that okay?"

"Whatever you want, honey."

"Will you take all of this to our room? I'd like to help my mom finish the tables."

"Your father and I can do it, sweetheart, you go get ready." Her mother plopped a miniature rose bush with tiny white buds into another purple pot.

"I want to help."

"The caterers will be out shortly to set up the dishes. I can't believe you found someone to do the job on such short notice," Colt said to Luna.

"I won't tell you what that short notice cost to have them drive in from Bozeman."

Colt took the garment bag and packages from Luna's hands. He gave her another soft kiss. "Whatever the cost, it was worth it. This is our night."

"It's bad luck to see the bride," Tanner announced.

"That's the thing about loving someone, Tanner," Colt began. "You'll risk anything to be with them." He leaned in and kissed her again, this time lingering for a few seconds longer. He broke the soft kiss, pulled away just enough for her to look him in the eye, and whispered, "I love you."

Colt stood tall again and handed off several bags to her brother. "Let's take these inside."

Luna watched them go, her heart in her throat. She loved that man so much it swelled inside her until she thought she'd burst.

"I worried you were taking things too fast. Not thinking things through, or taking the time to get to know each other well enough before you got married," her father said. "Seeing you two together, the way he is with Tanner, I'm not worried at all."

"He's a good man." Her mother echoed Luna's words to Wayne, to her parents. It pleased her that they saw it, too. Even if they didn't, she'd still love him, because she knew Colt and he knew her. Somehow, they'd found their way to each other, and they fit.

She looked around the backyard and the tables still not finished. Now all they had to do was pull off a wedding they'd planned in less than a day. No matter how the decorations and food turned out, the most important thing was that by the time Colt took her to bed tonight, she'd be Mrs. Colt Kendrick, his wife.

"Now there's a smile a bride should be wearing on her wedding day," her mother teased.

"Mom!"

"I'm just saying." Her mother finished the bow on the next pot. "I like seeing you two together."

"I like who I am when I'm with him." Now all they had to do was get through tonight and the rest of their lives without any more interference from the Traverses. Not likely in the near future. A shiver of foreboding raced up her spine. Once they found out about the marriage, there'd be even more reason for them to come after her and Colt.

CHAPTER 31

Colt stood between Dex and Deputy Foster, his back to his and Luna's families, hoping no one overheard their conversation. The judge was ready to perform the ceremony. His family was chomping at the bit to know why Luna hadn't come out of the house yet. They needed to get this show on the road, but first Colt wanted some reassurance that they'd get through this night without someone getting hurt. Namely him or Luna.

"Well, are we all set?" he asked Deputy Foster.

"We've got someone on each of the Traverses. No one appears to know about tonight. They're all at their respective homes, though Josh tends to go out most nights for dinner or drinks according to the intel we've gathered on him."

Though Colt appreciated the added protection, especially tonight, he couldn't help but worry. "You're sure they can't sneak off without being seen and come here?"

"If anyone makes a move, we'll know about it."

"What about Agent Montrose? Anything happening with whatever trap he and Luna set?" Colt still hadn't gotten the down-and-dirty details on that one. He'd been too tired and in too much pain last night to talk through all the details. Once Luna said yes to his proposal, they'd spent the rest of the evening discussing the wedding. Today, he'd barely seen her, for all the running around they both did getting ready.

He checked out the backyard, surveying the elegant tables, flowers, and twinkling lights. If felt very much like a fairy-tale setting in the woods, with all the trees at the back of the garden area. He hoped Luna liked it. He wanted her to love it. He wanted her to remember this night forever.

Dex slapped a hand on his shoulder. "Go get your bride. Leave all this other stuff to us for tonight. We've got your back. Nothing is going to happen. Mixed in with your family and friends are three other deputies. Six private security guards are patrolling the property. Relax."

"I can't relax. Someone tried to kill me three days ago. If they ruin this night for Luna, they'll wish they were dead."

"Nothing is going to happen," Dex assured him again. "Go get her. Everyone is starting to stare and wonder what's taking so long."

"Get the judge ready. We'll be out in a few minutes."

Colt left Dex to covertly get people into position. He went around the side of the house and in through the front door to avoid his brothers or grandfather asking him again why they'd had to dress up for an engagement party. Rory and Sadie had a good ol' fashioned barbeque. They expected him and Luna to do the same. Weren't they going to be surprised?

Colt stood outside Luna's bedroom door and straightened the silver tie Luna bought him. He smoothed his hands down his jacket lapels and checked the shine on his black boots. He jolted and stilled, realizing that for the first time, he was nervous. His gut went tight and his throat went dry. He slipped his hand in his slacks pocket and pulled out the aquamarine bracelet Luna had given back to him in the hospital. He rubbed his thumb over one of the butterflies. This is what he wanted. Luna was the only woman he'd ever love. He didn't want to wait another moment to make her his wife.

He rapped on the door and waited, not wanting to rush her. The door opened and she stood before him, a vision in white. The inch-wide, see-through straps over her shoulders came down to a scoop neck that showed off her cleavage, hugged tight in gathered satin. Dozens of rhinestones spread over the band around her ribs, sparkling like tiny stars. The rest of the dress dropped to the ground in sheer white material over satin.

She'd put her hair up in an elegant style that had her bangs swept over part of her forehead, the other side pulled back. Her dark hair combined with the white gown was striking, but then she'd done her eyes in a soft, smoky gray and her lips in red. He'd never seen any woman look this glamorous.

"God, you're beautiful."

"You are so handsome." He'd tried his best to clean up and make her proud. The dark gray suit fit well. The silver tie set it off. He'd even combed his hair into some semblance of a style.

She reached for him, sliding her fingers around to the back of his neck as she smiled. "You are one sexy-hot cowboy, but dressed in a suit, oh man, you take sexy to a whole new level."

"I want to kiss you so bad right now, but I don't want to mess you up," he admitted, afraid to touch her.

"Come here, cowboy. One last kiss as a single man before you're tied down for good."

"Honey, you can tie me down any time you want."

She laughed, and the sound made the knot and tension in his body ease away like they had never been there to begin with.

"I don't want to tie you up, honey. I like those hands on me too much."

That's all he needed to reach for her. He slipped his hands around her back, his fingers gliding over the silky soft material. He drew her close and kissed her softly. She leaned into him, her hands coming up to rest on his face. She ended the kiss, playfully rubbing her nose against his.

"Are you ready for this?" she whispered.

"I had a strange moment of nerves right before I knocked, but then I saw you and all I want to do is hear that judge say you're mine forever."

"You don't need a judge to tell you that. I am yours forever. Nothing and no one will ever change that."

"I feel the same way, Luna. I don't need a piece of paper or a ceremony to know that I'm yours until the day I die."

She gave him a wicked smile. "Then let's get married, make it official, then kick everyone off our land and spend the night in each other's arms."

He pressed his forehead to hers and smiled back at her. "You are the smartest woman ever. That's a plan I can get behind." He set her away and held out the butterfly bracelet. "This is something old." He latched the bracelet around her wrist, then dipped his hand inside his suit jacket and pulled out the black velvet box he'd stashed there earlier. "This is something new." He flipped open the lid and revealed round aquamarine stud earrings inside.

Luna gasped and pressed her hand to her mouth. "Colt, they're beautiful."

"I got them for you today."

"After all the errands I sent you on, you still managed to buy me a gift?"

"My wedding gift to you."

Luna plucked one and then the other earring from the box and put them in her ears. She smiled brightly at him, tilting her head to show them off. "You like?"

"They're almost as pretty as your smile."

"Aw, you're sweet."

"So all you need now is something borrowed and something blue."

"You've thought of everything. What am I borrowing?"

Again Colt pulled something out of his pocket. He held it enclosed in his hand and looked Luna in the eye. "I don't remember my parents that well. My memories are flashes that seem more like a dream than reality. I wish they were here to see me marry the woman who made me feel something other than the emptiness I carried around in my heart missing them. I don't know if my mother wore this often, or who gave it to her, but I'd like you to wear it tonight."

Luna placed her hand over his closed one. "Of course, Colt."

"I want to give it to you. I think it's actually perfect for you. But I didn't have a way to ask my brothers if it's okay that I keep it and give it to you without telling them why. So for now, you can borrow it, and I'll know that a piece of my mother is a part of the ceremony."

Colt opened his hand and revealed the tiny ring he held in his palm.

Luna gasped. "Oh, Colt, it's beautiful."

"It's a star sapphire." He held the smooth, deep blue stone up so she could see the white streaks that crossed the stone as the light hit it. He slipped it onto her right hand and stared at his mother's ring on her finger.

"Some things are meant to be, Colt." She reached up and touched his cheek. "I have something for you." She walked to the dresser and opened the drawer. She pulled out a small black satin drawstring bag. "Sadie gave this to me last week to take to the jeweler to have it fixed. The post had bent and she wanted you to wear it to her and Rory's wedding. She wanted each of you to wear something of your father's. She picked this for you." Luna opened the bag, pulled out a small tie tack, and held it up to the light. The blue star sapphire sparkled in her fingertips.

"No," Colt said, astonished. "I've never seen that."

"Your grandfather showed Sadie some of the things he'd kept tucked away for you boys." Sadie pulled Colt's tie from his jacket, fastened the pin for him, then tucked the tie back in. She smoothed the tie with her right hand, the ring and the tie tack a perfect match.

"I don't care what my brothers or grandfather say, we're keeping these."

Luna leaned in and kissed him. "They're here with us, Colt."

He had to admit, right now, he felt them close.

Colt took her hand and kissed her palm. He held it to his face and leaned into her soft warmth. "Ready?"

"I can't wait."

He kept her hand in his and walked down the hallway to the living room. He took the small bouquet of lavender roses from the vase, then handed the larger white bouquet to Luna.

"I'll send your dad in. See you in a minute." He gave her a quick kiss, took one last, long look at his beautiful bride, then left her with a reluctance he couldn't shake. He didn't want to be without her ever.

He stepped out onto the patio with the bouquet tucked behind his back.

"Where have you been, little brother?" Ford asked.

"What have you done with Luna?" Rory called.

"Mr. Hill, Luna's inside waiting for you," Colt said.

He walked past Colt, whispering, "After tonight, it's Joel or Dad. You pick." Mr. Hill gave him a smack on the back as he passed.

A little stunned, Colt had to suck in a breath. He'd never called anyone Dad. At least, he couldn't remember ever doing so. After tonight, he'd actually have people to call Mom and Dad. It kind of messed with his mind, but he set that aside for another time and focused.

"Ah, Luna will be out in just a minute. We'd like to thank all of you for coming tonight. It's a very special occasion."

"Yeah, who knew you'd ever get someone to agree to marry you, especially a bright, beautiful girl like Luna," Ford teased.

"Well, she did say yes. And now I need to ask you, Rory and Ford, if you'll stand up for me at my wedding."

"Of course we will," Rory said.

Ford nodded his agreement.

"Great. If you'll make your way to the garden where Judge Spitzer is waiting, we'll get started."

"What?" Grandpa Sammy yelped. "You're getting married now?"

Colt nodded. "Right now."

"Did you knock her up, too?" Ford asked, referring to Rory getting Sadie pregnant before he asked her to marry him.

Colt shook his head, trying not to laugh in front of

his future mother-in-law, who eyed him suspiciously. "No. She's not pregnant. But she agreed to marry me, and we're not inclined to wait."

"You're serious?" Sadie asked. "But she didn't say anything to me."

"We wanted it to be a surprise." Colt pulled the flowers out from behind his back. "Will you stand up for Luna as her maid of honor?"

Tears sprang to Sadie's eyes. She came forward and took the bouquet. "Of course I will." She held the flowers to her chest. They complemented her pretty purple dress. Sadie looked around again at the backyard, then back at him. "It's beautiful, Colt. Just like she always talked about. A wedding under the stars."

It touched him that Sadie said so and that he'd pulled this off in less than a day. Relieved he'd given his bride the wedding she wanted and dreamed about, he got a bit unexpectedly choked up.

"Let's all gather by the garden."

Colt walked down the path. Rory and Ford fell in on either side of him, each slapping a hand on Colt's shoulder. Colt ignored the wave of pain and focused on the anticipation filling him up.

"Damn, brother, when you make up your mind, you make up your mind," Rory said.

"We've got our reasons for doing this so fast, but it doesn't change the fact this is what we both want."

"We'll talk about it later," Rory said.

"That's a nice tie tack," Ford commented. "I think Dad had one like it."

"It is Dad's." Colt took his place beside the judge. Rory and Ford stood to his left.

Sadie took her place on the other side of the judge. "I gave that to Luna to get fixed for our wedding, Rory."

"I've got something of Dad's," Colt said to his brothers. "I gave Luna the matching ring that belonged to Mom. I told her she could borrow it, but I want her to have it. It means something to me. I'm sorry I didn't ask you guys first."

Rory hooked his arm around Colt's neck and hugged him close. "You want them for your special day, they're yours, Colt."

Rory released him and Ford nodded his agreement.

Grandpa Sammy came forward and straightened Colt's tie, though it didn't need adjusting. He placed his hand on Colt's chest. "It's perfect. Your father would have wanted you to have it. He wore it on his wedding day. He gave your mother the ring as her wedding gift, just like you did for Luna. Some things are meant to be, son."

"Like her." Colt nodded toward the house and his beautiful Luna standing at the edge of the garden on her father's arm. Luna's mother tapped play on Colt's MP3 player, starting the music on the stereo system he'd set up. The wedding march began. His grandfather gave him a tap on the chest, then stepped back to join their gathered friends. Some Colt had invited, others were Luna's friends from the diner, the guys who worked on the ranch, along with Dex and Deputy Foster. Only their closest friends and immediate family, but enough for them. All they needed was each other, but it was nice to share this special occasion with the ones they loved.

"She's beautiful," Sadie whispered. "Look at that dress."

Colt smiled and tried not to fidget or go after her and pull her down the path so they could get this done. Instead, he took her in again. So lovely and elegant in her dress, her hair pulled back just so, and that sweet, sexy smile she gave him as she drew near.

"Damn, bro," Ford whispered.

Colt stepped forward and took Luna's hand from her father. "Thank you, sir. I promise I'll take care of her."

"All I ask is that you make her happy."

"Every day," Colt swore.

This time he gave into his urge and pulled Luna forward to stand in front of the judge. She held her flowers in front of her, his mother's ring sparkling in the soft lights strung overhead. Her other hand remained firmly in his.

She smiled at him, then tilted her head back and looked up at the stars. He did the same, taking a moment to take in the night sky overhead.

They both looked back at each other at the same time.

Judge Spitzer smiled at both of them. "Before we begin, the bride and groom have each requested a moment to say something to the other."

The judge nodded for Colt to go ahead. He and Luna had both agreed to the short vows the judge would have them repeat, but they'd each wanted to say something personal. He hoped the speech he'd agonized over meant something to her.

"Luna, just like your namesake, the moon, you brighten up the darkest parts of me and light my way straight to you. I want to be the peace in your life. The happiness that makes you smile. The quiet that settles your busy mind. The man who makes you laugh and fills your heart. You are all those things and a thousand more for me."

Luna's eyes glassed over at his simple but heartfelt words.

"Colt, if I'm the moon, then you are the stars that light up my night sky, my heart, my life. If this love we share started with a kiss, then I hope we share thousands more and that love builds into a lifetime of happy memories. We've been given so much, but the most important thing we share is the love we have for each other. As long as we have that, we have everything."

Colt squeezed her hand to let her know he agreed.

He lost himself in her unwavering gaze as he, then she, recited their vows. The judge paused once again, allowing them time to exchange rings. Colt pulled the wedding band from his pocket and held it up in front of Luna.

"A symbol of my never-ending love, my promise." He slid the simple gold band onto her finger.

Luna handed her bouquet to Sadie, turned back to him, and pulled the ring he hadn't seen from her thumb.

"When did you have time to get that?" He didn't really expect her to have a ring for him. He thought they'd pick one out later.

"I made time. Believe it or not, this took longer than finding my dress." She held the thick gold ring up. Two polished gold bands on either side of a hammered gold center band. She turned the ring so he could see the engraving inside.

A small butterfly, then the words "You are my everything," ending with a tiny half moon.

"Luna." Just her name. He had no other words to tell her how much the ring, the sentiment, her love meant to him. Overwhelmed with it, his heart swelled so big in his chest he could barely breathe.

"A symbol of my never-ending love, my promise." She slipped the ring on his finger and smiled. "It fits."

"You fit." He pulled Luna in for a deep kiss, too

consumed with his love for her to do anything else but show her how much he loved her.

"Well, you got the kiss part done," Judge Spitzer said, a laugh in his voice. "All that's left for me to do is say, I now pronounce you husband and wife."

Colt hadn't stopped kissing Luna, but the words that she was his wife made him pull back just enough to smile down at her. "Mrs. Kendrick."

"Oh, I like that." The smile on her lips, the light in her eyes, everything about her made him so damn happy.

A cheer went up from their family and friends, breaking him out of the bubble he'd been in with Luna. His brothers gave him a hug and a slap on the back. At this point, Colt was numb to the pain in his shoulder. Luna held Sadie close, the two friends caught up in talk of her ring, the dress, the flowers, and the inevitable pout from Sadie that Luna pulled this all off without Sadie's help or telling her a word about it. Rory and Ford didn't seem to care he'd kept the secret.

Grandpa Sammy pulled him aside for a moment while Luna hugged her mother and father. "I'm proud of you, son. I wish you and your lovely bride all the happiness and a long future together."

"Thanks, Granddad. Maybe you'll even get another great-grandbaby soon."

"Take your time. Enjoy each other."

"What? This after you hounded us for the last year to get married and have babies?"

"Like I told Rory. I wanted you boys to find true and lasting happiness. The way you look at her," Grandpa Sammy shook his head, a wistful look in his eyes, "I see the magic there. You've always had family, but now you know what it's like to have more."

Colt hooked his arm over his grandfather's shoulders and pulled him close. "You were right. More is better." His life was better because he had Luna in it. "We want to make our life here, the kind of life Wayne had with his family, though Luna and I will do it our way."

"And better, I hope. I don't like this nasty business with his family."

"That's about to end."

His grandfather eyed him, questions on his mind, but Luna flew into Colt's arms, so Colt let it go for a little while and focused on the best thing in his life presently kissing his neck. Tonight was for him and his wife.

They ate, they danced, they toasted their new life together, and accepted all the good wishes from their family and friends. By the time he lay in bed with his well-satisfied wife tucked against his side, her hand resting over his heart, her wedding rings sparkling on her finger, he almost believed that the joy they experienced tonight would last, but deep down he worried about the days to come and the threat still very real in their lives.

CHAPTER 32

Simon sat at his kitchen table, staring at his laptop screen, the cursor blinking away. Taunting him. He picked up the bottle of Scotch and poured another double, thinking that drinking probably wouldn't clear his mind or allow him to make the right decision.

He'd kept *this* option in his back pocket. Insurance.

As often as he told himself he could do it, the thought of getting caught stopped him.

He'd rather do anything than work on the ranch. He hated the dirty, hard work. He excelled at sales, marketing, and especially schmoozing clients and potential buyers. He'd rather be the guy giving the orders than taking them. But that wasn't going to happen now. Not when she'd gone and taken it all away. Again.

His finger hovered over the mouse, but he didn't click the confirm transaction button. He slammed his fist on the table and made the bottle and glass shake. He picked up the hand-delivered letter from his father's attorney and smashed it in his fist, chucking it across the room, completely frustrated when the light paper fluttered to the floor instead of slamming into the wall with a satisfying crash.

He moved his hand to tap the mouse and just do it,

but he stopped at the last millisecond and stared at the half-million-dollar check he'd received along with the letter that read she and Colt had married and she'd invoked the other terms of the will.

As much as he wanted to hate her, he couldn't deny that she tried to be fair. Underlying everything she did and the talks they'd had about the ranch, she wanted to do the right thing. He'd felt she held something back. Maybe just the part about her marrying and taking over the ranch for herself, but a niggling feeling deep inside said there was still something more.

Simon believed the test his father had put forth, which would allow him to inherit more, was still in play, and that flicker of belief kept him from hitting the send button on his computer. It had kept him working at the ranch each day until she'd ordered him to leave after Colt's accident, even though it had been clear to him, Luna, and everyone who worked there that he wasn't cut out for the job.

He understood why she'd ordered him off the ranch. He'd seen her with Colt. It didn't take a genius to put together the way they looked at each other, the way they couldn't keep their hands off each other, the way Colt protected her, making sure someone on the ranch was always near to keep her safe. He'd never seen a woman light up the way Luna did when Colt was around. No woman ever looked at Simon the way Luna looked at Colt. Based on the way Colt relaxed and smiled, like everything eased and was better just having her near, the feeling was mutual.

Luna married Colt because she loved him. To protect him, she'd taken the ranch away again. His father had left Luna the ranch because he'd believed she'd take care of it. That truth tasted bitter on Simon's tongue.

Knowing all the arguments, Simon tried to understand why his father did this, but still Simon couldn't reconcile it in his mind.

Reality sucked. His options seemed even worse.

The house phone rang, but he didn't pick up. Josh already called twice without leaving a message. Sure enough, the recorder clicked on and Simon listened to his brother's angry voice.

"Damnit, Simon, pick up the damn phone. I know you're there. Aunt Bea and I are meeting in an hour to talk about our options. That bitch won't get away with this. I'll make sure of it. If you're in, meet us at my place. You don't want to be left out of this. We will get everything back."

Simon didn't want to get caught up in whatever they planned. He didn't want anyone to get hurt. After what happened to Colt, that terrible car accident that was no accident, Simon thought he'd take the money and run. The thing was, he had an odd feeling that letting it go would be far more beneficial and less stressful than looking over his shoulder the rest of his life.

Simon wondered how close Josh and his aunt had gotten to each other, grieving in their simmering pot of rage, roiling together in their shared hatred of Luna, rattling the lid on the boiling cauldron of righteous indignation that smothered their grief.

Simon didn't want to get caught in the middle when the outrage boiled over.

Colt had already been hurt. Would somebody finally have to die before their greed subsided and they started thinking clearly and they understood that nothing they said or did would change the outcome but would inevitably make things worse?

Simon didn't want to fall into that category, which

was probably why he couldn't bring himself to collect on his own insurance policy.

He hadn't ruled it out completely. Even now, when he wanted to give in to his anger, feed off his family's, that something inside niggled that there was more to what Luna was doing than met the eye.

But what?

That question kept him from diving headfirst into the mire with his family and goading them to take action against Luna. He didn't really have to do anything.

Josh wouldn't stop until he got what he wanted, no matter the cost.

Yeah, Simon would keep that insurance policy in his back pocket. It just might come in handy if they pulled this off. Whatever *this* was. He didn't want to know. Plausible deniability.

Even if they did get away with it, he'd take it all away. They didn't deserve it after what they'd done. He blamed his fucked-up logic and his next move on the booze.

He called Luna, surprised she'd pick up.

"What do you want?" she asked.

He said only one thing, then hung up. "You may think this is over, but it's not."

CHAPTER 33

A week after the wedding and that ominous phone call the following day, Simon's warning still rang in Colt's head. They knew this wasn't over, so what were the Traverses waiting for? The waiting drove him crazy. Luna jumped at practically every little sound. He hated the dark circles under his wife's eyes, the way she agonized over her decision to keep the ranch and cut the Traverses out, and especially the fact that the longer this thing went unresolved, the deeper the fear took hold of her and left her afraid to walk out the door each day. She fretted about him driving into town. He had to admit, his stomach tied in knots on that long stretch of road they'd taken him out on once, but he remained cautious and vigilant. The stress was getting to them. So much so that when he'd walked in the door last night, Luna had actually snapped at him about being late and not telling her where he'd gone. Not that it was a big deal, but with things the way they were, it was a big deal to her.

"Colt," her sweet voice called from the front of the cabin he'd been working to get ready for Tanner to move into next week.

"Back here, honey." He set the paint roller in the

tray at his feet and wiped his hands on the bandana he pulled from his back pocket.

Luna appeared in the doorway, her hands braced on the frame. He smiled at his rocker country girl, wearing tight jeans with a frayed hole in the thigh, her favorite black cowboy boots, and a tight black Def Leppard T-shirt stretched across her breasts. Her dark hair hung forward, but it fell back when she looked up and past him at the new color he'd painted the walls.

"I like it."

"Let's hope Tanner does." This was the third time he'd had to change the color because Tanner didn't quite like it. It had to be the perfect shade of tan. The first had too much brown in it. The second turned out too yellow. This much lighter and brighter tone better be right, because Colt didn't want to paint again.

"If he doesn't, bring him back at a different time of day and tell him it's a different color. Eventually, he'll accept it."

"Why didn't you tell me that after I painted the last time?"

"Because I didn't like that color either. This one is perfect." She walked into the room and right into his chest, wrapping her arms around his neck. She stared up at him. "You're perfect."

He eyed her. "I take it you're not mad at me anymore for running into town to buy more of your favorite ice cream." A treat and a surprise he'd hoped would take her mind off everything, if only for a little while. Instead, he'd run into an old buddy in the parking lot and gotten to talking about the cop following him, getting married, and moving to Rambling Range. A half hour later, he'd gone back into the store to get a new container of ice cream because the first melted. Then he'd headed home and straight into Luna letting loose her pent-up emotions, which had left her out of breath and apologizing when he'd handed her the tub of rocky road.

"I wasn't mad." The words rushed out of her mouth. Her gaze fell to his chest. She slipped one hand down his still sore left shoulder and the trail of bruises that led straight over his heart. "I was scared," she admitted, her voice soft.

He pulled her close and kissed her soft hair. "Nothing is going to happen to me."

"It already did." She touched the stitches on his head. "They nearly killed you. If I lost you . . ." Sadness laced with the fear in her voice. Her nails bit into his back, she held him so tight.

"Luna, honey, you've got to stop worrying so much. We can't keep living our lives waiting for the next bad thing to happen. We need to find a way to let it go and live the life we want."

"I'm trying."

"Then stop treating me like a two-year-old who can't be out of your sight."

"They want to use you as a target to get me to do what they want."

He held her by the shoulders. "There is nothing they can do now. You own this place. It's done."

"Tell them that."

"Dex told them. He'll keep telling them. We talked about this." Every day for the last week. "Wayne would want you and me to run this ranch, to raise our family here. To protect what he built and make it better."

"I don't like that his family is so upset and aggressive."

"Is that a polite way of saying, *They're out of their ever-loving minds*?"

"Wayne wouldn't have wanted this for us."

"He wanted you to be happy. We're newlyweds, yet my wife barely smiles anymore. People are going to start thinking you regret marrying me."

Her mouth opened on a gasp. She smacked him on the chest. "No they won't." Her eyes narrowed and turned sultry. "Not when they see the way we kiss."

Her mouth swept over his in a light caress. That's all they needed to dive in for more. No, no one would think his wife unhappy with him. He pleased her well in and out of bed when it came to the physical stuff. He wished he knew how to erase all this upset. He wanted her to go back to being the carefree, happy, fun-loving woman he fell so hard for he couldn't help but be drawn into her world and want to be a part of it forever.

Lost in her, he ignored the first time someone cleared their throat to get their attention. And the second.

"Hey, you two. Get a room," Ed said from behind Luna.

Colt cupped Luna's beautiful face, pressed his forehead to hers, and stared down into her hungry eyes. "Later," he whispered, a promise filled with intent he meant to keep.

To Ed he said, "We're in a room. Alone. Until you showed up."

"The paint color looks great. I think Tanner will like this one."

Colt didn't want to go there. He'd paint the room a dozen more times if it meant Tanner felt at home and at peace here, but Colt didn't have to like it.

He wanted Luna to feel safe here more than anything.

"What are you doing here?" he asked Ed.

"Patrol car and Dex just showed up in the driveway. They're waiting up by the house for the two of you."

Luna shot him a worried look.

Colt spread his hands wide, then let them fall and hit the sides of his legs. "Let's go see what they want."

"Do you think they finally got the evidence they need to arrest the Traverses?"

"Let's go find out."

Luna hesitated. He suspected she feared getting more bad news. One more delay. One more day they'd live wondering if the Traverses would pull another stunt and hurt one of the animals, one of them. She feared something happening to him so much that she clung to him in the night and watched him like a hawk during the day.

He wanted this to be over just as much as her. If the cops didn't get it done soon, he might just issue a few threats himself to get them to stop. Enough was enough. He refused to watch his wife tie herself up in knots every second of the day. The toll it took on her was too much for him to bear.

"Ed, would you mind cleaning up the paintbrushes and roller, and pull the tape off the trim?"

"I'm on it." Ed moved into the room and dropped to one knee. He closed up the paint can and gathered all the other supplies into the tray to take to the sink and wash out.

Colt took Luna's hand, brought it up to his mouth, and kissed her palm. He wrapped his arm around her shoulder and walked out of the cabin with her by his side. She tried to keep the pace slow, but he ushered her up the gravel road to the main house. Sure enough, Dex and Deputy Foster stood on the porch waiting for them.

"We got them," Dex called, a big smile spreading across his face.

Luna stopped short. "Them?"

Deputy Foster stepped down from the porch and met them on the path. "Harry and Josh. Harry will be charged with theft for stealing your truck, a handful of other misdemeanor charges, and the much more serious attempted murder for hitting Colt."

"Are you sure it was him?" Colt asked, surprised the older man would do such a thing. In his mind, he'd pegged Josh for the crime.

"During the accident, Harry face-planted into the airbag. We've got his DNA."

"How did you match it to him?" Colt asked.

"We didn't yet, but we will now that we have him in custody and a warrant to compel him to give us a sample to compare. We lifted his print from the door panel and driver's-side window. The latex gloves he wore when he stole the truck must have broken during the accident when the air bag went off. Stunned by the force of the accident, he didn't realize it until it was too late and he was getting away. His prints are on file from a DUI arrest a couple of years ago. Wayne got him out of that trouble."

"And this is how he repays that kindness, by undermining Wayne's wishes." Luna shook her head, her lips drawn into a tight line. "How did he get away? Did his wife help him?"

"He says no, that he had another vehicle stashed nearby."

Luna's brows drew together. "Who made the call to me?"

"All the prints on Colt's phone were smudged. Harry says he made the call."

"I don't believe that for a minute." Luna swept her bangs aside. "He's quiet. His wife does all the talking. She made that call."

"When I left the station to come here and tell you what we've got, she was raising the roof. Still, we have no proof she was in on it. Harry refuses to give her up."

"Blind love," Colt said. "He did it on her order."

With nothing more to say about Bea's involvement, Deputy Foster moved on. "We put Josh here the night he made that call to you and threatened to shoot Colt."

"His name wasn't on the caller ID, how do you know for sure it was him?" Luna brushed her hands up her arms and kept them crossed over her middle, thinking of that asshole creeping around outside their windows.

"We checked local places within a ten-mile radius of his home to see if anyone remembered him buying a disposable cell phone. We actually got a hit. Some teenage girl working behind the counter at a drugstore remembered him."

"He's a good-looking guy. I can see that," Luna said, drawing Colt's *What the hell?* glare. She smiled indulgently at him and patted his arm. "He's cute. You're gorgeous, honey. Relax."

"Stop checking out other dudes, especially when they're pieces of shit like Josh. You're my wife."

"Yes, I am. Now. And forever more."

"Damn right."

"Anyway," Deputy Foster broke in, "we got a copy of the receipt and the number for the phone. We got a warrant to have the phone company triangulate where the phone was used on the day in question. Then he went and made things easy on us and kept the phone hidden between the seats in his car with your number still in the call log."

"Idiot." Colt grinned at Josh's stupidity.

"Criminals get caught all the time for making stupid

mistakes. Josh is arrogant. He never thought he'd get caught."

"Compared to what Harry did, his offense isn't that bad," Luna pointed out.

"No. But he will be charged with peeping, trespassing, threatening Colt, and, uh, I don't know how to tell you this, but he, uh, took pictures of you two . . ." Deputy Foster made a suggestive gesture with his hands in a kind of clapping motion to symbolize her and Colt making love.

Luna's face flushed red, partially from embarrassment, but mostly with a rage that made her gasp and narrow her fury-filled eyes. "That bastard."

"Exactly," Deputy Foster agreed.

"And Simon? What has he done?"

"Nothing as far as we can tell, or prove. If he was in on any of it, Josh and Harry didn't say."

"Have you spoken to Agent Montrose? Any movement on the computer front?"

"Nothing," Deputy Foster confirmed.

"Okay, so who poisoned the horses?"

"While we've confirmed someone tainted the food, we have no evidence of who did it. Simon seems the likely suspect as he had access and motive, but we also placed Josh on the property, so it could be him."

"So Simon is still a wild card." Luna turned to Colt. "What do you think?"

"He did the work asked of him here. He seemed genuinely surprised by the vandalism when you moved in. While I don't think he'd have lasted doing the manual labor here on the ranch, he might have finally come around to realizing there is a lot of other work he could have done and shared the burden with you. I think he was still on the fence between playing things straight and taking the easy way out and robbing you blind."

"I think so, too. But the horses, that still gets to me. If he's capable of doing that, what else might he do now that he's got no chance to earn his piece of this place?"

"I know it's way out there, but I peg Bea for the rats and the horses," Colt said. "It's cruel, and she comes off as not caring about anyone but herself if she'd put her husband up to killing me."

Luna held herself tighter, shaking her head. With nothing to say about Bea, because Colt's assessment rang unbelievably true, Luna went back to Simon. "Now that Harry and Josh have been arrested, let's see what Simon does. Side with them? Turn his back on the family and renounce what they did? Help with the investigation against Bea? Or come after us again?"

"Harry and Josh will be arraigned tomorrow. Josh will probably get bail. Harry may be denied, unless he's got a really good lawyer," Deputy Foster said, putting things back on track. "I'll keep you up to date as I get information. Until then, enjoy your evening knowing we got them."

Dex stepped forward. "Let me know if you need me to do anything, Luna."

"Get a judge to issue a restraining order against all of them," Colt demanded.

"Now that we have actual evidence, you should be able to get it," Deputy Foster acknowledged.

"I'll get started on it immediately. I'll ask Judge Spitzer to hear our argument. Since he married you, I think he'll be sympathetic to putting it through immediately." Dex shook Colt's hand and patted Luna's shoulder before heading to his car.

Deputy Foster followed and got into his own.

Alone in front of their house, Colt held Luna by the shoulders and stared down at her. "What's wrong?"

A shiver rocked her body and vibrated up his arms. "Why don't I feel like this is over?"

"Even if they don't pin anything on Simon and Bea, Harry and Josh's arrest should make them back off now."

"It should." She said the words with so little conviction even Colt didn't believe it.

Maybe it was her uncertainty and fear that gave him a creepy sense of inevitability that they hadn't heard the last of the Travers family.

CHAPTER 34

Simon walked into the sheriff's department and didn't need to be directed where to go. Aunt Bea stood over a deputy sitting at his desk and pointed one perfectly manicured pink nail right in the poor guy's face.

"You let him out right this minute," she demanded. "This is his lawyer."

"Ma'am, I told you a hundred times, he'll be arraigned in the morning. Until then, he's not going anywhere."

"Mrs. Murphy, please come over here and let's discuss our options," some guy in a suit pleaded with his aunt. Had to be the lawyer she hired. He'd gotten here fast. Simon just got the call from Josh about his arrest not even half an hour ago.

His cousins, Anne and Kelly, took their mother's arms and pulled her back from the deputy, though they still remained standing in a clump next to his desk.

"They can't hold him like this. He didn't do it. She paid the police to fabricate evidence," Aunt Bea ranted, a touch of hysteria in her voice.

Simon rolled his eyes, wishing he could be anywhere else. Maybe he should just walk out the door and leave them all to face the consequences of their plotting and scheming.

"Mom, please, we need to talk to Mr. Lindy about getting Dad out of jail," Kelly pleaded.

Mr. Lindy took the opening. "Mrs. Murphy, the judge will hear the evidence tomorrow and we can ask for bail."

"Yes, we'll bail him out." His aunt eyed the deputy, letting him know she was still pissed he didn't do her bidding.

"Do you have sufficient funds available? With the charges against him, the bail sum could be substantial," Mr. Lindy explained.

"We can put up the house," his aunt spat out.

"Do you own the home or have enough equity to do so?"

The realization that widened his aunt's eyes and made her gasp hit Simon at the same time. "Wayne bought me the house and property."

His dad had done the same for Simon and Josh. Holy shit, they didn't own their houses. Luna did. Simon had never put it together until right now. She'd never said a word about it. Neither had his father's lawyer. But he and Aunt Bea both got it right now. Luna got fucking everything, including the roofs over their heads.

"So you don't own the house." Mr. Lindy confirmed the worst.

"No." Aunt Bea's denial came out on a soft exhale of disbelief. "That fucking bitch who stole everything does. This is all her fault."

"Mom, you have the money Uncle Wayne left you. You can use that to get Dad out of jail," Anne pleaded.

Anne and Kelly read the sad, resigned, and shameful look that came into Aunt Bea's eyes better than Simon did, because the two women released their mother's arms and their faces turned into angry scowls.

"You spent it all, didn't you?" Kelly accused.

"You wasted it on online shopping and TV shopping networks." Anne swept her hand up and down in front of his aunt. "When will all the shiny things you buy be enough? When will you finally get it that no matter how sparkly you look on the outside, it will never make you feel happy on the inside." Anne's eyes teared up.

"Your shopping addiction cost us everything," Kelly accused. "You're the reason Uncle Wayne had to buy us a house after you and Dad filed for bankruptcy and lost the other one."

"If your father had only followed in my brother's footsteps and built the business into something that made us money instead of sucking us dry." The words dripped with Bea's unwarranted scorn.

Kelly fumed. "You sucked the business dry. Daddy had to pay off all those debts you racked up. Every time he tried to get ahead, you dragged him down. You dragged all of us down, stealing money from Anne and me when we worked part-time jobs in high school. Our babysitting money. We had to hide every dime we ever had, to keep you from taking it." Kelly's eyes shined with unshed tears.

"How many times did we have to leave the grocery store without any food because the credit cards were maxed out and the bank account was empty? No one would take a check from you," Anne spat out, her hands clenched at her sides.

"And still you wouldn't part with one of your precious baubles. All that crap you bought, but never once did you think of us," Kelly accused.

"I bought you things, too," Aunt Bea responded, trying to justify her behavior.

"We wanted you to stop," Kelly shouted.

Simon had no idea his aunt had a problem. Every time the families got together, he never suspected anything was wrong. Sure the girls seemed put off by their mother when they were younger, but he figured that was just the way things were with kids and their parents. He'd butted heads with his dad and mom all the time.

His aunt dressed in designer clothes and wore an audacious amount of jewelry. Even now, he wondered how much the gems and gold weighed on his aunt's hands. She must get tired waving them around all the time. The necklace with the three-inch-square purple stone surrounded by dime-size round stones must have cost a fortune. He and Josh used to joke that Aunt Bea pretended to be royalty with all her giant jewels. Now "Country Queen," their childhood nickname for Aunt Bea, didn't seem so funny. The woman had a problem, and her family had suffered because of it. No wonder his dad had to send them money all the time. No wonder he and Bea hadn't gotten along. Wayne had to have been tired of supporting her habit. She might not be doing drugs, but her addiction was no less destructive when she chose fanciful items over feeding her kids.

"If he hadn't left it all to that bitch . . ."

"You'd squander it all away," Anne finished. "We know why he did it, so you wouldn't spend it all on everything, anything, and nothing that meant a damn thing."

"I'm glad he left it to her," Kelly said. "The ranch means a lot to her. She and Colt are married now. They'll run that place and be the kind of family we never were."

"How can you say that? How can you take her side?" Aunt Bea raged.

"Because she paid off the credit card debt you put on my card when you stole it from my wallet. She paid the two-year lease on the apartment I rented so I can go back to school. She isn't a bad person. She helped Anne, too."

Anne nodded. "She paid off all my debt so I can start fresh. She even gave me an interest-free loan to start my own business."

"What?" Shock filled Aunt Bea's voice.

The same shock that rushed through Simon. He had no idea his cousins contacted Luna and asked for her help. He had no idea that Luna gave it so easily and generously.

"That woman you want to condemn isn't out to keep it all for herself. She didn't ask Uncle Wayne to leave it to her. She's trying to do what he asked of her and take care of what he left behind. That includes us," Anne added.

"But you want to take it from her and you don't care who gets hurt. Daddy loves you. He'd do anything for you, and you use that to hurt him again and again." Kelly's voice cracked.

"It stops now." Anne's voice held conviction, along with the sadness she couldn't hide. "You've gone too far, Mom. He's facing serious jail time. He could have killed Colt. Do you have any idea how much he's agonized over that since it happened?" Anne asked.

Aunt Bea looked stricken, like she'd never considered that Uncle Harry might regret helping his wife.

"Of course you don't," Anne went on. "You only think of yourself. You don't see the dark circles and bags under Dad's eyes. You don't see the strain you've put on him. Oh, he'll cover for you. He always does. He'll come up with a dozen and one excuses for what you made him do and why. He helps you, but you can't help him."

Kelly turned to Mr. Lindy. "She can't pay your retainer or the bail money. I'll contact Luna and see if she will help. I don't know if she will, seeing as how her husband was the one who got hurt, but I think she'll have enough compassion to at least pay for a lawyer for my dad."

Aunt Bea's face turned dark red with rage. She vibrated with it. Even from ten feet away, Simon felt it radiate off her.

A deputy brought Uncle Harry, his hands cuffed behind him, out of the back, where they must have had him locked up. Kelly and Anne ran to him, wrapping their arms around his middle and hugging him close. Uncle Harry bent and kissed each of them on the head. His head came up and his weary gaze landed on Aunt Bea, who seethed, looking at her daughters' obvious allegiance to their father and not her.

"She won't get away with this." Aunt Bea stormed past Simon, whipping him in the side with the chain strap on her designer purse as she headed for the door. She threw it open and walked out without another word, not even a *Sorry* for hitting him.

He might not have noticed it before, but that bag probably cost a fortune. A fortune she didn't have to begin with. He rubbed his hand over the small hurt, easing it almost instantly.

"Simon, what are you doing here?" Kelly asked.

"Josh called," he answered. "You two going to be okay?"

"We're used to dealing with Mom's messes." Anne hugged her dad again. "We'll get through this one even though it is a million times worse than anything she's ever done. Losing Uncle Wayne really messed her up."

Yes, it did, if she was willing to try to kill someone and use her husband to do it.

"Girls, your mother is grieving. She needs time . . ."

"Stop it, Dad. We don't want to hear it," Anne snapped. "Now come over here and talk with Mr. Lindy. He'll tell you what you need to do to avoid spending the rest of your life in prison. You will do as he says," she ordered.

The group moved off to use a small conference room at the other end of the office. A deputy stood guard outside, making sure Uncle Harry didn't decide to make a break for it.

Another deputy led Josh out of the back.

Simon didn't have time to deal with his brother. He turned for the door, some inner sense telling him to go after Aunt Bea. He didn't like the way she looked when she left, and he feared she'd do something even more stupid than what she'd already instigated.

"Simon, wait! I need your help. Post bail for me." Josh stood before him with his hands cuffed behind his back.

"Did you help Uncle Harry try to kill Colt?" Simon asked, eyeing the door his aunt left through, knowing he shouldn't stall but go after her. Right now.

"No. I had nothing to do with that."

"Then what did you do?" Simon nodded and said what he already knew. "Peeping through her windows, making that threatening call."

Josh's gaze fell to his feet. "I might have also taken some rather graphic pictures of them in bed together."

"Let me guess, you thought you might blackmail her with the pictures."

Josh couldn't help the grin that crept across his face. Simon saw it appear every time Josh got caught for something he thought funny but was really just wrong.

"Maybe," Josh confirmed Simon's suspicions.

"That's really fucked up, you know that?"

"It's child's play compared to what Aunt Bea and Uncle Harry did."

"That doesn't make it any less despicable."

"She deserves a little public humiliation after seducing our father, taking our inheritance, and hooking up with that cowboy so she can keep it all to herself."

Simon shook his head, finally seeing everything more clearly through his grief and disappointment that his father hadn't trusted him. His dad had a point. Kelly was right, Dad had left it all to Luna because they couldn't be trusted with it. They'd have tossed it all away without a thought and wondered why there wasn't more being handed over to them.

"Dad left you quite a sum of money. Bail yourself out."

Simon spun around and went after his aunt, hoping she'd gone home to cool off and maybe order some useless shit off the Internet. Deep down, he feared he knew exactly where he'd find her.

CHAPTER 35

Luna jumped at the sound of breaking glass. She flipped off the burner beneath the skillet of frying ground beef and rushed around the counter toward the living room. Colt had gone down to the stables a half hour ago to check on the horses one last time before they ate dinner.

"You fucking bitch," Bea shouted, swiping her hand across the foyer table and sending the planters and framed pictures crashing to the floor. She'd broken the front door side window pane so she could reach in and unlock the door.

Luna stopped in her tracks, shocked by the sheer rage and destruction before her. Bea grabbed the photo of Luna with Wayne off the wall, held it in both hands, and smashed it against the side of the table. Glass went flying everywhere.

"Bea, stop," Luna coaxed in a soft voice.

"You did this," Bea screamed, slamming the frame down on the table again. Her heavy purse bounced at her side, but it didn't fall off her shoulder.

Luna didn't know if Bea meant that Luna or Wayne had done this, but it didn't really matter. Bea's anger remained squarely pointed at Luna.

Bea dropped the frame with a clatter on the tile, then pointed one bedazzled finger at Luna. "You spoke to my girls. You turned them against me." Tears shimmered in Bea's fury-filled eyes.

"I've spoken to both your daughters. You've raised two lovely women." Luna hoped her outward calm eased Bea, but it only agitated her more.

"You gave them money."

"They asked for my help and I gave it to them. Wayne would have wanted me to do that for his nieces. He spoke of them often. He loved them dearly."

"He always wanted a daughter," she said absently.

Luna felt as if he'd found a little piece of that dream with her. He'd certainly treated her like family.

Colt bolted onto the porch and stopped short just inside the front door, looking at her first, then down at the mess Bea made. He ran past Bea and came to her, taking her by the shoulders. "Are you okay, honey?"

"I'm fine," she assured him.

"What the fuck are you doing here?" he demanded.

Luna saw the swift change in Bea and wished she'd had a few more minutes to wind down Bea's anger.

"He took the piddly amount of money our parents left us and built this place from nothing. Oh, he paid me back the money I gave him to get started, but he should have left me half of this place. He wouldn't have had it without me!"

Luna clamped her hand on Colt's forearm to silently ask him to be quiet.

"Sounds like you sacrificed during those early years to help your brother."

Bea's mouth compressed and her eyes narrowed. "I did. We came from nothing. Nothing! And how does he repay me, he leaves his whore everything."

"Watch it," Colt warned.

Luna held Colt's arm, even as he took a step toward Bea, ready to toss her out of their house. "Wayne wanted me to look after this place and his family."

"How are you looking out for us?"

"I helped your daughters." Luna pointed out the very thing Bea already knew but hated to acknowledge, because all she really wanted to talk about was how Luna was going to help her. Or more accurately, that Luna would hand everything over to her. "I paid out the rest of the million to Simon even though I didn't have to. I'm trying to be fair."

"Fair. Is it fair my husband is in jail?" Bea yelled.

"He tried to kill me," Colt said evenly.

"He wouldn't have done any such thing if you'd just sold the ranch and given me my money. I thought I made it clear when you moved in you weren't welcome here. I thought you'd see that you're not cut out for this place. You can't even keep your horses healthy." Bea's eyes shined with hysteria and mirth.

"You vandalized the house. You poisoned the horses." Luna couldn't believe it. She didn't want to, but she had to face the truth that Wayne's sister would stop at nothing to get what she wanted.

Bea stuffed her hand into her purse and pulled out a gun. "You took everything from me. Now I'm going to take everything from you." She leveled the gun and pointed it directly at Colt's chest.

Luna jumped in front of Colt and held up both hands. His settled at the sides of her shoulders. He tried to pull her out of the way, but she held firm, protecting him. "Don't do it. Don't do this to your daughters. They need you. Your husband needs you." She needed Colt. She wouldn't let anything more happen to him because of her.

"He's going to jail. My daughters think this is all my fault." Bea shook the gun at her. "It's yours."

Luna kept one hand up and took a tentative step toward Bea. Colt tried to hold her back, but Bea shot her gaze toward him, moved the barrel of the gun in his direction, then back to Luna and back and forth until Colt stilled, knowing he could very well set off Bea and she'd just start shooting at both of them.

"Bea, I understand you're upset."

"Upset. I'm pissed off that you get what you want and I'm left with nothing! It's not fair," she whined. "You can't have it. It's mine."

"Aunt Bea, put the gun down," Simon said from the doorway.

Bea's head whipped around to her nephew, as surprised as Luna was to see him standing there.

Luna seized the opportunity and the split second Bea took her gaze and aim off her and Colt. She rushed Bea and grabbed her wrist, trying to pry the gun out of Bea's hand. "Let go."

"No," Bea wailed.

Luna fell forward with Bea as Colt tackled the older woman from behind. The gun went off, kicking back in both their hands, then dropping from Bea's fingers. Colt held Bea down with his hands braced on both her arms, his big body holding her, wiggling, to the floor.

Luna sat back on her knees and grabbed the gun off the floor before Bea could get hold of it again.

Colt moved off Bea and flipped her around to face them. Bea screeched and tried to slap Colt across the face. He grabbed her wrist before she smacked him, then held it tight. "Stop, or so help me God, I'll deck you."

Hysterical, with tears and black makeup streaking

down her face, Bea didn't give up the fight. Angry that Bea would try to hurt Colt even now, when he had her at a complete disadvantage, Luna held her hand back and swung, slapping Bea right across the face, whipping her head to the side. Luna's hand stung, but she got what she wanted. Stunned silence.

In that moment, when they all held their breath from the sickening crack Luna's hand made against Bea's cheek, they finally heard Simon's garbled gasps and looked up toward the front door, where Simon lay on his back, half in and half out the door. Bright red blood spread over his chest.

"Colt, call an ambulance." Luna bolted for Simon and slid to her knees beside him. She tossed the gun onto the porch and pressed both hands over the hole in Simon's chest. Blood oozed through her fingers. He stared up at her, his eyes filled with pain and disbelief.

"Hold on, Simon. Help is coming." Luna turned back to Colt, who'd pulled his cell from his pocket, put it on speaker, dialed 911, and rattled off the address, simultaneously tying Bea's hands together with the cord he'd ripped free of the broken lamp Bea trashed along with all the other stuff on the table.

Bea sobbed uncontrollably. "I didn't mean it. I didn't mean to shoot him. It's all your fault."

"Shut up," Luna shouted.

"It should have been you," she yelled back.

"Say another word and I'll gag you, too," Colt snapped.

Simon gasped for another breath, then stopped breathing altogether. Luna took her hands from his bleeding chest and waited to see if more blood pumped out. It stopped, along with the rise and fall of his chest.

"Nooo. No. No. No." She placed her hands back

on Simon's chest and pumped. "Come on, Simon. It doesn't end like this. Come back," she demanded, pushing up and down on his ribs.

Colt slid in beside her, leaned down, and gave him a breath.

A sheriff's vehicle pulled into the drive, lights flashing. Luna knew the odds of saving Simon's life were slim to none when they were this far out of town.

"We need a med flight," she yelled to Deputy Foster. "Now."

"It's on its way," he called, rushing toward them.

He disappeared into the house, then dragged a kicking and screaming Bea out by holding her around the waist and pulling her along. Luna took a kick to the back, but barely noticed.

"Get that crazy bitch out of here," Colt yelled.

Luna kept pumping Simon's chest. Deep down, she prayed he lived. A weight settled on her left shoulder and a sense of calm came over her. She couldn't explain it, but she felt as if Wayne were with her. After all, the last time she saw him had been eerily similar to this.

"You have to live, Simon. Your dad would want you to live."

Luna locked eyes with Colt. He reached over Simon and placed his hand on her cheek as she bounced up and down on Simon's chest. "You've got this, honey."

His confidence in her gave her the courage to keep going, keep trying, because Wayne would want her to never give up on his son.

Everything happened so fast and too slow. Time seemed to speed up and slow down at odd moments. Like waiting for the helicopter that seemed to take forever. The way the life-flight medics rushed Simon on board. The questions she and Colt answered at length and over and over again until she finally stopped talking altogether and stared down at her bloody hands, until Colt covered them with his own and kissed her on the forehead.

She didn't know when everyone left. She couldn't even say who came and went. She didn't know how she ended up clean and in bed, tucked up against Colt's warm body in the dead of night.

She stared into the dark night at nothing. Numb from the inside out, she stared and waited. For what, she didn't know.

Out of the dark came a soft voice she recognized so well. It drew her back from the emptiness and made her reach for the love that made everything in her life better.

"You're okay. I love you." Colt hugged her close with the arm he kept banded around her waist. Her head rested on his other arm. She turned her head and pressed her lips to his big biceps.

She rolled in his arms and faced him, pressing her palm to his rough cheek. He cupped her face and stared down at her, though it was hard to see him in the dark. She didn't need to. She read the worry in the way he touched her.

"I love you," she whispered. "If she'd . . ."

"Ssh. No more. It's done."

"Is Simon . . ." She couldn't finish the sentence.

"He's out of surgery and in ICU. The next couple of hours are critical."

She sighed, a sense of relief coming over her. "He'll make it."

"If he does, it's because of you."

"He might not have gotten shot if I hadn't gone after the gun."

"She might have shot you and me instead if you hadn't. I can't believe you stepped in front of me like that." The anger simmering in his words covered the real reason for it. She'd scared him. The thought of losing him scared her more.

"I'd do it again to keep you safe and by my side." She pressed her forehead to his chin.

He shifted and planted a warm kiss on her skin. His big hand went over her head and he held her close. "Don't ever scare me like that again."

"I'll do whatever I have to, to keep you safe. Including giving up this place. I don't care what Wayne wanted. If it comes to it again, I'll let it all go, because having you in my life is more important than a piece of property or the money."

"Okay, but wherever we end up, you're painting Tanner's room," he teased.

"Deal." She hugged him close and let the smile come, because that was Colt. He didn't care about the land or the money. He loved her the way she loved him. Totally. Completely. More than anything in this world.

CHAPTER 36

Luna stood beside Simon's hospital bed days later in her matron of honor gown. Colt stood at the end of the bed, dashing in his tux.

Simon glanced from Colt to her. "If I'd known this was a formal occasion, I'd have dressed up."

The stupid joke actually made her smile, because it meant Simon was truly on the mend. The doctors had assured her he'd recover fully, but seeing he still had his sense of humor helped alleviate Luna's concerns.

"Well, you know, only the best for you."

"Right. Because we're so close, and it doesn't really matter that my family tried to kill you."

"I don't hold that against you." Luna meant it. To prove it, she kept her steady gaze on Simon and squeezed his hand.

"She blew a gasket at the sheriff's department. I thought she might go after you at the ranch."

"You came to warn me."

"She had a head start. I came to stop her."

Luna believed that, too. "I've retained Mr. Lindy to represent your aunt and uncle at Kelly and Anne's request. They'll probably be locked up for a long time. If and when they do get out, I've promised Anne and

Kelly that I will do as they wish and deem suitable for their parents at that time."

Simon nodded and let out a sigh. "It's far more than they deserve."

"As for your brother the perv."

Simon snorted and looked away, unable to meet her eyes after what his brother did.

"He's got a lawyer of his own. He'll probably get a slap on the wrist for all he's done. If those pictures ever surface, I will bury him right after Colt kills him."

Simon met Colt's steady gaze, then turned to her. "Uh."

"No need to say anything. I've already had my attorney advise Josh to stay away, or Colt will beat the living shit out of him."

Simon glanced at Colt again. Colt nodded, that same intense look he'd held all the while firmly in place. Colt could intimidate an angry bear with that look. Simon read it and looked away, not wanting to instigate anything with her badass husband.

"Last, but not least, you, Simon. I'm keeping the ranch. If you can't live with that, and you come after me or Colt, I will not stop at taking everything you hold dear away from you."

"The one thing I've realized from this near-death experience is that I don't have anything I hold dear. Not like you." Again, Simon looked from her to Colt and back again. "Not like my dad did. He loved that place and what it stood for in his life. He was right, I don't have his cowboy heart. That place is in good hands with you and Colt. I get that now."

"Good. I suggest you think about what it is you love to do and find a purpose for your life." She squeezed his hand again. "You're not getting out of here for at least a week. Plenty of time to think. Use that time wisely. You never know what the future might hold. You make something of yourself, you might just be rewarded for your efforts more than you ever thought possible."

Luna left Simon with those words, took Colt's hand, and walked out with him by her side, their future together more assured now that she knew Simon didn't harbor any ill will toward her. He wasn't like the rest of his family. He'd earned a second chance. She'd give it to him and see what he did with it.

CHAPTER 37

Colt escorted Luna into the hotel where Rory and Sadie's wedding started in half an hour. He spotted his brothers and Grandpa Sammy in the seating area just outside the bar. He stopped Luna beside him, cupped her face in one hand, and leaned down and kissed her softly. She'd been quiet on the ride over from the hospital, but he felt a shift in her. Like she finally believed this whole mess was over and they could finally start their lives without a threat hanging over them.

Rory walked up to them. "Sadie's upstairs waiting for you. She's in room 202."

"I'm headed up now. Are you ready?"

Rory glanced at his watch. "She's about a month late from when I wanted to get this done. I should have done what Colt did and marry her the day after she said yes."

"It worked for us," Luna said, smiling at Colt.

He loved that smile. He'd missed it these last weeks. "Go hurry her up. No one said the bride couldn't be early for her wedding," Colt coaxed.

Luna didn't rush off. Instead, she turned pensive again and reached up and touched the scar on his head. "I really have left a few marks on you."

He took her hand and kissed her palm, then held it

against his face. "Your love is branded on my heart, honey. I am a better man, I have a better life, because of you."

Rory slapped him on the back. "Amen to that. Now go get my bride, Luna," Rory ordered, his voice gruff.

She gave Colt a soft kiss, then stepped back. "On it."

Colt didn't move from his spot until Luna disappeared behind the elevator doors.

"You're lost, man," Rory said from beside him.

"I found everything I ever wanted when I fell for her. I didn't think I wanted a wife, but God, I always wanted her."

"You saw Simon this morning. Everything good?"

"Yeah. He's got his head screwed on straight."

"Good. Then you and Luna can move on with your lives."

"That's right. Starting today, no more looking back, just our bright future ahead of us. Like you and Sadie."

"Let's drink to that." Grandpa Sammy handed them both a shot of whiskey, then took the spare one Ford held. They stood in a circle, their glasses raised. "To Rory and Sadie. A long and happy life together." They clinked glasses and downed the shots.

Colt hooked his arm around his grandfather. "Two down, Granddad. One to go."

"I'm still waiting on baby news from you and Luna."

"We're going to take some time practicing for that one," Colt teased. "Enjoy Rory's little one for a while and let Luna and me settle into our life on Rambling Range."

"Take your time. Enjoy each other for a while, but I want that great-grandbaby."

"Harass Ford for a while." Colt shoved his grandfather toward Ford's retreating back. "You can't get away,

Ford. You're next." Colt laughed when Ford gave him a death stare over his shoulder. As much as Colt had thought getting married was not in his near future, he couldn't be happier being married to Luna. It's what his grandfather wanted for them. Love. Happiness. Colt had both now. More than he ever thought possible. He wanted that for his brother, too.

Luna stood behind Sadie and stared over her shoulder at their images in the mirror. "Sadie, you are so beautiful. That gown is gorgeous."

Sadie smoothed her hands over the pretty lace and her slightly swollen belly. For the first time, Luna felt jealous of her friend. The thought of having Colt's child left a warm glow in her chest. They hadn't really talked about having a baby. She'd like to settle into their life on the ranch before they had a child. Still, the thought stuck in the back of her mind.

"I love it." Sadie tilted her head and studied her reflection. "Am I going to look pregnant in all the photos?"

"Only because you know you are. No one else will notice." Luna stood behind Sadie and wrapped her arms around her friend, seeing the sadness Sadie tried to hide because her mother wasn't here to help her dress and do her hair. Her father wasn't here to walk her down the aisle. Her brother sat in a cell day after day with no remorse for what he'd done. Luna hugged Sadie from behind and tried to give her the words Sadie's mother might have said. "You are the most beautiful bride there ever was. I love you, my friend. You and Rory are going to have a beautiful life together. The love you share is everlasting."

"Like yours and Colt's," Sadie said, her hands over Luna's at her waist.

"Yes. Today you will marry the man you love. The family you lost will always be in your heart, but today you'll have a new family."

Sadie pressed the side of her head to Luna's. "And a sister."

Luna smiled. "We were already sisters. This will just make it more official."

"Then let's go make it all official."

Colt felt a punch to his gut when Luna walked down the aisle in her pretty blue dress, holding a bouquet of white roses. Seeing her walk toward him brought him back to their wedding under the stars. They'd had such a perfect night.

Luna smiled at him so brightly that he knew she was thinking about their wedding, too.

The wedding march played and Sadie walked down the aisle on Grandpa Sammy's arm. Colt barely paid attention, he only had eyes for his wife standing on the other side of Sadie. He wanted to go to her and hold her hand, recite the vows Sadie and Rory exchanged, and kiss her the way his brother kissed his new bride. The joy he saw in Rory and Sadie's eyes and smiles when they turned and faced their family and friends filled him up when Luna's gaze met his and he saw all the love and longing in his heart reflected back at him.

Rory and Sadie walked down the aisle together toward the reception room. Colt held his arm out to Luna, who hooked her arm through his, looked up, and accepted the kiss he planted on her lips as they walked down the aisle after Sadie and Rory. Ford and Grandpa Sammy brought up the rear.

Rory and Sadie were already on the dance floor, lost in each other's gazes and the music. Everyone attending the wedding gathered around and watched the couple. Colt only had eyes for his wife. When Sadie and Rory pointed at them and beckoned them onto the dance floor, he was only too happy to take Luna in his arms and sway with her to the music.

The next song started and Rory took Luna from Colt, so he stole Sadie and kissed the bride.

"You're glowing," he commented.

"I must look just like Luna did when she married you."

"I'm glad you brought us back together."

"I love both of you. I just wanted you both to be happy."

Rory and Luna stepped up to them. "We are happy. Now give me back my husband, and I'll give you back yours."

Sadie beamed Rory a smile. "I'll take him." They danced away into the growing crowd on the dance floor, which included Grandpa Sammy with Dr. Bell and Ford with one of Sadie's friends from the diner.

Colt wondered if Ford would stop pining away for the girl he'd given up and they'd all end up with one of the diner girls. Probably not. Like Luna, some girls just marked you in a way that never went away.

He took Luna back into his arms. "I'm keeping you," he said.

She held him close as they moved to the slow, sultry song, her gaze locked with his. "Good. Because I'm keeping you." She tilted her head, her bangs sweeping over her eyes.

He touched her forehead and swept them aside.

"Did you ever think we'd get here?"

He smiled, then kissed her softly. "This is just the beginning."

EPILOGUE

Luna and Colt pulled up in front of the Travers Wholesale and Manufacturing warehouse. She stared up at the sign in wonder, knowing that a year ago this hadn't been in Simon's plans at all. He'd found his way this past year. He stumbled a bit after getting out of the hospital and recuperating, but eventually he came up with a plan that combined his talent for sales and his new girlfriend's love of supporting local products.

Simon didn't ask Luna for a dime. He used the money he inherited from his father and built the business on his own. It was still struggling, but well on its way to being profitable. She helped out in another way, throwing some business Simon's way in the form of using the oats, cherries, and nuts they produced on the farm to come up with a line of Rambling Range granola bars. All natural. Locally sourced ingredients. Luna came up with the recipe. Simon manufactured and distributed the product. She made a tidy little profit on the venture. Simon expanded his business.

"Having second thoughts?" Colt asked, because she hadn't gotten out of the truck.

"No. You?"

"We discussed it. I'm all for this. Wayne wanted him

to find his way. He did. The last time we saw him, he looked happy. Settled."

"I think so, too."

Josh, on the other hand, hadn't changed a bit. He'd gone back to his old job, changed to another, and yet another. He'd even hit Simon up for a job, but Simon held him off, not wanting to let Josh use him for a paycheck Josh had no intention of actually earning. That one decision earned Luna's respect and helped solidify her decision to do what she was about to do now.

Simon walked out of the building and waved to them.

Colt opened his door and slid out, looking back at her. "Come on, honey, time to fulfill Wayne's wishes in your way."

Yes, they didn't have a lot of time. She had two therapy sessions later this afternoon. She had twelve kids in the program and more on a wait list. She needed to hire more help. She loved spending time with the kids. Tanner thrived having people around who were in some ways like him.

Luna took Colt's hand and slid out of the truck on his side. They walked to meet Simon.

"Hey you guys, why didn't you come in?" Simon gave her a quick hug, then shook Colt's hand They weren't exactly friends, but they'd grown closer over the last several months.

"How is everything?" Colt asked.

"Business is good. Great. We just signed a deal with a local candy maker to do the direct shipping of their online sales orders."

"That's fantastic." Luna meant it. Online sales mailing opened up a whole new avenue of business for him.

"Thanks. Rambling Range sales are up, too. Is that why you're here? Quality check the manufacturing?"

She laughed. He always thought she was looking over his shoulder, keeping an eye on her small piece of his business so he didn't steal from or sabotage her. In fact, she was looking at him. He knew it. Accepted it. Never developed a chip on his shoulder because she didn't quite trust him. Yes, a test, she admitted to herself, because she'd never forgotten that he slipped some spyware on her computer and at any moment could have wiped out her accounts.

He never did. Not in a whole year, especially when he needed the money for the business. He didn't take a single penny from her.

"No, we came because today is . . . a special day," Luna finished awkwardly, remembering Wayne and her last conversation with him at the diner. He'd told her to fix things with Colt. A year later, they were so happily married that they couldn't keep their hands off each other, and they laughed every day. What more could she want?

Simon's eyes filled with sorrow and regret. He stuffed his hands in his pockets. "I miss him. I wish he were here to see that I took his advice and found something that I love to do. He was right. It doesn't feel like work." Simon glanced back at the warehouse with his name on the sign.

"He'd be so proud of you, Simon."

"I think so, too. Plus, he'd be excited to know I found someone to spend the rest of my life with who makes me really happy. The way you did for him." He held up a hand. "Not the way you have with Colt, but in a way that made his days less lonely, someone he counted on and trusted as his friend."

"He was a very good friend to me," Luna said, choked up, trying to hold it together and not cry before she got everything out. "I'm so happy for you and Alicia. When is the big day?"

"Money is kind of tight right now. We're going to wait and maybe do it next year."

Colt squeezed her hand. "Luna can help you out with that."

Simon held up a hand and shook his head. "No. We want to do it ourselves. Besides, if we wait, we'll have more time to plan. I want her to have everything she wants."

"The help I'm giving you isn't because you're getting married, it's because it's what your father would have wanted." Luna took a breath to stave off her sadness. She pulled a thick envelope from her purse. "This is for you." She handed the papers to him.

He took the envelope but didn't open it. "What is this?"

"The inheritance you earned."

His eyes narrowed. "I don't understand. You canceled the terms of the will. I can't earn my half of the ranch."

"No. Because you don't really want it. Your father knew that about you. He wanted you to find your own path and gave me the authority to give you what you deserved when the time came."

"You mean *if* the time came. I take it Josh isn't getting anything today."

"No. You've earned this, Simon."

"What exactly is this?"

"You now own your home outright. The deed is in your name. Free and clear. The warehouse and this piece of land is yours, too."

"You bought this property?"

"The money you used to pay rent can be put back into the business now."

Simon raked his free hand through his blonde hair. "Wow, I don't know what to say."

"There is also a check in there. It's not the ten million you'd have gotten if I sold the ranch, but I think you'll be happy with the sum."

"Go ahead." Colt coaxed him to open the envelope.

Simon gaped at the check he pulled out. "Two million?"

"Don't spend it all on your wedding. Save some for the honeymoon," Luna teased.

"Wait, what is this other contract?"

"Sign that and you own the Rambling Range brand. You'll continue to buy the ingredients from the farm, but you will own that piece of the business."

"So I own a piece of the ranch after all."

"In this way, yes."

"You mean in a way that suits me, the businessman."

"One of these days you'll realize your father never meant for you to be a cowboy. There's a lot you could have done on that ranch. You just didn't see it. You didn't see the potential of what that place could be in your life. Now you do. In this way, you are still a part of what your father built, but you've made it your own."

Simon shook his head. "I never saw that one coming."

"I know. You'll be kicking yourself for that one later."

"I am right now. But I do have some ideas to expand the line into cereals."

"Great. We'll discuss it next week when you come to the ranch to pick up your order. I'm sure between you, me, Colt, and Artie we can come up with a few different ideas."

"I'm looking forward to it." He held up the check and the envelope. "Thank you. This means a lot. Especially when I know you didn't have to do this."

"Yes, I did. It's what your father wanted. Since you kept your hands off the accounts and did something with your life, I decided it was time to reward you. Keep it up, you never know if I'll do it again."

Simon gaped at her. "You knew about that?"

She smiled slyly. "The FBI has been watching and so have I," she warned just to get his goat. She didn't think he'd try anything now.

"Too late, huh, you changed all the passwords, I bet."

"Yes, I did. And I deleted the spyware. This morning before we drove over here."

"You left them all the same just to see if I'd steal the money?"

"Yes. But you passed with flying colors. If only the rest of your family had come to their senses the way you did."

"I talked to Kelly last week. She loves school. Anne is loving her job, and running her own business. I never thanked you for what you did for my aunt and uncle. They may be in jail, but the lawyer you hired got them a fair deal."

"I never wanted everything, Simon. Wayne didn't want me to keep everything. But he did end up bringing the most important thing back into my life."

"Colt," Simon guessed.

"Yes."

"I'll see you at my wedding?" he asked.

"We'd love to come." Luna hugged Simon goodbye, feeling like they'd let the past go and forged a new friendship. She'd done what her friend asked of her. It felt done. Settled.

But she still had one thing left to do to tie up the loose ends of her past.

"Come on, cowboy, I owe you a beer." Instead of

heading for the truck, she tugged Colt's hand and pulled him toward the bar at the end of the street.

"It's about time you paid up," he teased about their running joke.

"What? It's only been a year."

Colt held the door for her when they got to the bar. She walked in and took a seat. Work hadn't quite let out at the surrounding businesses, so the place wasn't that full. She and Colt had relative privacy, with only two other guys at the other end of the bar and a few people occupying some of the tables.

"What can I get you?" the bartender asked.

"I'll take whatever dark beer you've got on tap. She'll have . . ."

"A Sprite."

Colt's gaze narrowed on her. "You don't want a beer?"

She shook her head. "I can't."

Colt picked up his frosted glass and took a sip. "Why?"

"Because we're having a baby."

Colt's hand fell to the bar. Beer sloshed over his glass and hand, but he didn't notice. His gaze locked on her, then dipped to her belly, and back up to her face. "Are you serious?"

They'd only started trying two months ago. Turns out they only needed to try once to make it happen. "I'm two months along."

He cupped her face in his hands and pulled her close. His lips met hers again and again with a dozen soft kisses. His hands swept down her arms to her hips. He held her close. He pushed her back and looked down at her belly again. "You're pregnant." The words held a wealth of wonder and so much excitement that she smiled at him.

"Yes."

"I'm going to be a dad," he announced to the bar. "Next round's on me."

A cheer went up from the dozen patrons in the bar. The bartender started pouring drinks for everyone.

"I thought I was buying you a beer," she teased. "At this rate, I'll never get it done."

He kissed her again. "I love you. I can't believe we're having a baby."

"Wait until Grandpa Sammy finds out he's getting another great-grandbaby."

"He's going to be so damn happy. But not as happy as I am." Colt held up his beer and handed her the glass of Sprite. "To Wayne for bringing us back together."

They clinked glasses. "You know, he told me you'd be crazy not to fall for me."

"I'm not crazy. I'm yours." He kissed her softly, then stared at her, something definitely on his mind. "When I saw the two of you together, I thought it'd be nice to have a beautiful woman like you doting on me in my old age. Then I thought I'd rather just have you by my side."

"Then it's a good thing I'm yours."

Keep reading for an exclusive excerpt from
New York Times bestselling author
Jennifer Ryan's sixth Montana Men novel,

HIS COWBOY HEART

Ford never expected the woman he gave up so many years ago to come home a hero. The haunting look in Jamie's eyes tells him she's been to hell and is still trying to claw her way back. Ford is determined to see her happy and well again—even if that means he has to use some tough love to nudge her in the right direction—and back into his arms.

After a terrifying bombing and shootout sends Jamie home from the Army wounded in both body and mind, she's hoping to find a little peace and quiet. Instead, her PTSD and the black hole of missing memories are slowly driving her insane. But her erratic behavior and short temper don't deter Ford, the man she loved and hated to leave.

When a dark truth is revealed that leaves Jamie reeling, she'll risk everything, including her future with Ford, to save herself and avenge her fellow fallen soldiers.

PROLOGUE

Eleven years ago . . .

Ford stared down at his listless grandfather in the hospital bed, trying to hold back the tears stinging his eyes. Granddad's pale face and sunken cheeks warned of his tenuous health. They didn't know what was wrong, only that he'd collapsed in the house and lay motionless on the floor for God knows how long before Ford walked in and found him several days ago.

The same fear and crushing pressure squeezed his chest tight just thinking about it.

He and his brothers, Rory and Colt, had been taking turns staying by his side since the doctors admitted him to the hospital. Ford needed to get back to the ranch to cover for Colt so he could have his turn.

"He's going to be fine," the nurse assured him. "The doctors said it's the concussion from hitting his head on the floor that's the worst of his ailments. They're working to get his blood pressure down and to make sure there isn't anything else wrong with his head or heart."

"When do we get the results of the echocardiogram and MRI?" Ford asked.

"The doctor should know in a couple of hours," the nurse answered, touching his arm in comfort before she left the room to check on another patient.

He didn't feel any better for it and worried more about what the results might tell them. He and his brothers feared the worst and didn't want to admit that this brought the death of their parents too close to the surface. If they lost their grandfather and the failing ranch, what would they have left?

"It's not your time to go." He patted his granddad's leg. With his heart in his throat, Ford left the room, hoping he got to see his grandfather again.

He drove home without remembering the drive at all, his thoughts on family, the ranch, and the decisions he had to make.

Some decisions had been made for him by circumstances and family obligations and love.

Jamie sat on the tailgate of her brother's truck, sun-kissed legs swinging her tiny feet back and forth. Her face lit up when she spotted him pulling into the yard. She hopped off the end of the truck and ran to him. His heart did that funny flutter thing it did every time he saw her.

Ford slipped out of his truck and stood before the most beautiful girl in the world, her golden-red hair luminous in the sunlight, soft green eyes squinting against the harsh light beating on her pale skin. He desperately wanted to hold on to her, but knew he had no choice but to break her heart. They stood in the middle of the yard on his family's ranch, horses roaming in the pastures, his brothers out chasing stray cattle they couldn't afford to lose past the river. His gut tied into knots of worry about his hospitalized grandfather, sagging cattle prices, and what it all meant for his future with Jamie.

They didn't have one.

The ache in his chest throbbed.

God, how he'd miss her pretty smile that lit up his world.

Her head tilted in that cute way it did when she studied him too closely and saw too much. "What's wrong?"

I miss you already.

Deflecting, he asked, "What are you doing here?"

"Escaping."

He read the hurt in her eyes too easily. "What did she do this time?"

"Same thing, different day." Jamie huffed out an expressive sigh. "She's impossible. And delusional. She accused me of throwing myself at my stepdad. Again." Jamie's lips scrunched into a sour pinch at the distasteful thought.

Her mother read into simple, innocent interactions with a twisted jealous eye, heart, and mind that had no basis on Jamie's part or whatever guy was in the picture before Jamie's mother drove him away. According ing to Jamie, it started when she was eleven after her real father left her mother for a much younger woman, never to be heard or seen again.

"She kicked me out. Shoved me out the front door more accurately." Jamie pulled up her sleeve and showed him the red marks on her arm.

Things were getting worse if her mother was putting her hands on Jamie. Though she wished for her family to be loving and close, it would never be. Jamie had been left to her own devices practically her whole life and done well in school and taking care of her little brother. She'd taken care of him for more than a year. No one cared about him the way Jamie did.

She only knew how to pull it together and forge onward even when her choices were limited and none of them particularly good. He like the way she made the best out of everything.

"I think she actually meant it when she said, 'Don't come back.'" Fear and anger darkened her eyes.

He wanted to comfort her, but didn't because he was about to hurt her far worse than her mother's warped taunts, accusations, and empty threats. Some women weren't meant to be mothers. Too selfish and self-centered.

Jamie was sweet, kind, and sensitive. Her mother's disapproval sliced away at Jamie. One cut stung. A thousand made you bleed and ache and wish for it to end.

She needed it to end. Now. Before it made her as angry and bitter as her mother.

He didn't want that for her. Jamie didn't deserve such poor treatment. He wanted her to be happy. Always. He wanted to be the reason she was happy.

Never going to happen now.

He tried to keep her away from her mother as much as possible. He drove her into town and home from her job at the day care center. One less thing to ask of her mother. One less thing for her mother to use against her and demand she be grateful.

Jamie loved the job, playing with the children and rocking babies. Nothing made her happier than sharing all the love in her heart with those kids. She lavished that love on him too.

She squirreled away her paychecks. She dreamed

of leaving her mother's house and living the life she wanted—a life with a bright future without the storm cloud of her mother's negativity darkening her world.

A life that wouldn't include him. Damn, it hurt like hell. Deeper than the ache in his chest, it ripped a searing path to his soul.

He wanted to beg her to stay here, give up everything she wanted, but he couldn't do it and watch her happiness shrivel and die along with the love she felt for him.

Some things can only be fixed by doing the hard thing, even if it wasn't what you wanted to do.

She pressed her palm to his chest. "Let's do it, Ford. Let's leave this place behind and buy that house with the wraparound porch on the ranch you want. You'll run the cattle. I'll help you with the horses. We'll raise our own family." She smiled sweetly, thinking of the kids they'd never have now. "I'll plant a garden just like your mother and my grandmother had when we were kids. We'll pick tomatoes and zucchini, cook them up, and eat together on the porch and watch the sun set."

Her enthusiasm and the picture she painted sounded like everything he'd ever wanted, especially with her by his side. He saw her on the porch swing, a blonde baby in her arms, her smile so bright he wanted to join her rather than do anything else.

"I can't leave."

Her grin dimmed. "I know we talked about leaving in a couple of months, but I don't want to wait. I can't. I want to start my life with you. I don't have all the money I wanted to save, but I'm close, and you've got what you saved. We can do it. Together."

They'd talked about leaving. Him because he wanted her away from her mother and to start his own ranch one day. Something of his own. To take what his father taught him from birth and run his own business outside the one Rory ran for them on their parents' ranch. He thought to take her to Wyoming. Far enough away they'd have their own life, but not so far he couldn't come home to his family whenever he wanted. She could visit her brother, Zac.

He didn't even consider it, because he couldn't leave. But she needed to go.

She needed a guy who could go all in, hold nothing back. As much as he wanted to be, he couldn't be that guy right now.

"I can't go to Wyoming."

"It doesn't have to be there. We could visit my cousin in Georgia. Her husband is in the military. She said we could stay with them as long as we need. Her husband has a ton of friends. He can help us get jobs until we find the perfect place to settle down."

Georgia seemed a million miles away.

"I didn't know you were close with your cousin."

"I'm not really now, but when we were little girls, you'd have thought we were sisters." Excitement for her new plan filled her bright green eyes.

"Sounds like you found the perfect fresh start. I'm happy for you."

"You're happy for us," she corrected, narrowing her gaze. Confusion dimmed her enthusiasm.

He gave into his need to touch her, knowing it may be the last time he ever did, and traced his fingers down her long blond hair. The streaks of copper shimmered in the sunlight.

Her head tilted to the side, rubbing against his palm. "Let's leave today. I'll go home and pack. You pack and finally tell your brothers we're leaving." Her eyes pleaded with him to say all the things she wanted to hear.

He'd held off saying anything to Rory and Colt because it had been the three of them since their parents died. They did everything together, including keeping this ranch running and a roof over their heads. Yes, they had their grandfather, but this place had been left to them. Now, they might lose their grandfather and their home. He couldn't walk out on them. Not when they needed him the most.

Rory would push on, working himself into an early grave. He'd take care of Grandpa Sammy and make sure he got the medical care he needed. Colt would step up, take his share of the load. But Ford couldn't add his burden to his brothers' shoulders and ask them to carry it for him so he could run off with his girl no matter how much he wanted to make a life with her.

Some things just weren't meant to be. This wasn't meant to be right now. Maybe one day, he'd find a way to make it right.

"I'm sorry, Firefly, but I'm not going with you." He'd given her the nickname the first time he saw her. Glowing with golden energy, it was a wonder she didn't take off and fly.

He stuffed both hands in his pockets to keep from holding on to her.

Her brows drew together, crinkling her forehead. "What do you mean? What's changed?"

Ford sucked it up and said what he had to say. "You want to go. You need to go. I get that, but my place is here."

"I can wait."

No, she couldn't. She'd endured her mother's torment her whole life. She deserved every happiness, but she'd never find it here.

"It's not about when."

"You really don't want to go with me?" The crack in her voice tore open his heart and made it bleed.

He didn't know if he could endure the pain before he gave in and told her the truth.

"No." He nearly choked on the word, but he got it out. For her.

"Is that why you've been so distant this past week?"

Not really. Worries about the ranch and his grandfather's poor health crowded his mind, making it near impossible to think of anything else. All the late night talks with his brothers, pouring over the dwindling accounts, sorting through which bills to pay now and which to hold off, arguing about selling off a piece of land or trying to get a loan to tide them over, all of it one big headache after the next, leaving them with few options.

He didn't answer her question, because if he told her about his grandfather, she'd stay to help the only father-figure she'd ever had in her life, but if things kept going the way they were, he'd lose the ranch and have nothing and no way to provide for her. The money he'd saved to go away with her, he had to put back into the ranch to keep it going. They'd have mounting hospital bills to overcome too. No matter how he worked it out in his head, it was all too clear that he had to stay here and fight for his family's ranch and do whatever he had to do to make sure his grandfather got the care he needed.

Jamie stepped close and put her hand on his chest again. "I love you. I don't want to go without you."

His heart thrashed against his ribs. Sure she felt it, he didn't let his roiling emotions show on his face. He had to do this clean, so she'd go with no regrets and move on with her life.

"Like you said, you'll stay with your cousin. Find a job. Start a new life in a new place."

"I thought that life included you, the home we dreamed about, the family we both want."

I wish, but not anymore.

His chest went tight. He barely managed his next words. "You'll be fine on your own. You'll figure out what you really want once you're away from here. I'm a rancher. This is where I belong."

"You really don't want to go with me." The disbelief in her whispered statement tore another strip off his battered heart.

Ford didn't move a muscle. He didn't answer that statement by word or deed, because the honest to God truth was that he did want to go with her. Hell, he just wanted to be with her, here, there, anywhere.

"Did I do something? Say something? If I did, I'm sorry." Tears glistened in her eyes as she struggled to come to some kind of understanding for why he'd do this to her.

Her mother always made her feel like everything was her fault. He hated to do this to her. Hated it. Hated himself for putting her through this.

He choked back his emotions. Had to. For her. "We were great together, but now you need to go. I get it. I'm sorry to see you leave, but I guess this was always the way it ended."

Someone should shoot him. Put him out of his misery. Avenge her for his making this seem like it was her fault. He didn't know if he had the resolve to keep this up much longer. She needed to go before he took her in his arms and begged her to forgive him for being an asshole. Before he begged her to stay with him even though she needed out.

He wouldn't trap his firefly in a cage and watch her beautiful spirit and light dim and die.

He loved his family, the ranch his parents' left to them, but sometimes it was a heavy burden, despite it being his heart and soul.

She opened her mouth to say something, but he cut her off. "Pack your bags. Leave today like you wanted. Get away from her, this place, all the bad memories, and start *your* life."

Jamie shook her head, golden red hair swishing across her back and shoulders. Tears glistened in her eyes. "Why are you doing this?" Her voice cracked with the plea in that complicated question.

"You want to go. I need to stay." That's as close as he'd come to telling her the truth. "Go, Firefly. Fly away."